Voice from the Planet

An Anthology of Living Fiction

Edited by Charles Degelman

New York

Harvard Square Editions

2010

CONTENTS

Preface...vii

The Ground beneath My Feet by Paul-Anthony Delor...............................1

Dark Lady of Hollywood by Diane Haithman................................9

Consultation by Ruben Varda 27

Gates of Eden by Charles Degelman...35

Under the Poinciana Tree by Carlos Victoria 55

The Vale of Cashmere by Sean Elder 67

A Cultural Revolution by Teresa Hsiao......................................85

Patchwork by Dan Loughry 103

Sunflower by Susan Lindheim..121

Estella and the Gringo by Joel Willans..135

A Date with the Unknown by Eitan Olevsky 151

Polis by J. L. Morin 163

The Fire Dancer by Maria Pavlova 179

Your Mother by Alisa Clements 197

Frenching My Sister by Jay Boyer..211

Marion Terry, who might have been a singer . . . by Vivien Jones 219

Lily Dale Assembly by Sharon Dilworth 225

A Dream at the End of the World by Ben Cheetham...............241

Boisterous Devotion by D.E. Tingle...261

Jameson's Letters by B.R. Bonner 279

I'm Prudence by Joanne Groshardt..287

Bucktown by Dave Woods 293

The Catalytic Seduction of Brian White by Andrew Binks 297

Learning to Crawl by Ben Mattlin 311

Remordimiento by Hélène Valentina de Portu...........................321

Don't Think You're Calling Too Much by Wickham Boyle....................327

Scherzo by David Landau 341

What Happened to My Mother by Paula Brancato 355

When Conrad Aiken Lived Upstairs by Kalman Applbaum....................371

Soldier Red by Lauren Handman...391

Reunion by Walter E. Gourlay..405

Permissions 421

PREFACE

For centuries, much of the world has been excluded from the literary dialogue between the United States and a few Commonwealth Countries, mainly the United Kingdom, Canada, and Australia. Most of the top English-language book prizes are limited by national interests: the Pulitzer Prize for fiction goes strictly to American authors, preferably ones writing about American life; the Orange Prize is limited to UK authors; and only Commonwealth Country citizens are eligible for the Man Booker Prize. Likewise, most anthologies are limited in their themes to a particular country or town, reinforcing this entrenched literary nationalism. A rich canon of international literature has been denied to many English-speaking readers.

Enter the Information Age. The cyber apocalypse, a communication revolution. The thirty authors from around the globe gathered here in *Voice from the Planet* have been interacting via the world wide web in an effort to bring you a new, Living Fiction. They played an unprecedented part in the cyber revolution downloading cross-Atlantic messages that would have taken months to reach them twenty five years ago. Their voices are varied and unique, with award-winning and new authors from Congo, China, Peru, the United States, Bulgaria, Belgium, Canada, Brazil, Scotland, Finland, England . . .

Most of those involved in this endeavor have never met. Communicating via e-mail and the Internet, they cast about for new work from far-flung and gifted writers, explored common ground, developed new, digital editorial processes and structures, and formed new friendships to create the volume you are holding in your hands.

The result? We believe *Voice from the Planet* has developed its own, unique theme — an expression of cyber liberation at its best. This anthology presents short fiction and novel excerpts from around the world, all submitted, edited, and polished over the internet.

Voice from the Planet is published by Harvard Square Editions, a new, independent press that grew out of a discussion group on the Harvard University web site. Award-winning author and editor Charles Degelman has gathered these voices into an anthology with authors donating net proceeds to the Nobel Prize-winning charity Doctors Without Borders.

We invite you to let your mind wander off on a literary adventure through a world of fine new fiction. We also hope you join us in our celebration of Living Fiction by logging in to comment on your favorite *Voice from the Planet* stories using the authors' digital contact information at the end each story and at www.harvardsquareeditions.org

The Ground beneath My Feet

—— ☙❧ ——

by Paul-Anthony Delor

My mother left me this morning. You may think she made the decision to leave, but she didn't. She didn't know death was coming. She didn't want it, she couldn't have. I know it. I can see her, I am facing her and I can't breathe. My eyes are swollen, they are burning with pressure but I will not allow the tears to fall. I can't. She told me not to. Big boys don't cry! Now get up, brush that dirt off your knees and finish that work. And I finished the work, I did. But things are different now, I cannot get up this time.

Sweat is running down my face, down my neck and arms, I can feel it run over the sand, soil and dust covering me, cementing me into a coffin of mud. Flies circle around me, crawl in and out of my sagging, oversized shirt, jealous of the perspiration on my body, and of my moist, jaundiced eyes. I can't think, I have to stop, close my eyes.

Obscurity, everywhere. All that I have seen has been covered by a blanket of black silk, giving me a chance to breathe, to rest, to forget. Behind the blanket prevails a deep and hollow melody, reassuring by its regularity and steadiness, lulling me into a dream. My mind is lost in nothingness, my body is stunted, flesh and bone, but my heart still beats as strong as the march of a thousand soldiers, who, every single one, believe in their decree. It is to my heart that I shall turn, and imitate its endurance, strength and determination.

The wind slaps sand onto my face, onto my neck and onto the cuts and gashes upon my forearms. It tickles, and I enjoy it. I am away, elsewhere. But my quiescence is short-lived, too short, indeed. The next second I am torn from my dream and dragged by my feet into reality. I press my eyelids together and claw at the silk. But light pierces through and the black silk is pulled apart. I can hear a woman's voice, thank God.

"God be blessed! Ngoyi you're alive. What do you think you are doing you devil! Get up, I must get you to a hospital!" says the shaking voice from behind.

The voice is that of Aimée, my neighbor, erect on a carpet of debris. There is no dirt on her dark, hardened skin, no blood staining her decrepit dress, no trembling in her limbs. But there is a kind of feverish hysteria in her eyes.

"I . . . I don't understand," I utter. But my words are nothing but air, strangulated by the grip of exhaustion, submerged and dying in the soiled waters of existence, of survival.

A silence follows. The sun is at his highest, scorching the decayed, oxidized iron of what might once have been a car, spreading a hot smell of warmth — a smell I have smelt many times in the past. The sand below me is sweltering, but I don't mind. I can take it. Fair white clouds are projecting shadows onto the land, shadows that play on roads, escalading buildings before jumping off and racing to the next. Children too are playing, oblivious to what happened, or maybe just unaware. Many have retained their smiles, why can't I?

"I'm sorry . . ." says Aimée in a husky voice, "Uncle Chiumbo was wounded by the attack, I must go to him. Come meet me at the blue building, that of the UN, or whoever. I must look after you, do you hear me?"

But I do not answer. No matter how much I like her, and how much I know she likes me, I can't let her take over from my mother, let her compensate for her when she is still here, in front of me, lying desolately amidst the collapsed edifice, that which she had worked so hard to build. The ground beneath my feet is still, ghastly still.

"I'll see you there!" is her response to my silence. "God keep him safe!" she says as she turns around and leaves. Aimée is now running towards the main road, lifting her dress to her knees, losing her sandals, but not caring, too absorbed in catching the nearest bus. I am now alone, again.

I feel sorry that she left, why was I so cold? She has always been good to me, and I have always tried my best to return her caring and affection. It made her happier. I should have made her happier a minute ago, when she most needed it. But no matter how hard I try I never manage to do things right. I have tried, many times, but my small achievements are worth nothing - helping Khamisi catch fish after school, or running to the market to get Dr.Gwandowa's prescriptions for his never-ending patient list that have brought them temporary solace, but Khamisi still starves every night and Dr.Gwandowa's patients still die. I don't do enough, it's useless.

On the horizon, oil pumps hammer the earth, dancing with delight in the heat wave. Why is it that the rich and powerful dance? These metallic villains steal all that we have, transport it elsewhere and enjoy themselves in the process, dancing to the idea of their pockets being torn open and dripping with gold. The gold is red to me, it's red to all of us. How tired and worthless are the uses of this world!

Oh, Africa is a rotten place. Its flesh has been infested, its soul has been corroded and its bones have been broken and crushed by the weight of unneeded exhaustion. How can a fortuneless beggar bear the consequences of a fat man's greed? How can a man pluck another man's feathers to blow them purposely into his face? How can this all happen? How can a loving mother be murdered by people who share the same blood, the same skin and the same flesh as she? How?! It isn't right, it isn't fair!

Ugh, I'm a fool! We are but animals, at the very bottom of the food chain, at the very bottom of society. Why bother? There is no point. I should adapt as we always have, live a happy depression. What do we do other than harvesting our shadows? Whilst at the same time, in the distance, a whole universe is making its escape, abandoning us to our fate.

In these slums, in these lost cities, we cling to the belief that we can arrive at a better life. We offer many smiles that bring assistance, that contribute strength to those who most need it. But all is wasted in my heart. True existence is non-existent. True existence is dead.

I dissolve in my thoughts, suddenly imagining life without rancor. Is this really a crime? An unreal combination? My senses are ignited. A chaos of honey, cinnamon and sugar appears like thunder, and suddenly I drift into a daydream. I imagine a death without chagrin, a crime like a mad desire, infinitely subtle. I am overcome by an insidious drunkenness, I am ignited. I turn my back to the sun and stiffen at the shade projected in front of me. Are my thoughts perverted?

Get up, brush the dust off my kneecaps, and start walking. Where to? I can't tell you, but I've made up my mind. The streets have come to life. They had always been alive, but my mind was too numb to notice, too numb to care. I carve my way towards the increasing heat of the high street and all is very loud. People are brushing past me in anarchic, disorganized waves. My nostrils fill with the distinct smell of the city; a mixture of sweat, kerosene and garbage. I used to love the city; it was the centre of life, animation and spirit. People looked different, they smiled in different ways and it was a pleasure to watch them, to observe life in its different forms. But now all these people look the same, wearied — stunted body and soul by life.

I make my way to the marketplace, or what remains of it. It too has been targeted by the violence of everyday life. A man is standing atop the wreckage, looking for something. The ashes and bent metal have not yet cooled, the grounds are still fuming. The man is forlorn and alone, in the same way that I am alone. Something is intriguing about him, this shape amidst the smoke. I want to talk to him, find out what he's lost, why he is alone. But I can't, I promised myself I'd keep on walking.

I'm now in the shade of a narrow street. Wet clothes sway in the warm breeze, cooling the air and masking its heavy stench with soap. I can hear the radio playing music from inside the tin-roofed houses, and people laughing, clapping their hands and holding their heads in playful disbelief. The street is full of life, full of sparkle. Children are playing cards on their doorsteps, betting stones, pushing each other playfully. But as I continue down my route, the music and laughter is replaced by a pale and deathlike silence. I feel my heart compress. A woman is standing outside her house. She is wearing a robe and sandals, and is holding a worn-down and fatigued handbag carrying very little food. Her house has burned to the ground, and so have the twenty others or so at this end of the street. She, too, stands on ashes and the blackened, bent metal that made her roof. Her sunken eyes are staring at the washing lines behind me. She is alone, in the same way that I am alone. I want to speak to her, but I can't.

I've left the streets and finally I reach my destination, but I'm not staying. I'm just picking up my bag. I'm not staying. Something blunt is digging into my back, just like the books did when I used to walk to school. I'm smiling. The feeling of the blunt object is uncomfortable, yet comforting. I make my way back to the streets, cross a few of them, head lowered, and find a tree facing the Lubumbtu Miranda School, my old school. It's made of mud, crumbling and spoilt, but those dark, stuffy rooms have the generosity and incorruptibility those soaring glass towers will never have. Those buildings just . . . Gah, I need to sit down, to rest.

I remember when I used to run to get here. I had no reason for coming. I wasn't paid, wasn't fed, but I still came, just like all my friends, they who lived so very far away. We'd rush in through the gate and compete for the first desk. Our teacher Rachel let us share the first desks and the girls would complain, as they couldn't see the board. But it was all fun, for the girls too, even if they didn't want to admit it. We learnt letters, numbers and the existence of all kinds of desert creatures in the Sahara. Myombe would chase us through the playground, making horrible sounds, and the girls would gather up in groups and watch us discretely, giggling. We boys always acted tough, but liked their attention. We liked the attention of our teacher Rachel, too. I was never alone. But I am now, with a bag at my feet.

My eyes are swelling again, burning. The school, just like the few narrow streets, is but a boat in a sea of trouble; a capsule of life which tries its best not to be drowned by the growing despair. It's all part of the past, the school and all. I must leave. Back on my feet, the bag seems a lot heavier. It is pushing down on my shoulders, draining the little energy I have left. I must move on.

On my way I stop again, this time to stare at a scene that is too common: a woman victim to violence in these dusty streets. It happens so, so often. This woman looks like she's in her thirties but it's safe to guess that she's no more than twenty. Fatigue has clawed at her face, hope has evacuated her eyes, and now this. She is being held by a skinny, starved man while a despairing boy is rummaging through her bags and pockets. The woman is wearing no emotion, and neither are the tens of bodies staring at a distance, including myself. I close my eyes and leave, breathing deeply, not knowing how to feel.

It is strange how men behave. At times showing care, and at other times displaying neglect and inattention. I wonder if it's security that makes men affectionate, and the lack of it that turns them cold? Do we only care for people we feel safe with? I felt safe with my friends, and with our teacher Rachel, and with Aimée and with my mother. I cared for them. But why didn't I stop for that lone man in the market, and that woman on her doorstep? Did I fear them? Did I fear becoming like them? I am like them anyway. My bag is getting heavier, my head hurts.

I've reached the main marketplace, the bigger one, and am quickly submerged by its swing. Waves of people clash with waves of cries, each side trying to get a better deal from the other. This is the place ordinary people come out of their silent, numb shells, this is the place they throw away the shyness of human acquaintance to replace it by a desire for connection. But these people don't care for each other — on the contrary. The marketplace is another battlefield. A milder one, but one nonetheless. Exasperation reverberates through the stands as merchants are unable to rid themselves of their stock. Hungry crowds are begging to see the prices lowered, and children are trampling each other, desperately trying to catch everything that falls to the ground. People are driven to this, it isn't them. I make my way to its center, and I am now standing still.

Memories arise in my mind, throwing light over darkness, warmth over frost. I cover my eyes with the same blanket of black silk, pushing reality away to make space for my thoughts. My mother is now beside me. I know that she is unreal, a mere illusion, but I can't wave her away, for she is all that I have. She is smiling at me, telling me that she is sorry. The bag's weight has disappeared and there is nothing left but her and me, all in a pool of quiet. But this doesn't last. Cries pierce through, and I am pushed to the ground by a swearing salesman. I am confused by the movements around me, there is pain in my left arm. That's it, pain. Always pain! To hell with it, I've taken enough. All these people have taken enough. It is not their fault, but I can't do it in any other way. I need to pass the message, I will honor the cause.

But this can't be the right . . .

The ground shook beneath my feet.

Paul-Anthony Delor is a new writer, and *The Ground Beneath My Feet* is his debut work of fiction. Born in Kinshasa, in the Democratic Republic of Congo, but having spent most of his life in Europe, Paul-Anthony feels strongly about the African continent. Aged seventeen, he has undertaken several voyages across Africa, and these recent voyages haven given rise to an urge to communicate what he saw and felt.

Currently living in Brussels, he wishes to continue writing about the people he meets and wishes to meet in very different geographical and social contexts. *The Ground Beneath My Feet* marks the beginning of what he hopes will be a thread of works that he believes will turn people's attention to situations they are unfamiliar with, and make them discover characters of whom they are unaware. Contact: delorpa@hotmail.com

Dark Lady of Hollywood

—————————— ଚ୬ଓଃ ——————————

Excerpted from the novel
by Diane Haithman

"See, here's the *thing*, Kenny . . ."

I'd forgotten how my supervisor, Danny Gordon, never really shook hands; he'd just put his in yours and leave it there, like a small, limp package waiting for UPS. We'd been holding hands like this ever since he walked into my office to welcome me back. Sweet.

"The thing?"

"The . . . *thing*." Dan nodded, then fell silent. I decided it was up to me to end the non-handshake, and gently disengaged myself. The pause was clammier than his hand. "Say whatever the fuck it is you have to say, Dan," I suggested pleasantly.

Danny winced; he tended to take profanity very personally. "The thing is, Kenny, I've been in communication with the writers, and they don't think they can work with you anymore, Kenny."

That was one too many Kennys. I willed myself to stay calm but my heart began to rocket around inside my ribcage like the metal pellet in a pinball machine. I pressed one hand against my chest in the guise of straightening my tie.

"They . . . *know*, Ken," Dan said.

"Know?" I asked, keeping my heart in my chest with my hand.

Dan's thin fingers played over the premature, thirty-five-year-old bald spot in his dark hair; swear to God he had less hair than when he came in. "And, as much as they personally love you — and I do mean that, they *love* you, Kenny — they just aren't going to be able to write jokes if they feel bad. And this whole — well, you know, *thing* — definitely makes them feel *bad.*"

"Why should it make *them* feel bad?"

"This isn't me talking, Kenny, it's the network." The apologetic whimper had come crawling back into Dan's nasal voice. "Do me a solid, Kenny. 'Patty's Going Out' and 'He's On the Force' both got canceled after two episodes."

"Yeah, saw it in Variety. Thanks for not calling me." After saying it over and over, week after week, meeting after meeting, I'd honestly begun to believe that "He's On The Force" would be the perfect comeback vehicle for former child star Donny — *Don* — Calder after two years in a minimum security prison.

Now our only hit was a sophisticated nine-thirty sitcom starring white-hot stand-up comedian Bert Cherry. Following in the footsteps of his father, Bert's character had become a veterinarian. Problem was, he didn't like animals, and animals didn't like him. It was called "Bite Me."

"I think that we both know there's only one thing standing between us and ratings disaster," Dan said.

"'Bite Me,'" I replied.

"Correct. The anchor of our Wednesday night comedy block. Perfect demographics; men 18 to 49. Kenny, we've finally stopped *skewing old.*"

"I know. I launched that show, Dan."

"Reality television, Kenny; we're up against *reality television.* These people will eat live bait and you don't even have to give them scale."

Reality, Danny; I'm up against *reality.* "If they want reality, they should turn it off," I grumbled.

"I'm not trying to be difficult, Ken, but this is my call, not yours." Dan squared his stooped shoulders. "Besides, it's not just the writers who say they can't work with you anymore. It's . . . well, it's Cherry."

"*Bert?*" Okay, that was a slap in the face. "But Bert and I . . . we have a *relationship.*"

"I'm sorry, Ken. I wasn't going to tell you, but you had to push . . ." Dan was now actively pulling out strands of his own hair. "Your baby is now our franchise. We own it. We love you, but . . . we don't *need* you."

"So . . . I guess I need a new franchise," I said, my voice tightrope-walking. "I'm sure you have a brainy suggestion, Daniel?"

Dan brightened. "I think I've got a win-win for you, Kenny. There's a slot for a development director over in Movies and Minis ("Minis" was short for mini-series, which was short for TV that was going to go on way longer than it should). "We were just saying the other day that you'd really be a great help to movies, you know, when they deal with . . . issues like yours."

"Okay," was all I could think of to say.

"It's the best way to protect our franchise: 'Prime Time is *Your* Time.'" Dan stopped, then erupted into giggles. "Kenny, the writers have *such* a great story line for the next 'Bite Me.' Working title: 'Taming of the Shrew.' It's from Shakespeare."

"I know where it's from, Dan."

"How cool is *that*? I had to take Shakespeare at Palisades High, but the only thing I remember is the kid next to me having to memorize the line 'Alas, poor York, I knew him well.' "

"It's not 'York,' it's *Yorick*. And it's not 'I knew him *well*,' it's 'I knew him, Horatio.' Hamlet's talking to Horatio. He's standing next to an open grave with Yorick's goddamned dried-up skull in his hand, and he's talking to fucking *Horatio*."

"It's all good, Ken." Dan let out a long, shuddering sigh. "Listen, I've got to get to the ten o'clock . . ."

"And I don't . . . *kidding*."

"I know, right? Anyway, I'll send someone to move your stuff over to movies. Do you know where it is? In the Old Hacienda Building."

"I've been with the network for five years, Dan; I know what's on the other side of the fucking parking lot."

"We'll re-assign you to a parking space in front of the Hacienda."

"Cool." I knew this was not so I could park closer to my new office, but because the spaces by the aging Hacienda were smaller. I could already see the dings in the shiny silver paint on my Mercedes. "Do

I . . . get to keep the plant?" The plant was a gift from Standards and Practices, creepily grateful because I'd agreed to cut the word "balls" out of an early "Bite Me" script. Little did I know how quickly the network would return the favor.

"It's . . . a little hot and dry over there for a bromeliad, Ken. But do what you think best."

I nodded.

"It's going to take them awhile to get you moved; maybe you want to take the rest of the day off, and we'll have everything ready for you tomorrow morning?"

"Sure, I'll take the rest of the day off," I said.

"And if I don't see you on Monday — or, you know, again, ever . . . well, take care, Kenny. I mean, that was stupid, *duh*, of course I'll *see* you." He backed out of my office so fast he ran smack into a passing mail cart.

And whether we shall meet again I know not. / Therefore our everlasting farewell take. "That's Shakespeare," I murmured. "Julius Caesar."

"*What's* Shakespeare?"

I guess I hadn't said the line; I only thought it, because I'm losing it. "Nothing. Later," I said.

I left my former office and headed for the parking lot. I paused to switch from my regular specs to sunglasses in front of the corner drugstore, located beside the soda fountain on a street of eerily regular faux cobblestones. A Wright Brothers-style bicycle shop and a peppermint-striped barber pole added to the illusion of some indefinite but comforting period in American history. These plywood storefronts have stood in for the good old days in more TV shows than I can name.

The good old days. A studio tram loaded with visitors rattled by over the cobblestones. I waved. They waved back, in case I *was* somebody. I took it as a good sign. It was only a matter of time before I returned to my slot as V.P., comedy development. I was fine.

I was a straight white male, thirty-six years old, right in the middle of TV's most desirable demographic, men 18 to 49. I'd been in network television long enough to know that the demos don't lie.

But demographics did not explain why the lenses of my cool new Oakley sunglasses suddenly fogged and blurred with tears.

How could I hate Alice for offering to stay with me, despite the minor complication of not loving me anymore? She was planning to put all formerly outlined plans to leave me on indefinite hold. In fact, she would devote as much unswerving energy to not leaving me as she did to defending her guilty clients downtown. She always followed the impartial path of justice, and even the no-longer-loved have a right to legal representation. How could I hate Alice for that?

I didn't know, but I was sure as hell going to try.

Alice helped me locate a small condo-for-rent in that vast amorphous zone known as "Beverly Hills-adjacent." And one night, about a month after leaving our beach house on Pacific Coast Highway, I awoke, Beverly Hills-adjacent, jolting out of foggy dream in which I sat in my former living room wearing nothing but Oakley sunglasses, desperately trying to coax a ring of silent men in white lab coats to explain what insidious cosmic force had chosen to fuck with my desirable demographic. I didn't drink, I wasn't fat, I didn't smoke. No family history. I *worked out*.

They didn't answer me; instead, they turned in unison, raised hands and pointed at the TV.

Terror triggered an urgent need to urinate, but I couldn't stand up; the bedroom was spinning way too fast. I was going to have to slide off my bed like a crab, then crawl to the bathroom on my knees.

It was dark, and I was dizzy. Instead of rounding the corner with my usual expertise, I whacked my head hard against the corner of a metal bookcase that had come with my new, furnished, single-guy rental condominium.

Lightning shot through my cranium. I reached a hand up to my forehead to check for blood. No blood. Groping further in search of pieces of my head, my fingers met the cracked spine of a large, heavy book.

I'd had some stuff moved here from our house, including the random assortment of boxes I'd carted with me every time I'd moved since college. Never unpacked 'em, just kept moving 'em. A couple of these boxes were full of books. I'd taken the volumes out and put them on the bookshelf, to make the place look — hah — homey. As I unpacked, I paid no attention to what the books actually were.

I lifted the big volume and tucked it under one arm. I hauled it along with me as I made my way back to the bedroom, still on my knees, Jesus, head splitting right down the middle of my brain.

When I reached my room, I grabbed the doorframe and pulled myself to my feet. I switched on the light; it hurt my eyes. When I could open them again — squinty, tearing, one at a time — I looked at the book tucked under my left arm, a thick, worn out, pea-green volume, embossed in gold: *The Complete Works of William Shakespeare*.

I'd had the book since UCLA, where I had managed to score an "A" in "Introduction to Shakespeare" without actually reading any of his plays. Hey, I was eighteen, and I had the notes. You can get by on the notes.

During the next eight long, solitary months, I read all the plays. Seriously. Every word. I really never planned to keep reading the stuff, but it made sense, it made sense to me in a way that nothing else ever had.

I've always worked in comedy. But for Shakespeare, my feeling is that tragedy is definitely the better franchise. I like to think I know a little bit about humor after executive positions in comedy development at two different networks for more than ten years and, frankly, most jokes written in the early 1600s just aren't funny anymore.

This may explain why tragedy helped me more than comedy. When you're inside of a Shakespearean tragedy, it's impossible to think of anything else. Everyone in them always winds up dead at the end — and I'm talking bodies *everywhere* — but there was something so clean, so pure, so just, so . . . fair, I guess that's the word I'm looking for, so fair, that kept me hanging on.

I have to admit it though; my introduction to Shakespeare also scared the shit out of me. Sometimes I had to put down the heavy, pea-green volume for an hour or two, and go back to watching repeats of "Bite Me." With TV, I wasn't sure I liked where I was standing, but at least I knew where I stood. I was on dry land. As much they drew me, Shakespeare's tragedies were . . . water, deep, black water with no bottom that I could see.

The water was so very, very, black; so very, very deep. And it was not until I reached bottom that I discovered her: the Dark Lady of the Sonnets.

I'd finished all of the plays, and now I didn't know what to do; I just knew I had to do *something*. But there wasn't any more; sixteen hundred pages of tiny, tiny type and I'd already read every word.

But then, as I turned all the pages I'd already read, faster and faster, I found something at the back of the book: The sonnets; Shakespeare's sonnets.

I thought I liked, loved, the tragedies. And I do. But sonnets — whoa. Here was instant gratification in fourteen lines. And the final couplets were truly high-concept — the whole thing in two sentences, no need for further explanation.

But the only thing I cared about, as I turned pages with shaking hands, with numb, tingling fingers, was the Dark Lady of the Sonnets.

"Sonnets 127 through 154 deal in either an abstract or literal way with a mysterious woman with a dark complexion, and perhaps dark hair, who was the mistress and Muse of the poet," said the introduction to the Complete Works. "The language suggests the Dark Lady would not have been considered beautiful by Elizabethan standards." Probably not beautiful by Hollywood standards, either, judging by the amount of blond hair with black roots being tossed around in this town.

The Dark Lady might have been married, a lady-in-waiting in Queen Elizabeth's court. Or she could have been a winemaker's daughter No one knew for sure if she was a lady or a whore. Not only did this woman bedevil Shakespeare's mind as he wrote the sonnets, but some of the women in his plays might be modeled after her. Maybe Hermia, Rosalind, Cressida; Cleopatra, or Hamlet's nervous gal pal, Ophelia.

I was happy to see that Lady Macbeth was not on the list, confirming my original theory that she was just a bitch.

Shakespeare had his Dark Lady; he was not alone. I would not be alone, either, not any more, not so terribly alone adjacent to Beverly Hills. No, Alice, no, Danny Gordon, I would not be alone. Never had anything felt so right as this.

No scholar had ever been able to discover the true identity of the Dark Lady of the Sonnets, not for four hundred years. But to hell with scholars, I had an even tougher job ahead of me. Christ — I had to find her in *Hollywood*.

The next morning, I had a change of heart. I stopped by my old office, shook hands with the twenty-four-year-old who had replaced me in that many hours, and picked up the plant.

If I was going down, so was the bromeliad.

As I walked into the Hacienda, I could hear a young secretary — excuse me, *assistant*, there's no such thing as a secretary in this business — on the phone, chattering away about how work was going. "It's crazed, I'm like so crazed, I'm like, *dying*!" she gasped. "With this new job, I don't even have *time* to be bisexual!"

I'd already met the head of Movies and Minis because, at one point earlier in our careers at another network, I had fired her. Blair Smith was about fifty now, with threads of gray in her thin, straight blond hair. "Good to see you again, Kenny," she said, her tone making very clear that it was not. "I'm very sorry to hear about your, ah, situation, but we're all excited to have you on board."

"Thanks." I grinned at Blair. That was so nice that I was willing to get past the insincerity. "And, Blair, I want this to be business as usual."

"Agreed," she said. "And that's why I've got your first project right here in my hand. It's a Peters/Brown movie about a woman who's got... " her voice trailed off into nothing.

"I know. I read the coverage."

"Good." Blair cleared her throat to make sure the word she'd been about to say hadn't gotten stuck in there and screwed up her cells or anything. "Tyne Daly. But they've got no script, just a star. I mean *this* is the script, but it's no script." She placed a huge stack of white paper in my arms, way more paper than ordinarily required for a two-hour story.

"I'll do what I can."

"At least this assignment is geographically desirable." Peters/Brown Productions had their offices on our lot, due to an exclusive production deal with the network. "The writers would like to talk to you this morning, if you're ready. They're very anxious."

Of course they were anxious; they were writers. "Tell them to give me fifteen," I said. I had something to take care of.

I was already on the Peters/Brown area of the lot when it became clear to me what a bad idea it is to swallow a handful of new prescription drugs on an empty stomach. I stopped walking as my world slipped sideways. I lost control of the Tyne Daly script; random sheets of paper fell from my grasp. Even in this alarming moment of dizziness, I couldn't help thinking this script was probably no worse with the pages missing.

Luckily, I was near the open door of one of the sound stages on the lot; I could go inside, get out of the sun. I stumbled up the four small steps to the narrow side door that led into the cavernous sound stage.

"Hey, the line starts back here, asshole!" I turned to see who had spoken. It was then that I noticed a long, restless line of people waiting to enter this particular studio. Pale, overweight people with tote bags and disposable cameras. These people were shooting pictures of celebrity *parking spaces*. That said it all. The unruly crowd waiting here in the heat today could be none other than a live studio audience.

Confused, I looked back at the sign beside the entrance to the building: Peters/Brown Studio 7. *Studio 7*. Shit — of all places. Everybody in the country, probably the world, knew what show was taped here in Studio 7. TV's most outrageously popular daytime talk show: "Hey, Girlfriend" — hosted by the reigning queen of American pop psychology, Kelley Jenks.

I knew Kelley Jenks from the giant billboard, on one of the outside walls of the lot. The big, bright sign featured tiny Kelley sitting right in the middle of her overstuffed pink sofa, clapping her small hands with delight in response to some unknown stimulus and wearing an oversized pair of pink bunny slippers

There were two things everybody in America knew about "Hey, Girlfriend" — all the guests were women, and each guest was required to take off her shoes and put on slippers before she joined Kelley Jenks on the pink sofa. Like a big pajama party. Kelley would always smile and pat the cushion next to her; come, sit next to *me*, girlfriend.

"Hey, you — asshole!" Same message, different voice.

"Sorry — I'm not cutting in front of you, I'm from the network," I gasped out. Without waiting for a response, I yanked the door open. "I'm sorry sir, we're not letting people in yet!" A perky, college-aged page in a bright blue blazer, her shiny black hair pulled back into tight ponytail, rushed over very importantly to block my entrance. She was swinging her glossy tail of hair on purpose, and her gold nametag said she was Peggy Chen.

"It's all right, Peggy, I'm with the network — development." I gave perky Peggy Chen a wink, which she of course just ate up. "I'm sitting in today — just wanted to grab a seat in the back before the crowd comes in. Okay?" Smiling, Peggy Chen waved me in and pointed to an empty seat in the top tier.

I slipped past her — then, instead of climbing up to my seat, ducked into the tiny men's room and, as quietly as possible, threw up everything I'd eaten since "Cheers" went off the air.

I splashed some cold water on my face before making my unsteady exit. I was obviously going to miss my writer's meeting. Clinging tight to the railing, I half-walked, half-crawled up to my seat in the back row, and then waited in the dark, alone in the empty stands. I'm pretty sure no one could see me up there.

And then, suddenly, there she was — Kelley Jenks, striding out onto the stage, surrounded by an entourage of thin, worried-looking female assistants dressed in various shades of black. She was five feet tall and no more than ninety pounds, most of it cleavage. She had a gleaming, shoulder-length pile of that Hollywood hair, bright blond, its roots a black starfish washed up on a sandy beach.

18

But right now, Kelley Jenks wasn't smiling her delighted, billboard smile. She was screaming, her pink-frosted rosebud lips parted in *shrieks like mandrakes' torn out of the earth* — that horrid, wrenching sound the freaked-out teenage Juliet so aptly described while considering the unwelcome possibility of meeting dead relatives in the tomb: "These are the wrong fucking slippers!!! Get me the right ones, goddammit!!! NOW!!!" I really hate to argue with Shakespeare, but when it comes to what goes on behind the scenes in the entertainment industry, apparently sometimes the fault *is* in our stars.

And then, out from behind the back wall of the set, clutching a pair of pink bunny slippers exactly like the one that had caused Kelley's sudden meltdown, emerged the loveliest creature in the world.

Most radiant, exquisite and unmatchable beauty! My exhausted brain borrowed this from "Twelfth Night." I'm not a writer; I'm a suit.

Even though the bright stage lights made my head ache like a son-of-a-bitch, I just had to look at her. A cascade of warm, brown curls that glinted with golden lights, as unruly as Kelley's straight, blond hair was clipped and coifed, flowed down the back of her soft white dress, almost to her tiny waist. Her flawless skin was the color of sweet honey dripping from a spoon. From whence could a person who looked like this possibly have come? What country, what century, what planet?

She also had these really great tits. I look at tits. I'm not fussy about size or anything. I like them all.

Without saying a word, the creature took away one pair of Kelley's size-four pink bunnies, and replaced them with the other. Then, carrying one of the wrong fucking slippers in each hand, she disappeared.

Before I knew it, the show was over. Kelley Jenks had worked her talk-show magic on the audience; they appeared excited and happy as they grabbed their tote bags and cameras, scuffling out of their seats to head for, I don't know, Universal Studios or Knott's Berry Farm or somewhere.

They had to step over me on the way out, though. I had pulled out of my dreamy trance, only to realize I felt not a whole lot better than I had when I came in. I closed my eyes and motioned my fellow audience members to go past me, which they seemed only too happy to do. Yeah, definitely going to Universal Studios.

"Excuse me, sir, are you all right?" I sensed a hand on my shoulder. Not a particularly light touch — a firm, warm hand. It felt odd; it had been at least eight months since anyone had touched my arm who wasn't poking around for an available vein. I opened my eyes to behold the woman with the unruly hair and the green-gold-silver-amber eyes, staring down at me with an expression of deep concern. She was here.

I lifted my head, and stared back. "Yeah, thanks," I finally said. "I . . . came here right from a workout at the gym, and I forgot to eat anything. I'll be fine."

"You need carbs. Maybe you should have some fruit juice. We have all kinds of juice backstage."

I shook my head. I shouldn't have; it hurt. "I'm fine. Terrific. Really."

She did not look convinced. "Well, okay. But if you need anything at all, just let me know. I'm Kelley's personal assistant. I've got to get backstage. I don't know what Kelley wants yet, but it's always *something*." She wrinkled her cute nose for a split-second, but very quickly her smile returned. "Just call down for me. I'm Ophelia."

Her name was *Ophelia*? Ophelia, as in *Hamlet*? *Chaste treasure, maiden presence — sweet Ophelia*? Hello. This wonderful, not-at-all-blond person, whose roots miraculously matched the rest of her hair, had to be the Dark Lady, the Dark Lady of the Sonnets, the Dark Lady of Studio 7, the Dark Lady of television's most popular daytime talk show, "Hey, Girlfriend." *My* Dark Lady.

I had not even had to look for her. She had found me. She had touched me.

"Wait . . . I think . . . maybe some juice might help after all," I called after her. Actually, I was suddenly feeling a great deal better. But it was much too soon to let her go.

"Sure." She seemed pleased to be able to do something. "Back in a sec."

Almost immediately, a whole bunch of those thin young women in black, led by Ophelia in her flowing white dress, began appearing

20

at my side. They were bearing bottles of juice of all kinds and colors, their faces contorted with anxiety.

"Thank you all, but this one will be just fine," I said, motioning at whatever it was Ophelia held in her incredibly soft hand. *Her* hand had to be soft, didn't it? "The rest of you can go."

I gave Ophelia a calculatedly weak smile as she placed in my hand a frosted plastic bottle containing, Jesus, what was this, a banana-coconut smoothie. It was thick, slippery, and sweet. Not a beverage, not solid food, but something wretchedly in-between.

"This is wonderful, thanks," I murmured. I shook her hand. Very soft indeed. "I'm with the network; development. Ken Harrison."

"You're a network executive?" She seemed to like that. "I'm very interested in development. I've been working for Kelley Jenks for the past four years, but actually I'm an actress."

An actress? Oh, great. No matter what kind of encounter I tried to have with an actress, it always turned into an audition. But, at this moment, her acting aspirations just might be something I could work with. "Really?" I managed to sound surprised. "I'm involved in a lot of casting for the network shows. Right now, I'm in movies and mini-series."

I had said the word "casting" in front of an actress. Her eyes began to sparkle. "Ophelia, I'd really like to thank you for helping me out today. Let me take you to lunch this week. We could talk about . . . your career."

"Ophelia, I need you." bellowed Kelley Jenks.

Ophelia jumped from her seat and made a face — not at me. "Um . . . when?" she asked, hesitantly.

"Tomorrow?" I said quickly. "I'm booked for the rest of the week, but I had a cancellation. Things have been just *crazed*."

"Oh, yes, here too! I'm just *dying*!" Ophelia nodded happily.

"Ophelia!"

"All right — tomorrow . . . Ken?" Ophelia said.

"Noon, then. I'll drop by." I gave her an enigmatic half-smile, the kind that sometimes worked with women, and always worked with actresses. "Say, did you ever . . . do any Shakespeare?"

I don't care where you're going, or how late you are; you just don't climb over another person like he's not even there. Shame on all those people in the studio audience — their mommas ain't raise them right, as my grandma on my mother's side always says.

At first I was just going to leave Ken alone, even though my job description as Kelley's assistant includes "maintaining audience equilibrium," because that story about the gym — well, I'm not saying I didn't believe him, but there are a lot of people with serious drug problems out here in Hollywood — it's sad, but oh, so true.

Now, if I were to go back home and tell my grandma on my mother's side how many very wealthy, successful, powerful Hollywood executives, men with everything in the world, still have a taste for illegal substances, she'd probably say something along the lines of: "White folks is a mess." In fact, that's exactly what she'd say. She'd be just as critical of a person of color who violated her rules of propriety. She's a bigot, my Grandma Nettie Mae, but an equal-opportunity one, I believe. No, that's not true; she's really an awful, awful woman. But at eighty-nine she still bakes the most extraordinary chocolate chip brownies, knits me cable-stitch sweaters, and I love her dearly.

But gosh, those people just made me so angry; I had to do something. Besides, he looked so fragile, sitting there with his head in his hands, swimming in that gorgeous, slate-gray Armani suit. His sandy hair was short, like a military buzz cut that's grown out about half an inch. We invite a lot of military personnel to join our studio audience; they usually seat them right next to the Make-A-Wish kids and pan the cameras there for a moment before every commercial break. One might see this as manipulative, but I figure the chance to be part of a live studio audience *has* to make a person feel better about being shipped out to Baghdad.

Then I realized I had to be wrong — no military man could possibly afford this suit; this was a network executive suit. This was exactly the kind of suit they mean when they call someone a "suit" in Hollywood. I never much cared for that expression; it sounds like there's no one inside.

I also had to be practical. The ghost-pale man in the Armani suit, though perhaps bravely on his way to conquering his addiction, did look as if he were going to be sick — and I had no desire to face Kelley's reaction should this occur in her newly-remodeled, white-maple, state-of-the art studio.

You can't really thank a person for not vomiting, but in the end I was grateful to Ken for making the right choice. I think it was the banana coconut smoothie. You just can't feel bad with one of those in your hand; it's like your own private tropical vacation.

And I was so surprised and flattered that he asked me out to lunch! Although it does happen to me a lot here in Hollywood. I'm embarrassed to say I get taken out to lunch so much I don't even really know how much lunch costs anymore.

Still, I really am surprised and flattered each time I'm asked. It's like getting fresh flowers, and who ever gets tired of birds of paradise, blue irises and tiger lilies?

I do lunch even when I'm not hungry. Although I usually am — unlike most women in the industry, I have a very healthy appetite, probably because my grandma on my mother's side always told me: "Clean your plate or I'll go upside yo' head." Doing lunch is my calling here in Hollywood. I do it for my budding acting career, one must *network*, but I also do it because I feel sorry for men like Ken Harrison, mid-level creative executives charged with the overwhelming psychological burden of making a great deal of money while having no particular skills.

I don't want power, I prefer flowers. I am an *artist*, thank you very much. I could never be a power player in the entertainment industry, not even at mid-level — in fact, the whole idea of even being a *man* makes me feel completely exhausted and even a tad depressed; maybe it's the limited clothing options. But that doesn't mean that I'm not . . . curious, sometimes. I know, silly me, but I wonder what it would be like to be Ken Harrison — or, heck, if I'm going to wonder, I might as well go ahead and wonder what it would be like to be Ken Harrison's boss, or *his* boss, or — just hypothetically — the head of the entire network entertainment division.

One day my acting career will blossom like a bower of bougainvillea, all bright magenta blooms, I just know it, but it's been ten years and . . . well, every once in awhile I wonder what it would be like to be a suit, to have the power to run Hollywood.

Sometimes, when I'm driving up here on Mulholland Drive, the Southern California sky a big blue blank, winding around the curves past big houses with decks cantilevered out over the hillside on tall stilts, pools, lounge chairs and umbrella tables just hanging out there over nothing — I wonder what would it would be like if, one day, at the end of the day, all the maids, gardeners, nannies, and pool men locked the gates and wouldn't let the owners back in. I don't wonder every day, but some days I do, especially when there's not a cloud in the sky.

Of course, I never tell anyone about my daydream, and certainly not the suits — I mean, the *men* who hold the power. After doing lunch for ten years, I understand them well enough to know they wouldn't understand.

But this time there was something in his eyes, mournful gray eyes the color of a Midwestern thunderstorm, looking up at me with dazed wonder when I put my hand on the shoulder of his gorgeous Armani suit, that made me think that maybe this suit, Ken Harrison, would.

Diane Haithman's *Dark Lady of Hollywood* was a finalist in the William Faulkner Creative Writing Awards competition, novel-in-progress category.

Diane was an Arts Staff Writer for the *Los Angeles Times* until October, 2009 and is now a major contributor to Nikki Finke's Deadline Hollywood industry website. She first joined the *Times* covering the television industry before moving to the fine arts beat. During her tenure, she spent the Spring, 2000 semester at the University of Southern California as the *Times'* Writer-in-Residence at the Annenberg School of Journalism and is currently on the Membership Committee of PEN USA.

Prior to joining the *Times*, Diane was West Coast Bureau Chief and Hollywood columnist for the *Detroit Free Press*, based in Los Angeles. She has been a Critic Fellow at the Eugene O'Neill Theater Center's New Playwrights Conference.

Diane is an honors graduate of the University of Michigan with a joint degree in English and Psychology. She is co-author of the book "The Elder Wisdom Circle Guide for a Meaningful Life" (Penguin/Plume 2007). Contact: dianehaithman@gmail.com

CONSULTATION

─────────── ℘℧ ───────────

by Ruben Varda

"You're making progress, Kit, I like your universe. You managed to achieve rapid stabilization. This promises long life without any shock. Tell me, how do you see its future? What might its zest, or uniqueness, be, so to speak?"

Kit smiled, flattered by the words of her Professor.

"You are right, Professor, it is stable, that's true, but because of this it is not very lively. Not much happens there. At the moment I do not see any zest, and I'm afraid I have to add one more spatial dimension."

"And if you continue to play with the initial conditions, without adding a new dimension?"

"It is possible, of course," Kit hesitated. "But first I will continue as planned, and if it does not work, then I will follow your advice."

"Fine, but remember that not much time is left, examinations are coming soon. If you need my assistance, come and see me."

"Thank you, Professor, certainly I will show you the results again and will consult you."

"Is there anyone left behind the door?" asked the Professor. "Tell them to come in."

"I believe only God is waiting," Kit said, gathering her papers.

"Come in, God, come in. As usual you're the last," mumbled the Professor. " Well, is there any progress since our last meeting?"

"I took into account all your remarks, Professor, and look what I got," said God, unfolding his paper.

"Well, and what have you there, God?" asked the Professor in a tired voice. This group of students was his biggest, and they exhausted him with the results of their numerous simulations.

"You see, Professor, since your last consultation I have considered many different models. You know, my specialty is bio-universes, so I tried to build a model of the universe where at some stage of the development bits and pieces based on silicon or carbon emerge. In the beginning nothing good happened, and even when I succeeded for a short time in creating large molecules, they soon broke up into component parts. But once I got lucky: I managed to create quite a complicated and twisted helix molecule, after which the process went with astonishing speed. And then I set a goal: to create, firstly, a biological object in my image and likeness, so that in its appearance it would be like me, and secondly, to ensure that sooner or later the object would realize that by its very existence it is indebted to me and only me."

"Modesty, God, humbleness! You're still a student and look at your ambition! You think I do not know where this new fashion comes from? Creationism, or so they call it? And what good is it? What have you achieved with it, God, tell me."

God's mood began to worsen. He had expected praise and support from the Professor, and it turned out that all his efforts were in vain. Noticing this, the Professor felt his duty to support the talented, but somewhat presumptuous student.

"Do not worry, God, if it does not work with this one, build another universe. Your universe is just a file, and it can always be deleted."

"I would like to leave it and see what will happen with these amusing creatures."

"You can leave it if you like, but for me everything is clear: your universe has entered into the nonlinear mode. You managed to create life, but it turned out that to sustain one life another one should be destroyed. These amusing creatures, as you call them, will continue to deteriorate and, eventually, they will destroy this very life for which you created your universe. My advice to you, God: Go for a new universe. By the way, how many dimensions did you have there?"

"Initially there were many, but eventually only three spatial and one time dimension survived."

"That's it! And does time flows back and forth there, or only in one direction?"

"Only one, Professor," mumbled God.

"All clear! With only one time coordinate you make them forever hurry, jump like grasshoppers and overtake time, whence all this aggression. Why not try to build inverse bio-universes with one spatial and three time dimensions?" the Professor suggested cheerfully.

"I did try, Professor," God sighed sadly. "Even worse: they crawl along a single spatial coordinate and perpetually fight, either with ancestors or with descendants, and even with both simultaneously."

"Well, I do not know what to advise you, God. I am afraid that as long as you stick to your creationism, nothing sensible will come out. Look at Kit and other guys. They created quiet universes. It is a real pleasure to look at them."

"You know, Professor, I would have removed this universe and started a new one long ago if not for some amusing creatures. You laugh, but I have become attached to them."

"I do not understand, God." The Professor was genuinely surprised. "You mean to tell me that you learned to work at the level of individual creatures? There should be billions of them there! How do you do it?"

"I wrote a little program called "Guardian Angel." It follows the life of every amusing creature from birth to death, after which it automatically enters the data into the archive and destructs itself. As soon as a new creature is generated, the program copies a new guardian angel for it."

"And how do you distinguish one creature from another?"

"This is just something simple. I put into the program a random name generator, and to each creature it ascribes a name of several words. Sometimes the names are rather hilarious . . ."

"Like . . .?" The Professor became interested.

29

"Like, for example, Theophrastus Phillippus Aureolus Bombastus von Hohenheim — this one I like more than any other."

"Can you sum that up?"

"Yes! Paracelsus, meaning "greater than Celsus"* — so he nicknamed himself. With him I have fully succeeded. He teaches that amusing creatures "are made by me, God, from the alchemical 'extraction' of the world, like in the great laboratory, and bear the image of the Creator." I am not sure about the 'extraction' but, as you can see, Paracelsus realized whom he looked like and who created him. And he is not the only one who has cracked me."

"If so, then you deserve praise, God, you accomplished a lot!"

"Ah, Professor, if it were not for one thing: These amusing creatures are mostly busy destroying each other. With each new cycle of the program they create increasingly sophisticated weapons to kill their relatives."

"I do not want to repeat myself, God, but your single time dimension causes the problem. It leaves them no alternative; so be it, keep these three spatial dimensions, they are certainly accustomed to them, but introduce at least one additional time dimension, and you'll see it all will change for the better."

"I'll try, professor, but I fear that this would come as a shock for them."

"So introduce it cautiously, slowly, so that initially only scientists can guess the existence of the second time dimension — there should be scientists there, right? And so on, until you reach the politicians, and then these will decide how to proceed," the Professor suggested with sarcasm in his voice.

Knowing that the sarcasm was caused by the Professor's recent failure in the elections, God in his own way wanted to comfort him:

"Professor, you should see how my amusing creatures hold elections. Recently the opposition there has won sixty percent of the vote and, nevertheless, lost."

"It cannot be true," the Professor was astonished. "I do not believe it! You mean your amusing creatures have been able to think of nonlinear logic?"

---

* 2nd century Greek philosopher

"Yes, imagine that . . . but not the scientists, no. Scientists out there were persecuted for centuries! A few hundred cycles ago they burned at the stake a philosopher who claimed that the creation of only one universe is unworthy of me, God."

"Imagine that! They managed to hit upon it! What insight! And what was your philosopher's name?"

"Giordano Bruno,"* replied God.

"Nice name, I like it," the Professor said thoughtfully, and unexpectedly added: "Excellent! Really, I did not expect this much from you, God. I will recommend your work for the prize."

The Professor looked at God, wanting to see the seeds of joy on his face, but God was silent. He sat with his head bowed.

"Is something wrong, God? You're not happy with that?"

"I am glad, of course," God sighed. "But, you see, Professor, the data of these two visionaries, Paracelsus and Bruno, are long in the archives, and few of the amusing creatures are aware of them. There are now various fashionable theories about the origins of the amusing creatures. While some do recognize me, God, as the creator of the universe, for some reason they have decided that I did this in six days, in the end personally sculpting from the clay the first funny creatures. Complete misapprehension of the problem. Then there are those who believe that the theory about six days is a fairytale, and argue that funny creatures emerged during the evolution of other, equally funny though less intelligent creatures. That is closer to reality, but they have completely eliminated the possibility of my very existence, while, in fact, I conceived and wrote the program that really drives their evolution," God said with undisguised bitterness in his voice. "And one of the highest authorities in this school of thought is trying to convince everyone that I, God, am just some mental virus that gets into the heads of funny creatures in early childhood. I do not know what to say. Me — a virus?"

"Do not worry God," said the Professor. "One cannot avoid surprises in such a complex problem. But that's why it is so interesting!

---

* The great Italian philosopher and poet Giordano Bruno was burned alive at Campo dei Fiori in Rome in the morning of 17th February 1600 after spending eight years in the jails of the Holy Inquisition.

I was wrong. Do not delete this universe. Leave and continue to monitor its development. At the same time, here is my advice: make a backup copy and cautiously enter the second time dimension — you will see a lot of new interesting things. But only after exams!"

Ruben Varda (Vardapetian) was born in Yerevan, the capital of Soviet Armenia. He wrote and later published in Moscow his first fantasy novel in Russian: *The Girl with a Lute*. Ruben is now writing his second novel.

Ruben received a PhD in physics from the Moscow Lomonosov University and then worked in Armenia, teaching and doing research in the Yerevan University and in the Academy of Sciences. In 1992 he moved to Denmark and in 1996 was posted by the Danish Ministry of Research to Brussels. Since then he has lived in the Belgian capital, mainly occupied with the management of R&D projects, the latest being on EU-Russia cooperation in nanoelectronics. Contact: arsos@mail.ru

GATES OF EDEN

— ℘☊ —

Excerpt from the novel
by Charles Degelman

Months before the assassination, Barry Shear resigned his lecturer's post at Harvard to take a promised position in John F. Kennedy's new international aid program, the Peace Corps. The appointment was delayed by the bad joke of a bureaucratic bungle, strike three after a broken marriage and a death in the family.

"Screw it," he mumbled.

Five days later, Harry disappeared from Cambridge to take a job teaching history at the most unlikely place he could find in America — Bronco, Texas. Period. In a further capitulation to impulse, he rented an Airstream trailer parked in a grove of cottonwoods down by the river and settled into watery, contemplative seclusion.

School opened. An already-restless Barry Shear launched a project to inject inspiration into his listless Texas students. "What's going on out there?" he shouted at the somnambulant teenagers. "What are these new governments in Africa all about? Who's Patrice Lumumba? Why is Guatemala mad at America? What are these crazy guys with the beards doing in Cuba?" He rattled on like a brainy Gatling gun, never waiting for answers.

Shear's energy and urbane sense of humor confused the kids at Bronco High. Teachers were supposed to be staid, boring. The students gossiped about him in the halls. He was a communist, a weirdo. The guys thought he was a homo; the girls thought he was cute.

On the other hand, Bronco High senior Roger Wolfe looked upon Shear with curiosity: *Who was this guy? Where did he come from? What was he doing in Bronco?* He was different, this Shear guy, and Roger enjoyed probing the man on everything from racism to rock and roll.

How different he was from Roger's father, who, on his rare visits home, spoke of the faraway lands he visited with drunken contempt. Holding a beer or a bourbon in his hand, lips loosened with the booze, the old man loved to comment on how filthy and disgusting "those people" were — the Africans in Nigeria, Indians in Guatemala and of course, the deadly ever-present depravity of commies everywhere, in China, in Russia, in Cuba. When Roger questioned his old man about his travels, Dick Wolfe would wave his drink in the air, blink with annoyance and snarl, "none a your business."

Barry Shear on the other hand, seemed to get a big kick out of Roger's questions. He took time to answer. He suggested that worlds lurked beyond the horizon, worlds that promised novelty, adventure and hope. This prospect excited Roger, and he began to feel a sense of kinship with the Northerner, a kind of closeness he had never known before.

One day, Mister Shear took Roger Wolfe aside after class. "You know, Wolfe," he began, "I suspect you may have the potential to evolve into a human being. Stranger things have happened."

"What're ya pickin' on me for, Mr. Shear?"

"I'm not picking on you, kid. I'm offering you a shovel so you can dig yourself out of this shit heap."

"What shit heap?"

Shear laughed. "C'mon, Wolfe. Look around you. What shit heap you think I'm talking about?"

"You mean Bronco?"

"Bingo, Roger. Bronco."

"What's wrong with Bronco, Mr. Shear?"

"Oh, nothing. If you're a go-nowhere dumbbell with a future full of oil rigs and cow shit. Nothing wrong with that, Wolfe. Problem is . . ." he grinned. " . . . there's something wrong with you."

"Huh?"

"You're different. You don't have the same crapped-out attitude everybody else's got around this dump." His features softened. "You don't even know it, do you?"

"Don't know what?" Roger asked.

"That you don't fit in." Shear pointed a pencil at Roger. "You don't belong here."

"Who says?" Roger was popular among his classmates, most of whom he had known since he was six or seven. He had grown into a handsome teenager. Brown eyes warmed the Nordic features he had inherited from his mother, Dottie. Nevertheless, he often felt alone in Bronco. Other kids had parents, a family. Roger's mother had just been diagnosed with cancer and he had stopped calling his father "dad," mainly because the old man was never around. Now Barry Shear was telling Roger there was a reason for his loneliness.

"Look, I don't have time to fuck around," Shear said. "Neither do you. I'm gonna be outta this place verrrry soon, and you're going to graduate in June. So I'm taking a chance here. I'm telling you the truth."

"What truth?"

"You have a brain. You have spirit. And somewhere, hidden beneath that atrocious cowboy hat and those dirty fingernails, you've got class. It's your senior year." He pointed the pencil toward the door. "Get your ass down to Austin." He stood to leave. "Go to college. I hear they let cowboys in for free."

Shear left Bronco the day after John F. Kennedy was assassinated. Nobody saw him go; he never said goodbye, not even to Roger. Shear was gone, but the line stuck in the young Texan's head. Go to college. *I hear they let cowboys in for free.*

By June, the cancer had reduced Roger's mother to a nightgown-draped skeleton. The cigarettes she had smoked since she was a teenager tarred her alveoli and mutated her cells. With her husband perennially out of town, Dottie turned to Roger as she had so many times before.

He accepted his responsibilities with a loyalty electrified by fear. Every day he would stop home after school to make sure she had eaten, taken her medications or kept a doctor's appointment. Then he would race off to pump gas at the local Texaco. Despite his care, Dottie continued to waste away. As she did so, she retreated from the world, leaving Roger helpless and guilt-ridden. *Why was she leaving? What was he doing wrong?*

When she was too weak to walk, the doctor ordered her into 24-hour care. Two orderlies took her — still strong enough to curse and look good at the same time — from Roger's arms and escorted her to the county hospital. Dottie Wolfe died on a Thursday afternoon while Roger was pumping gas beneath a bright, blue Texas sky.

He called his father in New Orleans. "Mom died."

"Shit."

"What? What did you say?"

"Nothing. It's just bad timing."

"Yeah, well . . . " Roger felt his anger rise. "It was bad timing for Mom, too."

"What's that supposed to mean?"

"Never mind." He sighed into the phone. "Can you come home?"

"It's gonna take some doin' . . . "

"Please, Dad."

"Can't stay for long."

Dick Wolfe stood at the fringes of a small cemetery crowd, arms crossed over a skinny tie and white shirt, watching his son and a sprinkling of Dottie's friends grieve over his dead wife's casket. Afterward, father and son drove to the gas station where Roger unlocked the garage doors, turned on the pumps, and silently gassed up his father's rental car. The old man was heading back to New Orleans and the shelter of his FBI cronies.

"Don't you miss her?" Roger asked.

38

"Sure I do."

"You miss me?"

" 'Course I do." He cracked his knuckles. "That's one helluva question for you to ask."

"But you can't stay."

"No, I . . ."

"You got important work to do, right?"

"You better believe it, buddy." He gave Roger's shoulder a squeeze.

"I took good care of her, Dad. Best I could, anyways."

"You're a good man, Roger."

"I'm a man now? That's what it takes? My mother dyin'?"

"Hey, take it easy. We're all pretty broke up here."

"Bullshit. You don't say 'shit' and 'bad timing' when you hear your wife is dead. You say 'shit' when you run over a skunk and it stinks up your tires."

"I said, take it easy."

"You barely make it to the fucking funeral and now . . . you're gone again. You call that 'broke up?' " Tears blurred his vision. He clenched his jaw. He wouldn't let his father see him cry. "You're not supposed to treat your wife — the people you love — like that."

"I have my reasons for comin' and goin'."

"Yeah?" Grief wrenched a sob out of his gut. "Like what?" He jammed the gas nozzle back in its cradle with a metallic clash. "Like what?"

"National security is a big deal in this day and age, boy. You know that."

"They can't spare you for a minute?"

"I'm protectin' you . . . "

"From what?"

"I'm not at liberty to say."

Roger laughed a loud, harsh bark. "Mom didn't need any fuckin' national security. She needed somebody who cared about her." He retreated into the gloom of the garage, looking for a rag to wipe his hands. "Only, knowin' you," he emerged from the shadows, "she didn't need that either."

Dick Wolfe grabbed his son by the arm. "Look, you little bastard. The world is a dangerous place. While you're fiddle-fucking around here with your girlfriends —"

"I don't have a girlfriend."

" — I'm the one keepin' you people safe."

"Thanks a pantload, dad."

"You don't have to like what I do. Shit, boy, you don't even know what I do. But goddammit . . . " He pushed his son backward with flat-handed shoves to the chest. "I know my enemies. Do you?"

Roger thought about Barry Shear and the half-serious, half-hilarious position he took about America, past and present. "Oh, I know all about it. You think the enemy's out there." He swept an arm across the horizon. "That makes you a fuckin' idiot, Dad." He folded his arms and leaned against the car. "The biggest enemy is right here. Right here in the U.S. of A. It's the fucking Pentagon-assed, military-industrial complex, that's who the enemy is."

The elder Wolfe paused. "Who taught you how to talk like that?

Roger laughed in his face. "You did." He folded his arms and leaned against the car. "Mom dies alone while you play hero? In my book, that makes you the enemy."

Dick Wolfe's hands locked around his son's throat, throwing the teenager off balance. They stumbled against the garage workbench, knocking a tray of socket wrenches into the grease pit behind them. Wolfe found Roger's shin with the inside of his boot and drove straight down. Roger screamed in pain. Locked together, father and son tumbled into the pit.

Roger scrambled to his feet first, leg and ankle burning. Wheezing from pounded lungs, he bent over. His father lay still. Oil and a thin trickle of blood blended into a viscous mess on the grease pit floor. Outside the garage, the afternoon light angled from the west, lengthening the shadows of the cottonwoods, darkening the cluttered interior.

Roger knelt over his father's form. Beneath his shaking hand, the older man's chest rose and fell. He was breathing. Pressure built behind Roger's eyes. He couldn't cry, not again, not over this, not now.

Hands shaking, he locked the gas station, drove the rental car behind the garage, parked it, locked it and threw the key into the alfalfa field beyond. Roger didn't want his old man mobile. He climbed into his old, red Ford pickup and drove to the bungalow on

Edna Mae Street. Edna Mae Street, where he had lived his life, where his father had shared his table like an alien, where his mother had lain in bed, reading magazines and dying.

He opened the door onto the barren living room, neglected during his mother's demise — the rug filthy, the drapes dingy, the naked, oriental-lady lamps broken. The West Texas sunset bounced off five hundred miles of red New Mexico dirt and burst into the near-empty home, projecting a perfect square of rich orange light across the blank living room wall.

He put on a Sinatra record, one of his mom's favorites, and limped into the bathroom. He turned on the shower and shed his funeral clothes. The whole front of his shin had been scraped blood red. "Bastard," he spat out loud, hoping hatred would defeat the fear. He could picture his father lying in the grease pit.

Please don't let him die, too.

With his raw leg smarting, he soaped down before the water got hot. He had to leave — that night. He was going to begin his life, right now, tonight, just like Barry Shear said he should. He'd get out of town, head for Austin and the college they had there. They let cowboys in for free, that's what Mister Shear had said.

Madeline Singer dragged herself out from under warm covers in her chilly East Village flat. Shivering, she rapidly donned a man's blue work shirt and jeans. She pulled on a baggy V-neck sweater and laced up a pair of hiking boots. She tucked a wild sphere of curly black hair into a red bandana, but stubborn ringlets still cascaded around her baby-smooth features and olive skin. Teeth chattering, she put on water for coffee while she packed a gigantic Indian-print shoulder bag she had purchased on Bleecker Street the summer before. It had been tough to get out of bed that early, especially when it was still cold, but she was determined to follow through with her plan.

Days earlier, she had picked up a leaflet from a guy in the NYU student union. They called themselves Students for a Democratic Society. They seemed cool and she liked the straightforward logic of the writing.

41

The war hurts the Vietnamese people.
The war hurts the American people.
SDS says U.S. get out of Vietnam.

Madeline resolved to cover the protest march SDS was organizing in Washington, D.C. She was sure she would find a story.

"I want to write this up." She spun the leaflet onto the desk in front of the newsroom crowd at the NYU paper. "It's against the war."

"What war?" the editor asked. At 22, he had already affected the attire of a *Washington Post* columnist — bow tie, suspenders. "You talking about the Indochina thing?"

"Vietnam. SDS is putting together a mass demonstration this weekend. It sounds cool."

"Cool. Boring speeches. Aching feet. Sweaty liberals. But for you . . . ?" The blond sportswriter looked up at Madeline. He didn't see a young journalist with press credentials and a camera bag. He saw an exotic piece of ass, a goddess dressed in black, her Egyptian makeup framed by the corona of curly black hair. A short skirt hugged her butt and a Capezio leotard telegraphed "no bra, no bra" through horizontal red-and-black stripes. Slim hands grasped a tie-dyed canvas bag.

"Vietnam? That's no war," the editor replied. "They got the Peace Corps over there, running clinics and shit."

"Yeah? And so why did Kennedy just send gobs more troops over?"

"Come on, Madeline." The editor rolled his eyes. "They're just advisors."

"Who says?" Madeline asked.

"*The New York Times*," the editor snapped. "That's who."

"Oh! Well. Hey. If *The Times* says so, shucks. They must be just advisors." She feigned chagrin. "Silly me."

"So instead . . . " The editor passed the pamphlet to the sportswriter. "You want us to believe this crap?"

"I don't care what you do. I'm going to Washington." Madeline snatched back the pamphlet. "And I'll bring you back a story so big . . . " She stopped at the door. "You won't dare publish it."

Roger Wolfe hit Austin about 10 a.m. After a night full of driving, his head reeling with images of his gaunt mother and bloodied father, the young fugitive desperately cast about for an anchor, a place to land in the midst of his panic and confusion. After an hour of wandering through the unfamiliar streets, he stumbled upon a boarding house near the campus filled with pasty-looking guys who called themselves "grad students." The landlady called them "beastniks," but they paid rent by the semester and rarely "raised a fuss," she assured him. She looked the young, red-eyed refugee up and down but, "seein' as how you can't judge a book by its cover," she took his thirty-five dollars for the week and let him drag his paltry belongings upstairs.

In the days that followed, Roger used his truck to land odd jobs. He got lucky helping the landlady's sister move, hauled a neighbor's trash to the dump, straightened a lopsided gate and patched a leaky porch roof, anything to augment his dwindling cash and to straddle a seat at the local diner where he hunched protectively over cheap breakfasts, cheese sandwiches, and truckers' chili. He spent evenings on the campus, juggling his daydreams and watching the pretty college girls walk by, books and notepads cradled against pastel-colored sweaters.

He couldn't stop thinking about Mister Shear and what he had said. 'There's something wrong with you.' And he had meant it in a good way. He missed Barry Shear but Roger knew he belonged here. "They let cowboys in for free." Saying it out loud made him grin.

"What's the joke?" A dark-skinned face floated above him, framed by a shaggy explosion of dark hair and a greasy fatigue jacket. A sheaf of mimeographed leaflets drooped over one arm.

"Nothin'. I was just thinkin'."

"That's a novelty. Most of the idiots around here avoid it like dogshit on a hot sidewalk."

Roger laughed. "Who're you?"

"Albert." The boy extended a chubby paw. "Like Einstein. The genius."

"Roger." Albert's palm felt warm, smooth, comforting.

"I've seen you hangin' out around here," Albert continued. "You in a fraternity?"

"No."

"You into politics?"

"You mean like voting?"

"No, man." Albert laughed. "I mean like throwing yourself on the gears of the machine."

"Huh? What machine?"

"The university. The machine. That's what Mario Savio calls it."

"Who?"

"Mario Savio."

"Uh, cool." Roger had no idea what the guy was talking about.

"They shut down a whole university. In Berkeley."

"Where?"

"Oh, man," Albert said. "In California. Near San Francisco."

That sounded cool. Mister Shear had talked about San Francisco like it was some kinda heaven. Roger had seen pictures. It looked nice with the ocean all around it. So Berkeley had a college. "So this college . . . who shut it down?"

"The students. And this guy Savio. A bunch of other people, even professors."

"Why'd they do that?"

Albert sat on the wall next to Roger. "This is a good sign."

"What is?"

"You ask questions. Look . . . " Albert stared down at Roger. "What you doin' tonight."

"Nothin'. Why?"

"Why don't you come to this meeting?"

"What meeting?"

"Students for a Democratic Society."

Crossing the campus with Albert, Roger realized he hadn't thought about his father or mother all day. For the first time. Maybe there'd be some chicks at this democratic society thing. He sure was lonesome.

Washington reminded Madeline of Paris. She had visited the great French city twice with her parents, once on the Bastille Day that followed the fall of Dien Bien Phu, the French Waterloo of Indochina. Madeline had been only six but she remembered gun shots. The streets had been filled with demonstrators, and government troops had fired at angry crowds.

Now, she wondered — Had the Paris protestors been celebrating or mourning their Indochina defeat? What had triggered such passion? Here in Washington, nothing moved except for the traffic on Constitution Avenue. Madeline feared that no one would come to this protest.

Doesn't anybody care?

As the sun rose above the buildings to the southeast, the Washington monument walked a perfect shadow across the Mall. In the shadow's wake, a scattered crowd of demonstrators began to trickle onto the grass, many of them students, but others, older, formally dressed like churchgoers. Negroes marched in the ranks, carrying signs.

One Man, One Vote — Selma or Saigon
Make Jobs, Not War

An awkward young man sporting an ill-fitting suit, a blond crew cut and heavy black glasses held a hand-lettered poster.

FORGET DEMOCRACY
Make the world safe for hypocrisy

Madeline wrote down the slogans she liked in her notebook. The procession grew, flowing around her like an indolent river dappled with hand clapping, snatches of song, laughter. A poorly played bugle blatted into the bright April air. The burgeoning crowd began to rally around the base of the monument.

As the gathering reached critical mass, a guy in a baggy corduroy sport jacket clambered onto the speaker's platform. He approached the microphone, gazing over the crowd that had spread away down the Mall. "Wow! You should see yourselves out there. You look great! So many of you!"

The crowd hooted and whistled.

"This war is like a razor," he began. "It slashes away any illusions about our government. We see them standing naked before us, fighting a war they did not declare. They act like they own Vietnam. They act like they own America. They act like they can use our country — and us — the way they want. But they don't own America. We do. And they can't use us. Not if we don't let them."

The crowd roared.

He made such simple sense and it seemed to turn people on. Madeline scribbled in her notebook.

The speaker stood motionless, startled by the impact of his words. Others joined him on the stage. Together, they reached into a box beside the podium, raised handfuls of paper in the air. "SDS gathered these petitions from all across the country. Fifty thousand signatures!" He grabbed another handful. "They shout out, these signatures. 'No more bullshit battles for democracy!' 'No more U.S. in Vietnam!'"

Madeline watched as the speaker joined a cadre of students who lifted the box of petitions to their shoulders and set off down the Mall toward the dome of the Capitol building. As they approached the Capitol, shouts of "one, two, three, four, we don't want your dirty war" found a rhythm and pushed the crowd forward.

A double line of helmeted cops waited at the foot of the Capitol steps. Grasping nightsticks, they linked arms, forming a chain.

"One, two, three, four, we won't fight your dirty war!" Chanting protestors took on the speed of a river forced into the narrows. Armed with voices and numbers, they would storm Congress!

"Stop!" An SDS leader shouted into a bullhorn. "Please stop! Please!" The SDSers formed a line, a fragile barrier between the charging demonstrators and the blue police line. "This is a non-violent demonstration, people! Stick to the plan . . . please."

The feisty vanguard subsided, hissing like a spent wave.

Madeline stopped with them, breathless, shaking. At one with her companions, she had wanted to rush the cops, to throw herself against the blue wall, to kick and punch and bite.

46

The SDS squad regrouped around the petitions. Diminished by the granite mass of the Capitol, they hefted the box like pallbearers and carried it, coffin-like, up the steps. A frightened government clerk stood at the top, dwarfed beneath the great rotunda. The petitions were delivered into his arms.

The April afternoon cooled, the sun set behind brick and granite. Their mission accomplished, the crowd dissolved. Lines of tired demonstrators drifted back to their buses. Madeline flowed with them, exhausted by the collective exultation of the march and confused by the sudden isolation she felt. She wished the demonstration would never end, that they could be pressed together, moving forward, forever.

The next morning, the sun flowed white across Madeline's pillow. The hypnotic bus ride home and a deep sleep had aroused great longing in her: She wasn't sure what had gone down in Washington, but she wanted it to happen again.

She threw on yesterday's jeans and work shirt and loped down five flights of stairs to the newsstand on the corner. "Hiya Morty," she said to the overweight newsie who ran the stand.

"Hiya, sweetheart," Morty wheezed. "Cold out still. And it's already April."

"Yeah," she said, absent-mindedly as she scanned the front page of *The Times*.

Washington Rally Attracts Thousands

"Thousands!" she muttered. "There were like a million people there!" She flipped the pages, reading snatches aloud. . . *Students clogged the sidewalk.'* " She glared up at the wheezing newsie. "Shit, Morty, They're lying! There were all kinds of people there. Black ones and white ones and old ones and young ones. We all marched together to the Capitol building with a huge pile of petitions. Don't they even say that?"

"Whaddya . . . You was there?" He looked skeptical.

47

She thrust her face into the paper. " '. . . *beards and blue jeans!*' Who cares what they wore!" She read on, incredulous, while he huffed and puffed in the background like a locomotive. What about the petition? What about Joan Baez and those songs? What about the guy who spoke? They didn't even give his name. He was so cool. "This isn't the way it was, Morty." She thought about her dumbass NYU editor and his childish faith in *The New York Times*. "This isn't the way at all!" She offered Morty a quarter.

"Keep it, sweetie," he said. "If *The Times* gives a person that big a charge? They owe you."

She scuffed back upstairs. *So this is how they do it,* she thought. *They don't lie . . . It's all about what they leave out. And why? What does* The New York Times *have to lose from a bunch of people saying a war shouldn't happen?*

The kettle whistled.

She brewed the coffee, sat down at the kitchen table and opened her notebook. She'd tell it like it was and the boys at the NYU paper would have to publish her story. Next time, she'd bring a camera.

"I wanna enroll."

A lady with bejeweled harlequin glasses glanced at Roger from behind a desk piled high with paperwork. "Good start, sugar." She resumed her work, head down. "You'll still need your completed Texas Common application, your name and Social Security number, two admissions essays, an official transcript on your school letterhead and the signature of your high school principal."

She clacked on stiletto heels across the room to a stained coffee pot. "And don't forget, hon," she called across the desks, "you'll want your SATs sent directly. Them scores on your high school transcript will not satisfy this requirement." She poured half a bowl of sugar into a mug, added coffee, and stirred.

"You're supposed to let cowboys in for free."

"You do have to apply, sweetheart." She dropped a postcard and a pamphlet on top of his wrinkled Bronco transcripts. "Even if you're Gene Autry."

"Shoot, ma'am, I don't hardly have an address."

"That's fine, dear," she answered vacantly, already on to the next task. "Give us what you got on that card."

Impatient and disappointed, Roger scribbled his name and the boarding house address down on the postcard and stomped out, boot heels clicking on the marble floor.

Outside, he blinked through the sunlight at the pamphlet. This wasn't going to be easy. A long wait. Red tape. An application fee. Favors from Bronco. This required a dad on one side, a mom on the other, a phone number, a principal's support. He had none of that.

Days later, a tired-looking detective in a rumpled blue suit appeared in the admissions office, looking for a Roger Wolfe. The harlequin lady fingered through the "W" file. "No Roger here. I got me a Deborah Wolfe."

"Deborah Wolfe didn't beat her old man half to death."

"Mercy me!" She embraced her cheeks with manicured fingers. "Wait a minute . . .There was a kid in here last week with that name. Wanted to enroll."

The detective pulled a greasy little spiral-bound notepad out of his coat pocket. "He fill in an application?"

"Nossir. I told him he'd have to wait for the spring semester to apply."

The detective turned to leave.

"Hold on here. I think he filled out a card. For the application notice." She opened a second file.

"What'd he look like?"

"Cute fella. Looked kinda like James Dean."

That evening, the landlady stood up from the oven when Roger walked into the kitchen. "There was a man came 'round, askin' after you," she said.

Roger's heart corkscrewed. Had his old man caught up with him? "Did he have a little moustache?"

"Oh, no, he was a detective." The landlady stood up from the oven. "I know him. Went to school with my son." She set a pan of corn muffins on the sideboard and fixed him with a sad, steady stare. "Have you done something wrong, dear?"

Upstairs, Roger packed his duffel bag, left $35 on the bed, and drove back to the campus. He had no idea what to do or where to go. He'd been busted. Busted for leaving his old man in the grease pit of a garage in a West Texas oil town. *Now what?* In his confusion, he tracked down Albert. "I gotta get to Chicago," he lied. "My mom's sick."

Albert took one look at his stricken friend and called the Chicago SDS office. "I got a volunteer for you. He's down here at U. Texas but he's comin' up there. Name's Roger." He hung up.

"I'm no student," Roger said. "What'll I tell them?"

"No one'll check. They need help. Just work your ass off."

That evening, Roger drove north toward Chicago, hoping the old Ford pickup would hold together.

Madeline stood in a forlorn Chicago neighborhood, exhausted but cranked on caffeine, snapping shots of the SDS national office with her Pentax. The headquarters for the rapidly growing organization huddled on the second floor of a crumbling red brick edifice east of Hyde Park. Weeds and broken glass stretched away from either side of the decrepit hulk. The rusty buttresses of the Chicago El wrapped themselves around one corner of the building.

She had been assigned to cover an upcoming campus protest at the University of Chicago and had just arrived, bleary-eyed, after a non-stop drive from Boston. Two years had passed since Madeline had filed her first anti-war story at NYU. The response was gratifying: The NYU chapter of Students for a Democratic Society quoted her continually. Her bow-tied editor and even the preppie sportswriter had been forced to acknowledge that Madeline had brought back a big story. Since then, her free-lance reputation had spread. After she graduated, Madeline moved to Boston where she fell in with a news collective that had started their own underground weekly, *The Back Bay Rat*.

Now, she climbed the splintery stairs to SDS headquarters. The door yawned open. "Anybody home?" *Strange*, she thought. Most movement offices kept their doors locked, even barred, a cautionary measure generated by repeated break-ins, trashings, and other poorly disguised forms of harassment, usually by the FBI and the local cops.

Inside, her eyes adjusted to a room full of battered desks, improvised tables, greasy typewriters, and an ink-stained Gestetner mimeo machine. In the kitchen, paint and plaster hung in curls off the ceiling. Over the sink, the bearded visage of Che Guevara confessed:

At the risk of sounding ridiculous, let me say that the true revolutionary is guided by great feelings of love.

Down the hall, a toilet flushed. A blue-jean-clad guy emerged from the bathroom. He strode toward her, buttoning his fly. He looked well built, the muscles of his arms and chest squared-off, his waist devoid of the usual politico paunch.

A phone rang from the parlor office. She wove through the maze of tables and rickety chairs, located the source, and picked up the phone. "Hello?"

"Hey, how's it going?" The voice at the other end of the line sounded familiar. "I'm looking for Brooks. Brooks Robinson."

"I don't know if he's here. I —"

Strong hands grabbed the phone and pushed her away.

"Hey!" she shouted. He smelled of soap, sweat, and hair oil.

"National office. Roger speakin'." He inspected her with soft, brown eyes. "Somebody'll be around. You know where you're headed? Yeah. Up Lakeshore. You got it? Right. Right. Yeah. Later."

"Who was that?" she asked.

He slammed down the phone. "Who are you?"

"Madeline Singer."

"What're you doing here, Madeline Singer?"

"I'm a journalist."

"Oh, great. Which side are you on?"

"Wow," Madeline said. "Who put a hair across your butt?"

"Just tell me what you're doing here. I've never seen you before and that ain't good."

"I'm writing a story. About SDS and the draft . . . "

"For who?"

"For whom."

"Fuck you. Who you with?"

"*The Back Bay Rat.*"

"I know, I know. Boston, right?"

"Right. And you just got us off to a terrible start, you lunkhead. I talked to Brooks Robinson on the phone. He said to come on ahead."

"Sorry. We been hassled a lot by the cops lately. And . . . " He shrugged. ". . . we been dragged through the mud by the media."

"Yeah," Madeline said. "By the *Chicago Tribune. The Sun Times*, the Bumfuck, Nebraska *Tweedledum*. Straight newspapers. That's not me. Come on, man." She presented herself to him. The stance was more than disarming. "Do I look like an establishment journalist to you?"

He scrutinized her black jeans, scoop-neck cotton blouse, and hoop earrings. As usual, a bright, cotton bandana failed to contain Madeline's curly black hair. "Not with those boots," he replied.

"What about the boots?"

"They're all scuffed-up. You know, like shit-kickers."

" 'Shit-kickers?' " She wrinkled her nose.

"Yeah. Shit-kickers. You know . . . " He broke into a sudden, sweet smile.

Despite herself, Madeline felt her heart flutter. *I'm here on assignment*, she reminded herself.

"Looks like you been raised on a farm," he continued. "Not the kind of outfit a snitch from the *Tribune* would be able to assemble."

"Okay, Sherlock. So I got the right kind of shit-kickers. But I don't live on a farm and I don't like the smell of cow poop. So . . . When can I talk to Brooks Robinson?"

He let his eyes roll freely down her body. "I've got work to do. You'll have to wait on your own."

"That's cool," she said. "I'm already working. You're a story all by yourself, buster. What kinda story, I wouldn't want to say . . . yet." She pushed a sleeping bag, a frayed sweatshirt and a dog-eared paperback out of the way and sat down on the end of the cot that ran beneath a bay window. "So where is everybody?"

"Up at the university."

An elevated train roared by the window outside, shaking the building.

Roger sat down at a table surrounded by a pile of mimeographed literature. He folded a pamphlet and stuffed it in an envelope.

"Why aren't you up there with the rest of them?" she asked.

"I'm not a student."

"If you're not a student . . . " she asked, "what are you doing at Students for a Democratic Society?"

"Fuck!" He spun in his chair. "You don't want to find out what's happening. You want to find out what's wrong!"

"I'm trying to get some information."

"I'll tell you what's wrong here," he said. "The fucking war. That's what's wrong. Why don't you go write about that? What's the matter . . . don't got any connections to the Pentagon? No inside line to Lyndon B. Johnson?"

"No, I don't," she said. "I'm trying to cover the Left, not the Man. Besides, I don't see anything wrong here."

He turned away.

"Can I help you?" She sat down at the table opposite him.

Outside, a slow-to-come rain first spattered, then steadily increased, sending the smell of summer-hot brick and pavement wafting up through the open windows of the stuffy second-story flat.

"I thought you'd never ask."

Charles Degelman is an award-winning author, editor, and producer living in Los Angeles. His first screenplay, *Fifty-Second Street*, garnered an award from the Diane Thomas Competition, sponsored by UCLA and Amblin Entertainment. His first novel, *A Bowl Full of Nails*, was a finalist in the Bellwether Competition, sponsored by Barbara Kingsolver. His impressions of two trips to Cuba have been published in *Cuba* by Travelers Tales. Co-founder of Indecent Exposure, a Los Angeles-based theater company dedicated to creating original work for the stage, Degelman has also written and produced a spate of documentary and educational films, including a feature-length biography of filmmaker John Huston and an award-winning Internet biography of Mozart. "Gates of Eden" is excerpted from a novel set in the anti-war movement of the 1960s. Visit the web site at www. charlesdegelman.org. Contact: chas@chasdeg.com

UNDER THE POINCIANA TREE[*]

--------------------------------- ℘℃℞ ---------------------------------

by Carlos Victoria
(translated from Spanish by David Landau)

On a night in Cuba during the dry season, while working as a watchman, I found a dead man. He was lying under a poinciana tree with his legs bent up to his chest, his head leaning on a root and his shoulders and back smeared with dirt.

I was guarding a warehouse near Camagüey where they kept foodstuffs and rum. The city lights twinkled in the distance. The warehouse, quite empty, was a big old ruined shed in the middle of a pasture, near a dirt road; my job was to spend the night in a sentry box and walk around the building every half-hour, with an unloaded rifle, to discourage prowlers.

During the watch, I liked to lean against a fence and peer up at the sky; after a few months I was able to recognize the stars. At times a friend came with a bottle of wine and we drank ceremoniously, clinking our tin cups as we toasted an uncertain future and the faraway splendor of other lands. But then my friend fell victim to a spiteful brother-in-law who turned stool pigeon and got him thrown in jail for selling clothes on the black market.

---

* Translated from "La ronda" in *El resbaloso y otros cuentos* (Miami: Universal, 1997), stories by Carlos Victoria.

Most often I made my rounds to the accompaniment of singing crickets and night birds. Once in a while an owl went squawking by, wings flapping in the darkness. Trucks beamed their headlights on the dirt road, the walls of shrubbery and sugar cane, then clanged away trailing billows of dust. At midnight, behind the warehouse, I often heard a rider scold his horse over the animal's reluctance to cross a rickety wooden bridge. The animal's hooves dug in stubbornly at the same place before the first plank, and the rider uttered a string of curses. I used to hear the angry voice and stick my head out of the sentry box to catch a glimpse of the man's shadow, raised up in the saddle, as he got the horse moving and the pair disappeared behind the sugar cane.

Mostly, the watch was uneventful — until I found the dead man.

Out of boredom, I sometimes took a path and followed it to an abandoned house that I thought I might use for making love, in case anyone attractive showed up and I could get her to do it. Night watchmen are always thinking up such things. As I walked along, I parted the flimsy shrubs by swinging my gun like a broom; I pulled leaves and twigs off my clothes and crushed big watercress leaves with my rifle-butt. All at once I saw a body near the trunk of the poinciana. I drew close, thinking it was a drunken man curled up in sleep. I grabbed and shook his arm. It was like shaking a piece of cement.

Quaking and drenched in sweat, I hurried back to the sentry box and phoned my chief.

"Come at once. There's a dead man here."

"What do you mean, there's a dead man? Did you kill him?"

"Of course not! How would I kill him?"

"Who is he?"

"I don't know. I've never seen him before."

"How can you not know?"

"Did I fail to mention he's dead? I can't talk to him. Get over here and call the police."

Two patrol cars arrived along with an ambulance, a motorcycle and the chief's jeep, full of militiamen. It was the biggest event the desolate spot had seen in many years. The militiamen, a bit soused, put severe looks on their faces and shook their heads, walking about in whispers with hands clasped behind their backs. A lieutenant with an idiotic face questioned me two times, all the while taking notes with a dull pencil. He kept telling me: "What I need to know is how he kicked it." Then he took up the phone and called his wife, or his sweetheart, and spoke softly to her in what sounded, by their honeyed tone, like phrases of love. The dead man was removed, covered with a flour sack that had Russian letters printed on it. The cleanup went on until dawn.

Later the chief told me about the investigation's finding: this was neither a murder nor a suicide. The doctors, it seemed, had ruled it a death from natural causes — a clot on the brain or perhaps a heart attack. No one could say what the man was doing under the poinciana. He had lived on the other side of the city with a son — his wife having remarried and moved to a town in Matanzas province. One morning, the week before, the man had left his house to stand on a bread line. By afternoon his son was looking for him in the food store but no one remembered having seen him. He was forty years old.

The night after, I felt quite a lot of fear. I wouldn't even make the rounds of the warehouse. I kept in the doorway of the sentry box, looking at the leafy silhouette of the poinciana, which stood out majestically on the large, level terrain. The nearby shrubs gave a stunted, sickly appearance, while farther off the bristling sea of sugar cane stretched across the horizon. The crickets and birds were quiet; only the insistent barking of a nearby farm dog broke the silence. More than an angry bark, it was a lament, as if the animal were sounding a disappointment. The barks became less and less frequent until finally the dog calmed down.

At that moment I heard a squeaking sound from the dirt road. It was a bicycle with a rusted chain that someone was pedaling with difficulty. When the bicycle reached the fence the rider got off, leaned the bike on a post and walked over to me. It was a young fellow with a big head of hair and a beginner's moustache. He was wiping his hand over his face, as if to hide the downy fuzz that hadn't yet turned into a beard. His open shirt exposed a broad, hairless chest.

"I'm the son of the dead man," he said with a bravado that discouraged any expression of sympathy. "Are you the one who found him?"

"I am. Have you had the wake?"

"This afternoon. They said we couldn't wait any longer."

I looked squarely into his keen, penetrating dark-green eyes, which were like a cat's. He met my gaze with an insolent attitude.

"When I found him I thought he was sleeping — or drunk," I said.

The boy's mouth twisted into a scream. "My father didn't drink! And I don't either!"

I was surprised and took a step back, not really understanding his anger.

"There's no harm in that. It's quite enjoyable."

"Drunkards make me sick," he said more calmly.

He's just a difficult kid, I told myself, and now he's in a bad spot. I stroked my rifle and asked him: "What's your name?"

"Daniel Semper. My father was Arturo Semper."

"It's an interesting last name," I said, making conversation. "In Latin, 'semper' means 'always.'"

The boy bent over to tie his shoes. When he straightened up he said without looking at me: "How nice, that you studied so hard to become a watchman."

Without answering, I turned around and started toward the warehouse. Low-lying clouds had hidden the moon and stars. After a few minutes the boy came over.

"Where did you find him?"

"Under that tree."

"Do you have a flashlight? I haven't got one on my bike."

I strode ahead, lighting up the path. Daniel followed so closely I could feel his panting breath on the back of my neck. When we got to the poinciana I trained the yellowish light on the base of the trunk and said: "That's where he was."

He lay down on the grass and leaned his head against a root. "Like this?" he asked.

58

"No. His head was on that other root, the biggest one, and he was on his side, like" — I was about to say "like a fetus" but I thought that might offend him. "He was all curled up in a ball."

"Like this?" he said, trying again to get it right. The faint light made his face look pale.

"That's pretty close."

"Pretty close?" He got up and said: "Then why don't you show me exactly how it was."

His tone was cutting. I was about to tell him no, but without thinking further I gave him the light, got down on the ground, put my head on the root and curled my legs up to my chest. I closed my eyes and went motionless. When I opened my eyes I found the light in my face, and the boy gazing at me in puzzlement.

"Are you sure it was like that?"

"I am."

I got up and brushed off my clothes. Without any thanks he returned the light to me and we started back toward the sentry box. Again I went ahead, lighting the path, but this time he loitered; I slowed down to let him catch up, and once more he fell behind. I took him over to the post where he'd left his bike.

"Didn't he leave a note?" I asked.

"Why should he leave a note? He wasn't going off to kill himself. He loved to walk. He was always walking here and there. He couldn't stay still. I'm just the same."

"Some people are like that," I said in a very low voice.

"No, I'm like that because he was like that, and I was his son."

He got on his bike. As he rode away, he shouted, "And you're like me! You're not cut out to be a watchman!"

Two nights later the owl returned with its squawking. It passed by the sentry box on its flight heavenward. The owl's path across the sky fascinated me, and as I watched I realized Daniel had spoken the truth. A part of me just wanted to fly away.

In the wee hours I heard a noise under the poinciana. At first I didn't dare move, but then I realized that if I didn't go and see what it was, my fear wouldn't leave me alone. With light in one hand and gun in the other I went along the path, moving my arms about in

59

an exaggerated way to puff myself up with courage. I really didn't need the light; a full moon was shining on the field, and in that glow nothing could hide. Daniel was curled up beside the trunk. Keeping his eyes closed, he said to me: "I don't feel like talking."

"What are you doing here?"

"What am I doing? I'm going to sleep."

For a few minutes I stood there watching him. His face was twitching; a scratch on his cheek had made a line of coagulated blood. His body reeked of sweat.

"If you need anything, let me know," I said.

He didn't answer. I turned off the light and stood under the branches, scratching my arms, looking at the pasture lit up in blue. Then I went back to the sentry box, dragging my rifle on the chewed-up grass like a soldier who's lost his honor and knows he'll never amount to much.

Toward dawn I went over to him again. He saw me coming, scrubbed his face with his hands, circled the tree slowly and stopped in front of me.

"They say he died in the morning. He must have walked all night and gotten here when the sun was coming up. I think he came that way, by the sawmill road, along the stream. That's how I did it last night."

"Where's your bike?"

"I walked. I'm almost sure he got as far as this tree and put his hand on the trunk — you see? Probably his legs were aching. Then he crouched, like this. He sat on the leaves, lay down and stretched himself out — like this, right? And he put his head here — didn't you tell me he put his head on this root? He curled up, as you showed me — wasn't it like this? And then . . ."

I thought he was going to say, "and then he died," but instead he said with emphasis, "fell asleep." Daniel closed his eyes. In the distance, roosters were singing and bantering — a simple language with just a few sounds. On a far side of the meadow the morning light began to shine, suffusing the ground with a greenish tint.

"I'm leaving in a bit," I said. "At six. You want to stay here? The warehouse people come at seven, and someone will probably see you."

"Don't worry about me," he said in a sleepy voice, rather irritated; his body was quite splayed out on the leaves. "No one will see me. Afterward I'll go back the way I came. I enjoy walking."

For a whole week I found him sleeping near the tree trunk. He got there at ten or eleven; as I listened for every sound, I always heard him. Sometimes I brought him cookies or a jug of coffee. I told him he'd better be careful during my nights off, because the other watchman was a real son of a bitch. Then he stopped coming.

A month later he showed up on his bicycle, with a girl sitting on the bar. Clear-eyed, olive-skinned, with overflowing breasts, she could scarcely conceal her excitement on dismounting and taking his arm for the walk over to me. Like Daniel, she was no more than twenty. Her short skirt let me see her thighs, fleshy but firm. She was carrying a rather bulky handbag, as if she were going on a trip. She seemed ready to jump or run, and her tongue was constantly passing over her thick lips. Daniel walked with a kind of awkward nonchalance and his face had a defiant attitude, like someone ready to be rude.

"This is my sweetheart," he said brusquely. "Her name is Raquel."

I bowed my head, and the girl let out a little laugh.

"I'm going to show Raquel the place. We'll be a little while. Come and see us later. We'll wait for you."

"If my chief happens to show up and sees her, he's going to scold me," I said with a shrug. "But I don't care."

"Of course you don't," Daniel said. "Come in a little while. We'll be waiting."

I saw them disappear on the path toward the poinciana. I kept looking at my watch and felt uneasy. I went to the fence and tried to calm down by looking at the stars. After fifteen minutes I couldn't stand it any more and took off in their direction, without my light or gun. There was no moon, only twinkling from the masses of stars.

They were spread out near the tree, lying on a sort of white blanket, naked and going at it. On the plushy material, their intertwined bodies were gleaming as if coated in oil. The girl, on seeing me, gave a cry and covered her youthful, enormous breasts. At the same time she slightly parted her legs, revealing shoots of dark fluff.

61

"Take off your clothes and lie down here!" Daniel said — and seeing me go motionless, he snapped: "Don't be a chicken!"

I was really dying to do it, but I was frozen by the image of a man curled up into a ball. Daniel seemed to read my mind. He turned over on his back, stroked himself and said: "My father is dead, but I'm alive. Come on, lie down here."

"I can't, thank you," was all I managed to say. I swallowed a mouthful of bitter saliva and went off with a tremble. My teeth were chattering and I shook from head to toe, barely able to walk. I got to the fence, collapsed on a bed of pine needles and brought myself off with eyes open, looking at the meadow, once and then a second time.

I lay down on the plank floor of the sentry box and fell asleep. An hour later or so I heard them leave; I pretended to be sleeping. In the distance the dog began to bark, as if commiserating.

That night was the longest I spent in my two years as a watchman.

A week later Daniel came back by himself, pedaling slowly on that rickety bicycle, under a faint rain. He stopped in front of the sentry box and shook his head to dry his hair, which the water had molded into thin strands. At that moment the cloudburst got more serious. It was the first rain in quite a while, and it drew a strong fragrance out of the earth. I asked him to come in and offered him the stool in the corner, while I sat on the floor.

"I'm leaving for Matanzas," he said as he sat down. "I'm going to live with my mom."

When he said "mom" I realized how very young he was. Still, his forehead was crossed with lines I hadn't noticed before; he looked like an old man in a boy's body.

"I think it's for the better," I said.

With a moistened finger, he began drawing circles in the dust on the floor.

"Why are you a watchman?" he asked abruptly.

I laughed. "Because I've got to do something! Otherwise I go to jail under the anti-vagrancy law. Being a watchman is a lot easier than working in the fields, which is the only other thing I'd be able to do. Ever since they expelled me from the university, doors have

62

been closed in my face everywhere. And, come to think of it, being a watchman isn't so bad."

"I want to be *something* but I don't know quite what. My dad was a carpenter."

The rain was beating on the tin roof. Thunder was booming in the distance. Lightning bolts, breaking through the clouds with a sudden brilliance, cast their beams on fragments of the meadow, exposing the rain-soaked flatland. Daniel stood up, turned his back on me and leaned against the doorframe.

"A man like that, a man who just gets up and leaves, is a man who loves nobody — isn't he?"

I kept silent. After a while, without turning, he said: "He always worked hard, he did a thousand things, he was a hustler. He made plans. But something always happened, and his plans didn't work out. Partly because he never finished what he started, he never stayed still, he was always going to and fro, always in a hurry, leaving people in mid-sentence, promising to come back, if not tomorrow then next week. He walked and walked. He didn't even have time to speak with my mother, much less with me. He used to ask me something and then he didn't hear what I said because he was hammering a piece of board or looking for a nail, or going to so-and-so's house, or saying that in the carpenter's workshop they were going to give him a raise, or they'd promised him a pig, or he was going to sell rice on the black market, or he was going to make a boat for me, or a baseball bat, or furniture for the bedroom or living room, and at times it was true but almost always it was a lie. The truth was he couldn't be at peace, because he couldn't get attached to anything, because at bottom nothing mattered to him, not even his son. When my mother took off he was quiet for a couple of days. He sat in a rocker on the porch and asked me to bring him water. That was two years ago. But then he went back to the same thing, his walking, his going to and fro. A man like that is better off dead — isn't he?"

He sat on the stool and looked me square in the eye. "Don't you think he's better off dead?"

I lowered my gaze. "I don't know. When are you leaving?"

63

"Tomorrow, on the train. I like the train." He got up abruptly, put out his hand and said: "The rain has stopped. I have to go." There were enormous puddles around the sentry box. In the darkness, frogs were croaking. His bicycle went creaking off, splashing through the water.

A few months later I was arrested and accused of some political crime, as happened to many people.

In jail, men lived like animals. Somewhere in those dungeons was a man with features like Daniel's, but his voice was nasal and muddy, his eyebrows too dense, and he never cut his fingernails. I didn't like talking with him.

Then came exile and the speedy years of life in America. Whenever I drove through the American countryside at night, I remembered my times as a watchman; the feeling of immensity was the same.

Decades after going into exile, I returned to Cuba as a visitor to see my family and friends. I rented a car and drove all around Camagüey, feeling perplexed. At night, in my hotel room, I couldn't manage to sleep. A weight had descended on my chest.

One morning I decided to go back to that place on the outskirts of the city where I had spent so many nights awake. People were crowded along the dirt road, waiting for transport; people with children on their shoulders, with bags and cardboard boxes. The road had become a huge mud pile, where earthen mounds crumbled under the wheels.

I got out of the car and walked around the old place. Of the sentry box, there only remained a pair of wretched, blackened boards. The warehouse had no windows or doors, only holes; grass was growing through cracks in the floor.

The poinciana was in bloom. Clusters of orange and red flowers, dappled in white, glittered at the treetop, a luminescent roof. Some yellow leaves were already ripe. Smaller leaves, intensely green, crowded around stems to make bigger leaves of sumptuous dimension. Branches curled, straightened and grew out to form a truss that gloriously spread the foliage. The main trunk had many slits from where, like a reddish honey, streams of hardened sap had flowed. And below, at ground level, in the cool air and shadow, there suddenly rose up the enormous root where one morning a traveler had put his head to rest.

Carlos Victoria (1950-2007) was a native of Camagüey, central Cuba. Literary success in his teens drew unwelcome attention from Fidel Castro's regime. Carlos was expelled from Havana University and imprisoned for "ideological deviation." In 1980 he grabbed the chance to go to the United States via the Mariel boatlift. Through a succession of novels and short-story collections published in exile, Carlos Victoria's fiction has become a favorite of audiences across the world.

David Landau is the translator of, among other books, Carlos Victoria's award-winning novel *A Bridge in Darkness.* Landau's story, "Scherzo," appears elsewhere in this anthology. Contact: pureplayed@live.com

The Vale of Cashmere

—— ❧❧ ——

by Sean Elder

While Floyd was out, Marcy tried to organize her mind. "You know, like those pill organizers they have, with the compartments for daytime and night? I wish sometimes I could organize my thoughts like that, seven days a week."

She had said this while getting her hair done a few months ago and everyone had laughed, so when she got home that went in the book. She was writing down all the things she said that made sense to her, with hopes of putting them all on cards or maybe refrigerator magnets and selling them; they could always use the extra cash! Which reminded her, so she checked her secret stash, not the money Floyd gave her like it was killing him, but a little something extra she kept in her brassiere. Sure as hell nobody would be looking in there.

Truth was, she used to be able to organize her thoughts like that, until Floyd retired. Now he was always hanging around, talking to her, asking what she was doing. Every time he went out, which wasn't often enough for her taste, he would ask her if she needed anything and then look angry if she did. Sometimes he'd look angry if she didn't. Now she looked for errands for him, just to get a moment's peace. When she sent him off for milk this morning she could have lived without it. But she couldn't have stood listening to him complain about the bus ride to Atlantic City before it happened, not non-stop for the next two hours.

"You're creating your future," she told him. "Whatever you're thinking and feeling, that becomes your reality."

"Don't give me that shit," he'd said, putting on his coat and hat. He had been wearing that same damned hat with the stingy brim so long it had come back in style.

"It's the law of attraction," she'd continued. "You can deny it all you want but that don't mean it's not true. Everything coming into your life you are attracting into your life. You're like a magnet."

"Well, this magnet's going to attract some milk," he'd said before going out the door.

He had made fun of her ever since she first heard Oprah talking about *The Secret* but deep down she thought that maybe he believed her. Or would, if he would just give it a try. He would come home so angry about something that happened out there — the security guy asleep in the chair, or someone who wouldn't give his seat up on the subway — and she would tell him, "Every bad thing that comes into your life, you make happen."

Sometimes that really made Floyd angry. "Is that right? Every bad thing? I made happen every bad thing that came into my life, Marcy?" He would tower over her, breathing heavily, staring at the top of her lacquered hair until she was silent.

She looked closely at the big digits on the clock by the bed. It was almost 8:30 and she still had not done her makeup. From the drawer in the nightstand on her side of the bed she looked for her own pill organizer and then realized she had already taken it out. She put it under the light, right beside that picture of her two boys, smiling in the lap of a black Santa, and looked at Wednesday. There were still pills in the morning box but the evening box was empty. Maybe she took the evening pills by mistake. Not that it mattered 'cause they were basically the same. Or maybe she hadn't filled the PM part.

Looking at the rainbow-colored compartments (Wednesday was green, Thursday red) she thought of Wilson, who had the hardest time with his R's when he was little — "Weeding Wainbow," he would say about his favorite show, and his brother would laugh at him. She felt overcome for a moment and then heard her husband's keys in the door.

She took the morning pills, four altogether, as Floyd shouted at her from the kitchen.

"Do you know how much they wanted for a half-gallon of milk?"

She imagined his face as he said the price and the way he would look at her afterwards. He might be looking that way right now, even though she wasn't there.

"Cost of everything is going up," she yelled back. Then she stood and headed for the bathroom. "I got to get a move on."

"Ain't you even going to drink your milk?"

She heard him swear as she closed the bathroom door.

The bus driver turned out to be some white guy who'd been sleeping in the back while people waited outside. The whole bus was talking about it, even after they got out of the Holland Tunnel and were getting on the turnpike, people tsk-tsking and hmm-hmming until Floyd wanted to yell, "Who told you to stand out there in the first place? It's not even cold." But he kept quiet and sat by a window, alone thank you very much, though Tommy, who acted like he was Floyd's best friend, insisted on sitting right in front of him, while Marcy huddled on the other side with a bunch of ladies. They outnumbered the men five to one anyway; he let Tommy represent, going back and forth across the aisle like some congressman making a deal. Each time he went over to the ladies he would say something so low that Floyd couldn't hear and they would all laugh and holler.

"I think it's about time for some music," Tommy said after one of his sorties. He had a gym bag with him that said Mets on it, and from it he pulled a boom box that he tried to balance on the seatback in front of him. He pushed play and Johnnie Taylor started in on "Who's Making Love" and the ladies all laughed, even though the sound was kind of wobbly. From the front of the bus the driver said something; they could see him looking at them in the rear view mirror, but no one tried to hear him. In fact Tommy stood up, with the boom box on his shoulder, and started to shake it in the aisle, which made the driver get on the mike.

"Sir, I'm going to have to ask you to sit down." He had some kind of accent, Russian or something, but no one really paid him any mind.

The hits kept coming; Tommy jammed the boom box between the headrest and the window so it wouldn't fall down and turned around to look at Floyd, but not before looking at the driver, who had his eyes on the road again.

"How 'bout a little taste?" Tommy said, taking a half-pint in a brown bag from the pocket of his jacket.

"Too early for me," Floyd said, looking out the window. To him it always looked like New Jersey was halfway through being torn down.

Across the aisle Marcy was in the middle of a conversation with the other ladies but she didn't feel quite right. It started as soon as she left the building; she had picked out a brooch to go with her blue blouse, a little gold tree with red apples on it, but she had left it sitting in front of the mirror. Now she felt naked, all that blue stretching out below her chin like an empty ocean almost and she felt like she was being pulled back from drowning each time one of them stopped talking. That meant somebody was supposed to say something; you were supposed to jump in like it was a game of double-Dutch.

"What I value most is the privacy," Marcy said, but no one answered. She had a feeling she had said that before. The topic was assisted living and how to know when you needed it.

"Until you wake up privately dead," said the lady in the Kente cloth. Marcy didn't remember meeting her before, a friend of Helen's was how she was introduced, but she didn't like her now. She had these gray and white streaks in her hair, extensions by the look of it, but it reminded Marcy of mud. Besides, she was probably the youngest woman of the bunch, what was she talking about dying for?

"My boy checks in on us every night," said Marcy and immediately wondered why she had. It wasn't true. Most times she had to call Eric and he never sounded too happy to hear from her. He did come to visit though, once a month at least. They saw less of him after his divorce, though you'd think it would be the other way around.

"Where are we?" she said suddenly, looking out the window. Everything looked the same.

"You keep asking that," the lady in the Kente cloth said, or maybe she said. Marcy wasn't looking at her and the music Tommy was playing made her feel lost.

"Sending this one out for all you ladies," said Tommy, like he was some deejay, and they all laughed but Marcy didn't think it was funny. It was that song about sitting on a park bench that always made her sad.

I see her face everywhere I go
On the street and even at the picture show
Have you seen her?

There was a hospital up there high on a hill and for a second she felt that the bus was going to take off and fly straight up to its doors. She closed her eyes and felt herself rise.

They parked in the lot of the Showboat casino. Though they could have gone anywhere they wanted, the thirty-odd passengers that disembarked made for the Showboat as if summoned, shuffling and limping toward the entrance in a broken conga line.

"No one says we got to go to this casino," Floyd said to the crowd of ladies leading the way.

"The Showboat has a Mardi Gras theme," said the lady in the Kente cloth. She turned around to give Floyd the fisheye, pulling down her glasses as she did. "Besides, we got coupons for the Showboat."

He fell in line sullenly beside Tommy who offered him another drink. Floyd took a swallow this time without pulling down the brown paper to see what it was. It tasted like mouthwash.

"Jesus, what the hell you drinking?"

"Little peppermint schnapps." Tommy tried to slap Floyd on the back but the big man danced away, handing the bottle back as he moved.

"What she mean by a 'Mardi Gras theme,' anyway?" Floyd said.

Tommy shrugged. "As long as they got free drinks and blackjack I don't much care."

Seagulls screamed overhead. Floyd saw his reflection scowling in the window of a parked Humvee. He went to New Orleans during Mardi Gras when he was in the Navy, how many years ago? He got lost and someone stole his wallet. A man dressed as a woman tried to put beads around his neck, he remembered. You could have your Mardi Gras.

Marcy was among the first of the women to enter the casino and the air conditioning hit her like a cold wave. "Good thing I remembered my shawl!" she said but no one answered. The music and the sound of the slot machines, dinging and ringing with sirens going off every five minutes as if some crime was being committed, swallowed her voice.

Marcy had thought to bring rolls of quarters and silver dollars. While the other ladies were getting change she was already pouring her silver into a red plastic cup provided to her by a girl in the shortest skirt she had ever seen.

"You must be freezing!" Marcy said but the girl didn't seem to hear her. Maybe she just got tired of people trying to talk to her.

The slots area had thousands of machines and at noon it was already half filled, mostly old-timers like her and Floyd. He and Tommy had set off in the other direction like there was a sign saying 'Men, That Way.' The carpets were in a pattern of red and orange and gold that reminded her of a kaleidoscope and the ceiling was made up to look like stained glass, though she knew real stained glass when she saw it and this wasn't it. She felt like if she didn't sit down she might just fall into the colors. She sat down at a quarter machine and began feeding it. She didn't know where the other ladies had gone and looking over her shoulder left her none the wiser.

"Y'all gonna have to find me," she said, and as if conjured, a different lady in a short skirt appeared.

"How you doing today?" she said. She had a tray filled with drinks and a notepad tucked into her belt. "Can I get you something to drink?"

"Well I suppose you can!" Marcy turned in her chair to show her appreciation. "My name's Marcy by the way, I come here from Brooklyn with a bunch of folks from my church group."

"Now isn't that nice? My name's Kim Sue. What can I get you?"

Marcy smiled and opened her mouth. But she could not think of the names of any drinks, not just the fancy ones but any drink. She felt a trickle of sweat run down her back underneath her blouse.

"It's funny," she said, embarrassed. "My mind's just a blank today."

"Sure, no problem!" Kim Sue smiled back at her like one of those Chinese dolls, her name right there on her badge. "We have beer and wine and soda and mixed drinks." She kept smiling at Marcy and continued. "I could make you a nice white wine spritzer, if you like."

"Oh, that sounds nice," said Marcy, and it did sound nice, like a sprinkler in the summer time, the kind the boys used to play in. Kim Sue left and Marcy returned to the machine. Cherries and plums rolled past, never stopping at the same time.

Eric used to chase Wilson through the sprinklers in the park and sometimes when Marcy wasn't looking he would hold his little brother down and try to pull off his shorts in front of all the other children. She would get so mad at him, always teasing like that, knowing it would make Wilson cry and come looking for her, but she had a job then, looking after a little white boy named Oskar whose parents lived in Park Slope and worked all the time. Oskar's parents didn't mind too much when she brought her boys with her when she took him to the park. "As long as you remember," the father said, "that Oskar is your first priority."

Well of course he is, mister doctor man! Why would my own flesh and blood come before your little prince? Good gracious, the things that man would say. If the wife heard him she would weigh in and try to soften the blow. "What my husband means is that we don't want you to get too distracted. Three children is a handful."

Now that was the kind of thing only a white person would say. Where she came from, three children was just getting started, even if she was done after Wilson, something her own mother could never understand.

"Oh, don't worry, ma'am," Marcy would say. "I won't ever let Oskar out of my sight."

All these people thinking someone was going to steal their child, like the whole country had gone crazy. Soon they'd be putting their

73

pictures on milk cartons and billboards and on TV during the news
— "Have you seen Brandon?" Usually white kids. If a black kid went
missing generally people knew who took him.

"Here you go, ma'am."

Kim Sue was back with her drink. It was in a big plastic cup with
a straw that went in curlicues, like a roller coaster, like this was for a
child. She started fishing in her coin cup.

"Drinks are complimentary, ma'am."

Like I didn't know that. She pulled out a Susan B. Anthony and
put it on her tray. "That's for you," she said.

"Very nice of you, ma'am. And if you need anything else you just
let me know."

She turned to leave and Marcy was afraid to see her go. "Kim Sue,
it's like your momma gave you two names."

"Kim is my family name. Family name comes first in Korean."

"Is that right?" said Marcy. "Well I think family should come first,
don't you?"

"Yes, ma'am."

Marcy thought that was something else she should write in her
book but realized that she hadn't brought it with her, and then forgot
what she had said. "But they probably don't spell it like that in Korea,
do they? The Sue, I mean."

"No, ma'am, we have a different alphabet."

"Now isn't that something?"

She was balancing a tray full of drinks while she talked so Marcy
let her go, disappearing into the big Tiffany lamp around them. A
band was playing Dixieland and Marcy strained her eyes to see them.
The music seemed to be coming from everywhere at once, "When the
Saints Come Marching In."

"Let me tell you another," she said, sipping on her drink.

The lady at the machine next to her looked at Marcy and then
moved away, taking her quarters with her. Marcy watched as the
drink spun up the straw when she sucked. Here we go loop de loop.

Sometimes Eric would help her push the stroller as they went
around the park, and Wilson would run so far ahead she would
shout after him. "Don't go where I can't see you!" she'd holler, and

74

Oskar, too big to be pushed around in a stroller, would try and stand up and yell after her. "Go where I can't see you!"

Wilson would hide like that at home as well; hide so good she couldn't find him sometimes. They were living in Prospect-Lefferts, more house than they needed but you could afford those big limestone buildings then, even on a Con Ed salary, and Wilson would go into different rooms and be so quiet that she would get hysterical, be practically beside herself by the time her husband got home. Then they would hear him laughing. "Got you!" he would say and emerge from the cupboard or from behind the sideboard and Floyd would get so mad. That one time he came out of her closet wearing her bra and Floyd just about went crazy; took off his belt and chased him.

She put in a coin and pulled the lever: a watermelon; a bell; the number seven in gold.

"What numbers are you playing today?"

She turned her head but nobody was there. Who had spoken? Just turning her head made the colors around her move and when she looked at the floor she saw the pattern there was moving too. It was like a flying carpet, the Vale of Cashmere —

The Vale of Cashmere! That was the name of that strange corner of the park where she took the boys now and then. They were getting older; other boys took the place of Oskar, and Eric got too big to want to be with them. But Wilson kept her company as she made the rounds, bought the kids ice cream and wiped their sticky hands. People used to call it The Swamp and there was a muddy pond okay and some hanging trees.

"How come you don't play with boys your own age?" one of the kids had asked him once.

"I just like to help my momma," he'd said.

He was the one who found out the real name of The Swamp, checked an old book out of the library and showed her on the map. There was a poem that went with it and Wilson stood up by the pond and put one finger in the air as he read:

Who has not heard of the Vale of Cashmere
With its roses the brightest the earth ever gave?

Another babysitter saw them by the pond once and came over to warn them. "You shouldn't be down in there," she said, afraid to come too close with her stroller in front of her. "They say men get together down there."

And after that Marcy noticed them, lurking about, standing in the trees. Once when she came down with Wilson and a stroller two men ran out, going in different directions.

She didn't think about it again for years, until Wilson was grown and still living at home, and he came back one night that first time with his face all bloody, drunk or high on something and smiled at her, blood on his teeth.

"Hey, Momma, I been to the Vale of Cashmere!"

That's when Floyd said no more.

"What numbers are you playing today?"

She turned and the colors whooshed like a scarf being wrapped around her head. She saw her this time, a little woman, no bigger than a dragonfly like the ones the boys chased in the park, Wilson would put them in a jar with holes punched in the top, while Eric tried to cover it up with his hand so they would smother.

"I'm looking for three sevens," Marcy said to the dragonfly woman. "Are there some other numbers to play?"

"That is the question, isn't it?" said the faerie. "Are there other numbers to play?"

And then she flew away, just like a little hummingbird, and Marcy got up to follow her, passing into the pattern of colors and leaving her cup of coins behind.

Floyd went through all his money the first hour. Not *all* his money but all the money he'd meant to spend, the money he put in his shirt pocket, seemed to fly off the table. Dealer beat him every time: if Floyd had 18, the dealer had 19; if Floyd sat on a 19, the dealer hit him with two bricks.

"I guess this lady feels like she has to show us what a blackjack looks like," said Tommy, when the dealer drew her third in ten minutes. She apologized to them both, even though they didn't tip her, and Tommy's luck was better than hers: He doubled down twice and made a hundred bucks in the blink of an eye. All Floyd could do, once he had spent the money he had earmarked for this outing, was sit there and simmer in his resentment while Tommy's chip pile grew.

That was when Helen, the lady in the purple pantsuit, came and asked if he knew where Marcy was.

"I thought she was with you," said Floyd. It came out like an accusation.

"Well, we agreed to meet for lunch at three," she said, "but then nobody could find Marcy. We figured maybe you two went off together."

And that's how well you know us, Floyd thought. "Maybe she just went off to another casino by herself," he said. Even though he was losing, and wasn't even playing at the time, he didn't want to have to leave his spot and go look for his wife. "There's no law says we got to stay here."

"Blackjack," said the dealer, flipping another ace.

But after a minute he did get up to look, as he knew he would, leaving Tommy, who still had a hot hand and no doubt wondered what all the fuss was about.

"Did you try the ladies' room?" Floyd asked Helen.

"That was one of the first places we looked. They have sofas in there, you know." She paused. "Do you think we should call security?"

The suggestion made his blood pressure rise. "No, I don't think we should call security. Christ sake, grown woman goes off for a few minutes and you want to call the cavalry?"

"Does she have a cell phone?"

"Our son gave her one but she couldn't figure out how to use it." Eric had given them each one last Christmas, and neither of them could figure out how to use it. By the time Floyd got the hang of it he realized that the only person he would call was his wife, which was kind of stupid since he saw her all the time anyway.

They looked all the places that they had already looked and the lady in the Kente cloth joined them, acting more concerned than Floyd felt. "We need a system," she said, as they circled the room for the second time. The place was more crowded than ever and Floyd could hardly hear what she was saying. "How about I go stake out the buffet and you stay here?" she suggested to Helen.

"How 'bout *I* go stake out the buffet?" Helen said. "I haven't had lunch yet."

Floyd said they could both go feed themselves and take their time doing it; Marcy would turn up. He stood like a sentinel beneath the bells and sirens of the Mardi Gras slots, scowling most of the time. He hated slot machines; there was no sport in it, as he often told his wife. With blackjack at least you were playing the odds. Slots to him was just dumb luck, like a rabbit betting it wouldn't get run over when it ran across the road. Twice he thought he saw his wife, and each time he took pleasure in anticipating just how much grief he was going to give her. But each time he was wrong.

By four o'clock they were back together, Tommy too, and they began to set out in search parties. They were a small group: most of the travelers didn't want to leave their stations, since the bus was scheduled to leave at six and this whole business had already cut into their time as it was. The lady in the Kente cloth, who finally introduced herself as Niobe, took charge. She contacted hotel security, who seemed to have some experience with old folks wandering off, and as the witching hour neared, and the day-trippers started heading back toward the bus, she went out and argued with the bus driver, who was pretty adamant about leaving on time.

"You can't just go off and leave an old lady alone," she scolded him. The engine was already running, gently shaking the bus, while the AC gusted out the door in heavy welcoming breaths.

"I won't be leaving her alone," the driver said. "I will be leaving you to find her."

He agreed to wait as they made one last search. A handful of them fanned out, going to neighboring casinos and restaurants, off the boardwalk and into the side streets. Floyd couldn't help but think that Marcy was messing with him the whole time, and when he saw the impatient faces of the other folks on the bus — they'd lost their money and had their fill, they just wanted to go home — he couldn't help but side with them.

As he wandered, most of the people he saw were wearing shorts and T-shirts. Used to be people would get dressed up to go someplace. And when did everybody get so fat? Walking down the boardwalk, bag of French fries in your hand, what did you expect? The new motto for the city was "Always Turned On," which he found kind of creepy. There was nothing that he saw that turned him on.

Doors were open, air conditioning blasting out, cooling nothing. Floyd took to popping into places and doing a quick look around, not even asking half the time if they'd seen anyone who looked like his wife. One, they couldn't hear you with all that noise and two, half of them couldn't speak English.

"You seen an old black lady?" he shouted at one girl scooping ice cream. Her nails were so long he figured they might end up in somebody's cone. "Blue shirt, about this high?"

She stared at him like he was the one with the language problem.

He kept walking. Going in and out of the summer sun was making him thirsty. He wished for the first time that Tommy was with him. That man would always stop for a drink. He saw people in those rolling chairs, being pushed by young people, girls sometimes. And you wonder why you so fat?

Down at one end of the boardwalk he found what looked like a real bar. The crowd had trickled off as the sun sank lower in the sky. Go on, get out of here. A lot of good you been. Floyd ducked inside and felt the rivers of sweat roll out from under his hat and chill on his face and neck. His glasses steamed as he took a seat at the bar and ordered a gin and tonic. He perched on the stool and looked up at the game on TV. The waitress brought him his drink and man, did that taste good. No skimping on the gin, either. He forgot to ask her about Marcy. His wallet was bothering him; he felt like he was balancing on it. When the waitress asked him if he wanted to start a tab he simply nodded.

"You got a phone?" She pointed to an old-fashioned booth in the back, the kind Superman used to change in. The place was filling up, young couples waiting for dinner. Once inside the paneled wood booth he forgot who he was going to call. Eric, right. He searched the scraps of paper in his wallet for the number he never had cause to memorize and let it ring, go to voicemail, and then dialed again.

"Hello?"

"This ain't no telemarketer."

"Hey, Pop." He did not sound happy to hear from him and Floyd had already put enough change in the machine so he cut straight to the point.

"We in Atlantic City and your mother's gone missing." He backtracked from there, explaining the whole afternoon in greater detail than Eric needed, but never did his son sound any more excited than Floyd felt. He asked the obvious questions — had they called the police? Who else was looking?

"Did she have her cell phone?" he asked, pointedly.

"That's why I was calling," Floyd said. "I figured maybe she'd called you."

Eric was silent. Floyd imagined him at home, still in his work clothes, the sound on the TV muted, his eyes on the game. From his perch in the booth Floyd could see the TV over the bar. Jeter was trying to steal.

"I'm sure she'll turn up, Pop. I mean, where's she gonna go?"

"I know that."

"You got your cell phone with you? So I can call you if she does?"

Floyd muttered something and got off the phone. That boy would go to his grave asking about those damn phones. He should just wrap them up and give them back to him for Christmas. Turn 'em into salt-and-pepper shakers.

When he got back to his seat at the bar Jeter got picked off and he ordered another drink. Now they could send the search party out for him. The tumblers were tall and when he turned in his seat he found he had company. Big old white dude with long hair and a pointed beard. He was sipping a Budweiser longneck and looking at the screen. His arms were covered in tattoos; dragons, snakes and skulls disappeared into his shirtsleeves.

"Fuckin' Yankees," he said and turned to look at Floyd. "Nice hat."

Floyd turned to face his own reflection in the mirror behind the bar. "You wouldn't believe how long I had this hat," he said.

"There isn't much I wouldn't believe," the man said.

They got to talking. Turned out he worked in a tattoo parlor on the boardwalk, which explained all the ink. Halfway through his second drink, Floyd was feeling generous in his opinions.

"Back in the day," he said, "man had a tattoo it meant he'd been someplace. In the service, in the joint, you know."

"I hear you," the man said. "These days it just means you been to the mall." He drained his beer and held up the empty. "Buy you a drink?"

"Let me buy *you* a drink," said Floyd, and pulled out the fat wallet that had been giving him such a pain and laid it on the counter. Soon he had the pictures out and was showing him snaps of Eric, bragging on his son's job even if he wasn't exactly sure what he did. Then one of the whole family, when everyone was young.

"Where's your other boy?" the stranger asked.

Floyd made a face like he was sucking on a lime. "Wilson got killed in a hold-up ten years ago," he said.

"Oh, man, I am sorry. They catch the guy who did it?"

"No, it was in Prospect Park one night. Lot of crime in there."

"That's why I could never live in the city," the man said, which struck Floyd as funny. Most people would be scared of this dude, even in Brooklyn.

"So what happens when folks get old?" said Floyd, changing the subject. "Maybe they don't want all those tattoos any more."

"Shit, you don't have to wait 'til you're old to regret something stupid you did." The man laughed and Floyd got a glimmer of a gold tooth in his head. "People come in all the time wanting to have tattoos taken off, usually the name of some girl that don't love them anymore."

"Can you do it?"

"Sure," the man said. "Hurts like hell and costs twice as much. But we can do it. Easier just to change it, though."

"How do you mean?"

"Well, there was this one girl who loved a guy named Chris and had it tattooed on her ass. Until she found Jesus and then we just added a 'T'."

He didn't smile at first and it took Floyd a minute to figure it was a joke. "Hey, I got one," Floyd said. The stranger's eyes gleamed in anticipation. "There was this guy who loved this old girl so much he had her name tattooed on his johnson."

"Now that's gotta hurt!"

"Hell, yeah." Floyd wiped his mouth. "Then they broke up, you know, and soon he started missing her real bad. So he went all over looking for her, from Wisconsin all the way down to Jamaica. Then he's in the bathroom one day and he looks over and he sees this other guy's dick." He stopped for a minute. The stranger kept staring at him. "Now I can't remember that girl's name."

"Is it important?"

"Yeah, it's the whole punch line."

"Uh, oh. Better have another drink."

Floyd felt flushed and excused himself to go to the bathroom. There he stared straight ahead at the wall and read all the graffiti as if looking for a message. And by the time he got back to the bar, he was not surprised to see the stranger was gone and with him, Floyd's wallet, though all Floyd could feel was a keen sense of disappointment: He remembered the end of the joke now. He had remembered that old girl's name.

Sean Elder's writing has appeared in the *New York Times Magazine, National Geographic, New York Magazine, Salon, Slate, Vogue, Elle, Men's Journal, Men's Health, O: The Oprah Magazine, Gourmet, Food & Wine, Details* and many other publications. The essay he contributed to the collection of men's writings *The Bastard On the Couch* (Morrow, 2004) was reprinted on three continents; his essay on ecstasy, included in the collection of drug writings entitled *White Rabbit* (Chronicle Books, 1995) was called "seminal" by *Granta;* and a piece he wrote about being a stay-at-home dad for *Oprah* was included in her best of O collection, *Live Your Best Life* (Oxmoor, 2005).

Elder has co-authored several books, including *Websites That Work* with designer Roger Black (Adobe Press, 1997) and *Mission Al Jazeera* with former Marine captain Josh Rushing (Palgrave, 2007). He also works as a book doctor and helped edit *Making Rounds with Oscar* by Dr. David Dosa (Hyperion, 2010). He lives in Brooklyn, New York with his wife and daughter. Visit him at www.seanelder.com. Contact: elder.sean@gmail.com

A CULTURAL REVOLUTION

— ℰℭ —

by Teresa Hsiao

At Chinese School, students always kept to their own kind. Donnie Chang and his friends always hung out by the clay statue that was supposed to be of Abraham Lincoln, though it was only about four feet tall and had duct tape holding up the arms. Those who sucked up to Donnie hung out by the boys' bathrooms across from where the mini-Lincoln stood, occasionally dispersing whenever an unspeakable stench wafted in from the neighboring territory. Those who hated Donnie hung out at the corners of the hall, where they could prop their books up on the radiators, and though they were not an organized group, they were unified by their devoted loathing and disgust.

On Sundays, when the students at Chinese School gathered in the hallway for class, they would fortify themselves in these established locations. Donnie Chang would assume his regular position and wrap an arm around the disgraced, pint-sized Lincoln. "Okay, so guess what happened," he would say, like he always did, his legs wide, his hands waving emphatically, though careful not to break off a taped arm. "There's this kid Mack, right, this white kid at my high school, always talkin'. And he's talkin' in homeroom, and he's just sounding like an idiot, going on and on about his baseball skills, man, he is gonna get his ass *kicked*. I mean the kid ain't even *good*. So I tell him like, 'Man, you suck at baseball. You ain't the man for shortstop, dude, you *suck*. You should do track, man.' And he goes, 'I should do what, Jackie Chan?' And I mean, *god*. Where do these white guys *come* from?"

And Ken Zhang would say, like he always would after one of Donnie's stories, "Donnie, you're whack, man, you are whack, dude," from across the hall.

And Jerry Ming-Foster would yell from the corner, "Shut up, Ken, stop kissing his ass."

And then a teacher from the Chinese School would come out of the bathroom and yell at Ken Zhang for being in the way, and Ken and his kind would scatter, but eventually regroup on Donnie's command.

And then Donnie Chang would pull one of his acts on the teacher.

And Ken Zhang would get kneed in the balls.

And Jerry Ming-Foster would throw his *Contemporary Chinese History* book at them, and then scramble over to get it back.

And the disgraced teacher would tread away cautiously, grumbling, reminding himself never to use that bathroom again.

It had not always been like this. The Chinese School had been founded almost a decade earlier, when an enterprising group of recent immigrants decided to start a school that would provide a "traditional" Chinese education for their sons. Donnie Chang's father, one of the founders, had feared that boys were particularly susceptible to rejecting Chinese culture in the Western world. Thus, the founders created a curriculum designed to educate boys about their heritage. Classes were held in an old red schoolhouse just outside of Boston, meeting for three-hour lessons every Sunday. Although the educational program had once mirrored the K-12 school system, enrollment had always been low for many of the older classes, especially once kids entered high school. Thus, a few years after its founding, the Chinese School changed its structure so that students would now graduate early, upon completing ninth grade.

The new ninth-grade teacher was a twenty-five-year-old graduate student from Shanghai who had just moved to Boston four months earlier. He taught the classes on Sundays to pay for rent, and during the week he studied computer science at MIT and took free English classes at a remedial school with teenage delinquents. When he arrived at the Chinese School, he found the ninth-grade classroom adorned with bright, colorful posters. Pictures of cows and sheep and turkeys lined the head of the chalkboard, with each animal's English and Chinese name written below in a curvy font. Paper lanterns made out of colored construction paper were strung across the windows. The teacher's desk faced the students from the front of the room, which displayed several handmade signs of American and Chinese proverbs. Above the door was the LOSING IS TEMPORARY, BUT RESPECT LASTS FOREVER sign, a sign that everyone knew Donnie's dad, now the principal of the school, had written in his shaky English. There was White-Out hiding the fact that the U had previously worn a cap, and the P in TEMPORARY had been squeezed in, though its precise lines and confident stroke made it look out of place.

Donnie Chang was in the ninth grade for the third year in a row, easily the oldest student in the Chinese School's history. He sat in the back row with his friends, flipping through car magazines and drawing mustaches on photographs of historical Chinese figures in the textbook. While Donnie and his pals sat in the back of the classroom, Jerry Ming-Foster sat in the front, listening intently to the graduate student's lecture on the Cultural Revolution. The teacher passed around photographs of churches with curved eaves and elaborately carved temples and pagodas that had been destroyed. Jerry scribbled furious notes on Mao Zedong, the revered Communist leader in China, hated Communist dictator in America. He stared at his textbook, trying to decipher unknown Chinese letters and meanings. He gaped at the pictures as he rolled tiny red and gold glass beads around in his fingers, his trusted link to this world of temples and pagodas.

Jerry Ming-Foster had been to a real temple once, after his father left, when his mother had retreated to China and taken her son with her. Jerry's grandmother, his mother's mother, had met them at the airport. She had cast a sharp look at his mother and disregarded her grandson, giving Jerry only a quick nod, as if he were anyone's child.

They went straight to the temple from the airport. It was a scorching day, and though the heat had reached record temperatures, the sunlight still struggled to make its way through the tops of the banyan trees, dotting the temple courtyard with spots of light. Jerry had been wearing a striped polo shirt and a blue Red Sox cap, feeling uncomfortable and somewhat disrespectful in such a quiet, sacred place; he could see his grandmother peering at him, her ears red. Never before had he seen so many people all reverently awed by a place in their culture — their culture, not his. He felt like an intruder. He took off his cap and bowed his head at the golden Buddha, awkwardly copying the actions of his mother and grandmother. He closed his eyes and mumbled the few Chinese words he knew: *hello, goodbye, how are you, may I use your bathroom, I don't know much Chinese.* He knelt on the floor, his arms resting on the partition in front of him, breathing in the lacquer and the flame and the incense — as if it were all a natural process.

When they were leaving he insisted upon visiting a gift shop on the street outside the temple, and although his grandmother crossly remarked that it was a place for tourists, his mother gladly yielded to his newfound curiosity. In the gift shop he bought a small stone, dark red with smatterings of a golden hue, which the vendor told him in steady English was jade, a stone that would guard him against misfortune and adversity. Jerry earnestly watched as the vendor wrapped his stone in rice paper, and he took the package from the man with two hands, bowing solemnly. He carried it delicately, this foreign object of value and significance and knowledge and *change.* He brought it out to show his mother as they got on the bus to the hotel. She looked at the stone in his hand, her eyes wide, gaping blankly at his eager face. She shook her head, pushing her eyelids down heavily, crinkling the corners of her makeup, a bluish gray stream trickling down her cheek. Jerry asked her what was wrong. His mother looked up and stared hard at his baseball cap, her eyes red. She whispered throatily that he had paid too much. His grandmother was less subtle. She snatched the stone from his hands and glared at him, exclaiming loudly, "This! This! Two American dollars and you can buy this in your Chinatown back in the United States! Or your grocery store!" She threw the stone against the floor of the bus, shattering it into shards of red and gold with a shrill *ping!* "Glass! You bought glass! You bought glass!"

A crumpled page of *Contemporary Chinese History* hit Jerry Ming-Foster in the side of the face, lodging itself between his cheek and his glasses, temporarily impairing his sight. Jerry turned to face Donnie Chang, who waved at him. The graduate student looked up tentatively from his notes, but Donnie gestured for him to continue. "Go on, Mr. Chao," he said, grinning smugly. "We're listening." The teacher blinked at the potted bonsai tree he now kept in the corner of the room, then dropped his head and continued his lesson. Donnie smirked at Jerry Ming-Foster, who glared back at Donnie, his brow furrowed in sharp trenches on his forehead. The teacher's face was now cloaked behind his notes, while the other students concentrated on their own papers, consciously removing themselves from the scene. Ken Zhang pulled on Jerry Ming-Foster's pant leg.

"Hey, *Jer*," Ken said, smirking a Donnie Chang replica smirk, "You wanna fail the class or somethin'? Go and take some notes for us, dude, you dig?"

Donnie Chang chuckled. Ken looked at him reverently and beamed.

"Yeah, Ken," Donnie grinned crookedly at Jerry Ming-Foster, flicking a finger in Ken's direction. "Go on Jerry. Go take some notes for that *dude*. You do *dig*, right? I mean, if *dig* is something you understand since no one says 'dig' anymore, got that, pansy?" He flashed a vicious smirk at Ken, who flushed purple. His pals snickering, Donnie Chang leaned over and grabbed a fistful of Ken's plaid shirt.

"Nice, Ken," he said, his eyes glinting darkly. "Like a fuckin' rodeo cowboy. Yeah, old American cowboy, Ken Zhang. This shirt almost makes you *white*." Donnie sneered. "*Almost* — like my pal Jerry here."

Jerry Ming-Foster's eyes flickered as he stiffened in his seat, but he didn't say a word. Ken raised his hand and asked to go to the bathroom. The teacher said yes without looking up from the line he was reading. Ken Zhang always had to go to the bathroom.

When he took the job, Nai Chao had been under the impression that these students were willing to learn. Although he'd been warned that there were a few troublemakers, he had assumed that they weren't really bad kids, just kids that needed motivation. On the first day of class, he organized a Chinese speaking game that he had played in kindergarten back in Shanghai (he had been told to start simple with this group). He arranged everyone in a circle along the back of the classroom, making an effort to involve Donnie and his friends as well, who had refused to move. Nai had stood in the center of the room and explained the game to them in Chinese, stressing that everyone was to participate in all future activities if they wanted a good grade. He'd looked pointedly in Donnie's direction, having been warned about him.

Donnie Chang had stared back at this new teacher, a crooked, amused smile on his face. Cocking his sunglasses to the top of his head, he started blinking, blinking fiercely. His pals guffawed, knowing what was coming next. "Mr. Chao, I . . . I don't un . . . don't under . . . don't underst-aaand," Donnie had stuttered, his mouth curled, the corners of his eyes twitching wildly. The other students in the room giggled. Suddenly Donnie stood up, his entire upper body shuddering, his arms convulsing uncontrollably, as if he were possessed. His eyes rolled to the back of his sockets, his body trembled vigorously, and then Donnie Chang fell over onto Ken Zhang's desk.

For a moment, Nai wasn't sure whether or not the kid really had some sort of mental problem. He reached out and touched Donnie lightly on the shoulder, careful not to get slapped by a wild arm. He whispered slowly, in his bad English, "Um, it is okay, ah, Donnie. It is okay. You do not play if you do not want to." He looked helplessly around the room of unfamiliar faces, then back at Donnie, who was now thrashing about in Ken Zhang's lap, crying, it seemed. "Do not laugh, classmates, he is not well. He . . . he has mental incapacities." Nai forced himself to use the biggest English word he knew.

"No!" Donnie shouted abruptly, elbowing Ken Zhang in the stomach, planting his arms on Ken's shoulders and hauling himself up. Donnie stretched his neck to one side and Nai could hear a loud *pop*; Donnie sneered at the teacher's bewilderment. "Sorry, Mr. Chao. I just had to go, you know?"

Nai blinked, partly because he was utterly confounded and partly because sunlight from the window was reflecting blindingly off Donnie's sunglasses. "I got to go peeeee," Donnie announced, enunciating the words pointedly, as if he were speaking to a child. "I gotta pee but the bathroom. . ." Nai pointed feebly at the direction of the door. Donnie continued, ". . . but the bathroom is out of order."

Donnie's eyes gleamed, calculatedly following Nai's outstretched arm. "Oh, but I can use your desk as a toilet? Your bonsai tree? Oh, man, Mr. Chao, that is way too nice of you. Too nice of yooou," Donnie repeated again. He strutted to the front of the room where Nai's bonsai tree sat peacefully on his desk. It had been given to Nai by his professor back in Shanghai, as a good luck gift in America. Nai had been eager to show the students examples of Chinese culture, but looking at it in Donnie Chang's hands, Nai was suddenly ashamed of the tiny bonsai, which looked strange, out of place. He tried to speak, to protest, but the words wouldn't come out in this brightly colored room, plastered with cartoon drawings of sheep and cactuses and turkeys ("*huo-jī*"). He watched mutely as Donnie placed the bonsai tree in the corner of the room and widened his legs.

"This'll be good fertilizer for it to grow and get strong, Mr. Chao," Donnie had said, as a stream of yellow trickled down on the gnarled branches. "Or else this little tree will never survive in America."

Donnie Chang kicked the chair in front of him, causing Jerry Ming-Foster to drop his pencil and Mr. Chao to look up from his notes. Donnie laughed. Damn, he couldn't believe that anyone could take Chinese School seriously. Donnie had always despised the lessons and the lectures, but this semester was the worst. His dad, who had been opposed to the early graduation plan, had forced him to re-enroll in ninth grade *again*, even though Donnie had already "graduated" twice now. They'd had a huge fight about it, but Donnie couldn't bring himself to tell his dad that he *just didn't care*. His dad, with his beloved trinkets and scholarly knowledge of Chinese history, put so much energy into running the Chinese School. He would be devastated if he found out that his son didn't care for any of it. So Donnie had given in, returning to the colorful room with its clumsy pictures and crooked paper lanterns, feeling like he was in kindergarten at age sixteen, where learning was futile and resistance was the only appropriate action.

Mr. Chao annoyed him. Jerry Ming-Foster annoyed him. Donnie couldn't see why they cared so much. Most times he wanted to get up and leave, but he stayed in class for his father's sake. He hated it, though. Sometimes Donnie hated it so much that he started to hate his dad, because he felt like he could never get rid of this *thing*, this feeling, whatever it was, that he *should* care. When his dad's voice came over the loudspeaker to read announcements, Donnie would cringe at his father's broken English. He didn't know why, but his dad embarrassed him. And this shame made him feel guilty. It killed him that his dad was not a part of the life he wanted the most, to play baseball and talk about movies and smoke cigarettes with the kids in school. But as Donnie slunk into his chair in the back of the classroom, he reckoned that he could never explain it to his father, who just wouldn't understand. He'd just pretend to care, like Donnie did every Sunday afternoon, in a colorful room with dizzying signs and paper lanterns he'd once helped to make.

Nai Chao peered at Donnie Chang now, as he watched him slide into the empty seat that had been vacated by Ken Zhang. He watched Donnie slouch in several angles, propping his feet up on the back of Jerry Ming-Foster's chair and kicking them back down again, stretching his neck agonizingly, trying to make himself comfortable. And if Donnie Chang wasn't comfortable, no one could be. When Nai had first taken the job, he'd felt that he could help this poor kid, get him to become interested in Chinese history and culture. After all, Nai was told, Donnie had lived in Beijing until he was five years old. But after the bonsai tree incident that first day, Nai knew that he had lost any chance of reaching out to Donnie, or even to the rest of the boys. They gossiped constantly about things they deemed important and turned in their assignments late, sometimes not at all. The students reminded Nai of the teenage delinquents in his English class; they just didn't care about what they were learning. It didn't mean anything to them; just showing up was effort enough, a symbolic gesture of respect for their parents' wishes. And so Nai, after a couple of months, gave up trying to teach them and caved. No longer did he spend hours designing quizzes and grading homework and preparing lectures. No longer did he give them speaking games or bonsai trees that he himself held so dear. It just wasn't worth it.

After that, the only student who still paid attention was Jerry Ming-Foster. Even though the other kids kept up the pretense of doing work with their scribbling (which Nai came to understand was just doodling), Jerry Ming-Foster continued to study diligently. This surprised Nai. He'd never seen a student so devoted and resolved to learn. Jerry pursued Chinese history and culture with an almost feverish craze. He wanted to experience the sounds of the lion dance, the smell of scallions, the taste of dumplings, the touch of bamboo. It concerned Nai, the immense magnitude of what Jerry wanted to understand. It was like he was chasing something he couldn't have.

There'd been a massacre; Jerry Ming-Foster had always known that about Tiananmen Square, but he didn't understand all the details. He gaped at the pictures that Mr. Chao showed now, angled in his direction. There was a man lying in the bloodied street, a mother cradling a lifeless baby in her arms, a student defiantly standing before a tank. Jerry could see the pain in the people's faces, the sense of purpose and understanding and knowledge and *change*. He rapidly took notes as Mr. Chao spoke, his pencil pressing harshly upon the paper, his eyes glancing up now and then to stare at another horrifying photograph, his breathing quick and uneven.

After their short stay in China, his mother no longer answered his questions when he asked her about Tiananmen Square, Genghis

Khan, the Revolution. She'd say that he never used to care about such things, so why start now? She told him that he didn't need to know anything like *that*; he should study George Washington or Abraham Lincoln instead, something his father would've liked for him to learn. She had even suggested that he drop out of Chinese School, which he had been attending since kindergarten. She didn't want him wasting his time, she'd said, grumbling; the students never learned anything *real* there — nothing of importance, anyways. Jerry would often catch her staring at him sourly, when he was pulling up his shin guards for soccer practice, or reading *Contemporary Chinese History* in the kitchen after school. When he'd ask her what was wrong, she'd simply reply, "Nothing. You just have your father's eyes."

Day after day, Jerry would read about this history, this past, this separate culture that he preferred. One day he almost burned down the apartment when he tried to make fried dumplings on the stove, the fire suddenly shooting out of control, enveloping the frying pan and flickering treacherously close to the ceiling. His mother had come to the rescue, smothering the flames with an enormous leather beanbag that had been his father's. It had been his father's favorite chair, made of pure American leather, his father had liked to say, from pure American cows. Jerry's mother had never approved of sitting in such a thing, though, and neither she nor Jerry missed it much when the fire department hauled away the charred remains. The next day, his mother went to Chinatown and bought him a green jade stone, real jade, top quality, she'd said, to keep you from burning down the apartment. Jerry had appreciated the gesture, but he kept the stone in his sock drawer, under a pair of gaudy Christmas stockings his father had given him, rarely taking it out. It wasn't fried dumplings or Chinese bamboo or even leather beanbag. It wasn't *authentic*, he groused to himself, turning the smooth green jade over and over in his calloused fingers; it wasn't jagged, or coarse, or rough like the red and gold fragments he'd picked up off the bus floor in China. Oftentimes he tried breaking the jade on the floor in his bedroom, but it always bounced off the carpeting intact.

Donnie Chang stared at the back of Jerry Ming-Foster's neck; he could never figure the kid out. He didn't understand why Jerry even bothered with Chinese School — everyone knew that Jerry was half and half, and rumor was that his American dad had left him and his mom last year for some blonde secretary. Ever since, Jerry had come in early every Sunday, sitting in the front row, all ready to take notes and listen to the graduate student's lectures. Donnie just couldn't understand it. Ken Zhang had told all of them that he overheard Jerry's mom talking to Mr. Chao one day after class, saying that she didn't care for Jerry going to Chinese School anymore, but that Jerry had *wanted* to keep going. Donnie had been shocked. Man, if he had a way out, he would've taken it like *that*, he thought. Ken had ended the story by acting out an imagined love scene between Jerry's mom and Mr. Chao, until Donnie slapped him upside the head. Damn Ken never knew when to stop talking.

Ken Zhang was always trying to act cool by cracking corny jokes and making ridiculous comments. Most times this annoyed the hell out of Donnie, of course, but secretly Donnie appreciated having Ken around. He knew that the poor guy looked up to him, even with all the teasing, and that made Donnie feel good. He looked toward the direction of the door now, hoping that Ken would show up and get horseshit over where to sit. *Damn.* That stupid sign was still up there, that stupid LOSING IS TEMPORARY, BUT RESPECT LASTS FOREVER bullshit. That goddamn White-Out blatantly obvious against the cream-colored banner.

Donnie had the same sign in his room at home, the quote printed in giant block letters in front of a starry black background. The varsity baseball coach at his high school had given it to him after tryouts, when he'd been cut yet again. In Donnie's room, his father had taped the sign onto the vaulted ceiling, too high for Donnie to climb up without a ladder and serious effort. So he'd left the quote up there, and pretty soon the same sign materialized above his classroom door in the beginning of the school year, this one homemade, and, again, out of reach.

God, Donnie hated that sign, almost as much as he hated Jerry Ming-Foster, or the fact that his dad probably didn't even know what the quote meant but paraded it around anyways, or the stupid white kids in high school who would make fun of anything that he touched. Jackie Chan, my ass, Donnie thought now, as he remembered the guy, Mack, laughing off his joke with the other white bastards, like it was funny. He could think of funnier things, man, and that wasn't even close.

That Mack was a complete bastard. All those kids were. He hated that he even tried to kick it with them, tell them things, like they could be cool. Donnie could remember Mack at homeroom one morning, squinting his eyes at Donnie, smiling a big dumb smile, then bending his knees and scuttling around, yelling, "Look me! I like play baseball, yah, you dig? But I no good! I just like shoot off my mouth to the team's star shortstop, yah, 'cause I think I a baseball expert! I wear polo shirt and pretend I am big jock, hah, but I am really big fucking pansy! I am great American heeeero, yah!"

Mack had stuck out his elbows and jabbed Donnie a good one in the side of his polo shirt. He'd plucked Donnie's sunglasses from his hair, U.S. Air Force aviator glasses that Donnie had gotten from a street vendor in New York, sunglasses that his father hadn't approved of and had tried to protest against but couldn't think of the English word for "expensive" fast enough. And Donnie had taunted his father, singing, "What's that mean? Huh, what's that mean? I don't understaaaand . . ." Mack took these glasses, dangerously twirling them around on his finger. Donnie had sat stiffly with his hands clenched to his seat, his eyes fixed straight ahead. He couldn't speak; he couldn't move.

"Who's the man, huh? Who's the man, big shot?" Mack had jeered, spinning Donnie's prized glasses around in his palm. "It's fucking raining out, what do you need these for? Huh?" He looked at Donnie closely. "Oh, I get it." He turned. "These glasses almost make you look cool . . . *Almost*." Mack spun around theatrically and faced the front of the room, his arms wide and welcoming, Donnie's glasses dangling from his outstretched fingers.

And then he dropped them, with a swoosh of an arm and a phony startled look on his face. The glasses fell to the floor, instantly shattering into hundreds of tiny, unfettered shards of glass. Donnie had stared at the pieces blankly, mutely, as if the destruction of his sunglasses was a natural occurrence. Mack had sneered, stretching his leg out from his chair, waving heroically at his bemused classmates like a Miss America winner strolling down her final runway. The teacher walked in then and grinned at Mack's pose, telling him good-naturedly to sit down, shut up. Mack, giving the teacher a sardonic smile and subsequent thumbs-up, complied, sliding into the seat behind Donnie. "Mr. Henry," Mack had said boisterously, "Wen-Don Chang dropped his sunglasses on the floor. But you don't hafta call the janitor, Wen-Don'll pick them up himself." He smirked at Donnie, smirking an authentic Donnie Chang smirk. Donnie could hear the other kids in the class giggling, amongst themselves, amongst their own kind. "Look, Wen-*Don*," Mack leaned in, his eyes narrowed, "Don't ever fucking tell me what to do again."

And Wen-Don Chang didn't.

Donnie hated himself for it, for not being able to fight back, for just sitting there, dumbly, humiliated. He hated his father for it, his father who named him Wen-Don and ignored any references to his nickname. And now, as Donnie looked bitterly around the ninth-grade classroom, he hated Jerry Ming-Foster, whom he just couldn't figure out. Sitting behind him, Donnie rapped Jerry on the shoulder, hard, but he didn't even flinch. Donnie flicked him on the ear. He could hear his buddies laughing in the back row. Jerry still didn't turn around. Donnie leaned his head in and practically stuck his whole nose in the crook of Jerry's neck. Then he thrust his fingers up in front of Jerry's face, wiggling them crazily, but Jerry wouldn't move. He wouldn't even turn around. All he would do was look down every once in a while and take notes in his notebook. Damn, Donnie thought: what would it take to break this kid?

Donnie moved his desk next to Jerry's, dragging the legs so that they made a shrill, screeching sound against the floor. Mr. Chao looked up momentarily, but he didn't say a word. With his desk right next to Jerry's, Donnie bent over and snatched away his notebook, and, in one quick motion, he hurled it at the door in which Ken Zhang was entering, just coming back from the bathroom. The notebook hit above the doorway with a *thud* and fell straight down, ripping into Donnie's father's sign. Ken, who had ducked, looked up as the disgraced middle of the banner floated down, leaving the two ends that had been most strongly fortified by adhesive up on the wall, so that the banner now read LOSING IS FOREVER, above Ken Zhang and the doorway of the ninth grade classroom.

And Donnie Chang laughed, pointed at Ken Zhang underneath the sign and howled, like he'd meant to do it all along.

And Ken Zhang glared at Donnie, snatched up the fallen banner at his feet and flung it at Donnie's face, yelling, "Asshole!"

And Mr. Chao sighed and dragged a chair over to take down the banner that remained above the doorway, while Donnie Chang scuttled in front of Jerry Ming-Foster, jeering, "Who's the man now, huh? Who's the man?"

And Jerry Ming-Foster shook his head and said, "And to think . . . your dad fixed that sign just for you, Wen-Don."

And that was it for Donnie, man, and he seized up and clenched his fists, and he punched Jerry Ming-Foster straight in the nose.

Nai Chao didn't see the actual punch, but he heard it. He spun around and saw Jerry Ming-Foster leveled backwards, flipping over Ken Zhang's desk, tiny red and yellow beads falling out of his pockets and bouncing to the floor. He saw Donnie Chang jump up on his chair, pound his chest, and scream, "I'm the man! I'm the man! Dammit, I am the man!" When he saw Donnie Chang's own pals yell at him to get down, looking panicky, Nai knew that this time Donnie wasn't pulling one of his acts. He quickly pressed the intercom and called for Donnie's father, knowing that this was all he could do. The boys would have to fight it out themselves, and Nai would let them do it.

Nai clicked off the intercom and turned around to see Jerry Ming-Foster, sitting up now, dazedly staring at the blood that had seeped out of his nose. Donnie Chang was crouched in the corner with the bonsai tree, favoring his bruised right hand, glaring, yelling at Jerry Ming-Foster, "You fucking bastard. You fucking bastard, you told my dad to fix the sign, didn't you? You think you had the right to tell him? You fucking think you had the right to tell him he made those mistakes? He could have fixed it himself! He would have figured it out, you fucker!"

And Jerry, curled up in the middle of the room, yelled back, "All I did was help him find White-Out! That was all I did! He fixed it himself. He said he wanted it to look like the sign your coach gave you, because you always liked that one better. I didn't do anything, man. All I did was get your dad White-Out . . ."

But Donnie didn't hear him, or didn't want to hear him, and crying now, he picked up the potted bonsai tree beside him and threw it, along with its glass base, at Jerry Ming-Foster, knocking out clods of dirt and shattering into pieces of glass on the floor. Ken Zhang caught a clump of dirt in his eye, causing him to flail wildly, shrieking, "I'm blind! I'm blind!"

Then Donnie Chang leapt out of the corner and struck Jerry Ming-Foster square in the face again, rolling Jerry over a textbook, and a car magazine, and the remains of the bonsai tree tray with a devastating crunch. And Jerry Ming-Foster was punched one more time before Donnie Chang's father ran into the room, and Donnie fumbled his way to his father and collapsed in his arms, crying, sobbing in Chinese, "I'm sorry, I'm sorry, I'm sorry Dad . . . I'm sorry."

Jerry Ming-Foster had to get his nose packed with gauze and five stitches over his eye, but doctors were confused as to how he had gotten a deep gash in his leg as well. "Well, I was wearing shorts," he told them, pointing to his exposed leg, "and there was broken glass on the floor, because Donnie Chang threw Mr. Chao's bonsai tree at me." His mother sat primly beside his hospital bed, her eyes red, clear streaks running down her face. He'd been surprised that she had come so quickly, and even more surprised to see her crying when the doctors brought her in. She'd hugged him vigorously like she hadn't done in a long time, the jade stone she'd bought him in Chinatown clutched in her hand, dangling from a red string. She'd gotten the jade strung into a necklace after she was cleaning out his sock drawer the other day, she told him, dabbing his forehead gently with a wet cloth. The jade necklace, she explained to him, was often worn as an ornament by gentlemen in Chinese history. She handed the necklace to him as he lay on the hospital bed, his eyes closed, his breathing slow and unhurried, and he held her hand with the necklace tightly enclosed between them.

The doctors, still perplexed by Jerry Ming-Foster's seemingly out of place leg wound — every other injury was from the shoulder up — discussed the strange appearance of the laceration. It looked to doctors as if something had fallen into the deep gash, and that it was infected perhaps by something Jerry had rolled over during the fight. Indeed, when the nurse was cleaning the area around the cut, she noticed a tiny glass bead protruding from the exposed flesh. When doctors examined the leg further, they found that several red and gold beads had become embedded in Jerry's leg. But, the doctors surmised, these tiny pieces of glass couldn't have caused the laceration, because the red and gold fragments they took out of his leg weren't sharp. They were smooth, as if someone had run their fingers over and over them endlessly, evening out the pointed edges and curving them into small glass pebbles, to their own satisfaction. However, there was one tiny shard of glass that hadn't been transformed, a piece so jagged that it pricked the nurse who handled it, expecting it to be flush and smooth like the others. They discarded this piece before giving the red and gold beads back to Jerry, who later threw them all out, as he couldn't believe that the glass had been entrenched in him for so long.

Teresa Hsiao graduated with honors from Harvard College in 2007, where she won the David Rice Ecker Short Story Prize. During college, Teresa studied economics and managed to land a summer internship at Lehman Brothers, which may have led to its eventual bankruptcy. Since graduation, Teresa has worked on the business side of a media company while continuing to juggle various creative projects, including blogging, composing short stories, and writing for television. In her spare time, Teresa enjoys playing squash and supporting the Boston Red Sox. Website: www. teresahsiao.com. Contact: teresa.hsiao@gmail.com

Patchwork

───────────── ℘℘ ─────────────

by Dan Loughry

"Let a little light in, would you?" Sal asked. He was washing breakfast dishes in the kitchen while peering into the dark living room where his lover, weak with AIDS, sat quietly.

Randy, rising slowly, drew the curtains back. The brash sunlight — so quick, so harsh — dizzied him. He rested on the sofa — a stiff vinyl monstrosity — and rearranged the fake tiger-print throw pillows against his lower back for support. He flipped on the TV with the remote control. Plinking new wave music played through the television speakers; some late 80's group with their current video.

"Your parents will be here in less than an hour," Sal said. "What are you doing?"

"Still dying."

"Well, before you drop that mortal coil," Sal hissed, "maybe you could dust."

Randy ignored him and continued watching TV.

A yellow Fiestaware cup wobbled as Sal placed it on the wooden drying rack. He felt an urge to smash the mug on the floor at Randy's feet. *Maybe then he'd move*, Sal thought. He propped his finger against the cup, ceasing its motion. "I cook, take care of you —"

"Do you bring home the bacon and fry it up in a pan?"

Sal placed his hands on his hips, exasperated.

"Of course you do," Randy said, watching soap suds drip from Sal's elegant fingers, " 'cause you're a woman."

"I'm *every* woman," Sal corrected. "Mother, sister, maid, nurse." He bit his lip, thrusting his hands in the dirty dishwater, and braced himself for the snotty response to come. But Randy — mute — gazed bug-eyed at the TV screen. *Don't just sit there,* Sal thought. *Fight back!* For a moment in the flickering light, Randy looked to Sal like the college student he had seduced at a fraternity mixer ten years ago. Randy'd been brimming with the promise of sex, recklessly flirtatious, cocksure. The devil-may-care glint in his eye was charming. *I wouldn't care,* Sal had thought at the time, *if he fucked me or fucked with me.* The video over, Randy shifted on the stiff sofa, and he struck Sal as diminished, a young man in his 30's with the face of a 60-year-old. His ribs stuck out from his ratty Heaven 17 t-shirt; the skin of his clavicle gathered loosely at the bone. Yet when he turned to address him, Sal noticed Randy's devilish grin.

"Oh Nurse?" Randy asked, his features animated by cruelty. "Could you come fluff up your poor little AIDS patient's pillows? Pretty please?"

"I'm off duty."

Randy lobbed the pillows onto the floor. "I'm tired," he mocked. "I cook, I clean —"

Sal hurled a fork into the sink, spattering dishwater on the wall. He stormed into the living room, ran a finger over the television screen — static igniting at his touch — and swirled dust between his fingers. "What's this?"

Randy pushed the mute button on the remote control, pointing it at Sal.

"Look!" Sal demanded, snaking his finger over the coffee table. "Everything's filthy."

Randy glanced at Sal's smudged fingertip. He followed it as Sal pointed out where the room could stand a little cleaning, but Randy didn't see dirt.

He saw waste.

He stood up to circle the room, consider their belongings. Everything they owned was mismatched. Tye-dyed textiles that

Sal made in college were draped across the corners of the room. A mahogany wet bar, given them by the long-dead owner of their favorite sex club, divided living room from dining area. A small end table sported ceramic figurines of the Jetsons cartoon characters in a nativity tableau, with George and Jane as Joseph and Mary, and Elroy as the baby Jesus. Cradling Elroy/Jesus in his palm, Randy felt disgust that someone had wasted time hand-painting these cartoon figures in day-glow oils. *Who would do something so stupid?* he thought, before remembering the afternoon he and Sal spent crafting a manger and cradle from popsicle sticks! "All this whimsy," he said, knocking Elroy from his cradle. What would his parents think?

He returned to the couch. Directly in front of him was their coffee table, a dolphin-shaped mosaic set on wrought iron legs. The table had been too ugly, too extreme not to buy — a private dare between young lovers. They carted it back to college in Sal's pickup. In a wheat field outside Moline, they took the table from the flatbed and proceeded to have sex on it. During their ferocious coupling they must have dislodged a cobalt tile, because afterwards Randy found it on the ground, put it in his pocket. He intended to glue the fragment back, but lost the tile soon after they returned home. Now he placed his hand over the glossy surface of the table, stroking the nick in the mosaic. A familiar buzz stirred his groin, yet the moment had dissipated by the time he recognized the urge as sexual. To have his own desire pass — barely perceived — filled him with dread. His dry mouth tasted of ash, of grief.

He began to shake, gasping for air.

Sal grabbed Randy's inhaler from a nearby desk. He slid on the edge of the sofa next to him, handing him the respiratory spray, all the while rubbing Randy's back over the outline of his ribcage.

Randy moaned under the touch of Sal's expert hands. *I remember this*, he thought.

Neither spoke, grateful for this moment of calm. It would leave soon enough, but they allowed their reprieve, stolen from the midst of chaos, to briefly disarm them.

"I should be doing something," Sal said.

"You are."

"Something else," he insisted.

"What else is there to do, Sal, except wait?"

Sal bore down on a muscle in Randy's shoulder. "You want to rot, fine. That's your business." He stood up, removed his apron. With one violent motion, he flung it at his lover.

"Thank you Betty Crocker," Randy said.

"Bette Davis!"

"BETTY CROCKER!" Randy screamed, rising from the sofa, the apron tumbling from his lap.

Neither moved. They stared at the apron bunched on the floor between them. Sal was rigid as a totem pole. Randy — woozy and faint — wondered why their apartment was always this goddamn hot. Sal put a hand out to steady him. Randy swerved out of his reach.

A good sign, Sal thought. *Feisty*. He forcefully grabbed Randy's forearm, his hand slipping around Randy's slender wrist.

Randy yanked his arm from Sal's grasp. "What do you want from me?" he said.

The directness of the question startled them both.

I want us to be well, Sal thought, pushing the idea away as fast as it came. A week ago, during a routine physical, his doctor — alarmed by a thick congestion in Sal's lungs — had suggested a blood test.

"For HIV," Sal had said, matter-of-factly.

"It could just be pneumonia," his doctor said.

"Right. Just pneumonia." Sal rolled up his sleeve for the blood test. He shouldn't have dared to hope, yet that's what he did, defiantly. When he received the results yesterday — positive, as expected — he grew enraged, slamming his fist on the doctor's desk. His anger didn't stem from the results — a predetermined outcome, he knew — but from the temporary relief of his own denial.

Sal had not told Randy that he had taken "the test" or of its outcome.

Randy watched the tight muscles set in his lover's face. He understood he was being shut out. *He wants to moderate everything*, he thought, *to control everything*. Bending down to pick up the apron on the floor between them, he lost his balance. Sal caught him, pulled him up.

Randy giggled. *Christ, he looks great,* he thought. Sal used to do housework nude beneath the apron, his pendulous cock straining against the fabric where there was now a threadbare space. Randy hooked a finger through the ripped cotton of the apron. He placed a hand on Sal's belt, weakly tugging at the leather.

"You're pathetic," Sal said, blinking back tears.

What are these tears for? Randy wondered. *Why is he crying? Is it about finally meeting my parents?* He lifted a corner of the apron to Sal's face to dab away the tears. He, himself, hadn't cried like that since the day he tested positive. He knew that Sal had seen their internist a week ago.

He dropped the apron.

Sal clutched it mid-fall before retreating to the kitchen.

Randy wanted to leave, go for a walk. He'd no idea what to say, so he distracted himself with busywork. He grew weary while attempting to gather throw pillows. He sat down with them on the floor instead. He grabbed one, fluffed it up. Puffs of dust flew out from the fabric.

Sal watched Randy grapple with his simple tasks. He wanted to help, but didn't budge. It was too easy to do everything for others, nothing for yourself. A year ago, after Randy's diagnosis, Sal decided to always remain calm, focused. Death would not scare him. Not Randy's. Not his own. Randy's fight was almost over; his own just beginning. He needed to pace himself.

Randy clutched a pillow to his chest, buried his chin into the supple down. It smelled musty, old. He knew what Sal was feeling, was thinking. He felt it in every immunodeficient cell of his body. And he knew they would never talk about his fear. When would the virus manifest into disease? How long would it last? How painful would it be? Their time together — what little there was left — would pass with mindless chatter, gabbing about this or this, but never *that.*

At the kitchen sink, Sal washed the same fork three times. He was transfixed by Randy, cross-legged on the dusty floor, rocking to and fro while hugging a pillow, the melancholy smile of a daydreamer on his sweet, aged face.

I should be by his side, Randy thought, *drying dishes*. He rubbed the gap of the missing chip in the mosaic table instead, thought of all that was lost between them, and all that had managed to survive.

Who will take care of you, he thought, *when I'm gone?*

Barbara Manning sat in the passenger seat of the Bonneville hugging herself to stave off the chill that had settled in her bones since she and her husband left home that morning. It was unseasonably cold for Iowa in May, and even though Ben had said it would be warm in the car — "hot as a henhouse," he had promised — it wasn't. "You call this warm, Benjamin?"

"I'd call it steaming," he said, his lanky frame stiff as he drove.

"Not nearly as steaming as the pile of garbage you're feeding me."

She'd been dreading this trip for weeks. Randy hadn't been home for over a year. Since Christmas, she'd suggested that her son visit. He was tentative, then blatantly evasive. Their last conversation was a relief to her, breezy and free like the old days. He invited them to Chicago to see a quilting exhibit. She said yes, caught up by his enthusiasm.

Barbara had mentioned the visit to a neighbor during lunch.

"Do you know what the 'quilt' is?" her friend asked, folding and unfolding a linen napkin in her lap.

Barbara lowered her voice, scanned the restaurant for familiar faces. "It's one of those *artsy* things." She blushed; 'artsy' was code for 'gay'. "Randy said it would be like a picnic!" She chuckled at the recollection.

Her neighbor didn't laugh. The set of her jaw was serious. "They call it the Names Project. It's an AIDS memorial quilt." She folded the corners of the napkin into tiny, precise triangles. "I can't believe he asked you to go."

Barbara dabbed at her clammy cheek with the back of her hand. Was Randy informing her — indirectly — that he was sick? He hadn't been to visit for so long! Did he have AIDS?

Next to her in the car, Ben — cheerier than usual — hummed his way through the Rodgers and Hammerstein catalog. He often sang to calm his nerves. Since she had not mentioned the Names Project to him, she wondered what had brought on his Broadway medley? There was one answer, no other. He knew. He knew about their son and hadn't told her.

As cold as she had been before, she now grew feverish. She rested her forehead against the cool window. White edged the fields. Within the borderline of snow Barbara noted patches of red soil, recently tilled, sprinkled with seed. Wheat would sprout in a few months. How sick was Randy?

"Are you okay?" Ben asked — he must have noticed her sudden pallor — and reached for her forehead to feel for temperature.

She slapped his hand away.

"I'd be better if you'd stop humming those damn tunes. You're not fooling anybody."

"Then let's talk."

"About what?"

"Anything," he said. "Randy."

"What about Randy?"

"Sal told me that —"

"Sal?" Barbara snorted in derision. "You mean 'Bela Lugosi.' "

Ben gasped at the mention of their private nickname for Sal.

" 'Bela Lugosi.' " She said it like an invocation, though she wasn't sure whether she meant to conjure Sal's image or cast it out. Either way, he was a demon. A decade's worth of photos proved it — from Randy's first days in Chicago when he sent pictures of himself alone until, over time, this man appeared alongside her son. Who was he? Why was he always standing so close to her son? His long face was capped by a tuft of spiky black hair. Beneath a pale forehead, dark deep-set eyes glared out, druggy and lifeless. She disapproved before she even knew he was her son's lover. Randy was all fun and frolic. 'Bela' — as she'd started to call him from the photos —

appeared melancholy, heavy-spirited. Anyone could see they were mismatched, her perfect angel and that, that . . . bloodsucker.

Yet she disliked him for another, more primal, reason: he'd stolen her son, the once-radiant center of her universe. He was still that, nostalgically, in joyful memories that took place before she knew he was gay. But once he declared his sexuality, she felt him recede to darkness — that place where 'Bela' waited; where women were tolerated though never truly welcome. She had felt doubly cursed. She was a mother who would lose her son twice. First to the world of homosexuals — *Bela's* world. And finally, oh, finally . . .

She groaned.

"You don't even know him," Ben said, sure her moan was meant for Sal.

"And you do?"

Ben had initially found Sal grotesque; thought him haughty, rude. Their contact was cursory, forced. A word here or there on holidays, on birthdays, instigated and orchestrated by Randy. But when Randy got sick, Sal told him what his own son could not. He came to know Sal as a man of reserve, of strength. When Sal answered Ben's questions with terse responses, he could hear his son in the background instructing him to lie.

"Tell him I'm fine," Randy once pleaded. "And not to tell Mom."

As wrong as he knew it was, that simple plea was enough for Ben to keep such a profound secret from his wife.

Ben phoned Sal at his flower shop twice a week. News was often bleak, but he was grateful for Sal's honesty. He felt a growing fondness towards the elusive, protective man at the center of his son's life.

"I don't want to startle you," Sal had told Ben a few days ago, "but it's fair you know."

"He looks bad, doesn't he?" Ben asked, bracing himself for the confirmation.

"He's thin," Sal said. Ben absent-mindedly twisted a paperclip. He could hear Sal's measured breath through the phone wires. "He's having night sweats."

Ben, silent, waited for Sal to clarify.

"He had an ugly bout with pneumonia last month. Now there's thrush, and toxi-plasmosis, and something else I won't attempt to pronounce. All these medical terms make me want to pull my out my hair."

He heard Sal shuffling through papers, looking for the name of Randy's latest illness.

"Who cares what it's called, Ben. There isn't much time."

The Mannings drove the last fifty miles to Chicago in an uneasy silence, broken only when Ben turned onto Wellington Street. He softly moaned, a sound Barbara interpreted as both a resignation to the day ahead and a signal that, though their son and Sal had been expecting their visit for years, they — slow in coming, having never been before — had finally arrived. If Barbara had asked him, Ben would have told her that she thought too much, that he was only responding to the beauty of Lake Michigan two blocks away in the late morning sun. But she wasn't thinking of Ben at all, only of her son. Would he throw open the door and playfully demand of them, of her, "What took you so long?," a harmless question Barbara couldn't answer, even to herself, without resorting to lies.

Barbara thought the apartment complex didn't look like much, just a brick enclave with an undernourished courtyard garden full of mud where perennials should be sprouting. But there was nothing growing here — no seedlings, no vines. The empty grounds were more than simply barren. They had the desolate pallor of neglect.

Yet once she stepped inside, the stairwells and hallways were warm, inviting. Mahogany banisters snaked to the upper landing. Floorboards, padded by worn carpets, croaked beneath the lightest step. Wall sconces held two plastic candlesticks each, their orange bulbs molded like flames. Their fake wax staffs were cracked and bent. Barbara wanted to straighten them but ignored her impulse, staring instead down the hallway at one after the other, each coated with light dust, each bulb dazzling with the glow of its electric stamen.

They hesitated outside the door of their son's apartment. 3G. Ben reached towards the apartment buzzer, though instead ran his fingers over the names printed in laminate beneath it. Salvatore Gagliardo. Randall Manning. The label was creased and peeling at the corners. He smoothed it with his thumb. The tag's weak adhesive stuck for a second before buckling again.

"Wait a minute," Barbara said as he extended a finger towards the doorbell. "Let me put my face on." She was palming a clam-shaped compact, tapped it with her index finger. The shell opened to reveal a mirror, a powder puff, and a circle of pale pink makeup. She stabbed at the compact with her applicator, loosening the cake of blush. She dabbed at her cheeks and forehead.

Ben had never seen her wear so much makeup. "Why didn't you do that in the car?"

"Hush." She saw delicate wrinkles in the magnifying compact. Ben reached for the doorbell. She swatted his hand away. "Give me a second."

"For what?" he asked.

She snapped her compact shut with authority and slid it into the pocket of her blazer. She smoothed her lapel with a few exact strokes. It had taken her nearly an hour to select an outfit that morning, obsessing over what would be appropriate. Black was too morbid. Red — confrontational. Yellow — frivolous. She settled on a neutral peach suit, bland yet not boring, with shirtwaist sleeves that exposed the elegant bearing of her wrists, and a calf-length sheath skirt that was proper but not frumpy. She wanted to dress well for her son, though Sal might think she did it to impress him. "How do I look?" she asked her husband.

"Stop fussing." He knocked on the door.

"I'm not." She twisted her pearl earrings, tugged at the edges of her jacket. The apartment door opened as she was checking the zipper of her skirt.

"That's a beautiful Chanel," Sal said, wanting to add 'Barbara,' but thinking it best to address Randy's mother more formally. He looked at her for guidance. He could see that — caught off guard — she'd not quite settled on the expression she wanted to present to him. Her smile was forced. Excess foundation struggled to hide her fatigue. There was a sagginess to her skin that caught against the tight curve of her smallish mouth. Yet none of this mattered when he noticed her eyes, alert with fear and disdain and — he could only imagine — bright when she felt compassion. Randy got his green eyes from her.

"Sal," Ben said. "Nice to finally meet you."

While shaking Ben's hand, Sal looked directly in Barbara's eyes. She was sizing him up. Randy had warned him that his mother could be distant. "Ben. Mrs. Manning. Come in." He retreated into the foyer.

Ben took his wife's elbow to usher her into the apartment, but she stood firm. She'd demonized Sal for such a long time, fantasized him as a pale gothic caricature, that she was stunned by his imposing presence. He had severe cropped hair, straight along the scalp with slight curls at the edges, black with natural gray flecks at the temples. Despite his formality with her, he seemed friendly; his brown eyes were certainly inviting. His lips were as she'd always pictured them in his villainy — ample red, yes, but with a comic purse that was delicately impish and all the more dangerous. There was a hint of flush beneath his olive skin, an imperfection that came as a relief against his disarming beauty. She needed a moment to process him, get used to his height, breadth, warmth. How was it that he seemed this healthy? Surely it was a ruse.

Ben tugged at her sleeve, placed his hand in the small of her back to push her forward.

"I can walk," she said.

"Then do it."

Sal lingered beyond the threshold. *This has to be tough for them.* He smiled and extended his hand to Barbara. "Come now," he said. "I don't bite."

"Don't believe him," Randy shouted from the living room. "He's luring you in for the kill."

Her son's soft, cajoling voice disarmed her, melted her reserve. She laughed, moving into the apartment, trying to peek around Sal

113

to see her son. When she did, she grabbed Sal's hand. Her son was emaciated.

"Trying to steal my man, are you?" Randy put up his dukes to spar with his mother.

It hurt her to see him. So she grabbed him, hugged him close to avoid looking at him. He must have been cold. He was shaking. She rubbed her hand across his back, the way she used to burp him as a child. The apartment felt oppressively warm and Randy, wearing a large University of Illinois sweatshirt, felt clammy. Fever? Cold sweat? Just nerves? Randy's banter was a mask to hide apprehension. To calm him — to distract herself — she'd play along.

"I wasn't going to steal your man," she said. "Only borrow." She glanced at Sal, who was glaring down at them. He stared at a lesion just below Randy's hairline. *Yes*, she thought, *take it in. Look at what you've done to him*. She cupped her hand over the offensive spot on Randy's neck. Sal's benevolent smile — the sadness in his gaze — astonished her. He had the reserve, the composure, of a killer.

Ben held back from the trio, patient for his turn with Randy. He shuffled his shoe against the floor, toe-to-heel in a soft rustle.

Randy heard the scuffing of Ben's loafers. "Hi Dad."

"Hello son." Ben expected the weight loss, the pallid skin, maybe even the gaunt cheekbones and sunken hollows that emphasized his son's slight overbite. But not the dull core of those green eyes or the lackluster hue of his once flame-red hair. These were all signs of his son's diminishment. He saw this. Then refused it. To him, Randy was the young boy in those photos on his study desk — red bangs dangling in front of his eyes, beaming at the prospect of discovering the world beyond Iowa. "You look good," Ben said.

Barbara felt Randy squirm in her arms, trying not to laugh at her husband's inane remark. "Look again, Benjamin," she said.

Laughter echoed in the foyer, none louder than her son's. She let him go and turned to her blushing husband. She hadn't meant to be insensitive, but had taken her cue from Randy and Sal, attempting to keep the day as light and irreverent as necessary.

"Where're our manners, Randy?" Sal said, aware of Ben's discomfort. "Take your folks into the living room. I'll get drinks." He moved towards the kitchen, away from the general unease, but called back to them, always the good host. "Make yourselves at home."

Barbara sat by her son on the rigid black sofa in a living room she could only describe — with forced generosity — as weird. *Too modern, too angular, too sterile*, she thought, as opposed to the practical, homey normality of the rest of the apartment. *Sal must have decorated this room*, she decided. Randy had her impeccable taste.

She took his hand between hers, rubbing it, content for the moment to be able to touch him. He turned away from her as she smoothed his fingers — one by one — with her palm. His visits home had grown infrequent over the years. She had always blamed Sal for this, but seeing Randy, she had to acknowledge that it was also shame that had kept him away. There were questions — basic, primal — that she wanted to ask him. When was Sal first unfaithful? When did he tell you? How did you let this happen? He'd be evasive with her, she knew that; deflect her questions with a playful change of subject. Her love for her son was strong, though their relationship had grown superficial since he told her he was gay. She'd let it happen by avoiding any discussion of his life with Sal. Yet as he sat next to her with his eyes closed, lost in thought, she wanted to know everything. "What are you thinking, honey?" she asked, stroking his hair.

Randy opened his eyes, smiling. There was an eager tilt to her head, anticipating his answer. But what would she want to hear? He was happy they were here, glad they'd come to see the place he called home, to meet the man who shared his comforts and, yes, now his pain. Yet his thoughts were of Sal — with him — and his mother would not want to know that. He said nothing.

Barbara sought out her husband, who was walking around the living room, looking at the vast array of strange objects scattered throughout it. He squinted at a popsicle-stick manger peopled with cartoon characters. His customary cheerfulness had abandoned him.

"Sit down, Benjamin."

"I've been sitting for hours."

She looked towards the kitchen where Sal was preparing iced tea. What was taking so long? Was it possible that he was being considerate, giving them time to be alone as a family? That was the least he could do! She looked at her men — Ben and Randy — one wandering around the room like a nomad, the other barely moving beside her. "I'm going to help with the drinks," she said.

Sal was scouring the stovetop. Barbara was surprised to find he hadn't fixed anything to drink, though there were four empty glasses, upside down, on the drainer.

"Finishing chores," he explained, sensing her confusion. "What can I get you, Mrs. Manning?"

She spotted a professional cappuccino maker on the counter. "Does that thing work?"

"You need something strong I'd imagine," Sal said. "Double espresso, coming up."

His mastery of the kitchen astonished her. This was his comfort zone. Clean, proportioned, well organized. He switched on the cappuccino maker, packed the filter, placed two clear shot glasses under the drip, got an elegant white cup and saucer from the cabinets above him, fished a lemon from a baggie, halved it, quartered it, peeled it, poured the frothy black shots into the bone china, and circled the rim with lemon rind before dropping it, with a twist, into the espresso. He handed her the coffee.

"Anything else, Mrs. Manning?"

"Yes," she said to him. "Call me Barbara." She scanned the mug in her hand. For what, she wasn't sure. She knew well enough that the disease wasn't born on the air or in a coffee cup. Still she examined it for any telltale traces, until she saw Sal staring at her. She lifted the cup to her lips, winking at Sal as she tasted his bitter espresso.

Randy and his father were in Randy's bedroom. Ben stood at the foot of his son's bed. Randy rifled through a sock drawer.

There was a red wooden toy-box near Ben, the one he'd made when his son was five years old, and where Randy had kept his playthings: a fire engine, board games, a G.I. Joe. Ben was moved that Randy still had the box, could tell it was valued by its shiny coat of paint and its polished brass lock. The toy chest looked better now than it did thirty years ago. Ben bet it was still filled with those old, untouched toys. He propped up the lid with his foot and saw a thick black dildo, a ribbed vibrator, a clutch of smooth red balls on a string. He couldn't name everything he saw though he knew, without doubt, how they functioned.

"Here we go," Randy said, pulling an envelope from the drawer. He turned as his father slammed the lid of the box. "I'm still using it to store all my unused toys."

Ben blushed. "What ya got there?" he asked.

"This," Randy said, loosening the red twine clasp, sliding papers from the mailer, "is the Last Will and Testament blah blah blah." Ben sat slack-jawed. "And you are the executor."

Ben stuttered. "I'd be honored, Rand, I would, honestly. But what about Sal?"

"He's done enough already." Randy was thinking of the future, beyond his own death, when Sal would face the signs of his body's betrayal. A cold that becomes pneumonia. A sinus infection that turns into shingles. Nausea. Blindness. Dementia. He handed his father the envelope. They sat side by side, shoulder to shoulder, at the foot of Randy's bed, reviewing instructions. Sal would get most of Randy's possessions. He'd left a few items for his parents, including the toy box. There were instructions for Randy's burial in the Iowa family plot. Explicitly, and most importantly as it was underlined twice in red marker: when the time came, Sal would be buried next to him. "You have to promise me this, dad."

Ben wasn't certain he could get his wife to go along with this. But that didn't stop his reassurances. "We wouldn't have it any other way."

With a little help from Barbara, Sal prepared a bland lunch — slices of kiwi and mango, watercress salad.

"I'm used to eating like this," he said, "so Randy doesn't feel like he's missing anything."

Barbara peeled the overripe fruit. Sal made Randy a macrobiotic shake. She watched him as he poured the thick goo from the blender. "Does he like this gunk?"

"Can't stand it."

"Then why?"

"Cleansing elements," he explained. "Easy on the colon. Something like that."

"Has it helped?"

"Does it look like it?" He said this as gently as possible, but he could hear the distress in his voice. "I'm sorry."

You should be sorry, she thought. If her son and Sal met in 1978, had been together for over ten years, the only way they could have been exposed to the AIDS virus is if they'd been unfaithful, if Sal had been — how else to put it? — fucking around. She ran her hands under the running faucet, her fingertips covered by the sticky juice of the kiwis. "I have no right to ask this, Sal, but —"

"Why Randy, not me?"

"If you'd been faithful, none of this would've happened."

He could only smile as she blamed him. He'd anticipated it. Still, she'd no right to be smug. He could explain to her that he and Randy had been devoted to each other. They'd been tender and constant, loving and companionable. Doting, even. But faithful?

No.

On occasion, they dabbled in combinations of three, that magic gay number. But Randy — how they laughed at the accuracy of his name — picked up men in bookstores, bathhouses, parking lots, anywhere. Sal — a few years older — was less compulsive, yet understood the need.

"Faithful?" he said to Barbara. "In a way, yes." He gathered the pile of fruit rinds on the counter and threw them in the sink, compacting them into the disposal.

She hadn't intended to offend him. She placed a hand on his shoulder.

"Don't," he said, flicking the disposal switch. The drain gurgled like air caught in the back of a throat. The cloying perfume of pulverizing rind lingered in the air.

She should have stepped away, attended to the business of lunch — setting the table, filling glasses with ice — but she persisted. "I just don't understand. You've been together since before this — this — the H.I.V. thing started."

"Mrs. Manning."

"Barbara."

"Mrs. Manning." He clicked off the disposal. "Your son is everything to me." His voice was barely audible. "*Everything.*"

She leaned towards him to hear what he was saying.

"I can't bear his suffering," he continued. "If I could die first, give you more time with him, I'd do it."

"That's not what I mean."

"But it's what you want. Why shouldn't you? I respect that. But this thing — AIDS, Mrs. Manning — it's no one's fault."

She couldn't help but admire his smooth restraint, his discreet denial. It was clear to her — as he refused to lay blame — that he was protecting himself, his culpability. She gathered slices of fruit from the cutting board, arranged them in a china bowl Sal had placed out for such a purpose. Didn't he just think of everything! She couldn't bear him. "Don't treat me with kid gloves," she said. "I need to know if —"

"If I'm sick? No. Not yet."

"But —?" She was dizzy with confusion.

"The H.I.V.?" he said, escalating the sounds of each letter like a question. He tilted his head, indicating to her that he was considering his answer, weighing it, but he was just looking into her hard eyes trying to determine if she might have one flicker of compassion for him. "Yes," he said. "I have the H.I.V."

How, she wondered, *was it possible*? There was one answer — one answer only — that she could keep at bay, and briefly at that, by phrasing it as a question.

"From my son?"

119

Dan Loughry is a novelist who has studied with John Rechy in Los Angeles, as well as a freelance writer and film and music reviewer for *Frontiers-IN Los Angeles* magazine and the website *Modern Tonic*. He is currently working on a second novel. Contact: dan.loughry@nbcuni.com

SUNFLOWER

—————————— ℰᴐℭℛ ——————————

by Susan Lindheim

"Wild sunflowers don't turn toward the sun," my brother Ben wrote, his tidy block print recognizable despite the smudged blue ink. "Unlike the domesticated variety, they aren't solar slaves." It was the first postcard he had sent me in years, and then, his last. Postmarked Malenkaya, Slovakia, January 17, 1992.

I scanned the Prague Central Train Station, unsure of exactly what more I really wanted to know. According to the police, three months ago, my twenty-five year-old brother hitchhiked to Malenkaya where he bought this postcard of a young girl standing in front of a plain white church holding a sunflower. A female postal clerk claimed to have seen him purchasing the stamp. She told the investigator from the American Embassy that she recognized the blurry passport photocopy because Ben resembled her own derelict son, all the while asking whether the Americans were offering any kind of reward.

The Czech and Slovak authorities were less helpful and clearly anxious to close the case. "Abducted by gypsies" was what the Second Deputy Chief of Police told me he had written in the file before it was sealed. "*Koshmarny,*" he added. "Malenkaya, big problems. No go you there."

The clock on the station's schedule wall read eleven-thirty in the fading late afternoon light, and the building smelled of diesel and damp stone. Pigeons flapped high above in the rusting metal rafters, and an occasional feather floated down through pale rays of sunlight to land on the soot-covered floor.

Everyone else had given up on Ben years ago, but I still couldn't. Not on the brother three years my senior who, when I was seven and our parents were in the midst of their divorce, spun his globe to a different spot every night, pointing out places like Irkusk and Tashkent and Vladivostok, imagining what could lie behind "that curtain made of iron. All that heavy metal might be there to protect *them* from *us*, after all, you never really know." Later, when he was in eighth grade and a mutual restraining order heralded the demise of Mom's subsequent marriage, he taught me to tune his short wave radio to the most faraway stations we could find, listening in late at night just to hear the accents, the oddly textured vowels and strange consonant combinations, static-laden promises of a different kind of life.

It *was* Ben who looked out for me then, I reminded myself, yet again. Sheltering me although no one had done the same for him. The least I could do was to press on.

I waited out the hour and a quarter until the next train by sitting inside a tiny store selling baked snacks on crusty white rolls. I sat on a creaky metal stool and munched on a *vegetarianáská* of tomato paste, onions, mushrooms and cheese, while I examined the map yet again. Still labeled Czechoslovakia despite the recent split; like so many others, the geographic publishers had yet to catch up. I looked up and noticed the store owner watching me.

"Where you go?" he asked.

"Malenkaya,"

"Tsk, tsk." He shook his head.

"Do you know if the train stops there?" I asked. He shrugged and retreated behind the counter. I stared at the small dot in the southeastern corner of the tangerine-colored map and forced down the rest of my stale pizza roll.

122

An hour later, the train station was more crowded, and the din of conversation echoed and distorted off the stone.

"Brilliant. Fucking brilliant."

The first words I understood. Spoken by a young British couple arguing with the man behind the ticket window.

"Two more days," the woman said. "Unbelievable. I hate this country."

Her companion tilted his head. "Come, come, Jenna. Be reasonable."

She swung a long brown ponytail into his face and walked off.

The man shook his head at her, then turned to notice me.

"Excuse me," I said, frantic to talk to someone who might understand. "Do you think you could help me?" I turned and pointed to the schedule on the wall. "I'm trying to get to Malenkaya, only I can't figure out which track to go to, or whether the train even stops there."

"That one should," he said, pointing to the far right of the station. "In theory, at least. Around here, you never really know."

"Thanks," I said.

"At least she's polite," he yelled toward Jenna.

Only a few other people waited on the platform, sparsely scattered the length of the train and cloaked in long winter coats. The older he got, the more Ben liked being anonymous so he could hide in plain view. By the time he turned sixteen, he was talking — when he was still actually talking to Mom and me, that is — about "camouflage for the soul. All the better to observe the clarity of real and actual truth." At the time, Mom had said she was sure it was just another passing phase, like the clove cigarettes and his stoner so-called friends. But not all endings are either crisp or clean, or timely.

Before anything else, I heard the rumble, low and steady, followed by the overpowering smell of diesel fumes. And then it arrived, the dark silhouette of the engine blotting out the remaining afternoon light. Covered in soot, the paint was once black and red with green borders and numbers. It was chugging along, powerful and fast, too fast. First the locomotive swept by us, then car after car was swallowed up into a trail of black smoke. Then there was the screeching, metal wheels against the metal track, so high-pitched and loud. Before the train even came to a full stop, the other passengers were picking up their bags and jogging to catch up with it. I grabbed my suitcase and scrambled to follow.

As I pushed my bag up the steep stairs and into the closest car, I noticed the English backpacker behind me on the platform, as if he, too, were waiting to board. A part of me wanted him to be here precisely because he'd followed me. But my gut told me no, no, no. Stay away. I wrestled my suitcase down the corridors and wobbly connectors for three successive cars until I found a cabin with empty seats. I took one for myself and another for my bag and tried not to think about omens.

"Mind if I join you?" the Englishman asked before I'd even had time to pull out my book. "My name's Nigel, by the way."

"Isabel," I replied, instantly sorry I had given my real name. "Should I save a seat for your friend?"

"What friend?" Nigel asked as he sat down on the bench next to me.

As the train moved out of the city, I tried not to make eye contact with Nigel.

I stared out the window at the stream of rectangular gray concrete apartment buildings with their lines of small square windows. "Regularity that numbs not just the senses but the spirit," that's what Ben would have said about this scene. But I wasn't sure I agreed with him, not entirely, not anymore. Regular was also reliable, and reliable meant predictable. It meant you could stop being so anxious all the time.

"You know the whole Velvet Revolution thing was staged," Nigel told me.

I stared at him for a long moment and tried to think of a reasonable response.

Clank, clank, clank.

124

Finally, I said, "What I saw on TV looked real."

Nigel tilted his head and smiled. "Oh, come, come. It wasn't. The communists knew their time was up, so they brought in a mob of students, stacked them all in Wenceslas Square and then pretended they were forced out." His eyes glided along my body as he spoke. Softly appreciative, I told myself, or at least not entirely sleazy.

I shifted in my seat and took *The Book of Laughter and Forgetting* out of my bag.

He continued, "The problem was, they didn't plan it right."

"Oh." I flipped the paperback open and stared blankly at the pages as I listened to the empty rhythm. Clank, clank, clank. After what seemed like twenty minutes but was probably only five, Nigel got up and told me he was going out for a smoke.

I stared out the window at the rain. Willow trees bent in the wind on the deserted road, the branches helpless and flopping, the leaves offering no shelter at all.

"Is it good?" Nigel asked. His voice startled me. I hadn't noticed him return. "Your book?" he said, gesturing to it.

"I just started it."

"Do you mind?" He picked up the novel and glanced at the back cover. "Kundera," he nodded. "Everyone's account of history airbrushed and unique." He handed the book back to me, took another cigarette from his bag and got up again.

"You should have just stayed in the smoking car," I said.

"Perhaps," he smiled as he pushed open the cabin door. "But the company's not nearly as good."

It was then that I noticed the postcard.

Peeking out of his rucksack, the bright colors were what struck me first, so familiar. I nudged it out slightly to reveal more of the picture: black shoes on a cobblestone street in front of a white building. I tugged the postcard slightly more and saw the hands of a girl holding the stem of a bright yellow sunflower.

The same sunflower. It matched the postcard in my bag.

On the back was the start of a letter to someone named Elizabeth. "Often we don't know the end until we're looking at it in rearview."

"There is luck and there is coincidence," Ben had told me once, shortly before he left for good, in one of those spaces between his angry bursts and the fugitive overnights when he could still be soft and kind. "But," he continued, "never the two together."

Nigel was reading a paperback with blocks of ice and penguins on the front cover, the words "Antarctica" and "One Man's Adventure" visible between his fingers. My eyes drifted back toward the postcard.

"Is your impolite stare at something in particular?" Nigel asked.

"Sorry," I said. "Must have been daydreaming."

Nigel kicked his bag under the seat for good measure.

I swallowed hard. "Where are you going?"

"Malenkaya," he said. "But don't worry, it has nothing to do with you."

Outside, the twilight had turned the gray sky a drab violet, and the leaves on the trees blurred into fuzzy olive blobs. I imagined finding Ben in the dim corridor of a dingy hotel. He didn't recognize me at first. Then he stopped to ask why I bothered to travel all this way. He didn't ask me to, he said, and he certainly couldn't imagine doing the same, not for Mom or Dad, or me.

Fighting the motion of the train, I grabbed my purse and headed toward the bathroom at the end of the corridor.

Malenkaya's train station was a single small waiting room the size of a tiny theater lobby with an unadorned ticket window built into the wall. Nigel had already gone and I was alone at the station, half wishing I had let myself trust him. Only one fluorescent light was working, and the back half of the room was dark. I searched each wall in turn for a posted map of the city but found none.

Outside, clouds turned the night sky a uniform black, like a lid. The cool night air felt electric, charged and magnetic, and a light wind carried the faint smell of pine. There was no taxi stand, not even a

126

bus stop, and as I dragged my suitcase toward the faint lights in the distance, I felt like I was watching myself in a black and white movie.

The city, once I got there, seemed stuck in another era. Sparse yellow streetlights, dark corners, the feeling of tired decay. The buildings were pockmarked with holes from bullets or shoddy construction, or both.

Toward the center of town, I stopped at a café bar to ask for directions. Two overweight middle-aged men with rosy cheeks and bushy gray mustaches — grandfatherly, I told myself — recommended a local hotel, or hostel, the translation was extremely rough. They offered to escort me there, and after some charades and mistranslations from my dictionary, I agreed even though I knew it was a mistake.

The first man insisted on carrying my suitcase, but I managed to hold onto my purse. The men mumbled at each other with too many consonants and elongated vowels. The one with my suitcase fell several steps behind. We turned a corner and I realized that the man with my suitcase had not followed.

I turned and went back, but he was gone.

"Where is he?" I yelled.

The man beside me shrugged. He pulled my arm and led me back down the street.

"But he stole it! He stole my bag!"

The man waved his index finger at me. "Tsk, tsk" he clicked with his tongue.

Up ahead was the sign for the hotel. I sprinted and easily outpaced my heavy escort. He did not follow me into the building.

A petite woman with highly bleached hair, too much black eyeliner, and long purple fingernails, was at the front desk.

"My suitcase was stolen." I told her.

"That happens," she said.

"Can you call the police for me?"

"No."

"Then, can you tell me how I can get in touch with them? I'll even go down to the station, if you tell me where it is."

"Not a good idea," she said. Her English was perfect, accent and all.

"If they didn't actually steal it themselves," a man's British accent told me from somewhere on the stairs, "they'll take everything in it before you get it back." Nigel. I turned to him.

"Thanks for giving me directions to the only hotel in town," I said.

"You didn't ask." He retreated up the stairs.

I turned back to the woman. In the pile of loose papers on her desk, I caught sight of a postcard of a girl standing in front of a white church holding a single small sunflower.

"That postcard you're holding," I said. "Where's it from?"

She flipped it over and glanced at the picture. "Some town nearby, perhaps," she said. "Definitely not Malenkaya. There's no church like that here." There was nothing on the back, save for empty boxes for the address and stamp. "There's a newsstand a couple of blocks from here that sells them, if you like."

The woman studied the blank postcard some more. "Maybe this girl has your suitcase," she said.

"A big middle-aged man has my suitcase," I said. "Or at least he did twenty minutes ago."

I asked the woman whether there were any rooms available for the night, and she said that if I paid in advance I could have the room with the single bed at the top of the stairs with a shared bathroom down the hall. I took the key and started upstairs, then turned back around.

"Have you heard of any people disappearing from around here?" I asked.

Her eyes widened, "People?"

"One person in particular. Tall American man with glasses and blond hair, about twenty-five?"

"Lots of things disappear," she said as she stored my registration papers away, "but I wouldn't know anything about it."

More than anything, I missed my toothbrush.

I woke up early in the saggy single bed, not feeling at all rested even though I had slept. I put on the clothes I had been wearing the day before and went downstairs.

I asked the woman at the hotel desk whether she remembered anyone named Ben Ashford staying here about three months ago. It was a different woman in the morning, and she didn't speak much English. She shrugged. She wasn't here then, she said. She can't tell me when the woman from last night will be back.

"That bastard owes me much money," a man called from the hotel restaurant in thickly accented English. He got up from his table and approached.

His gaze sliced through my clothing. "You know, there are ways you could help him," he said. His eyes were fixed on my chest. He thrust a business card at me. His breath smelled of greasy pork sausages and last night's stale alcohol, and the thick gold chain around his neck glistened in the lobby light. Poking out from his jacket, I made out what I thought was the wooden handle of a gun. "If you have interest, of course."

"I don't."

Outside the hotel, I paused to catch my breath. Even in the daylight, the sky and buildings were an unending solid shade of gray. A sloping red bus spewing black smoke lilted slowly down the street. As I watched its halting progress, I decided to try to find the newsstand selling the postcards, just in case there was something more to them. I wandered around for half an hour before I spotted a small kiosk at the end of a long narrow block.

Just then, I felt a soft lump under my right foot. A mound of bright green dog shit, smashed and stuck into the crevasses of my sole.

"You need help?" a thin old man asked me from a doorway across the street. He was wearing a stained coat and wrinkled pants and his glance made me cringe.

"No." I walked away.

"It's dirty," he called at me. "Very bad. Come here. I help you." I walked faster, a trail of green shit behind me. He crossed the street and followed me.

"Come here," he grabbed my arm. "I help you wash."

"Leave me alone," I said.

He grabbed my waist. The gristle of his beard brushed my face and his tongue touched my cheek. I pushed him away and he fell back into the building behind us.

"Let me help you," he yelled as he struggled to prop himself up. I turned a corner and ducked out of sight.

After another half hour of wandering through Malenkaya, I had uncovered nothing. I returned to the hotel and attempted again to question the woman at the desk. This time she merely grunted at me.

"She can't help you," Nigel said from the top of the stairs.

"And you can?"

"Perhaps."

In the hotel restaurant, over black tea in clear glasses with scorching metal handles, Nigel told me that I should look for a woman with henna-colored hair and a silver and blue pendant, Eva as she was known, although surely that was not her real name. She lived in the apartments on the far edge of town. As he smoked three cigarettes in rapid succession, Nigel explained the true workings of the "new business opportunities" in the area. Import, export, and distribution, he said with authority, but without ever clarifying his own exact role. Of so many things, he continued. Raw opium. Routed from Central Asia and Afghanistan to Moscow, it passed conveniently through Malenkaya on its way to Western Europe. "Via the Roma," Nigel explained, "the Travelers, the gypsies, or whatever you want to call them. Stateless people in the eyes of the government, the locals, just about everyone else." He paused to bring yet another cigarette to his lips. "They don't do the actual dealing or transacting, but they cloak and facilitate transport quite nicely. And, for a ridiculously small fee, the police have agreed to look away."

"So did you know my brother?"

"No."

"Then why are you helping me now?" I asked, leaning in toward him. "The honest reason, please. No airbrushing."

"I have a sense about you," he said quietly as he reached for his lighter again. "You remind me of someone."

"Someone who's still talking to you?"

Half a mile outside the city, on the same road as the train station but far past it, there was a small, untended patch of dirt surrounded by sterile concrete apartment buildings with laundry spilling out. Next to the buildings, a few old Fiat campers were parked alongside rusting vans. Sparse tufts of grass poked out from large patches of mud where several boys played soccer in the steady drizzle.

Nigel stood where I had left him, half a block behind, holding guard.

Women loaded down with baskets and bags began to pile out of the vans. I scanned their faces for some kind of recognition, of anything. They looked down and away from me. Finally, someone who looked like Eva stepped out of one of the vans.

"Excuse me," I said to her.

She paused to look closely at me, then started to walk away.

"Please," I tried again. "It's Eva, right?"

She stopped and stared at me.

"You know my brother Ben Ashford." I described him again, watching her face closely for any kind of recognition, reaction. "I came here to find him."

"Don't."

She walked away.

I followed her into one of the buildings and up the dirty staircase to the second floor. Voices echoed down the concrete hallway lined with plastic bags and empty glass bottles. Once we were inside the apartment, I handed her two $100 bills.

"Please," I pushed the money into her palm. "I came all the way from San Francisco. It would mean a lot to me, even just to know what happened."

She closed her hand around the bills and let them rub against her palm. After a long moment, she nodded. "Follow me."

Eva took me up several more flights of stairs and out onto the roof. She pointed beyond the cluster of buildings and vans to a flat field surrounded by trees. The last time she saw Ben — the last time anyone had seen him — he was running toward the makeshift cemetery in that field. He looked afraid.

"Why?"

"I'm only watcher," she said. "Ben helped me once with a man and a fight. Please, please — not get more involved."

I grabbed her arm. "You know more than that. I can tell."

She sighed and wriggled her arm free. "*Ano*. Matti drove Ben in his truck." Matti, a cousin or uncle or brother, it wasn't clear, would occasionally pick up men like Ben to break up the routine of driving, to improve his English, to recruit new faces to help transport the drugs.

"But with Ben was too much," she said.

"What do you mean?" I asked.

"Bad luck," she said. "Matti had to curse his own truck to get rid of it. He had to destroy everything."

And then, as I stared at her in disbelief, I noticed it.

Next to the silver and blue pendant on her necklace, it was there on the chain. A gold ring, his gold ring, the one Grandfather had gotten him in Greece near the Acropolis, that oriental puzzle ring that Ben learned to put back together so smoothly and quickly that the solution became nearly unconscious, over and over, until all the yelling finally stopped.

Eva clutched at her necklace. "Present," she said. "He gave me."

"Sometimes we get what we deserve," Ben had told me after Grandfather's funeral four and a half years ago, right before he dropped out of touch. "Sometimes we don't. Sometimes there's little difference between the two."

The first thing I noticed about the cemetery was the girl. She was young, perhaps eight or nine, and she was holding a yellow flower in her hand. She stood in front of a grave in the middle of the field with a tall man who could be her father or brother. She looked nothing like the girl in the postcard.

The smell of earth was strong and heavy with metal, and the breeze pelted freezing rain onto my cheeks. Mud caked onto my shoes as I started back toward the apartments and town. Even from this distance, I could see him clearly. Nigel. He was smoking a cigarette as he paced back and forth across the empty space, waiting.

Susan Lindheim is an award-winning author living in Los Angeles. She won the UCLA Writing Program's Kirkwood Prize in 2007 for an excerpt from her novel-in-progress, *Baby Driver*. The novel is based on her grandmother's true-life experiences as a nice Jewish girl forced by her family to traffic heroin during the Depression. Her short story, *Travels With Gonzalo* was published in the *South Dakota Review* in 2003 and was performed as part of the New Short Fiction Series in Los Angeles in 2009. Lindheim also adapted *Travels With Gonzalo* into a screenplay which was a quarterfinalist in the 2006 Nicholl Fellowship Competition.

Lindheim speaks Spanish, French and some very rusty Russian. Her diverse professional experience includes: communications specialist for a Los Angeles based non-profit organization; business development for international media companies; technical writing and instructional design for high tech companies; literacy instructor for an after school program targeting at-risk youth; program officer for a non-profit organization engaged in work in Eastern Europe and the Former Soviet Union; privatization consultant to the Polish and Uzbek governments; and Fulbright-sponsored English language instructor at a high school in France. Lindheim has traveled to 38 countries, including several which no longer exist. Contact: amildsunshine@gmail.com

Estella and the Gringo

— ℰℛ —

by Joel Willans

I was shelling peas in the courtyard when Mama shouted at me to come say hello. Radio Panamericana was blasting out *merengue* and the dogs were yapping, so I pretended not to hear, sure that it would be the son of a bitch *padre* or one of Mama's dumb friends. When I looked up and saw it was a young gringo, I was so surprised that I knocked the bowl over, spilling peas across the concrete. The gringo grinned like it was the funniest thing he'd ever seen. I cursed him under my breath until he knelt down and helped me pick them up.

"Sorry, I don't normally have that effect on people," he said in sloppy Spanish. He smoothed down his messy maize-colored hair and shook my hand. "Nice to meet you, I'm Doug."

Close up I could see he was older than I first thought. Twenty-five at least. Perhaps more. He had a long face and a nose that took up too much room. His mouth was pretty though, like a girl's, and his eyes were a fine-looking river green. A gold stud glinted in his eyebrow. He touched it when he saw me staring.

"I got it in Rio. It seemed like a good idea at the time."

"I think it's very pretty," Mama said, putting a painted fingernail to her lip.

It was then I realized that she'd curled her hair and put on the yellow blouse she normally kept for the *padre's* visits. I sniffed the air. Perfume too. She'd known a gringo was coming and hadn't said a word.

"What are you doing here?" I asked.

Mama patted me on the head as if I were one of the dogs. "Oh, don't mind this one, Señor. Estella may be almost nineteen, but she still has plenty to learn about manners." She grabbed Doug's elbow. "Now, your room is ready. I've made it up very nice."

"Thanks," he said. "That's very kind of you."

The way she put her hand over her mouth and fluttered her eyelashes, you'd think he'd told her she was the most beautiful woman in the world. Doug didn't notice anything. He was too busy looking around the courtyard. "You know, this place is just amazing. My mum would love these flowers."

"They are my babies, Señor. I treat them well and they keep me happy with their color."

I bit my tongue. It was true. The flowers were beautiful. I loved them all. The yellow angel's trumpets with a fragrance that gave you strange dreams, the cantutas, the lilies and the purple orchids stuffed in old paint pots, hanging over doors and coating the walls. But if they were her babies, why in the Virgin's name was it me who had to water them every morning?

"Give me a little while and I can show you around our town," Mama said, hands flittering like butterflies.

"That's okay. Once I've dumped my gear, I can check it out myself."

"I need to buy some bread. I'll come with you," I said.

Mama's mouth puckered up like a dried plum, but she didn't say a word. She didn't have to. I knew what she was thinking.

While Mama showed Doug his room, I counted on my fingers how many gringos I'd seen in my life. Seven, that I could remember. Three missionaries. Two doctors. One NGO woman and a man who came through town once on a motorbike. Doug didn't sound like a preacher or look like a doctor, so he had to be a charity man.

When he returned, he'd changed into army shorts and a t-shirt that said Born to Surf. A big camera hung around his neck.

"Ready?" I asked.

"I'm always ready."

I led him through the courtyard and out into the street. A *campesino* was herding his goats, making dust rise into the air like mud-colored fog. Doug pointed his camera at them. "Damn, this place is cool."

"You think? Surely goats are goats everywhere?"

"Yeah, but you don't see them wandering down the high street where I'm from."

As we walked, he turned his head this way and that as if he was looking at the world for the first time. When we got to the plaza and saw the statue of Bolivar riding his horse, he went *loco*.

"I bet he's a hero 'round here, right?"

"Who?"

"Bolivar."

I laughed. "Don't be stupid. He's been dead a hundred years."

Doug got on his knees and started snapping away again. "I've read all about him. Not many people who've freed a whole continent, hey? Just shows you can do worthwhile stuff when you travel."

I shrugged. "What are you doing here?"

"I'm going to teach English at a village school in the valley. My dad says I'm a bum just traveling around, so I'm going to show him different." He spun round, taking pictures of the church, the mountains, even Don Miguel sprawled on a bench.

It was funny to see the way people stared at him and the way he just grinned back at them. *Mamitas* held their knitting still, men froze, cigarettes hovering before their mouths. Kids stopped their games and giggled. When some *chicos* I used to play football with pouted their lips and made kiss-kiss sounds, I gave them the finger.

Despite his accent and the way words chased each other out of his mouth, I liked his chatter. He was full of energy, like a child after too much cake. I was concentrating so hard on his words that I didn't notice the *padre* until he put his hand on my shoulder.

"And who have we here, young lady?" he said. Even though his sunglasses covered his eyes, I knew he was looking down my top.

Like always, I imagined spitting in his face, but instead I just shrugged him off and nodded at Doug. "Why don't you ask him yourself? He speaks Spanish."

The *padre* stroked the scar on his chin. The one he said he got in the service of Christ, but, as I'd overheard him tell Mama, was really from falling off his motorbike drunk.

"Thank you for such a polite introduction, Estella."

Sticking his chest out, he stared up at Doug. The *padre* knew everyone in the plaza was watching, and made a big show of grilling Doug as if he was sitting in confession. Doug waved his arms around a lot and answered all his questions with a smile. The longer they talked, the more the *padre* ran his hands through his slick gelled hair. When he strode off, he didn't say goodbye.

"What's his problem? Has he got a thing against foreigners?"

"Maybe."

"I thought these religious dudes were meant to be all kindness and light."

"How can you be a teacher and still be so dumb?"

He laughed. "Give a guy a break! I only arrived this morning. So come on, tell me. What's the lowdown on the little man in black?"

I wanted to shout at him that the *padre* was a son of a bitch hypocrite. That after fat Sergio's daughter had caught me with Alejandro in the forest, *padre* had preached about the whores of Babylon leading good people down the road to ruin. And that two nights later, I saw him kissing Mama in the moonlight and that the bastard came around my house all the time now, and once he'd even tried to grope me between the legs. But I didn't have the guts, so I ignored the question and instead asked Doug if he wanted to take my picture.

Doug took the *colectivo* bus into the countryside the next morning. When he saluted me from the window, I waved back, ignoring the gawping *campesinos* and the sniggering kids pushing their faces against the dirty glass.

It was two days before I saw him again. I'd just got back from the market, and was weighed down with *granadillas*, *cherimoyas* and maize. It wasn't just my shoulders that ached. My head hurt too. It was tiring ignoring the sniggers and the whistles, the whispers and the stares, especially when mama said it was exactly what I deserved.

I'll never forget the first time I felt everyone's eyes on me. I'd gone into town, the day after word had gotten out about me and Alejandro. People hissed and sneered at me like I was dirt. When I came home and told mama, she said she was so ashamed that it hurt her to look at my face. She said that nobody would want to marry a slut who spreads her legs for a traveling salesman. She said I should stop moaning about the consequences, and think of her. Think of what I'd done to her reputation.

I felt bad then, as bad as the day I woke up and mama told me Papi had gone and he wasn't coming back. If I'd have known about her and the *padre*, I wouldn't have grabbed her arm and begged for her forgiveness. I would've told her that she might be all high and mighty on the outside, but she was no better than me. Worse even, because I'd never get it together with someone I didn't love. And even after all those months of gossip and stares, and even when Alejandro told me he didn't want to see me again, I still loved him.

I was thinking of him when I walked into the courtyard. I must've looked down, because Doug jumped up as fast as a cricket and rushed over. "Let me take those before your arms fall off." He grabbed the bags and nodded at the *granadillas*. "Can I have an orange?"

"*Estupido*, that's no orange!"

"Well, it sure looks like one."

"Try and peel it then."

He did as he was told. The peel cracked and white fluff puffed out.

"What on earth is that?"

"Pull the skin off."

He worked his fingers over the surface. When he spied the slimy green insides, his face screwed up as if he'd just opened a parcel of pig liver. "I'm not eating that. It looks like something you cough up when you're ill."

I laughed. "That makes you a coward."

"I'm no coward," he said. "Watch." He threw back his head and gulped the green jelly. "Man, that tastes fantastic!"

"See, bravery has its rewards."

It felt good to show someone as educated as him something new. I was about to ask him if he liked football so I could show him some of my tricks, but Mama leant out the window, her hair in curlers. "Estella, where have you been hiding yourself? The toilet needs scrubbing, and I've got *Señora* Lida coming over for a *cafecito*. Get to it, girl."

"Why don't you get to it yourself?"

"By all the saints, I don't need your lip. I give you a roof over your head and you talk to me like I'm nothing. You know where the door is if you're not happy." Her face froze. "Oh, Doug, I didn't see you there! I'm just making some lunch. You'll eat with me, won't you?"

"Okay. If you like."

Mama's head disappeared as she shouted. "Yes, yes of course. I want to hear all about your time in the *campo*."

"Is your mum always like that?" he whispered behind his hand.

"Like what?"

"Hassling you."

"Yes. She has no respect for me."

Doug looked at his nails. "My dad's the same. Bitches me big time when I'm at home. Reckons I'm selfish. Me. Can you believe it?"

"I don't know you well enough to tell."

Mama reappeared with her hair free of rollers. She looked stunning, like someone out of a Columbian soap opera. Doug stared at her, just like all the men did whenever Mama made an effort.

"Come, Doug. I want to hear all your stories. Did the *campesinos* disturb you? It pains me how they live like animals and how ill-educated they are."

Doug followed her into the kitchen. A hungry puppy after a bone. When I put the food into the pantry, I heard them laughing.

That night, lying in bed listening to Olga Tañón sing *Muchacho Malo* on the radio, I thought of the *padre* and Mama. I wondered what went on in their heads. How could he, a man meant to be wedded to the church, bring himself to lecture us every Sunday about sin? And what about Mama, who said I was a slut for giving myself to a married man, when she was sleeping with a priest? It made me so angry that I wanted to scream. Instead, I punched my pillow over and over. One punch for Mama. One for the *padre*. It helped a little, but it was nowhere near enough.

A few days later, Doug caught up with me while I was walking to the park. Although I didn't have time to play football anymore, I liked to go there to watch the kids play. It reminded me of when Papi was still around.

"Guess who?" Doug said, putting his hands over my eyes.

"The President of the Republic?"

"If only. Where you going?"

"To the forest. Want to come?"

I took him the same way I went with Alejandro, but this time I made sure we walked further away from the path. Maybe he knew what I wanted, but he didn't do anything, so I took us to sit by the river. For a while we said nothing. Just listened to the birds and the crickets.

"You have pretty fingers," I said eventually.

"You think?"

I took his hand. "They are soft too. Like baby skin."

He laughed. "Don't tell my dad. He thinks I haven't done a hard day's work in my life."

"You always talk about your papa."

"Do I?"

"Yes. Do you miss him?"

"You must be joking.'"

"Is he handsome?"

He threw a stone in the river. "If you're into bald men with glasses."

"Do you think my mama is pretty?"

"Yeah, for an older woman."

"She wants you."

"What do you mean?"

"As her lover."

"What?" He clapped his hands together. "Don't be stupid. She's just being friendly."

"I know her and she's after you. She thinks because you're a gringo you're rich."

I edged closer. "Have you ever kissed a Peruvian girl?"

He arched his back and ran his hand through his hair. "Oh man, if this is going where I think it's going, we should be heading back."

"Is it that you want my mama or are you just too scared to try? Like you were with the *granadillas*?"

He blinked and licked his lips. "No! I'm not scared. It's just I came here to do something worthwhile, not to party."

I caressed his neck. "I think you're scared."

"Yeah?"

"Yes."

He grabbed my face and kissed me hard. His mouth tasted of mint and cigarettes. He pushed his tongue deeper than Alejandro and I remembered what they said about all gringo girls being easy. Even though I didn't like his smoky taste, I made sure I didn't pull away.

After that, whenever he was back from the countryside, he tried to find a way to be alone with me. And even when Mama was in the same room, he'd squeeze my elbow or bang into me and pretend it was an accident. Mama was too caught up in her own head to realize anything. She still made Doug take lunch with her and still dressed herself up like a soap star.

The *padre* suspected her of something, though. He may have been a sleaze, but he was no donkey brain. One Monday, he stopped me in the plaza and asked how long the gringo was staying.

"Why do you want to know?"

"I'm curious, that's all." He smiled with his too-white teeth.

"Worried he'll take your place?"

"What are you talking about, girl?"

"You know."

His smiled stayed fixed, but his nostrils flared like an angry horse's. "Do you think anyone will listen to a word that comes from your filthy mouth? You ooze sin from every pore. I'm counseling your mother. Helping her deal with the sadness you have brought her. Understand?"

I laughed. "Counseling wasn't what the boys at school called what you and Mama do."

"You are going straight to hell, Estella Galindo, as surely as night follows day."

142

The way he marched away, chest out, arms swinging like a soldier's, I knew I had got to him. The thought kept me singing all day.

A couple of weeks later, while I was feeding the chickens, Doug told me that Mama had asked if he thought she was beautiful.

"And?" I said, tossing grain in big handfuls.

"I said yes, of course."

I spun round and threw the chicken food at him.

"Hey, what are you doing?" He flapped like one of the birds.

"You've never told me I'm beautiful."

"Well, course you are. Beautiful women have beautiful daughters. And you are, you're real beautiful."

I let him kiss me then, but I could tell by the way he pressed himself hard against me he wanted more. When I pushed him off, he said something in English and kicked the wall.

"I'm leaving."

"Why? Because I don't let you kiss me when I'm feeding chickens?"

He crossed his arms. "No, because you're mother is trying to get into my pants. And because you won't let me get in yours."

I pinched him. He yelped like a kicked dog.

"What about trying to prove to your *papi* that you can do something worthwhile with your life?"

"Damn, I've been here long enough," he said, rubbing his arm. "I've emailed him the pics. I've shown him I'm no waster. "

"If you go I want to come with you."

"Don't be ridiculous, Estella. You live here."

"I don't want to live here anymore."

He sat on the step and rolled his head around his shoulders. "I can't take you with me. I'm cruising around South America until my money runs out and then I'm going home."

"You're just like Papi."

"What do you mean?"

"You run away from your problems."

143

"Listen, I don't need any of your psychoanalysis, okay. You're a sweet girl, but I was never going to stay forever. And now your mum is freaking me out. It's time to hit the road."

I grabbed his hand and pulled him to his feet. "If that's how you see things, I want to give you something to remember me by."

"You do?"

I sat in on his lap. "I do."

"When?"

"Meet me in the plaza just before noon."

"You've got a date," he said grinning.

The rest of the morning I praised myself for keeping calm. When I'd wanted to slap Doug's selfish face, I'd caressed it. When I'd wanted to kick him between the legs, I'd sat on his lap. Just like everyone else, he said one thing and did another. If he'd come to my town to help people, what was wrong with helping me? If he had money to travel around South America, he had money to take me with him. I pretended to look happy in front of the mirror before I went to meet him in the plaza, but my smile looked as fake as a plastic doll's.

He was waiting beside fat Sergio's ice cream trolley, playing with two *campesino* girls. Their ponytails swung back and forth like black rope as he chased them in circles. He was good with *niños*. One day, he might make a good husband and father to someone. I took a deep breath, kissed the ring Papi left me and marched over.

"Hey there," he said, breathless. "These two are in my class." He nodded at the girls.

I smiled at them and took his hand. "Let's go. I haven't got much time."

"Where to?"

"Put your arm around me."

"Here?"

"Yes, here. You're leaving, no? What does it matter who sees us now?"

He shrugged and wrapped his arm around my shoulders. It felt good even when I saw *mamitas* nudge each other and point at us. The girls ran to get their friends. Nose in the air, I marched us towards the doors of the church just as the bell struck. Once I'd counted the twelve chimes, I grabbed Doug's face and kissed him.

Teasing him with my tongue, I grinded myself against him as if we were in the *discoteca*. Over his shoulder, I saw the church doors open. The *padre* strode out, sunglasses in his hand, squinting in the midday sun. When he saw us, he pulled his hands up to shield his face from the sun and stared.

"You're eager," Doug said, puffing his cheeks.

"This what you wanted, isn't it?" I glared at the *padre*. Even though his face was now in shadow, I saw his too-white teeth and his frown. I waited for him to say something, but he just carried on staring. He was still staring when I took Doug's hand and led him to the forest path.

The patio was quiet when we returned a couple of hours later. It felt as if the house was holding its breath. No dogs, no radio, no Mama singing. The only sounds came from outside. A cow's sad bellowing, beeping motorbike horns and *niñas* laughing.

A door slammed indoors. "Estella, is that you, girl?"

I didn't say anything.

Doug let go of my hand and stopped grinning. "What's gotten into her?"

Before I could answer, Mama burst out of the kitchen. She was breathing hard. Her hair was messed up like she'd been in a storm and her hands were clenched in fists. The *padre* stood behind her, shaking his head.

"Is it true what the *padre* tells me?" Mama hissed. "You've been whoring yourself in the forest again."

My face flushed hot. "The *padre* should know. He's an expert on whores."

Mama took two quick steps and slapped me so hard my cheek felt as if it had been whipped with nettles.

"I want you out of my house." She glared at Doug. "I want you both out of my house."

I rubbed my face and felt tears coming. It wasn't from the pain or because the *padre* was smirking and pulling Mama close like he cared.

145

No, it was the way Doug looked, like a little boy who's just been told that one day he will die. I grabbed his hands.

"I'd rather be a whore than a hypocrite," I shouted so loud the dogs began barking. "All these months you've made me feel bad, told me how I've let you down, and you're spending your time in the arms of a priest."

She grabbed the gold crucifix that hung around her neck with both hands, and shook her head. "Get out, Estella, and take your gringo with you!"

I dragged Doug upstairs, first to my room and then to his. He didn't say a single word until I started to pack his stuff.

"That was surreal." He sat on the bed, head in his hands. "I've never seen your mum so fired up. What's her problem?"

"She listens to the wrong people."

"Is she really getting it on with the *padre*?"

I nodded.

"That's crazy."

We got a taxi to the bus station. I think he was in shock, because he kept mumbling to himself in English. It wasn't until we got on the bus to Andahuaylas, and the driver turned on the engine, that he looked me in the eyes.

"Hey, I'm really sorry about all this. I never knew it would be such a big deal." Guilt covered his face like a rash.

I squeezed his hand. "It's not your fault."

The driver put the radio on. Huayño filled the bus. I recognized the song immediately. *Adiós pueblo de Ayacucho*. I looked out the window, hoping Doug wouldn't see my tears.

The next morning I sat on the balcony of our fine room in the Hotel Sol de Oro. Andahuaylas was much like my town, but the hotel was something very special. Everything shined like new. We even had our own TV. Still, I must have looked sad, because Doug massaged my shoulders and asked me how he could cheer me up. I squeezed his hand and told him I'd like a football.

146

"A ball? You've got to be kidding me?" he said, but he bought it just the same and laughed when I showed him the tricks Papi taught me.

"You were wasted feeding chickens," he said when I slipped the ball between his legs and ran past him as though he wasn't there.

"I know."

That was our best day. By the time we got to Cusco, things were different. The place he took me to had roaches and the sheets had stains and it was so hot my T-shirt stuck to my back. When I told him it was dirty, he glared at me and spat words. "I don't see you dipping into your pocket to get us anywhere better."

I shut my mouth after that.

He spent the evening flicking through his guidebook and sighing. Only once did he smile. "Hey, cool. If we stay a few days we can check out the Inti Raymi Festival," He clapped as if congratulating himself on his find. "What do you know about the Tahuantinsuyo Empire?"

"Nothing. I've never heard of it."

"What?"

I looked at my nails.

"This is your culture!" He waved the book around like preacher. "How the hell can you not know anything about it?"

I got up and grabbed the book from his hands. "Maybe because, unlike you gringos, I haven't had the time or money to go on big holidays around the world."

That night he didn't try to get it on with me like he had the night before. I was glad. It was better that I didn't have to push him away. The next morning, he got up early and said he was going out to get a paper and bring back some breakfast. He asked me if I wanted anything.

"I'd love a *granadilla*."

"What, that weird orange fruit?"

"Yes, please."

"Anything else?"

"No, that's all."

I watched him out the window, walking down the street. He would be away a long time. *Granadillas* were out of season. It only took me five minutes to find his money bag stuffed in a shoe at the bottom of his rucksack. He said he wasn't rich, but there were more soles and dollar bills than I'd ever seen. I took all the soles but left half the dollars. In the note I told him I was sorry, but that when I got work, I'd return the cash. I wished him good luck and signed it love, Estella. Because even though I didn't love him, I did love what he did for me. Then, with my football under my arm and my bag on my back, I walked out into a street where nobody stared and nobody hissed.

Joel Willans is an award-winning author originally from Suffolk in the UK. He has lived in Canada, Finland and Peru. Joel won the Yeovil Prize and Global Short Story Award, and in 2008, he was nominated for a Pushcart Prize. This year, his short story collection, *By Ma Biscuits or Kiss Ma Fish*, was shortlisted for the Scott Prize for Fiction. Joel's stories have been broadcast on BBC radio and published in more than a dozen anthologies and many magazines. Currently, Willans lives in a converted hospital in the Finnish countryside. Contact: Joelwillans@yahoo.com

A DATE WITH THE UNKNOWN

—————————— ℘Cℛ ——————————

Excerpt from the novel The Stone Collector
by Eitan Olevsky

There was eagerness in her smile, curiosity beyond words. She wanted a romantic encounter with him for so long — what had gotten into him! Meltus was acting differently after the day she stormed from his dorm. Maybe she should get angry with him more often. Her backpack contained a neatly folded pink pajama, her makeup, a toothbrush, a hair dryer and other essentials. She didn't want Meltus to see how messy her hair and face looked the next morning. A case of condoms hid in one of the backpack's compartments. Not that she ever had sex with Meltus, but there was always a first time. She wondered why they never had, questioning many times whether he was still a virgin. Maybe he was a little slow in those matters. She needed more patience. It took Meltus a while to finally ask her for this: a romantic night together. For the first time! She knew she had a dumb smile on her face. After all, she loved him despite how often he made a fool of himself; especially hanging out with those two idiots. Yes, Matt and George were the root of Mel's apathy. Men, they have too much pride in them.

If she managed to seduce him tonight, she knew he would stop following those two like a lapdog. This was her chance. She frowned remembering her pink-flowered pajamas. Why hadn't it ever occurred to her to buy sexy lingerie? Meltus and Matt were ten paces away from her. They talked in whispers and she pricked her ears to hear a few words. 'Alcohol' and 'scoring' were the two words she caught, but then raucous laughter muffled their words. Matt eyed her as she waited near the bench outside class. He shook hands with Meltus, gave him overabundant pats on the shoulder and returned to the faculty building. Matt knew she hated him.

Quickly she forgot about him and stared heartily at the smiling young man who came to greet her. She had not seen that expression in quite a while. His chubby cheeks were red. That was his shy way of showing how much he loved her.

She probably noticed, thought Meltus while he approached her. She had a quizzical smile, something he didn't understand. He stopped a pace short from her, afraid to kiss her. Shit, why was she acting so weird? Maybe she knew he was planning on having sex with her. It was embarrassing.

"Why are you blushing?" she asked. Shit, she actually knew.

"Me? Blushing? It's just the sun. I got a little sunburned."

"Aww, Mel, it's not even the end of spring yet. I think you are truly blushing," she said, pinching his nose playfully.

"Stop that!"

"Oh Mel, you are so funny."

"Let's grab that cab," he said, taking her hand. A yellow taxi stood in the corner. He dragged her to the vehicle and carefully opened the back door, waiting impatiently for her to sit; the back-door-thing had been Matt's advice. He peered at her from the front of the cab. She looked surprised but remained silent. At least she was docile today.

"So . . . where are you taking me?"

Why was she asking him this? Matt said he had to use the element of surprise, and that would be the best element to arouse her.

"You'll see . . . " he mumbled.

His mind was elsewhere. He thought of what he'd tell Uncle Arthur, the reason why he'd be staying at his place. How inconvenient could it be to simply show up after so many years? Arthur Fenning became a recluse in his own home after discovering the Shrine of Dionysus.

Maybe he hated the popularity that came along with it. Back in those days, every news channel in the island showed his face. Those were the times when Meltus' parents still got along with Arthur — when he wasn't an eccentric and people still thought him likeable.

His uncle took him there once, two months after its discovery. Back then, the shrine was half-covered by the Mestas mountain ranges, a few kilometres near the open sea. It was an exciting time. Lots of men digging deep into the earth revealed what looked like an archway and a dome.

Again this put his uncle on every network. Meylach's Reality Channel made it a special coverage, a tribute to his efforts to rediscover Meylach's ancient past.

Lydia tried clutching his hand.

"What are you doing?" he reacted.

"I . . . I am cold."

"That's impossible! It's springtime, you can't be cold." He heard her sigh. That trip to the excavation site was the last time he saw Uncle Arthur — five years ago, when he was fourteen and rumours began to spread of an ancient civilization that lived there a thousand years ago.

The Shrine of Dionysus was a historical breakthrough, a temple that would attract tourists from every corner: the eighth wonder. He regretted not seeing it later, when there was still a chance. It was an immense courtyard encircled by white open arches. Flagstone covered that large space, and in its center two thick pillars upheld the entrance to a temple carved out of white stone: the Shrine of Dionysus.

The general public never got to learn what lay inside. A week after his uncle had taken him there the Meylach Reality Channel transmitted live-breaking news. Arthur Fenning publicly resigned office as head researcher of the project. His parents had a big fight with Arthur one night, and from then on no one saw him again.

Even after his uncle's resignation, the government would not let go of a project of such a magnitude. The Shrine of Dionysus would provide a huge economic injection to the island of Meylach, meaning lots of foreign investment and tourism. To this day they were still working on the temple's restoration. Governments were inefficient. When his uncle was head of the project, it took six months to end the external excavations. It had been what — four years and the government was still working on the temple's interior. The few anthropologists that worked there were paid to keep their findings a secret.

"We're here sir," said the taxi driver, halting before a short and shadowy tunnel.

"Can't we go in?" asked Meltus.

"I'm not going in there," the driver responded, pointing at a wooden sign hanging askew. 'Trespassers will be shot', it said in bold black letters.

"Mel, are you sure your uncle knows we're coming?" asked Lydia.

"Of course he does," he lied.

Meltus paid the cabdriver, got off and took her along the short tunnel. The land opened over a green expanse. A hundred paces further lay the mansion. Mel had forgotten the magnificence of his uncle's house. Dozens of arched windows decorated the three floors of pale-yellow brick.

"This is where we are staying?" she said, gasping. She wheeled around and stared at the big garden.

Meltus nodded. "You like it?"

"Like it? Mel, this is a dream house! I can't believe you're actually doing this for me."

Two birds chirped away and clung to a marble statue of a boy carrying a vase with water. Meltus looked at his watch eagerly. Light would begin to fail soon. He needed to hurry if he wanted to arrange their accommodations.

"Wait for me here," he said. "I need a few minutes to prepare everything inside."

"Aww Mel, you are so sweet! I love you!" She gave him a loud kiss on the cheek.

"Gotta go now," said Meltus, nervously approaching the mansion's front door. Girls were so annoying. He stared at her as she unfolded a picnic blanket where she would sit to wait for him. She'd be blown away when she saw the whole place. The problem would be getting her in. What if Uncle Arthur saw her? How open-minded would he be? Even he might be unwelcome there. His heart pounded.

Two pillars guarded by a pair of stone tigers cornered the main entrance. "Never put your hand in the mouth of a tiger," his uncle had said millions of times when he was a boy. He plunged his hand deep into the jaws of the left stone tiger. However, when he removed the item in its guts he threw it to the ground in panic: a revolver. He was starting to regret coming here. He looked back, and Lydia waved a hand. She was too far away to see the problem. He had to pull through. Both Matt and George would ask him too many questions about sex.

"Be brave for once," he reassured himself. His hand slid into the other stone statue and as it went deeper, he touched something that produced a jingle. The mouth let out a set of coloured keys in a rounded keychain; he had known where it was since he was a kid. Uncle Fenning had told him something that was really curious about his keys. Each was made of a different material: silver, copper, gold and even plastic. Meltus remembered the place better than anyone. He grabbed the bronze key and opened the double door to the mansion.

It was dim inside and only a few seams of light entered through the window's shutters.

"Uncle Arthur?" he murmured, just to see if he was awake. The birds kept chirping outside, but inside, nothing indicated anything was alive in the house. He opened his backpack and turned on his flashlight. A circle of white light revealed a neat long hallway, with coloured plates hanging from walls and benches on every side. Uncle Arthur's mansion hadn't changed much. The only place to avoid was Arthur's bedchamber in the west wing. That's why he would head east — to the wine cellar. That meant not a chance his uncle would hear the feasting and squealing downstairs.

The hallway came to an abrupt end, and Meltus moved to the last door to his right. It was unlocked and led to a very small room. The circle of light aimed at the heaped, dusty pieces of pottery all around. In contrast to the clean, dignified hallways of the antechamber, the room looked like it had not been visited for years. Meltus held himself, wanting to sneeze as dust pricked his nostrils.

The center of the floor had a stocked concentration of vases and scribbled papers, the room of a madman. Meltus removed the items carelessly, and used his hands to sweep the remaining dust. His fingers finally found the metal bar. He clutched it and pulled it to open the concealed cellar door. Next to the ramp of stairs there was a switch, revealing a set of lights that began to flicker one by one.

Meltus sneezed but there was nothing to worry here. Nothing could possibly be heard from down there. The room felt cold and moist as he entered the sombre wine cellar. Flat-laid barrels in old canisters led him through an endless hallway, smelling a blend of putrefaction and old wood. It smelled bad, but at least they wouldn't have any trouble getting drunk.

The underground hallway ended in a chamber with a long wooden table with two equally long benches. Meltus opened his backpack and unrolled the red tablecloth. Then he got the candles and the lighter. 'Surprise her and you will have of her whatever you want,' Matt had said. The candles and the light were also Matt's idea. As long as he managed to impress the guys later he would be fine. He carefully opened the two styrofoam-packaged wine glasses. At this point, he needed to get the wine ready. 'Make sure she gets drunk,' Matt had said. 'Otherwise nothing will happen.' He had never seen Lydia drunk and it looked like the perfect chance.

Walking back to the hallway, he searched every barrel in the hope of making the right choice. The barrels were all alike except for the numbers marked to differentiate them. He stopped at one of them. It was out of its place a bit and had no number. He pushed the barrel back to its crate and felt as he did that something else moved as well, taking almost all his strength. He could have sworn it; something else moved.

Out of curiosity he pulled it back out again. His mouth dropped open with astonishment. The barrel was not a wine container but the camouflage cover to a secret door. There was nothing extraordinary about the door made out of dark wood, except it had no doorknob, just a yellowish keyhole. He grabbed the set of keys. Something told him it wasn't the bronze key he had to use, but the golden one. The door clicked and he pushed it forward.

Arthur Fenning was an eccentric. However, it was one thing to find a gun and a set of keys in two stone tigers and another to deal with an unexpected room in his uncle's cellar. Darkness engulfed the room, forcing Meltus to turn his flashlight back on. Everything from the soily ground to the cavernous walls looked like an excavation site. His light moved upon the rugged walls to reveal strange hieroglyphs.

He almost stumbled when something tangled his waist. Quickly he shifted his lantern. It was merely a rope, stretched horizontally along the walls to prevent someone from intruding into the area of excavation.

Meltus couldn't help but smile. No one could be better at demystifying his uncle than he. Imagine the popularity he'd get once he caught the press' attention. He never understood why his uncle vanished in the peak of his glory, from well-known newspapers, magazines and television. He had been a celebrity! After his divorce, many women had wanted to marry Arthur Fenning. But his secrecy and sudden disappearance scared even the most obstinate ones. His uncle had probably found something more paramount than anything any woman could offer.

Overlooking the ditch, a golden bowl held the remains of a skull. There were four other bowls, Meltus quickly noted, each with a head of a long-dead corpse. He hesitated for a moment, then crossed the rope and jumped in. His hand touched the bowl with excitement. It was solid gold! Shit, why had his uncle not shown this to anyone?

He heard the shuffling of footsteps above him. The light of a passing candle or torch illuinated the walls. He squatted to avoid being seen in the ditch.

"Who's in here?" the hoarse voice shouted.

What was he doing there? Maybe his uncle would be glad to see him!

"Whoever you are, you're going to wish you were dead after I find you."

Maybe not that glad. There was no mellowness in him anymore, only a dry, threatening voice. He had to get out. The footsteps got closer and Meltus crawled along the ditch trying to move away from it. He dodged two bowls. Then for a moment he stopped, plucking his nostrils. He wanted to sneeze, either because of the dampness or the filthy bones. His stomach made a rumbling noise. Some biscuits and cheese wouldn't be bad at this point. Meltus' whole body was revolting against him.

"Who's there!" said his uncle's voice.

Meltus crawled and turned as he got to the ditch's corner. Tired and hungry, he needed stimulation to keep going. Think there's macaroni and cheese at the end of the tunnel, he thought. But eventually he would end at the same place he started, trapped by a labyrinth that would soon force him to eat his own tail.

Just when he thought the trail would begin anew, a large stone foundation blocked the rest of the path. Above it, a glass box refracted the light of something in its interior. The stone foundation held a hieroglyph in its center. Below it, a piece of wood held what looked like a translation.

For all that matters — matter.

It made no sense. He read the inscription a couple more times before giving up. Taking a closer glance at the glass box dazzled his vision; inside it, a stone blazed, yellow and blinding like the sun. The stone was round in perfect proportions and was the size of a tennis ball.

Be rich and touch me, I am your reward, I am your cheese.

Was that his inner voice or was he going insane? His stomach growled again. Hunger was certainly playing tricks with his mind. If only he could smuggle the stone into his pocket. He hadn't come this far not to take it. The stone could be a priceless artifact and he could sell it for millions of dollars. Besides, what would it matter to his uncle? He was already too rich and selfish. Having such a huge mansion he never cared to invite me over for dinner. The crystal box had circular openings on every side. It was hard to reach, but easy to take, he thought, as his arm moved into one of the gaps. Despite its brilliance, the stone seemed cold in his hand — far too cold. Cautiously he opened his backpack to hide his new treasure.

"Shit!" He covered his mouth but it was too late. Almost immediately he heard running feet and then the strong torch light was above his head.

"You will regret trespassing in my home, thief."

"Uncle?"

"Meltus?" Is that you?" said Arthur nearing his torch suspiciously.

"My boy, you've changed so much! It's been years since I last saw you!" For a moment his face heartened, but upon seeing where Meltus stood he grimaced. "How did you get here?"

"Listen to me uncle, I wanted to visit you. I really didn't want to bother you so I found your keys . . ."

Arthur laughed, fixing his white combover with his fingers.

"Kids these days have a tendency to do the opposite of what their elders tell them to do."

"Wow, you're so lucky, you found ruins in your own house!"

"There's no such a thing. I discovered the ruins, and then built my house here. It was the perfect coverup to avoid those pesky government officers. But enough of that, what's with you?" Arthur said, forcing a smile.

"Can I spend the night here?"

"Of course you can! I have a room upstairs you can use, next to my bedroom."

"Well, I was actually wondering if I could sleep down here, in the wine cellar."

"In the wine cellar? Isn't that a bit cold and damp for you? I remember your mother used to talk about your allergies."

"Please? I just find it exciting to sleep here."

"Are you playing me for an idiot? I know exactly why you came here . . ." Meltus' heart skipped a beat. "The reason you want to be here is because you want to get drunk with all the wine I've got here. You can do whatever you want in my wine cellar, but this room is off-limits. I will lock this place and, if you don't mind, I'll have my keys back. Is that understood?

Meltus nodded. Of course he understood. Excavation sites were the least of his concerns now that a new problem had surfaced.

"Uncle, I need your help. I was simply looking at your objects, you know, and I couldn't manage to take this one off . . ."

Arthur Fenning's face wrinkled into a monstruous grimace.

"The stone, you fool!" he shouted almost as if about to commit murder.

"Please help me take it off, uncle. I'm sorry, I really just wanted to see it."

"Get out of my house," Arthur mumbled, gritting his jaws.

"I said I was sorry!"

"Out, you fool! You are either doomed or dead. So say the scripts. There is misery for those who touch the stone and I don't want to share your fate, boy."

"But it's just a stone," said Meltus showing his uncle the shining piece in his hand. It appeared smaller now.

"Stay back and leave!" he said as Meltus tried to approach him.

Arthur's head peered at the ground with sad eyes. "God, what have you done, boy."

"But — uncle . . ."

"Don't make me kill you. Get out of my house."

Meltus dashed through, passing the cellar and then the hallways until finally, the starry night embraced him with a cold wind.

"Lydia!" he shouted, trembling in fear. There was no Lydia. Flat on the grass instead, was a picnic blanket with something on its corner: a fluffy teddy bear with a silly smile. Its button-eyes had been torn off and in its tummy, small cursive letters read:

To Mel, the love of my life.

Eitan Olevsky is a Peruvian writer residing in Canada. Born in March 14, 1981, he is the author of two novels, *El Gran Maestro* and *The Stone Collector* and he's also written numerous screenplays, stage plays, lyrics, stories and poems both in English and Spanish. Contact: eolevsky50@gmail.com

POLIS

───────── ❧ ─────────

Excerpt from the novel
by J. L. Morin

When I posted the job, I had in mind an aggressive, young bull, bright on the future with no past. Someone to talk sports with when business was slow. Bottom line, I had to find a currency trader.

She didn't look up to see me peeping into the waiting room, weighing her. A listener, sad lips that knew only compromise. I went back to my office and sat down at my desk. Skimming her résumé, I could see that the job was a long shot. Below my window, the metropolis gave way to Hudson Bay. There beyond the -polis, was that blue horizon line.

I had résumés from all around the -polis. The last two guys I'd interviewed were qualified. There was a tall, fiery Duke graduate who played hockey, and a Latino black belt who crunched up a numerical *tempestuoso*.

They left me cold. They gave me that blank stare when I brought up Doo Wop. Hummed a few bars of *Give Me the Taco*. No one cracked a smile. I couldn't see myself making conversation with them for two years.

Next.

The only one left was Jerry, a nodding mop with the management potential of clay.

"Your four o'clock is here," my secretary said, her belly big in the doorway.

"She's early."

"You asked me to speed up the interviews. You know I'm going on maternity leave, right? She was the only one who —"

"Never mind. Send her in."

Jerry was already 'free', expectations deflated. Her shoulders slumped forward, giving her tweed suit the look of a coat pile. Dark curls mopped a doubtful expression. Her pale skin was translucent. A tilt of her head affirmed that she already knew what I was telling her: that Global Profit Bank was a second-tier institution grown out of early settler trade in coffee and gunpowder on the southern tip of the island. "We've made our share of HRE's, that's human resource errors, but we have a strong reputation for giving a man a chance."

Blue veins throbbed at her temples. Things had changed from the days of pencil sharpeners and suspenders, although I was still wearing mine. There were risk managers, quality control seminars, and master agreements. You hired the raw potential of an Armani suit.

"Our mission is to be the top tier-two bank on Wall Street before the millennium." I looked at her sunken shoulders in the chair across from me, and cursed Manhattan Head Hunters. She wore flat loafers and was holding onto an old briefcase, which she tried to hide behind her left thigh. A Southpaw. She looked like she was about to pitch it at me. If I called now, I could schedule another round of interviews for tomorrow.

Computer screens blipped across the trading floor. Phones murmured. Sasha, my Greek commodities trader, glided by in his summer wool. I grabbed Sasha and introduced him to the girl. His face lit up. "We need a good currency trader! There's a paradigm shift going on. Someone's got to make sense of European interest rates." He led her over to the oil desk, showing her off like an antique coin.

Where was that headhunter's number? On hold with the headhunter, my cell phone rang. It was a friend who had done me a favor with the admissions committee at my daughter's university. Butter was in her first semester coping with midterms. I was afraid she might not pass. "Hi Bernie." My back tightened. Good ol' Bernie. "What can I do for you?" We both knew I owed him one.

My eyes followed Jerry's long legs proceeding across the trading floor. She was wearing sheer black stockings. Hips wagged. Each step ended with a bounce.

"You see a little Robin Redbreast hopping around up there on the trading floor?"

I laughed loudly, holding the cell phone to my mouth. "How did you know I was watching a chick? That's uncanny, Bernie. What do you need?"

"Since you ask, I would greatly appreciate it if you could help the lady out." So the dame was connected, and it was Bernie who was on my case this time. "How far did you get with her?" Bernie asked.

"Not *that* far, if you must know. I'm interviewing her now, showing her around the shop. She's right here. Want to say hi?" She was sitting with the graying municipal bond traders.

I was about to hand her the phone when she interrupted me.

"Where is the bathroom?"

Decisive. Now it was what *she* wanted. Her untraditional approach took me by surprise, but since she was a friend of Bernie's, I told him, "Call ya back."

It was all men working on our floor, so I had to look for the women's bathroom key. I walked back toward the security guard out through the tunnel of mirrors by the elevators. Ten of me appeared in the hall mirrors, humming an a cappella from 1961.

In the sixties, I was so mixed up that I went around with a varsity sweater and hair down to my shoulders, trying to fit in with the jocks and the hippies. I grew a mustache, which I keep because I have thin lips, and felt disoriented trying to force my Russian background into the American mold. I think I succeeded in becoming more American than most Americans. I'm living the European dream: to break with the past, with the old world, I mean, still married after all these years to America in the 1950s. My savior was Doo Wop. Doo Wop music gave me the strength to hold a steady course as I went through the changes of the seventies, nineties, and the new millennium.

I came back, key in hand. My geeks had encircled her with their swivel chairs. "OK, so what's the square root of point one?"

She leaned her head back, shaking her dark mane as if someone had told her a joke — *women aren't expected to have opinions* — and snatched the bathroom key from my hand: *The position is filled.* That's how the divine forces set me up to go to bat for Jerry.

I took a deep breath before wading into the stale air surrounding the new Chief Financial Officer seated on his leather dais. He had just had his morning cigar. He ignored me for a minute and a half, and then faced me as if he had just switched me on. I overcame the urge to take a step backward.

Standing face-to-face with the new CFO, I hit him hard: "Mort, we have a new Ivy League candidate. She out-crunched all the others." I explained how well other Ivy League employees had done in their careers at the bank.

"A woman?" Mort said.

Time to play ball. I had a feeling about her. A feeling I hadn't had in a long time, not since 1997. I swung as hard as I could. "Not since our record year, before your time, Mort. Trust me on this one. We made a fortune in interest rate swaps. I can still taste the money."

The CFO licked his lips.

I heard the bat connect with the ball.

"I'm telling you, Mort, I got an itch in my nose. I only get this itch when there's a hunger that hasn't been satisfied in a long time. Don't laugh. This is strictly about our bottom line."

He called for Jerry. She skulked into the empty chair. Mort appraised her like a butcher considering how to chop up a beef. Jerry's bulky tweed seemed to baffle him. He shrugged and went into his Global Profit Bank spiel. I breathed with ease, with Jerry nodding and chiming in on the ends of the key phrases. He asked if she had any questions. She surprised me with, "What's your mission?"

He wheezed. "To be the top tier-two bank on Wall Street before the millennium." He asked if she had family in New York. She seemed not to hear, and he went back into the bank's mission. I wondered who was interviewing whom. I think I finally decided I was imagining her unwillingness to be forthcoming, but when I brought up the family a second time, she just looked out the window, watery eyes skimming the jagged skyscrapers.

Mort got a phone call. He watched her all the while. This second phone call was unnerving. Could she be *that* connected? Those lines in Mort's forehead meant that he was on the verge of acquiescence. He licked his lips again, took out the Mont Blanc pen I'd impressed him with at Christmas, and scribbled on his pad, all without taking his eyes off Jerry. "Uh huh," Mort said. I tried to quell my reservations, while she pretended to read a company brochure.

My curiosity got the better of me. "Don't you have any brothers or sisters?" I pressed, thinking about my own girl waving from the step of the dormitory porch. I tried to get Jerry to tell me how she knew Bernie. The life drained out of her eyes. Shaking my head, I disengaged from her stare. Not his type, I thought. Bernie liked redheads as a rule. With her nomadic legs, Jerry might be related, though. I hadn't noticed an accent, but the air of a southern belle lingered about her. A woman from the Deep South. It fit, probably some distant relative come up to the big city. I could tell Mort was sold by the way he hung up the phone.

Now the favor was almost done. The whole scheme was making me hungry. French or sushi? I would pick Bernie up in the Town Car at seven p.m., maybe call his contact at Butter's university on the way. Midterms were coming up.

I had said something wrong. Jerry was staring at me absently, large pupils open onto inner space. I just sat there in silence. "I have a twin brother," she said at last.

I knew it! A twin. I waited for more.

"We're not close, though." She added that he was temping part-time somewhere. She pointed out the window at the other Twin Tower. "Maybe over there." She didn't seem to feel the need to elaborate. Sitting next to her, I couldn't dispel a peculiar feeling. The hair on the back of my neck was standing up. This stubbornness of hers on the family issues didn't seem to matter to Mort, nor did the fact that she didn't fit the 'aggressive' cast.

When Mort changed the subject to numbers, Jerry was easygoing under pressure. I knew Mort was thinking that she'd be good for overhead — we'd only have to pay her 70% of what we were paying the boys. If only I had known about the harassment suit. I wouldn't have let him get carried away with her. A reference check would have stopped the whole snowball.

"I'm impressed," Mort said.

Home run!

The deal was done. Sasha left us alone together. A thick cloud enveloped our view out the bay window up on the 107th of the World Trade Center. "Jerry, the job is yours. Welcome aboard." She looked relieved. Things were falling into place. She mustered a little speech and accepted my offer. "You won't regret the confidence you've placed in me, sir." I shook her trembling hand. Her chest heaved under the lumpy suit. I had elevated a lump of human material 1310 feet above the -polis. She had me going.

How that lawsuit escaped me, I do not know. That is just the kind of thing I like to find out about right away in a phone call after the first interview. It still bothers me that I didn't put in any phone calls about her. Sometimes I go back to her laptop that we rescued from the investigators to figure out how I missed that, and other things. Like her mysterious twin.

And like the account of our first meeting I found on her old laptop: *My prayer was heard through the clouds, and the white-armed goddess cast a cloak over Destiny and allowed me to advance.* Here I am drawing conclusions from a machine. After all that's happened since 9/11, I need her company here.

Where is she? Sirens wail, time's up. This is a story in search of a mistress. She was here a minute ago. Long legs, curly hair, color: Ash Blond #8A. Have you seen her? Black eyes glared, and lit up her face. She was either in a hurry, or about to forget what she had to say. Couldn't follow a simple recipe, taking up too much space in a man's world. People didn't necessarily think of her as an outsider, but she was far, far away, with her own screwy logic for the destruction — as if clay could talk, *asleep under Athena's embroidered robe.*

The Hudson winked from below. I think I quietly noted somewhere in the back of my head that she'd put a spell on me. Screamin' Jay Hawkins, 1979. I followed her into the mirrored hallway. Her image splintered, and my reflection splintered. Me and the boys broke into *"You Put a Spell on Me."* We were singing to the train of girls in front of us, running on incantatory fuel. The girls turned around and shook our hands. Was it the real Jerry who opened her mouth?

No words came out.

Was anyone watching us? My gaze crossed the bond desk and traveled out over the -polis to the horizon. That solemn horizon line recalibrates my sense of proportion whenever I see it. Her hand trembled in mine but did not let go. I stood there holding her hand for I don't know how long until her reflections turned to go. They walked without touching the ground. A long line of ancestors accompanied her through the mirrored hallway to the elevators. Suddenly, they were gone.

My hands burned. They had let slip the reigns of power. I had been on Wall Street for twenty-one years, and tonight I would be paying my dues. It had been over-ambitious of me to expect to hire anyone normal, what with New York being so full of crazies . . . Maybe Bernie and me should start at that bar on the upper West Side with the terrace and the Brazilian waitresses.

I poked my head out into the waiting room.

There was a half-full cup of coffee in a saucer on the edge of the table next to my pile of *New York* magazines. Today's newspaper was refolded on the seat. A bird-like woman uncrossed her ankles. She looked up at me. Expectantly? What was she doing here? We had closed up shop. I'd hired Jerry, and that was that. No time to deal with a new broad. I had to find a restaurant for me and Bernie so I could hit him with Butter's midterms.

I leaned over an empty chair and snagged three magazines breathing in the leather scent of the little redhead's perfume. Draped over the back of her chair was a Hermes scarf with silken chains on ermine print.

What about that Japanese place on Fifty First where you could drink sake around a kidney-shaped bar? We could scoop up pieces of raw fish from those locomotive cars. I flipped through the magazines but couldn't find what I was looking for.

Manicured fingernails flipped lazily through the magazine I wanted, narrow foot tapping arhythmically, milky chin pointed down. Maybe one of these other magazines had a restaurant where Bernie could tell me about Robin Redbreast and I could hit him up for A minuses for Butter. I tilted my head to read the back of her magazine. Her red suit jacket opened onto the cleavage of an enormous bosom. Her golden zipper caught the light as it swung back and forth. Great blue eyes peeped out from frizzy red bangs. "Excuse me for staring." The redhead glared back at me. My eyes slid down to her read breast.

Bernie's Robin Redbreast?

My heart stopped. This was Robin Redbreast, not Jerry.

I ducked out and leaned my back against the door. The heavy metal latched under my weight. CLICK.

"Butter!"

There was no undoing the seed I had sown about Jerry in the CFO's mind. My legs felt like jelly. I wandered over to the spot desk and sank into a chair. I called my secretary. "I know there's a redhead waiting! Just cancel everything. You go home, too. You're welcome. You deserve it. Have a nice baby."

An hour later, I got a return phone call from the credit agency telling me that Jerry had no credit history. I hung up. The report was coming in on the fax, one piece of paper with a lot of white on it. There were no stains. Nobody had a credit report that clean. I'd hired a nobody. I had a feeling something must be very wrong. I skimmed her credit history. She seemed to appear out of nowhere a year earlier and since then had changed addresses every six months. I read over her application again and noticed that her home phone was an 800 number. "Putz." All this should have been done before I recommended her to the CFO.

Fudging for Bernie. Now it was up to me to smooth over the red flags. I had to laugh at myself as I called my daughter at school. "Study hard, Butter." Fudging for God.

It was dizzying. Who had I hired? I decided to lie down on the yellow couch Sasha had hijacked from the elevator on its way to the

CFO's office. Sasha had a way of coming up with the goods. He could take candy from a six-year-old. I kicked off my Guccis. My shoulders sank into the soft leather cushion. I welcomed the delicious guilt of being horizontal at the office. Whatever was lurking in Jerry's past, it was nothing that Sasha couldn't extract. Maybe the answer was in the yellow couch. Still, the room continued spinning. Little did I know that I was going to be getting used to this feeling.

I did a double take when my new hire stepped off the elevator her first day on the job. A myriad of reflection girls mimicked Jerry's curt half turn with a thousand bouncy new shoulder-length haircuts, all dyed blond. Gone was the bulky tweed, and in its place, a tight olive-green sweater-dress that divulged a generous bosom and curves even I hadn't guessed at.

I must confess I didn't know how to react. I watched Sasha fall over himself leading Jerry to her desk, and pulling out her chair for her. Half of the boys received Jerry and her new look with fascination. The rest surveyed her from the corners of their eyes. I was considering whether there had been a breach of trust, but for all my years at the bank, the only woman employee I had any experience with was my secretary. I knew that dames had the right to change their minds. It's just that Jerry had changed everything but her mind.

That's how Jerry took her place on the desk back in the days. We were rolling. Stocks were up, the dollar was strong, and some of the traders were making serious profits for the bank. The first two months she sat there, a yawning clump. When we did give her a bit of work to do, she jinxed it. Everything she touched went south. Customers got deleted, trades were put on backwards. She lost more money than she could count. I was ready to axe her, but the CFO was waiting for my *feeling* to bear fruit. I mustered a smile. There we were, up in the clouds with hundreds of organizations joined in a vast global network, trading for peace with Jerry. Mort came up and patted me on the back. "We have our first woman on the floor."

In the beginning, Jerry's only responsibility was to watch the boys and read anything she could find. I showed her the Bloomberg and my Japanese candlestick book on the coffee table next to the yellow couch, and I made it known that the desk was invited to use my yellow couch anytime they felt like it. The boys jumped all over the invitation, and there was no room for Jerry on the couch. Even when there was only one hairy lunk on it reading my newspapers, Jerry stayed away.

A few weeks later, I was commuting back up the elevators after a power lunch at Samy's, dreaming of a nice *siesta*. Whoever was on my couch was about to be kicked off. I threw open the door ready to tackle the whole bunch of overgrown teenagers. Jerry jumped up from the yellow couch with a startled look. They were holding *lattes*, and Sasha was laughing and crying at the same time.

"I didn't know you were funny," I told her. "I'll have to try you out in sales." Sasha made a big deal of changing the subject as I walked by their couch. "*Lattes*, huh?" I bought 5 September coffee futures. The atmosphere had lightened up with Jerry as our pet. We fed her chocolate and let her go at four o'clock.

I lay down on the couch waiting for Sasha.

"Your daughter's on line one," he said.

"Put her on hold." I heard Sasha's feet pad over. "Shoot."

"She grew up in a slum in New Orleans," Sasha said.

"N'awlins! Have you ever been down there?"

"No. I didn't know we had Jews in Gatorland."

"You have Jews everywhere, *malaka*. N'awlins is like another country. A culture of its own. It's a violent town, a black and white town, and to think, our little Jerry climbed out of a swamp."

"She said her mother was murdered."

"Holy — !" I choked on the fact. We let the phones ring. I felt sorry for the kid. "You *are* fast," I said.

Sasha rubbed his eyes. "She is hiding from someone."

"Who?"

Sasha's eyes swept around the room. He bent forward and whispered, "The murderer."

"The what?" I jumped up and looked around the office. The doorway was empty. The fax machine was printing a report. The Hudson gleamed below.

"Even her father doesn't know exactly where she lives. All he knows is she's somewhere on the East Coast. She calls her brother every couple of months from her home, a borough away, and says, 'I'll come visit soon.' She is a woman alone. You know what I mean? Looking for love in building windows."

"And she's hiding from the murderer? Does she know who it is?" I asked.

"She wouldn't say," Sasha said.

I let out a long whistle. "Holy smoke. We're not qualified for a mess like this."

"I know." Sasha could suggest a structured product at best. His parents had sent him to a Swiss boarding school where he looked at the mountains while he ate filet stroganoff with a waiter standing behind him. At least I grew up in Brooklyn among thieves and pimps. I would have been able to handle Jerry better if she *were* some kind of criminal. Still, I felt relieved that she was running away from somebody else. At least she was clean.

I'd been a little hard on her. I wanted to protect her, help her find out who did it, or just be there for her. All traders messed up in the beginning. We were going to see this through together. She really was here for a reason beyond human design. "She can stay."

Sasha paced the room with a look of determination. Neither of us had the slightest clue as to what she should do. Jerry came into the trading room and sat still in her swivel chair staring past us on the couch. She was vulnerable, folding in on her space. What next?

Her black stockings were sheer over red toenails resting on a pillow. Her high heels were sprawled under my coffee table. I pretended to read my computer screen.

"I was standing with my mommy in the tall backyard grass. We had just come off the swings." Sasha had her lying down on the couch! There was an empty *latte* cup in her hand. "I remember it so well. The grass was blue-green and full of wild flowers, daffodils, mulberries. I was coming out of a hiding place to try to convince Mommy to buy me a Barbie doll. She said, 'We can't afford it.'

" 'What's *afford*?' Mommy said she was saving up for college. That was better than toys. I said, 'What's college?'

" 'It's a school you go to when you're eighteen. You'll be seventeen, though.'

" 'What's the best one?'

" 'I guess Harvard.'

" 'I'm going to Harvard.' The grass tickled my feet." She turned on her side on the yellow couch.

"Is that all?" Sasha said.

"I remember lying on my mother's stomach, and mommy putting her arms around me and saying, 'Mommy loves you.' I felt close and floated off to sleep. Or Mommy would say, 'You love your Mommy, don't you, little Jerry . . .'

" 'Yes.'

"My beautiful Mommy came and sat with me on our green carpet at the foot of the staircase and said, 'Your Paw isn't going to live with us anymore.'

"I looked at my mother's white arms as they reached down to hug me. Mommy was sweet and wonderful, and all I wanted. How could I have known that my brother wouldn't see it that way?

"'Doesn't that make you sad?' Mommy said.

"I thought about it. If I could have Mommy, what more would I need? 'No,' I answered. Paw was usually angry with us."

It wasn't long before Jerry had us all bringing her *lattes* and competing to finish up for her at the end of the day. She gathered her gym bag and swept toward the door. "See y'all tomorrow." A chorus of goodbye's let her go.

I sat down next to Sasha on the yellow couch. "Anything new?" He didn't answer. "Come on. I know you've got something."

A smile crept across Sasha's big lips. "*Re,* do you want to hear why her parents got divorced? You're not going to believe this . . ."

I let her go at 3:45 so I could stretch out on the hijacked couch. "Sasha, I know I'm not the nicest guy to be around, and I'm not even particularly monogamous, but my kids have a father. The news is, it takes more than romance to make a marriage. Do you think I want my son to grow up gay, or my daughter to get raped before she has her period? Or Mommy to become Mom overnight, and never be at home? Those kids spend their childhood in resigned solitude. All they learn is drugs, alcohol, and fear of intimacy."

Sasha paced back and forth, as I lectured him from the couch.

"Are you saying she's damaged goods, man?"

"I'm saying, when you take away the father, it's the kids who are divorced. They change. The only thing they understand is neglect, and everyone wonders why they need more space and can't have a relationship. To the mother's boyfriend, the kids are an annoyance, if they're lucky. Divorced fathers don't provide financial support. They cut off their children."

Up in the skyscraper, we'd picked her up and brushed her off. Now she had me. *I* would finish her education.

What was it about her? Something made me need to find out which man caused her grief, not that I was sure it was a man, but I had to start somewhere. I had to piece her together, swooping down the wheel of fortune, turning back up.

"What is it, Jerry? Who are you afraid of?"

She pressed her nose into the yellow couch. "My twin brother."

"Your twin? Why?"

"Maybe he wants to kill me, too."

Sasha and I both crumbled onto the yellow couch next to her. She wrapped her arms around Sasha's neck. We sat like that for a long time.

In Russia you had to fight to have a family, and here kids were killing their parents. In the -polis, you didn't need to be happy to provoke jealousy. There she was, working with the boys at her steady job on top of the world, never suspecting in her misery that she might incur the jealousy of the Olympians, only slightly higher up.

Doubtful human material crawled out of her old skin and tried to live in the metropolis. Jerry had struggled through with the buoyancy of a statistic, became interested in statistics. I watched her develop as a trader. She became my best trader. Boy did she make money for the bank. She watched currency prices, identified with their momentum, understood anything that went up and down. Like the World Trade Center.

Did she understand the World Trade Center attack? She hadn't shown up for work for two days when it happened.

I still have the feeling of vertigo these days remembering September 11th. I have always been afraid of heights, but after watching what that inferno did to Brent crude, I'm a changed man. I can't stand to ride in an elevator higher than the 10th floor. I'm lucky not to have been pummeled to dust by what was once a universal symbol of world peace and international trade. To this day, in any suburb, you can't bring up 9/11 without eliciting another story about where someone was when the planes hit.

Gambling saved my life. I was in a hotel room in Vegas when the planes hit. I saw the Twin Towers collapse on TV. All trading was practically halted. I sat there on the bed watching my huge position on the little, black screen the morning of September 11th. Brent crude futures on the London International Petroleum Exchange surged $1.75 a barrel after the explosions. I couldn't believe it. I was long so much oil that for the first time in my life I lost track of my profits. On the news of the attack, I watched Brent extend its gains on the day to $29.20, the highest price seen since mid-June.

A pit opened up in my stomach. Most of the 50,000-odd workforce must be in there. The building started to peel, the windows came off and the towers melted down. I kept telling myself there was an airplane in there, and then one glided into the other tower, and I knew. It was war. I saw the fire going up floor by floor, thick black smoke and cinder boiling out of the glass walls, and was sure all my colleagues were dead. The building was disintegrating. People were jumping out of the windows. People on the ground were running in all directions, making their way all the way up to 14th Street on foot. Suddenly, floor by floor, the whole thing imploded.

Where does the self destruction stop? They point at the foreign war, an excuse to loot and rape. If we can kill our own mothers, what's to stop us?

One of the stacks of papers that keeps me company here is her diary. When I read it, I can hear her saying, "I move for men. Sadly acquiescing to whatever conditions. Throwing my things into a box." She had moved to Salonika for one, and to Paris for another one. I didn't realize she was so worldly. Maybe she just moved on. Red high heels? In the box. Moving domestically seemed like progress. Even with her break-up rate at one hundred percent, the warmth and comfort of a familiar face over breakfast outweighed any risk . . .

It's funny how the mind plays tricks on you. It makes you believe what you want to believe.

J. L. Morin, an award-winning author, grew up in inner-city Detroit. Morin's Japan novel, *Sazzae* first written as a creative thesis toward an AB at Harvard ('86-'87), won a Living Now Book Award in 2010.

J. L. Morin has three novels for future publication: *Traveling Light; Polis;* and *Trickster of Phraxos.* Morin's fiction, articles and translations have appeared in *The Harvard Advocate, Harvard Yisei, The Detroit News, Agence France Presse, Livonia Observer Eccentric Newspapers,* and *The Harvard Crimson.*

J. L. Morin traded derivatives in New York for six years while studying nights at New York University's Stern School of Business (MBA '97). Morin has worked for the Federal Reserve Bank posted to the 107th floor of the World Trade Center, as a TV newscaster on an island in the Mediterranean, and as adjunct faculty at Boston University. Contact: jlmorin@post.harvard.edu

THE FIRE DANCER

— ⚭ —

by Maria Pavlova
(Translated from the Bulgarian by Dr. Juliana Chakarova)

Joanna would never forget that first dance. Since then she danced every year on the day of the Saints Constantine and Helena. The power always came to her on this day, but the memory of her first dance was the clearest . . .

The fire was still going strong, it wasn't time to step in yet, but something golden in the fire was drawing her in. Joanna became more and more impatient, unable to resist — she felt like a butterfly drawn to a lamp. She wondered whether butterflies were fire dancer's souls that kept flying back and forth between the earth and the sky because they missed the warmth of the embers and didn't want to leave this world. The logs cracked and her fingers cringed from the cold. Silence with a hint of frankincense filled the meadow. She never knew where this fragrance came from, but it was there every year, and she felt it. Her heart sank and she tightened up remembering what had happened . . . The logs were cracking and her fingers turning white and numb. In a little bit the fire would calm down and it would be possible to step in, but some irresistible power was already pushing her in — it was becoming as big as the whole world and even bigger. Everything would fit in it: like a thread box that is so ordinary but you could find green thread and blue thread, brown thread too, a big needle and a small one, safety pins, and scissors, and a thimble . . .

Suddenly the fire looked as if somebody poured water over it, so she could step in without fear. The fire turned good and empty. Joanna was emptying herself too, just the suffering remained. It got smaller, but even after she danced it didn't completely disappear.

Five years ago her husband had died in the World War. It happened in February, during the last year of the war when she got the message that Vassil had been killed. The two of them had loved each other very much. He was so caring and would do anything for her. She took good care of him too: sewed shirts for him and smiled, kneaded bread and smiled. Her smile was always on her lips. They had known each other since they were kids, had married young and always lived happily. They had been through poverty and illness, but love was always there and nothing was missing. Their love was like a fireplace in winter and a cool breeze in summer. People talked about them a lot and tried to protect them from the evil eye by spitting over their shoulders.

In June that same year when she got the terrible news, Joanna danced on fire for the first time. Since then the power always came to her . . . She wondered if she would dance this year too. She always wondered. Tomorrow there would be fire again, for the fifth time since that year. Joanna sat on the bed. She was afraid to go to sleep. There was some bright light outside — was it the moon or a lamp, or one of Vassil's caresses, still alive, still shining? Her eyes dimmed, she sighed. If she could only go peacefully to sleep! That was all she wanted — to fall asleep and have no dreams.

When Vassil died, her pain was excruciating, but there was something worse than that. Sometimes, on occasion, she had a dream about him: he suddenly died and she didn't even know where he was, she couldn't find him, as if he didn't even exist. She looked for him and he was nowhere to be found, as if he evaporated . . . She would wake up with such heavy, dark pain in her heart that it was beyond all bearing. She would get up and walk around the house. This pain scared her — her heart squirmed, her soul too. Joanna walked from one room to another with her arms around her shoulders and wouldn't stop for hours. Sometimes she would even walk the streets. The dogs barked at her in the beginning but then stopped. Nobody could go to sleep on a night like that if they heard her because people knew that until this spell was over it would be a pain not only for her, but also for the Mother of God.

During those years she couldn't stop crying and grieving. Her eyes dried out. Now she was living again somehow, she even laughed on occasion. She planted rose bushes in the garden, but her dreams would come back and this unbearable anguish wouldn't stop. Joanna wasn't afraid of dying. She wanted to because she didn't want to live without Vassil, before the Mother of God stopped her.

Joanna wasn't afraid of living either, she would manage somehow, but she was afraid of waking up after such dreams. She wouldn't live through another spell like that, Joanna thought every time — her little heart would take no more pain. She was like a bird squeezed by a rock and felt as if she would pop. Only the fire would lift up the rock a little. Not that she could fly away, but at least she could breathe.

Joanna wasn't young, but was in good shape. Her thighs and breasts weren't drooping; she had a few gray hairs and some wrinkles around the eyes, but that was all. She hadn't given birth, they didn't have kids. They tried, but had no luck. Vassil wanted kids very much. He even suggested adopting, but Joanna refused. She was hoping they'd have their own child. She remembered his face, his warm eyes. She couldn't even bury him — the body wasn't returned. She stepped unprepared into this pain and her wound wouldn't heal. Her life shrunk, squashed, like everything in the village. Only the fire made her softer.

Those dreams came more often in spring. Everything woke up, only Joanna stayed the same. She would still feed the livestock and knead bread, but this was a habit, even her grief became a habit. It got worse after February, until the day of the saint. The only redemption was the fire. Sweet as cherry, almost bringing oblivion. It healed her. The minute she stepped into the fire her head would become empty.

If the dance was a lie, as one boy from town put it, it was a good lie. Far from everything else. And what a dancer she was! Nobody ever danced like her. Her dance was so light! As if somebody moved her, her arms, her body; something made her sweep the icon over the fire like wind — it was some power, invisible and strong. Her feet sank into the embers up to the ankles, but she felt like she wasn't even touching the coals. Joanna would scoop the embers with her hands, as if she was spreading stars, transparent stars — she was scattering beauty around.

Everybody that watched Joanna felt strange; she looked as if she was flying. During those minutes she had no age, had almost nothing to trip her besides the traces of her grief, but they were bearable and almost faded. The line around the fire would take her to a place where nobody — neither the fire dancers, nor other people that stepped in the fire — could follow her. They weren't able to go as far as she went. It was a gift, Joanna's gift. There, in the fire kingdom, she was alone and had the feeling that there was something waiting for her — she felt it better than all other people surrounding her in the village.

While Joanna was dancing the embers felt warm, but not hot. The first time she danced it surprised her. She also felt light and warm, but she knew she had to keep moving. If she let herself give in to this feeling she would stop and burn her feet. The others had told her this: she had to make sure she didn't fall into oblivion and had to keep moving.

That first year she almost died dancing on the fire. It would have happened if the Mother of God hadn't stopped her. That morning, after Joanna felt the power, she decided to join Vassil. She had already considered this, although it was a sin. But the Virgin Mary didn't let her do it. She told Joanna to change her mind. Joanna still remembered the Mother of God, as if she was standing before her now. The Mother of God appeared to her dressed in a neat gray gown that was simple and formal at the same time. She was wearing a necklace made of polished gems. Her hair was braided.

"Don't do it, Joanna, don't do it!" she told her sternly standing outside of the fire circle.

Joanna recognized her right away. The others froze as if they were painted there. The fire stopped too, became thinner. The moment the Mother of God appeared was a long one. She looked at Joanna severely, but with love. A little before that Joanna had stopped her dance. She froze, both her feet buried in the embers. She thought it was time. She didn't want to live without Vassil and couldn't bear suffering those dreams anymore. Nothing was keeping her here. And at this very moment a dragon jumped out of the calm fire — a dragon woke up, as if from the abyss, and jumped at her. An awful pain cut through her body. Joanna wanted to sink entirely into this pain and escape the long lonely days and even lonelier nights, her wretched wandering around the empty rooms and streets. Her grave would be here. And then the Mother of God appeared, looked at her and scolded her in a moment that seemed too long.

"Come back, Joanna! Where are you headed? It's not time yet! I know what you are contemplating, but you can't do that. You shouldn't! There is still something good waiting for you!"

Joanna screamed and stepped out of the fire. The Holy Mother's words scared her because Joanna was religious. She fainted to the wet ground. After this experience the healing process was long, but she came around and everything was okay. A miracle had happened and she had survived. The Virgin Mary had come to her, had bent and touched her feet, taking away the pain and the deepest wounds. That's why Joanna recovered, and it wasn't very painful when they put ointment and later urine on her wounds. Joanna didn't even have marks on her feet. The people in the village didn't remember any miracles like that.

Nobody appeared to her during the dance ever since. Joanna had visions, but not while she was dancing. Other fire dancers also rarely had visions while dancing . . .

Ever since that day, the Virgin had appeared to them with wounds all over her feet. All fire dancers would see her like that. Joanna cried when she saw her again. The other fire dancers and people who couldn't see her cried too. In August people would come from all of the nearby villages: the rumor about Joanna's and the Virgin Mary's pain had spread. People bowed to the icon in the church and silently cried.

183

"Poor Mother of God, why are you suffering like that for me? I should've died and gone to Vassil. You shouldn't suffer!" said Joanna when the Virgin Mary appeared to her the next spring.

"You have enough pain in your heart, Joanna. When you stop hurting, I'll stop hurting too."

The village, nestled in the woods of Strandzha Mountain, withered; like something inappropriate, children's laughter would startle the grown ups; the trees became smaller and the woods grew silent.

Joanna didn't believe that her anguish would go away and that something good was waiting for her. She felt sorry that the Mother of God would have red feet forever. She felt ashamed about what had happened. Nobody blamed her, everyone wanted to help instead. They tried to cheer her up. There was always a neighbor with her so she wasn't alone. Joanna came around and her face got back its color, but her dreams wouldn't go away. People would make the sign of the cross when they heard her wander the streets.

"Joanna, poor Joanna, don't do that, my daughter," the neighbor, Rada, an old woman, told her once. "Don't do anymore sins against your soul. Why are you doing that?"

"I'm like butterflies, grandma Rada, I can't find a place for myself."

"Well, Joanna, listen to the Mother of God," the old woman said and made the sign of the cross, "and there will be life for you!"

Five years went by in this way, until one morning before the big holiday. Joanna almost didn't sleep a wink because she had just had one of those bad dreams, and now she was terrified. She looked at the bag with that medicine some doctor from town had brought to her so she could sleep without dreaming. She took it a few times and fell into deep sleep, without any dreams. But then the Mother of God appeared to one of the old fire dancers, and asked him to tell Joanna to stop. Joanna obeyed, what else could she have done? Why was she still keeping the medicine? She took the bag to the river and threw it as far as she could. And that's when a man on a horse appeared before her, dressed like a policeman, with a hat and a gun — it was

Saint Constantine. Joanna recognized him, even though he appeared to her for the first time.

"Joanna, you have to do something today! Go to little Milenka and help her! Hurry! It doesn't matter where you go, but don't leave her alone! The Mother of God wants me to tell you this. Take it as an order. And tell the others to clean the holy spring well — last time it wasn't clean!"

Joanna was confused. "Milenka? Who is Milenka?" she asked.

But the man had gone, vanished. Joanna ran to old Neda, the chief fire dancer, and told her everything. Neda was quite surprised.

"Joanna, are you sure it was Saint Constantine himself? Is that what he said?

"Yes, grandma Neda, he said we should clean the holy spring better this year."

"We cleaned it already, but if he said so, we'll do it again. People don't have as much faith these days. No wonder they don't clean it well. I got that, but what about the rest?"

"He told me to take care of Milenka, to help her and not leave her alone. Have you heard anything about her?"

"No, dear Joanna, I don't know who Milenka is, but I'll go find out. She must not be from around here."

"But then why would Saint Constantine tell me about the Holy Mother's order?"

"I don't know, I'll ask and tell you as soon as I find out. You go now and take a rest. You look exhausted."

Joanna went home, but felt restless. She swept the front yard, cleaned the house, expecting the old fire dancer to come. Then some neighbors came and she told them about the holy spring and Saint Constantine. She asked them about Milenka too, but they didn't know who she was.

After this, when she was left alone, Joanna went into the big room and opened the chest. She rarely came into this room since Vassil's death. The memory of Vassil was the strongest here. She opened the chest for the first time since he was gone. There she kept her dressy outfits. She spread them on the bed. Ran her hand over the embroidery and a long gone feeling like a small spider crawled over her fingers. She touched her cheek with the soft material and paused like that. Closed her eyes and sighed. Then she put everything away and had a bite to eat. Soon after that old Neda and three more women came to her house. She invited them to come and sit down at her table, but they refused.

"Joanna," Neda shouted, "I found out at last! Milenka is from the nearby village. It's not that close. She is a little girl, an orphan. Her mom and dad died years ago. There was a storm and they went to check on the livestock, but a beam fell over them. A thunderbolt caused the beam to fall and started a fire. The house burned down too. A distant relative is taking care of the girl now since she has nobody else. But that woman has six kids of her own and can't afford to keep her anymore. That's what I was told. The family hardly made ends meet. Recently the husband got sick, so they are wondering what to do with the girl. Since the Mother of God ordered you to, you will have to go, Joanna! Do what she told you to do!"

"But why, grandma Neda? How can I be of any help to her?"

"I don't know, my daughter. You have to go and then we'll see. A cart is waiting for you outside. Ivan will take us there. We are coming with you too, how can we miss that! Hurry, get ready so we can be back before dark."

Joanna got ready quickly. She wondered why the Mother of God was sending her to see this little girl — how could she help her!? The cart moved and Joanna grew silent. Everybody was waving at them. Something strange haunted the village. It was so different from people's usual gray days and made their hearts quiver. Even the ones who didn't believe in fire dancers were waiting to see what would happen.

The village was small, but everybody felt that something big was happening. Maybe that's why the news spread so quickly. In the other two villages on their way people greeted them and wanted to hear first hand what the Mother of God had said, but Neda kept repeating that they were in a hurry, so they moved on without stopping. Some were pointing at Joanna saying: "That's her!" as if she were a leper. But there was no malice in their words. Instead they were filled with deep feeling. Joanna looked at them biting her kerchief — she felt uneasy about being the center of attention.

The cart finally arrived. The local people told them where they should stop the cart. The house was small, with a thatched roof, and looked even poorer than the other ones in the village. As soon as they arrived a woman came out to greet them. Two little boys ran after her and started chasing each other. She scolded them and then looked at the guests.

"Please, come in. I don't have a lot, but I can find something to put on the table for you."

"Don't worry, Kera. Isn't that your name?" the old woman Neda said. "We are not hungry. We came for something else. The Mother of God ordered us to come."

"I know, I know." Kera made the sign of the cross and was followed by the other women. "Which one is Joanna? Was that you that the Mother of God asked to take care of Milenka? Oh, the girl is good, but I can't afford to take care of her anymore. Even my own kids are starving. People are helping us, but they have their own cares. I have to give her to somebody else. It's not something I can do anymore."

Tears filled the woman's eyes. Startled, Joanna turned to her. She looked gloomy and very exhausted; her skirt was torn. At that moment her eyes were drawn to the door. There stood a little girl, about five years old. She had on a worn, but neat dress; her black hair was braided around her head. The girl was skinny and had huge curious eyes. She walked timidly toward them and stopped next to Kera.

"That's Milenka," the woman said and stroked her head.

Joanna leaned toward the cart. The girl was looking at her.

"Is it you the Mother of God sent to take me?" the girl asked.

"Yes, that's me," Joanna said and tried to smile, but couldn't. Her mouth was dry. She felt more and more uneasy: a lot of people gathered around. The girl came close to her, hugged her shyly and then drew back.

"Are you gonna dance on the fire tomorrow?"

187

"Maybe I will, maybe not. I don't know yet."

"I want to watch you when you dance! Doesn't the fire burn your feet? Is it true that because of you the feet of dear Mother of God are all burned? Is she in pain? We have a little jar with lard, you can give it to her and . . ."

"Be quiet, Milenka!" Kera scolded her. "Another time she wouldn't say a word, and look at her now! Enough asking, you shouldn't do that!"

Joanna didn't answer — she didn't know what to say. Then she asked Kera if they could go inside and talk in private. Joanna had a hard time stopping the other women from going with them. When they were finally alone she felt a little better. The house was poorly decorated. There was no bed. Kera's husband was lying on the floor in the other room. The two women talked for a while. Joanna told Kera about herself. Kera in turn told her about Milenka and about her husband's illness. Little of that was new for both of them, but they didn't know what else to say. Joanna started thinking how to excuse herself.

"I can't take care of the girl. I'm sick — I have problems with my nerves. And I don't know anybody from our village who could take care of her. I can find some clothes and food for her, but I can't do anything else."

"The Mother of God wanted that people hear about Milenka," said Kera and tears welled up in her eyes again. "Maybe somebody in town will hear about the girl and take her. There are rich and childless women in town, somebody may adopt Milenka and give her a home. It's a shame I can't take care of her, but we don't have enough food for my own children."

"Don't worry!" Joanna said and, for the first time, felt a little relaxed. "It's not your fault! You took care of the girl for one whole year! Maybe the Mother of God wanted what you mentioned. We are going to head on now, before dark. I'll find clothes and food and send them to you soon."

She went outside and told the old Neda about her conversation with Kera. Neda didn't want to leave without Milenka, but what would they do with her? Joanna couldn't sleep, she would scare the little girl if she woke up again and started wandering the streets. If somebody else takes her, they'll have to give her back too. They said goodbye and left.

Everybody was silent. There was something unfinished, but nothing else could be done. People in these lands were poor through and through — they also had poor imagination. They were expecting a miracle, but didn't know how to help or what to do.

Before she left, Joanna said goodbye to Milenka.

"Don't you want to be my mother?" the child asked quietly. "My mom died. My dad died too. The animals also died. They all burned. The lightning killed them. Only the cat is still alive. He is here, but doesn't worry and doesn't eat much. He is happy to have some bread."

Joanna looked at the girl. She felt sorry for her. What a pity she didn't bring anything to give to the girl. She promised herself to bring her gifts and remember her. She also prayed in her heart with the hope that a good woman from town would take Milenka and give her love and a home.

"I can't be your mother, Milenka, because I'm sick and can't even take good care of myself. Aside from that, I have a garden and some livestock. It'll be enough for us, but my health is not good. And you'll move to town anyway and go to school there. I also went to school. I can read and write; I have read books. My daddy wanted for us to be able to read and write. Then he died too and we became poor, but first we got an education. I lived there when I was a kid. It's nice there, you'll see. You'll see, everything will be okay."

Then Joanna gave her a hug and headed back with the others. The girl watched Joanna go away and waved at her until she was out of sight. They got back to the village in time. Again the news had already reached the village, but this time nobody waved at them. People looked tired. Joanna had a bite to eat and went to bed.

She woke up after a dream and heard the roosters. It was somewhere around three o'clock. Joanna listened. The night, torn by crickets chirping and dogs barking, didn't match the anguish she was filled with! Joanna got up quickly, put on her slippers and started walking around the house. Other fire dancers felt pain too, but it was different. It came from the power. It made them surrender and dance. It was bearable, but her anguish was impossible to bear.

Then Joanna grew angry with Vassil. How could he leave her alone! No man had touched her all these years; she wasn't feeling herself anymore. Why was she even alive, what kind of life was this? The clear spring night was cutting deep into her heart. Where was all this pain pouring from? "Mother of God, dearest Mother of God, why are you torturing me? I'm so exhausted. Let me go, I can't take it anymore! Why am I suffering?"

She started thinking about Milenka. *Poor girl, where would she go? I need to help her. I will send her some food and clothes.* And while thinking she suddenly realized that she had stopped walking. The spell had passed. The day was breaking, but by now she was feeling better. "Look at me!" Joanna scolded herself. "The poor little girl has nobody, has no home, no mom or dad, but is doing better than me."

Joanna couldn't go back to sleep and was tired the next day, so she decided not to go to the sacred place where, like every year, they would sacrifice a sheep as a part of the ceremony. Joanna liked to go there early, watch women decorate the icons with flowers and listen to the first sounds of the drum and the bagpipe, but this time she didn't go until noon. There was old Neda in the little building with some other women. They were cooking the sacred mutton soup and it smelled good. Joanna stayed there for a while, got sprayed with holy water, talked with the others and then went back home. She also used to like to go to the holy spring, but this time she stayed home. She lay down and drifted off. The moment she woke up Joanna felt that the power was finally coming down to her. That meant she was going to dance today. Like the other times, something like a slight haze started covering everything. The power came or more precisely was coming. It began to pull Joanna, took over, and she felt drawn toward the fire. It was pain, real suffering. It felt the same when she was thirsty — some power drew her to the water. Thirst didn't come all at once, but grew. What was happening now was neither good nor bad. She would just have to obey, that's all.

She got ready to go to the glowing embers that were spread in front of the church. It was already evening. Shivers were entering her body, one by one. A part of Joanna was putting on her clothes and shoes, but the other part was surrendering to the call of the fire and following it in a deep reverie. Her hands and feet got colder and colder, the cold crept up to her elbows and up to her knees.

When she reached the fire the dances had already started. The old woman Neda passed over the embers carrying an icon and then repeated the movement. She was up to her ankles in the glowing embers. Her face was tense, her eyes closed, her movements graceful and soft. After she danced holding another icon, Neda put it down. When it was clear she wasn't going to dance anymore, people started the circle dance.

Joanna stopped nearby. Her feet and arms were like ice now. She saw the others, heard them, but a big part of her was following the call of the fire. She almost heard a whisper: "Surrender, Joanna, surrender!" Her feet started moving on their own — back and forth, back and forth. Her hands went up, first to one side, then to the other. "Surrender, Joanna, surrender, don't resist!" The power was calling her, pushing her, and she finally surrendered. She swayed toward the fire, the way a ripe pear falls down from a branch. The fire was mild. To the others it looked dark and red, but to her, through the haze, the fire was somewhat tamed, touched with gold. She walked over the embers and didn't feel anything except for the rough surface. Then she took the icon and danced with it on the fire. She felt relaxed. She was here, but at the same time somewhere far away. She couldn't understand how her feet weren't burning, but didn't even try — it's God's deed, she thought. She had to keep dancing and the rest wasn't for her to know.

At last she stomped out of the fire. She still had power — this time the saint had given her a lot and her feet and hands were still cold. She was ready to go into the fire again, but something was bothering her. She was missing something. Joanna remembered last night. She started moving again. The others sensed that she was going to dance and gathered around her. Neda had always been the master, she had a lot of experience, but Joanna had no rival. When she danced it felt as if heaven spoke, as if it was giving the people something priceless.

Suddenly, before she stepped into the fire again, Joanna saw Milenka. She hadn't known the girl was there. Absorbed by the dance, Milenka was holding onto Kera's skirt. Perhaps the dance looked like a fairy tale to the girl, and the fire dancer — more important than a queen.

Joanna got out of the fire and approached the child. She greeted Kera and was thankful that Kera had brought Milenka. Joanna squatted beside the little girl and realized how much she wanted to see her again. The music stopped — everybody wanted to witness what was about to happen. The breeze faded, the woods trembled, the exhausted and wrinkled earth also prepared to listen.

Then Joanna grabbed Milenka, lifted her up higher than an icon and ran through the embers. The woman didn't know why she did it — maybe she wanted to share with the girl what she felt. Joanna didn't feel the weight; she ran again, and again, nine times. Finally she put Milenka next to the fire and squatted near her again. The girl was thrilled and everybody was excited — they had never seen anything like that. The bagpipe and the drum were silent.

"Milenka, you have a mother, you found your mother." Joanna whispered to the little girl, but even the people standing far away heard that. Then it became even quieter.

"What about your illness?" the child whispered back, as if they were sharing a fairytale secret.

"I'll take care of that now, you'll see!"

She waved to the bagpipes to start playing again and slowly turned to the fire. Fire dancing was Joanna's gift, and she was going to use it to heal! She ran, scooped the glowing embers up and they flew in the air as if they were feathers of a firebird. Then Joanna started the wildest dance ever — nobody's dance was ever that long and that magical. Even the hardest of hearts grew soft.

"Heart pain, I'm stepping on you, go away!" Joanna said suddenly and started stamping on the embers. She felt the power stronger than ever. Even Vassil was here with her — he was carrying her like before and was saying goodbye.

At this moment the night in Strandzha Mountain had two skies — the astral one and the sky of sparks from the fire. Joanna was saying goodbye to her love, her warm tears falling in the fire while she was burying her love. This lower sky was only a few meters, but was alive. She wasn't saying goodbye to a cold grave. It was warm. Soon Joanna knew that she had to get out — the fire felt hot.

The fire dancer sat on the ground barely breathing from exhaustion. Milenka ran toward her and touched the bottom of her foot.

"Are you still sick?"

"I don't know," Joanna replied and hugged her. "I hope not!"

And as she was hugging the girl Joanna saw the Mother of God smiling at her. The fire dancer recognized the Mother of God immediately — the night was bright. The Virgin Mary stood next to the fire, wearing the same dress as before. Joanna tried to get up, but couldn't. All she could do was hug Milenka and look at the image. In a little bit the image faded and then disappeared.

"If you are sick, I'll make you tea!" the girl comforted her and ran to join the other kids.

"I'm not sick, daughter, not anymore!" Joanna whispered behind her.

She breathed in the night air and finally managed to smile. Her smile lingered on her face for a long time. And that's when she understood. She felt the most important thing in life. She had lived according to this, but now she understood it. . . Joanna believed that if she lived according to God's rules, everything would be okay. She didn't want to live after Vassil's death, but the Mother of God ordered her to live and Joanna obeyed. She didn't even take the medicine powder as she was told to do from above. And she was bearing her pain. So, the Mother of God didn't lie to Joanna when she said that there were going to be better days for her. These days were here. Saint Constantine had told her about Milenka, so now she found a child and the girl found her mother. Joanna lost her love, but found affection. God didn't forget about her.

Joanna finally managed to crush the pain under her feet, to leave it there, to rise above it. Until now the fire had helped her to rise above her pain, but only for a short time. Tonight Joanna defeated it. She wasn't alone anymore — a child was waiting for her. She was expected to feed the girl in a little bit, tuck her into bed, tell her a story, kiss her goodnight, just like her dear mother used to do. Joanna needed the girl as much as the girl needed Joanna. They found each other because Joanna didn't renounce God's rules, no matter how hard it was for her.

Suddenly she saw Milenka run over the embers after the other kids, little Petar and Atanas. They were gathering coins and were probably making their twentieth round. She jumped to meet Milenka and Kera, and to rejoice in the little girl.

Joanna hadn't seen Milenka's first steps as a baby, but she saw her first steps in the fire. Her heart was happy.

This short story takes place after World War I and is based on an old tradition called nestinarstvo *that is still kept alive mostly in the Strandzha Mountain range near the South Black Sea coast in the Southeastern part of Bulgaria. Bulgarian* nestinarstvo *uniquely combines pagan and Christian beliefs. The manifestation of this tradition is dancing on glowing embers. The closest translation of the word* nestinarstvo *in English is the expression dancing on fire.*

Bulgarian fire dancers honor first and foremost the saints Constantine and Helena, whose feast day falls on June 3rd. Fire dancers believe that they receive their power from Saint Constantine. They feel that the dance is spiritual, physically purifying the dancer and, as a result, the whole village.

Nestinarstvo *in Bulgaria started to fade away in the beginning of the last century, its fires dying down one by one. During the last 10 to 15 years, dancing on fire is being brought back to life in the village of Bulgari and a few other places as a manifestation of will and technique, but its spiritual side is perhaps gone forever.*

Learning more about the ritual and its roots, the author became fascinated with its mystery and power. She witnessed and immersed herself in the charisma of the feast in the village of Bulgari.

Maria Pavlova (author) was born in the second largest city in Bulgaria, Plovdiv. She has a degree in Slavic studies and has worked as a journalist for various Bulgarian newspapers. Maria writes essays, poetry, short stories, and novelettes, some of which have been published in the press.

When she started working on her first novel, *The Rival*, Maria took a leave of absence so she could concentrate on the process of writing. The novel tells the story of a blind girl who simultaneously discovers love, life and the feeling for colors. At the moment Maria Pavlova is working in the field of graphic design and is finishing her second novel, *The Dual Life of a Witch*. Maria is married and has one daughter. Her fiction and creative nonfiction have been published in *Cezanne's Carrot, Forge, Yellow Medicine Review*, and *Etchings*. Contact: mariapav@abv.bg

Dr. Juliana Chakarova (translator) was also born in Plovdiv. She has a Master's degree in Russian Language and Literature and a PhD in Linguistics. Currently Dr. Chakarova is teaching The Theory and Practice of Translation, Cognitive Linguistics, as well as English and Russian at the University of Plovdiv. Her research papers, as well as translations (to and from English, Russian and Bulgarian), have been published in numerous journals and almanacs. She published a translation of *The Maker's Rage for Order: Theories of Literature and Culture* by Prof. D. Jenkins in Plovdiv in 2009 (Evro Print EOOD, 399 pp.). Contact: julianac@uni-plovdiv.bg

YOUR MOTHER

――――――――――― ℘℃ ―――――――――――

Excerpt from the memoir
by Alisa Clements

Your mother was back from her first year of college, stranded in a neighborhood of well-kempt lawns and whirring sprinklers. She moped, wrote in her journal, smoked hash on the sly, sometimes at the far end of the backyard, during nap time, or after her grandparents had gone to bed. She missed the incandescent friendships she had left behind and the pain of longing was compounded by envy: some of *them* would be sharing an apartment during the summer, living like actual adults. There was no real plan for her summer in Michigan: she would just find a job and hope the time passed quickly until the fall.

One night she had a dream that she was a hippie in San Francisco. The names Haight and Ashbury appeared on street signs, one above the other, facing in different directions. Upon waking, she thought she must have seen those names somewhere before, but could not fathom where; she felt a burning urgency to *get back, get back,* a desperate desire to return and reinsert herself into that life. The only other clear after-impression of the dream was the memory of a theater: there had been a theater there, called the Haight Theater, with crazy things happening in it, important things of which she'd been a part. It was devastating to be inhabited by such nostalgia for something that had never happened — or if it had, could never be revisited.

Then a possibility opened up: an aunt and uncle from Cincinnati would be driving cross-country to attend a graduation in Oakland, California. They could pick her up. It would only be for a few weeks; she would find a job when she got back. And there she was in the back of a car driven by relatives she barely knew, a bouncy six-year-old cousin beside her.

She'd never given a thought to the immensity of the North American landscape and was suitably impressed by it. The trip took three days; they spent the nights in low-budget hotels. She described some of what she saw in her journal, noting the insistent cropping up of 33s and 333s along the way.

The 333 phenomenon had startled her and her friends over the course of the previous months: the number started appearing repeatedly, then almost predictably: when you'd wake up for no reason in the middle of the night your clock would say 3:33; when you opened a book at random you'd find yourself at page 333; turn on the television and they'd be announcing "Case number 333," etc. One tried to be objective, of course, and acknowledge all the other numbers that turned up, but 333 insisted on distinguishing itself. The car that backed up and almost ran you over had 333 as part of its license plate, as did the one that went speeding the wrong way down a one-way street; the slip of paper that blew under your shoe was a convenience store bill for three dollars and thirty-three cents; the song that came on the radio just as you switched it on was called "Three Times Three." They found clues, your mother and her friends: apparently a fellow named Robert Anton Wilson, much given to delving into The Mysteries, had been plagued by the number 23. Satisfying as it was to read his list of related synchronicities, as well as his observation that 9 was also a significant number (he cited the Beatles' "Number Nine," among others), these still did not throw any light upon the *meaning* of the occurrences. 333 stood out, undeniably, but apparently that was all it did. Your mother drew her own private conclusion: three was held by several schools of thought to be the number of Manifestation; by tripling itself, and making itself so damn omnipresent, it reinforced this interpretation. And perhaps that was all there was to it! Manifestation making itself manifest, its significance lying in itself; it did not point one down any particular path, nor point at anything, really, aside from Other Principles — other than those one had been taught — at work at in the universe.

So it happened that during this trip she had a dream, experienced on the pillow of a hotel somewhere in Kansas, about the folks responsible for the appearance of 333. There was an office suite; the number on the door contained '333,' and the people in it were busy creating these "synchronicities" and recording the results on computers — the effects produced by each new instance on the thoughts and actions of those who noticed them. Printouts emerged from the computers on paper with little holes running down the sides.

Upon waking, your mother felt reassured. Reattached to her former life, despite the miles of unchanging prairie, the strained conversations in dreary dining rooms. Reminded of the importance of that which she could not understand.

One day, towards the end of the trip, as your mother was snuggled into the backseat corner listening to her Walkman, she discovered a curious thing. If she closed her eyes, she could see the landscape that was *about* to come into view, not the one the car was traveling through in that moment. She did it a few times before she was willing to believe that it was really happening. Simple extrapolation? No. At one point she saw a white steeple protruding from treetops in a kind of valley; when she opened her eyes the car was traveling between shelves of red rock that ran along the sides of the road with no end in sight. So much for that, she thought — until, about two minutes later, they rounded a bend and the wooded valley came into view, complete with white steeple.

So she was right. She was right to be there. She had a vague idea she might be a reincarnation of Wild Bill Hickock — an identification she'd made up sometime before the trip. Was that why the landscape looked familiar? Wyoming seemed to be the most beautiful state they'd passed through; and then the car broke down in Laramie, the town where Wild Bill had run into Calamity Jane. Nothing happened; the car was fixed and they went on, but your mother couldn't help thinking there was a *reason* she'd been made to steep in the Laramie vibes for a few hours.

In Oakland, there were more relatives; there was the graduation ceremony at the dental school. As soon as she was decently able, she made her exit: she would stay with a friend of her mother's in Berkeley until it was time for the return trip. Her first stop, though, would be to visit with Robert.

Robert was one of her friends from school; they had inhabited different circles that overlapped sometimes in the dormitory suite he shared with her two best friends. The arrangement grated on Robert — her friends were by far a coarser sort than he — but there was a stratum on which they all could meet, especially in the hours just before dawn when they would return from their various wanderings, devouring each other with gaping pupils.

She had phoned Robert — he was from Berkeley, originally — and he had set the meeting-place: the Café Med on Telegraph Avenue. A pleasant place, homey; she chose the upstairs area and settled in with a cup of coffee and her notebook.

Robert was late. At first he was a little late, then he was very late: over an hour had gone by with no sign of him. She was puzzled, annoyed, but more than anything she was curious. She started to write: I wonder why he's not here. As in: what is supposed to happen as a result of his not being here, that wouldn't have happened if he'd come?

Just then, she noticed that a man a few tables over seemed to be sketching her: he was bent over a pad of paper, drawing busily, glancing up at her every few seconds. Making a portrait without her permission? She was offended. After dutifully recording this latest development in her notebook, your mother stood up, went over to the artist and asked what he was drawing.

The man was small, disheveled, and apparently flustered by her question. Oh! Ah . . . don't mind me — he stammered — I'm crazy. I don't draw what's in front of me: I draw what's in people's heads.

He held out the paper for her to see. It was a portrait of Robert, complete with round glasses.

Before she could recover from her surprise, he asked in that same, breathless manner: Is your name Lisa? Are you from Oakland?

She was dumbfounded. He was only one letter off as far as the name was concerned, and she wasn't *from* Oakland, but she was definitely *coming* from Oakland.

He continued: Because they woke me up — the voices woke me up. They told me to hurry and get dressed and come to the café to meet Lisa from Oakland.

Your mother sat down with the man and listened to him. His name was Bluey, which had to do, he said, with a poem, which he wrote in spindly letters in her journal:

> *To the flowers so beautiful/The Father gave a name/Back came a little blue-eyed one/All timidly he came/And gazing in his father's eyes/And staring in his face/He said in low and trembling tones/Dear God, the name Thou gavest me/ Alas I have forgot/Kindly the Father looked him down/And said Forget-me-not.*

Bluey seemed to be a phenomenon on the order of 333: highly significant, there was no doubt about it, but the significance remained unclear. He talked a lot, his words tumbling over each other: she had to lean in to try and follow them. He had a Welsh witch for a grandmother. He had been struck by lightning and since then his head was like a long tunnel with doors opening off it to different places. There were children there; he could hear their voices. The way he got the body he was in at present was: a man had committed suicide in an elevator and he had stepped in and occupied the man's body.

Robert finally appeared, full of apologies, interrupting Bluey's monologue — but she was to hear a good deal more of it over the next couple of days. Robert ended up being called away on a concert tour — he was a violinist — and as your mother hadn't much else to keep her busy, she came back to the café frequently; as did Bluey.

The place was, she came to realize, more like an office than a café: tables took the place of desks, and the dividers were missing, but business was routinely conducted there by a number of different characters. One of them was a poetess whose picture your mother had seen on the back of a booklet in Robert's dorm room. This lady was famous for drifting about in long skirts and occasionally blowing streams of bubbles; she was a regular at the café. One day she marched up to your mother's table — nothing ethereal, despite the skirts — and plopped herself down. She wanted the thick silver band your mother wore around her wrist, an Algerian wedding bracelet. She asked to try it on and admired it, turning her wrist this way and that. What do you want for it? Your mother shook her head: she had no wish to part from the bracelet. The poetess insisted, bringing forth a small velvet pouch and shaking its contents out onto the table. How about a trade? There was a fetish bound with barbed wire, a ring with a secret compartment for storing poison, a few cheap odds and ends. Finally the woman saw it was no use; she thrust back the bracelet and flounced away.

When Bluey heard about this incident he became distressed. Oh, dear, he said; and: Did you put the bracelet on again right afterwards? Oh, dear.

He did not explain exactly what the problem was, but told your mother what she must do to remedy it. She was to put the bracelet on the table in front of her and look at it steadily, superimposing a mental image of her mother over it, while drinking a full glass of water. She obeyed his instructions.

Another time, she was sitting with Bluey in the upstairs part of the café, when a man stopped by their table, cheerful, apparently on friendly terms with Bluey. He'd be right back to sit with them if he might, he was just going to the bathroom first. Bluey smiled and nodded, but the distressed look came back over his face and as soon as the man was gone he whispered urgently to your mother: Don't say anything to him. Whatever you do, don't say anything.

There was no time to ask questions: the man returned and sat down. Your mother did not feel she could say *nothing*, but limited herself to minimal replies when questioned. The man did not, however, appear much interested in her. He was more interested in talking about himself, which he began to do after presenting her with his business card. The small white rectangle showed a picture of a clock, above which was a banner inscribed with the words: *Good*

Times, Past, Present and Future. Beneath the clock stood his name: *Peter OHalligan, Clock Maker.*

After giving her a second to look this over, Peter said, in hushed tones, I'm not *really* a clock maker. He then drew her attention to the fact that the time shown on the clock face was nine o'clock, and began to explain what his *real* line of business was: researching coincidences related to the number nine.

Imagine your mother's ears, your mother's whole *self* perking up, as he launched into his tale; imagine her bursting with the desire to confide Me too! Me too! and tell him all about her familiarity with 333 — but she couldn't: Bluey's gag order was in effect. So she listened keenly as the pseudo-clockmaker related the history of his involvement with Nine, citing Jung's particular interest in the number and giving her all the sorts of examples of recurrence she herself could have given him, with additional spectacular details, such as: Anywhere I go, in any country in the world, if I see a playing card lying face down in the street, I know when I turn it over it's going to be a nine. I have a whole collection of these playing cards.

He told how he had started an organization called the Liverpool School of Language, Dream, Music and Pun, in order to better research and explore this phenomenon. They had computers; they catalogued and tabulated synchronicities. And think of this — he pursued — he found the location for his school in a dream, a dream that led him right to a vacant building, and he knew that that was the right place because the number on the door was 18! And not only that, it turned out that that was the same street in which Brian Epstein, the Beatles' manager, first met the Beatles!

If your mother hadn't been entreated to stay silent, she would naturally have told him, not only about 333, but also about her dream of the office whose suite number contained 333, where synchronicities and their effects were being tracked. As it was, she said nothing, and when he had finished his exposition he declared what a pleasure it had been to meet her, exchanged parting salutations with Bluey and took himself off, clearly a busy man. Your mother then tried to explain to Bluey what a remarkable coincidence this encounter had been, but he seemed distracted, still troubled, distant.

Another time she was sitting with Bluey at a long table that filled up with people: several of them knew him, and then more showed up, and somehow Bluey slipped away. She was left among these people older than she, in their twenties or thirties maybe, conversing animatedly, though not with her. Then there was a collective rising and scraping-back of chairs: they were all going to hear Buckminster Fuller speak at Cody's bookstore.

Such an opportunity! Your mother had been turned on to Fuller earlier that summer by a kindly family friend who'd put into her hands — Here, you might enjoy this — a book that hooked her from its first sentences. She identified with Fuller's fervent convictions, liked his visionary earnestness, the way he would throw up barrages of the most convoluted syntactical constructions imaginable as if to deter all but the most persevering from finding their way, ultimately, to lucid conclusions phrased with the utmost simplicity. To actually hear him speak? She followed the crowd of young people to the bookstore.

What Buckminster Fuller said in his talk that afternoon did not end up making as much of an impression on her as the gleam of his balding pate and his humble, perfectly assured demeanor. She stared, hemmed in by the press of bodies all straining towards their object of worship. The question-and-answer session was interrupted by a man who stood up, introduced himself as a minister of the Church of Light who'd been involved in some way with Wavy Gravy's commune, and requested Buckminster Fuller's permission to perform a wedding ceremony then and there with the author serving as official witness. He produced the grinning couple, made a short speech, pronounced them man and wife, and then Fuller got down to the business of book signings and your mother wandered, a bit dazed, toward the door. Someone she recognized from the café said Hey, we're going to Lucinda's place in the Heights — wanna come? And your mother said Sure, and found herself in a car with several of these young people who didn't seem to want to get to know her at all, but took their role as tour guides for granted.

It was a neighborhood she hadn't visited before, in the hills of San Francisco: stately homes and an aura of money displayed with

204

tasteful reserve. Lucinda, a regal woman in her fourth or fifth decade of life, opened the door and your mother stepped into a fantastical environment. Every square inch of wall, ceiling, floor and furniture was covered with fabrics, papers, rubber, leather, plastic, bottle caps, pompoms, shells, feathers, figurines, masks, objects of all different shapes and sizes made of glass, stone, metal, wood and every other kind of material imaginable. The dimensions of the rooms were obscured, the passageways between them barely discernable.

Lucinda seemed accustomed to visitors and led the small group upstairs and downstairs, from one dizzying interior to the next. They settled in a room where Lucinda's companion and another man were exchanging reminiscences about a time they'd put LSD in the water supply of some college. The doorbell rang, and Lucinda went off to answer it, returning after a few minutes in the company of Peter OHalligan and a friend of his. Peter exchanged a nod of recognition with your mother. Clearly, it was his first time in that house, and after complimenting his hosts enthusiastically, he launched into the self-introductory spiel your mother had heard at the café.

There was not much more to the visit. Lucinda delivered them back to the front door, and once your mother was outside with the fresh breeze on her face, she realized her head was still spinning from the sensory overload, a sensation she had never experienced without first ingesting some chemical or other. They drove back to Berkeley and she was dropped off at the of the woman who'd known her since she was three and had provided the most wonderful hospitality for the duration of her short stay, including buying her own pack of Tarot cards, giving her free access to her stash of herb, and allowing her space to think and read and write and smoke undisturbed.

But the vacation soon came to an end — it was just a few days, after all. The relatives came from Oakland to pick your mother up and drive her back to the blander zones. Or did she take a plane? Before she knew it, she was back among the lawns and sprinklers, enveloped in the silence that stretched itself languorously over the neighborhood, broken only by the genteel peeps of bluebirds and the rustle of squirrels in the Dutch elms. Nothing had changed. It was hard to tell if she herself had. The whole shimmering California journey was swallowed like a rock dropped down a well: the surface closing over it, and no one the wiser. Or was she? She was so desperate, all the time, to *understand*, not knowing how to go about it: she had been told that true wisdom could never be attained by haphazard investigations such as the ones she conducted — though in fact it was more herself she allowed to be conducted, offered up to the swirling currents of happenstance like a twig borne off by a river. The mystery was all around her, it winked, it beckoned, it shouted . . . then skipped away, holding the key to itself far above its head, in the clouds, where she couldn't see it, let alone reach it.

The books said little; they proclaimed their visions but did not admit of other truths, which was suspect. Buddhists, Pleiadians, Crowleyites, Gurdjieffians: each could provide a schematic description of cosmic dynamics, a structure one could fit oneself into, the promise of reward in exchange for allegiance, even a glimpse of enlightenment if you were lucky or dedicated enough — only she didn't feel she could ever be, that she could swallow any one system whole. She found crucial bits and pieces here and there, like Robert Anton Wilson's numerical coincidences, and that was a relief, the relief of not being completely alone — well, her and her friends — but even Wilson put his discoveries into a framework involving the Illuminati and a conspiracy theory that didn't quite hold her interest.

What she had discovered in California was gratifying: she now had evidence of people older than herself traveling the same path as she, carrying the same flag, the one they had all inherited. But the trip hadn't really answered any of her questions, hadn't provided her with a Next Step, a Therefore; she supposed she had to be content with the confirmation of what she already knew. It did seem important — to accept that the world operated according to principles which were not generally recognized. Time was not linear in the sense she had always been taught, since precognition was a fact; causality was not as straightforward as it was made out to be, since people found themselves in the same place, at the same time, as the result of a series of independent decisions which had led to their convergence *for a reason*. Chance, in fact, revealed itself to be a dubious construct, a convenient scapegoat bearing the responsibility for that which one could not explain. Was it true that Bluey had gotten a "message" to come meet Lisa from Oakland at the café, or had he merely gleaned these details of name and place from her proximity? Telepathy, in any case, was a phenomenon your mother had experienced several times since childhood — it seemed a shame that its existence should be discredited simply because it resisted verification by "rigorous scientific methods." Your mother had once joked back and forth with a friend telepathically — their witticisms all the more devastating for being impossible to express in words, since the units of speech are too coarse to be able to capture the finest shades of meaning.

What a shame to ignore the evidence of these additional dimensions of reality, simply because Science was skeptical! Your mother was bitter, but then again, it didn't much matter what she knew or didn't know on those counts. They weren't subjects she felt like discussing with her grandparents, and it seemed like everyone else went about their business as if being alive were the most normal thing in the world.

That summer, nothing further was revealed to her. She wound up getting a job at a restaurant called The Money Tree, located on 333 West Fort Street in Detroit, and in the fall she returned, with great relief, to school.

Your mother sits back. All of that took place almost thirty years ago. Her friends are scattered, though they still keep in touch, mostly through the magic of the Internet. The Internet didn't exist in those days, although one of their group had visions of something very like it: he would describe it to anyone who would listen, though the reaction he got, more often than not, was a breezy Yeah, sure, that would be cool.

While she was in the middle of this tale, the other night, it occurred to your mother to look up the Liverpool School of Language, Dream, Music and Pun on the Web. Actually, she hadn't remembered the 'Language' part, but Google kindly filled her in.

There it was: the story of its origins, Peter OHalligan's dream that led him to the building, and the subsequent history of the School, which became a focal point for wacky Liverpudlian culture. A play was staged there, based on a book co-authored by Robert Anton Wilson; according to one of the other founding members of the School (whose voice delivered this information courtesy of an mp3 file), the play made it into the Guinness Book of World Records owing to its length — 24 hours.

Your mother found a particularly interesting paragraph on the page detailing the history of the Liverpool School of Language, Dream, Music and Pun:

> *Many other scientists have agreed with Carl Jung's opinion that the number of startling coincidences in the Net* [note: they were not referring to the Internet!] *increases sharply around anybody who becomes involved in depth psychology or in any investigation that extends the perimeter of consciousness.*
>
> *Arthur Koestler has written about this at length, in both* The Roots of Coincidence *and* The Challenge of Chance. *Dr John Lilly has whimsically suggested that consciousness research activates the agents of Cosmic Coincidence Control Centre.*

"The Roots of Coincidence?" "Cosmic Coincidence Control Center?" Your mother wonders whether, had the Internet existed back in the day, more of her questions would have found answers. As it is, she will probably track down the material in question . . . out of curiosity, but no longer, in her infinitely greater maturity — or weariness — in the hopes of penetrating the secrets of Life.

At the very moment your mother typed the word "Life," you said the word distinctly, in English, and then repeated it. You'd put a calculator on her lap and had been punching numbers into it while babbling in Portuguese; she had been wrapped up in her computer screen but heard the word, heard you repeat it before resuming your prattle. She seized your soft upper arm, hardly thicker than a hotdog, and shook it to get your attention. Hey, she said. Hey! Did you just say Life? You answered perfunctorily in Portuguese — Yes — and continued to hold forth.

Your mother has to laugh: the secrets only multiply, or else they vanish all at once. She'll be content with that, for now.

Alisa Clements decided at age seven that she would be a writer when she grew up. However, the exploration of other media, primarily electronic music briefly eclipsed her writerly vocation after she took a teaching-assistant position in the Harvard University Electronic Music Studio and later took the role of studio manager. Alisa entered the Studio for Interrelated Media program at the Massachusetts College of Art, in order to pursue her interests in experimental music, performance, and film, then became an instructor at the college. Her experience in this field — as a performer, composer, and teacher — enters into her first novel, *All at Once*, in the guise of arcane facts about the effects of audio stimuli on human consciousness. An excerpt from the novel was published in the anthology *Above Ground*. After a journey that has spanned several professions and four countries, Alisa is now settled in northeastern Brazil with her two children and has returned to writing. Contact: alisaslide@gmail.com

FRENCHING MY SISTER

※ ❧❦ ※

by Jay Boyer

When my mother phoned and told me Moira was acting inappropriately again it was because Mother thought I, and I alone, could talk sense to my younger sister and get her to listen. I'm my mother's only son and I have what my mother refers to as my father's *flinty resolve,* by which she means *business sense.* Ours is one of those old New England families of steady, no-nonsense bankers going back to the days of the Puritans. She assumes I came with that gene while Moira was born a *preterite,* the Puritan word for *passed over.*

"Just tell him what he's in for," my mother advised. "He'll get the point. I'll cut off Moira's allowance if I have to."

"That should get her attention," I agreed.

Moira has a long history of psychological disorders that date back to late adolescence — fugues and flights of fancy, manic stints leading to deeply dark depressions, some of these manageable through a protocol of drugs and some of these not. In the best of times she is as functional as anyone else; but these periods are just that, *periods.* We've learned to look for warning signs of still worse to come, *bumps in the road,* as it were, situations where Moira does something impulsive, against her best interests, something with questionable consequences, and the road, it seems, had grown bumpy of late. My mother's way of parenting my sister has always been to save Moira from herself well in advance of any damage she might do, but my mother was tucked away in Maine at our family house in Kennebunkport, and this time she didn't want to make the trip to New York City. She hasn't been herself since my father passed away. At nearly eighty, her health beginning to slip, not to mention that she was worn out with what she termed my sister's *shenanigans*, she was calling on my help.

"Take her riding perhaps. Just the two of you. By yourselves. That's how I'd begin. She loves the stables. Feel her out."

"Where's Moira at the moment?"

"She's in the Hamptons right now — I wouldn't be calling if this wasn't important."

"How should I approach this man she's been seeing?"

"A lunch, I think. Let Moira pick the place. Midtown is always good."

"Somewhere crowded where they don't stand a scene."

"Exactly. He'll have to break it off, Moira never will."

"Does he have a name?"

"Jeremy. It should be the three of you. Put an end to it though."

"How should I bring this up?"

"You won't have to. Moira will excuse herself once you call for the bill. Sit quietly and he'll bring it up himself. They always do. The married ones are guilty. Particularly where there are children."

"I'll be in the city next week. The Met's having its semiannual Trustees meeting. Is next week soon enough?"

My sister is fast approaching thirty. As near as Moira has ever come to holding a job was one my father secured at Manufacturers Hanover when she got herself in a pinch. He'd sent her off to boarding school in Switzerland believing she might find her footing if only she were left on her own and far enough from home. She lasted less than a term. There were reports early on of what sounded to me like harmless, rich-girl mischief and then Moira had one of her spells. What finally got her bounced was kiting checks on one of our father's Zurich accounts. She managed this swindle with surprising aplomb; it was only bad luck that she got caught, and our father (a Yankee, and a pragmatist to boot) took this to mean that since she had so little interest in anything else, it might signal an interest in finance.

The country was in a recession and Manufacturers Hanover had created a division specifically designed to deal in its hardship cases, writing down bad debts while going after their assets, foreclosing on family mortgages. It was here that Moira took hold. My sister is slender and she has always carried herself like someone older and wiser. Thin-faced, with soft brown eyes, she acquired at an earlier age than most women, skills at using those eyes to get her way. Most men are stupid where women are concerned. She'd acquired this knowledge as well, and so, doubly armed, she assumed — and pretty rightly, I have no doubt — that she could out-maneuver all but the most aggressive of customers, virtually all of whom were male. They were prone to have emotions that were dangerously near to the surface, having seen their families put out on the street and their businesses pulled out from beneath them like a cheap department store rug. This was where my sister came in. They still had their health and so did their children and wives. A vegetable could be a full meal if you knew what you were doing with simple foods. Maybe she just reminded them of the cool nights of summer and the warm afternoons when the leaves were turning, those first days of autumn. She probably said something about how one door never closes without another door opening, about how they were probably going on to better things, without speaking to what those things were, much less how, under the circumstances, they were likely to be better. What did it matter? It wasn't what she said. It was the hope they must have seen in Moira's beautiful, teenaged eyes.

You have never seen more animated eyes than those of my sister Moira. That's all it ever was though, animation. There was always something missing. It was like a heavy, velvet curtain had been pulled that blocked out the sun; my sister was like a movie camera that hadn't been loaded with film. Nothing got through that might make an impression. That can scare the bejesus out of you when those eyes belong to your sister. It proved a major plus when a client was arguing over collateral however. How are you going to tell them their credit line's kaput, now it's strictly cash and carry?

My father enrolled her at Spence at the beginning of the new year to keep her close enough to watch. Before he could get her back in school, she went from clerk to teller to becoming the personal assistant of one of the bank's junior officers, the head of this division, and I'm recounting that story here for two reasons, first, because I realized over lunch that Jeremy and that junior officer were one and the same, and second, Moira's eyes had changed.

The restaurant was one of their favorites, "Fiorini's" I think it was called. Moira's claustrophobic, though not enough to find it crippling. She can ride in an elevator, for instance. Nonetheless, you can see her begin to fidget and play with her food if a restaurant is too crowded or there are too many tables pushed too close together. A window helped. Jeremy and Moira were sitting with their backs to a window facing onto 56th Street. My chair was facing out. I watched as the sky darkened over a long lunch of three-colored salad, *cavatelli*, and a bottle of cheap red wine.

The first few minutes were tense. I was there when they arrived. Moira introduced me as her brother. You could see she was springing this on Jeremy. He'd assumed they were eating alone. When Moira claimed she'd gotten her wires crossed, he made that clucking sound that the French make when they mean to scold. It was annoying. I was protective of Moira. I didn't want her scolded. She couldn't have prepared either of us much worse than she did though. Moira had told me that her boyfriend Jeremy was in investments, if only in passing. I'd assumed this was roughly akin to one man saying to another that his lover had Knicks season tickets. She'd wanted me to think he might be of use to the family.

Over lunch I learned Jeremy was working for a firm that produces those splashy Broadway musicals that cater to tourists. I mean the ones that cost twenty million dollars to mount, and run in theatres the size of football stadiums. Part of the reason these musicals cost so much to produce is their load-in costs. The "load-in" can cost upwards of a million dollars. A load-in is when you haul sets and props from trucks and establish them up on the stage. Why this costs as much as it does has to do with union contracts and ways of doing business that go back fifty years. You could use day laborers off the street and get the job done for a few hundred bucks. Outlandish they are, these load-in costs, but a fact of life, just part of doing business, and that was Jeremy's niche. He had made his mark by keeping load-ins to six-figure billings, and, in return, he was being groomed to head production teams of his own.

You could see they were happy together. He was planning a trip to Los Angeles and they were working out the last minute details. He'd register at Shutters on The Beach in Santa Monica and Moira was going to be at the Casa Del Mar, which was virtually next door. He was flying to Los Angeles to negotiate something with the Disney people. Moira and Jeremy were deciding what she'd do while he was in meetings. Both hotels were at the ocean and the discussion was whether Moira preferred sunning herself on the beach to sightseeing. The list of things she mentioned was nothing I might have predicted. She wanted to go to Disneyland. She wanted to go on the Universal Studios tour. She was hoping Jeremy could get her in to the Ellen DeGeneres show. Everything was touristy, a place where you might take kids, and she seemed to be so delighted by each of these possibilities that even listing them in order brought light to her eyes.

Jeremy and I were comfortable with one another. Moira was sunny-bright, comfortable with us both. It was important to her that we meet. She had no idea why I was in the city except for the meeting at the Metropolitan Museum I've mentioned, and she was hoping we'd be friends. There was little enough chance of that, I suppose, but Jeremy seemed to be a perfectly pleasant person. He had both feet on the ground, and very firmly planted. Under other circumstances, I might have picked him for Moira myself. That's an odd thing to say, I know. He was decidedly older than Moira, a married man, a husband and father. He didn't take Moira for granted though. He could see that Moira was special. He cared about her. I could tell.

I'm not sure now how long we sat there. Rain began coming down, splattering the window at Moira's back, and anyone on the street was now bringing out their umbrellas. It was right about this time that we called for the bill and Moira went off to the ladies' room.

Jeremy rubbed his hands together once Moira was gone. I said what I'd come to say. I said we'd go to his wife and children if it came to that. He looked as if he was experiencing a sudden loss in body heat.

"This is a lot to take in all at once," he said.

"I know," I answered. "I know it is."

We sat there silently after that, nursing tiny cups of espresso until Moira got back.

The rain had stopped and the sun had come out and after lunch Moira suggested we walk. Jeremy had an appointment with some backers in the bar of the Peninsula Hotel on 55th so Moira decided we could walk west on 57th Street and Jeremy could cross over on 5th Avenue. I assumed they didn't want me along and made an excuse about needing to go in another direction. Moira insisted. We walked three abreast with Moira in the middle. Moira was right. It was a pleasant day now, a pleasant walk. Jeremy repeated what he'd said over lunch, namely that his firm was always in the market for new lines of credit, and while he didn't handle any of that himself, he could surely find a way to put me with the right people. Moira had been teasing me over the *cavatelli* about my weight — it was something on the order of *broadening my fiscal horizons* — and Jeremy was acting as if the joke had gone past him.

We had many things in common when you got right down to it. We liked the same music, the same sports, same pastimes. We laughed at the same things. The three of us got the same jokes. It felt right somehow, the three of us walking together and chatting. Jeremy was saying that if he never saw another musical it wouldn't be the end of his life — but you could see we had lost his attention.

Just as we were approaching Park Avenue, someone called out Jeremy's name. The fellow was wearing one of those foolish wool caps from Tibet that have flaps that cover the ears and strings that tie under the chin, and he looked silly in his cap, particularly with those strings of yarn left untied. I mean the day was springlike, and there he was in his cap. Jeremy traded glances with Moira, and Moira traded glances with me, and we were all thinking the same thing, Don't anyone mention his cap. But seriously, what's his problem? What's with that cap?!

When Jeremy didn't introduce us, his friend brought up someone they knew from the New York Athletic Club who was on a diet of plantains and rice. The dieter must have been some kind of marathon swimmer, because there was something about open water, a support boat and radio, and breaking a record for his age class. Then the fellow in the cap asked Jeremy which way he was walking. We could all see that Jeremy was making the situation worse by acting like Moira and I weren't there. I felt bad for him. He hadn't cheated on his wife before, I imagined. Moira wasn't something he'd planned.

Finally Jeremy introduced us, me first, then Moira, but only by her first name, as in, *And this is Moira*. Moira linked her arm into mine after shaking hands. Moira and I said our goodbyes, then we walked to the opposite corner as if positioning ourselves for an uptown cab. She raised her hand, which surprised me, because Moira wasn't a cab person as a rule, and got one right away. The cab pulled over and I opened her door. Before she got in, she gave me a deep, passionate kiss, long and slow and wet, bracing the back of my head with her hand. As I was closing her door, she said, "Thanks, buddy." Then the cab pulled away. I gave a little last wave to Jeremy and this other fellow, and after that I headed home.

J. Boyer teaches in the Creative Writing program of Arizona State University. Contact: J.Boyer@asu.edu

MARION TERRY, WHO MIGHT HAVE BEEN A SINGER . . . [*]

---

by Vivien Jones

There was a soft knock at the door. The scuffle of several small children stilled behind it. There was a pause, then the door was opened by a fair-haired woman, heavily pregnant and carrying a snot-smeared toddler on one hip. She could have been any age from thirty to fifty; she looked drained and weary, her apron was grubby but her smile was warm. She blocked the smaller children's escape attempts with her legs and broad beam.

"Mary! I did not know you were coming to visit. Do come in."

Marion urged her visitor into the hallway and down to the kitchen which was the only warmed room in the house. A ragtag of children tumbled after them.

"Oh Mrs. Terry, I did not know you had so many bairns in the house. I wouldn't have bothered you on such a small matter." Mary Elgin said, nodding to a pale woman sitting by the range nursing a snuffling infant.

"This is my sister in law, Polly, who has come to stay for a while — Polly, this is Mary Elgin who has a fine singing voice and sings in the Chapel with me. She is going to join our madrigal group after the summer." Marion Terry surveyed her kitchen to find a seat for her

---

* From the Papers of the Runciman Family. The character of Marion Terry, who lived in the late 19th century, is imagined.

219

visitor. Polly looked up from her nursing and smiled a wan smile. Marion pulled a stool forward.

"And don't be apologizing for coming, Mary dear, I have few enough visitors with this collection of cherubs cluttering up the house. Will you have tea?"

She was already filling a kettle and clearing the irons from the range to find the hottest spot. The children settled in small groups and played on the floor. There were eight children on the floor from three to eleven years old, and the two babes in arms. Mary knew that Marion had lost a daughter the year before and, judging by the size and lowness of her belly, was about to drop two more. Mary half rose from her stool to help find cups but Marion waved her back.

"Mary, sit yourself down. You're a visitor and will be treated as such."

Marion shifted the toddler from hip to hip as she, one-handed, arranged the tea cups and a jug of milk at the side of the range. She broke some oatcakes made that morning into small pieces and handed them round the children who gobbled them up and looked for more, but a slight frown from Marion cooled their hopeful gazing. Mary's, she put on a plate and gave it to her to eat on her lap.

"How is Mr. Terry?'" Mary asked.

"He is well, but not home until dark and then at his pupils' books until he cannot see by the lamp. I shall thank the Lord when the spring light comes. I think I must learn to bear the darkness better. The Lord will help me. Now Mary, what brings you here so bright-eyed in the afternoon?"

Mary's eyes were indeed bright.

"Oh Mrs. Terry, there was a visitor in the chapel last meeting. From London.

He was kind enough to remark on my singing. He has a school for young ladies. He has asked my father if I might take a scholarship in singing at his school. What do you think, Mrs. Terry?" Mary's voice was filled with a mixture of anxiety and longing.

Marion gazed at her, lost for a moment in a poignant memory of her own relinquished opportunity, of the Italian impresario who thought her voice good enough for the opera. It had been the talk of the village. She had allowed herself to dream of bright clothes and feathers for a day or two before accepting the impossibility of leaving her sprawling family to care for themselves. Her elder brother had died the year before and the rest were so young, so needy.

"Mrs. Terry?" Mary spoke quietly, breaking her reverie.

The toddler squealed in boredom. Marion set her down by a curly haired boy who was scribbling on a slate. The toddler smiled into her brother's face and both began to sing and clap hands.

"Cockle, take care of wee Marion for a while. And Ritchie, stop tormenting your sister. You can go and collect some sticks for the fire if you've nothing better to do with yourself. Jean, take Adelaide from your aunt while she rests a while."

For a moment there was peace in the kitchen. Polly, relieved of her suckling infant, promptly fell asleep and her own children gathered round her skirts like a bundle of puppies. Marion gazed around her extended family with a mixture of exhaustion and love, then back at Mary.

"What about Richard Ingram? Are you not to be wed in the summer? Are you promised?" she asked gently. Marion drew the broth pot onto the range and began to toss chopped neeps into the stock, but turned half towards Mary to show she was listening.

Mary shifted on the stool.

"We have been walking out a little. We have not spoken to the minister yet. But yes. It is our intention — eventually. Perhaps I could do both."

Marion quelled her impulse to chide the young and hopeful Mary for her vain hopes. She minded her own youthful hopes and her present weariness and was made gentle.

"What does your father say?'"

"He has asked me if singing in the chapel and the madrigal group would suffice. He fears my mother would pine if I went all the way to London." Mary admitted, but added fiercely, "But I am young, not yet twenty — and if I marry . . ."

She looked around the roomful of children, one for every year that came and went, and saw her own future in Marion's and Polly's bent backs and lined faces. The children were fine, much loved and as well looked after as any poor schoolmaster's could be, but the women . . . Mary knew if she married this summer, in a year she

221

would have an infant at her breast and her singing would be set aside. The tears came to her eyes unbidden. Marion, stirring and salting the broth, looked at Mary and knew her distress as her own.

"The Lord will guide you, Mary dear. We cannot penetrate the great mysteries of life ourselves. The Lord saw fit to bless us both with singing voices — my father too. He fills the house with joy whether it be hymns or Scots songs on his lips. We can sing anywhere and sing with a joyful heart if we are accepting of the Lord's will."

Mary sighed then gathered her courage.

"But Mrs. Terry, were you never sorry that you didn't go to the opera?" Marion stopped stirring the broth, trying to untangle her own vexed feelings and be honest with the young woman before her.

"I think it would be a terrible thing to be able to choose again. I would measure the many difficulties of my life against a dream, how could there be a wise decision made? I have been of service to my family. I do not know if amusing strangers would be anything but sand through the fingers. You must not ask me for advice, Mary. I am not impartial. Just trust the Lord."

Mary sighed again and Marion turned back to the broth. Wee Marion started to whinge and Marion scooped her up and began singing to her in her sweet contralto, allowing the child to stir the pot whilst she sprinkled in a cupful of barley. Polly startled awake and stretched in her chair, bringing the children at her feet to life again. Jean handed the sleep-reddened Adelaide back to her still yawning mother. The children's voices began to rise around the three women.

"Mama, I am hungry."
"Mama, the pussy scratched me."
"Mama, my belly hurts."
"Mama, sing to me too."
"Mama, I had a bad dream."
"Mama, Grandfather is calling."

Mary left quietly, shutting the door and the demands of the children behind her. She thought of the chapel and the first time she had ever been, a young girl who went to God's house and thought she heard an angel singing. She recalled the rapt face of Marion Terry, momentarily freed of all cares, her flaxen hair touched by pale gold, eyes on her inner vision as she sang, and Mary did not know what to do.

Vivien Jones' short stories have been widely published and broadcast on BBC Radio 4 and Radio Scotland — her first themed collection of short stories, *Perfect 10*, was published in September 2009 by Pewter Rose Press.

In autumn of 2009, her short stories were published in *The Yellow Room*, Horizon (Salt Publishing) and *Iota Fiction* anthology. A poetry chapbook, *Something in the Blood*, was published in February 08 (Selkirk Lapwing Press) and another, *Hare* (Erbacce Press) in March 08. She has twice performed in a *Poetry Double*, a performance event in which an experienced professional poet is paired with an up-and-coming poet, with Jacob Polley and Jen Hadfield and devises collaborative readings with music in performance at Book and Arts Festivals in Scotland and the north of England. She is currently working on a first poetry collection.

Vivien Jones lives on the north Solway shore with her husband and cat. She is a semi-professional early musician. Contact: vivien@freeola.com

LILY DALE ASSEMBLY

―――――――――――― ℰᏖ ――――――――――――

by Sharon Dilworth

They call it Silly Dale and Spooksville. They joke about ghosts and spirits haunting the place and stare at the residents like they're part of a freak show, as if the Assembly is there purely for their amusement. But despite all their unkindness and ridicule, they come. And most of them come back.

The husband and wife from Erie had the first appointment with my mother the day that Robert's son and Bella died in a car crash on the Pennsylvania interstate.

The wife was the one who had booked the reading with my mother. She was the one who needed the insight. She had brought her husband because she was afraid to do it by herself. Unfortunately, she was not the one who 'went over' that day.

The wife, Adele, had heard about the Assembly from the woman who colored and cut her hair. Adele had been going to the same place for twenty years so there was trust there. Her husband wasn't thrilled with the idea of fortune telling. But the Assembly wasn't that far from the Seneca-owned casinos in Jamestown and he thought they could at least stop and play a few rounds of blackjack and try the slots and, if nothing else, they might come out ahead.

Adele had not been feeling well. She was exhausted, slow in the bone; most mornings she could barely get out of bed. She found herself taking two-hour naps and then longing for bed as soon as she finished the dinner dishes. It felt as if something inside her body was broken and she had a sense it would never be the right again. She was afraid of doctors, afraid of what they would tell her. She dreaded a terminal diagnosis and hadn't even had a check-up since she had delivered the last of her four children. She dreamed of death and felt that her time in the world was coming to an end. She did not feel melodramatic, but scared.

People who come to Lily Dale worry about their money and their health — usually in that order. Profoundly afraid of the unknown, they want reassurance that bankruptcy, poverty and death are not forthcoming. Make them promises of long lives and golden pockets and they will leave feeling happy. Sometimes I thought we should just market some pills — *Long Life, Lots of Money*.

My mother, who believes her gift of second sight to be divine, would never be so calculating. Her clients — in the local parlance, we call them seekers — leave her house bothered; some are furious. A few threatened to sue, one promised to kill her. I don't think the honesty is worth the pain. It makes skeptics out of the believers and frightens the curious. Either way, people tend not to return if they don't hear what they want. I think of it as a childhood fairy tale. Most people don't mind a wolf, a witch, or a poisoned apple, but in the end they long for everlasting happiness, and not knowing what will happen to them gets them panicky. Mockery or not, reassurance is a good thing.

My mother has proved herself to be a genuine spiritual advisor. The board of Lily Dale Assembly, the largest and oldest gathering of spiritual mediums in the world, gave her credentials and she is registered with the national organization. Second sight and the ability to talk to the dead are not inherited traits. You either have it or you don't. I never showed any signs of that talent. It was not something I regretted, especially when I started to succeed in school. I had other plans for myself.

I had recently graduated from University but didn't know what I wanted to do with the rest of my life. I had come home that spring to try and discover my future. Everyone had advice for me; none of it was particularly inspiring. "You'll come into your own." My mother told me. "You of all people should have faith."

"You of all people should be able to tell me what I should be doing with my life," I said.

"You'll discover it soon enough." That was her wisdom. I was not the only one to receive this particular insight so I didn't feel special. I was, on the other hand, the only one who received it free and without a prior reservation.

My mother was confused by the man from Erie. His energy was strong and he was the one whose story she heard. When the two of them walked into the house that morning, she assumed he was the client. "Someone is waiting for you," she told him. "Your sister," she told the husband. "She's right here." The husband did not respond and my mother continued. "She's been waiting a long time to speak to you." There was still no response from either of them, so my mother described the visitor, encouraging trust. "Your sister is smiling. Happy as can be to be back in contact with you."

The man did not believe a word of what my mother was saying. Still, he was surprised to hear her talking about his sister who had been dead more than five years. He did not like to think about her. He had loved her and her death had caused him so much grief that he would go into the basement at night and cry. He had never experienced such loss and did not know how to make himself understand that she was gone and there was nothing anyone could do about it.

"She's wearing a Buffalo Bills sweatshirt, the one you gave her for her birthday that year they had that good season."

The husband was ready to bolt. Adele ordered him to sit. My mother assured him there was nothing to be afraid of. "She simply has something she's wanted you to know."

I was in the kitchen, relieved that my mother had a reading that morning. She was a firm believer in organic living and her kitchen was filled with herbal teas and hard chunks of dark bread. I guzzled Diet Coke behind her back, not wanting her to know about the caffeine headaches. She saw addiction as a character flaw; the idea of having more than one glass of wine at dinner was like suggesting we play Russian roulette. Back in Lily Dale without a clue where to go next, I got hired by the ground's crew to help readying the place for the upcoming season. My job that day, the day that Bella and Robert's-son were killed, was to give the dock a new coat of green paint. Later that month, we would put the dock in the lake, always the sign of the start of summer for me. I was bored. And worried. I couldn't believe that this was what I had studied for and I promised myself to get busy contacting former professors and throwing myself at their mercy.

I had just started on the dock when the couple from Erie came down the footpath and stood on the dock. They didn't see me. Lily Dale has owned the property for more than a century and half. This is an old-growth forest, trees that have never been cut, never been timbered; they are enormous.

"I never knew your sister killed herself," Adele sighed. The two of them wore Crocs, funny plastic gardening shoes that looked out of place in real life. Hers were purple, his red. It made them look clownish. "You never told me that."

"Of course I didn't. Because it never happened," the man was emphatic in his denial. "She just died. There was never any talk of her taking her own life."

"Then why did the woman say that?"

"Because she's a raving lunatic."

Adele stumbled on the soft earthen path. She righted herself and said softly. "She didn't seem crazy to me. She was actually very warm and inviting."

My mother is beautiful. She has clear soft skin and she keeps the gray out of her hair in a way that isn't noticeable. She has a charisma that she enhances with the way she dresses, bright gauze skirts with simple t-shirts. She wears silver bangles on her wrists and emerald earrings that shimmer when she turns into the light.

"She made it up."

"But how would she even know about your sister? How did she even know that she was dead?"

"Scam artists. All of them."

Grief is often connected to guilt, especially when it comes to suicide.

His sister had swallowed pills and feeling the tremendous grief of losing a child, had not put her finger down her throat to bring them back up. She did not love her husband and she no longer wanted children of her own. She sat on the bed and, staring at the pink roses of the spread, she simply stretched out to become a part of something still, of something that resembled beauty.

The man fumed. "Did you hear what that woman said? My sister wearing a Buffalo Bills sweatshirt?" He shook his head in disbelief. He would have been much happier down at the casinos.

"It is the kind of gift you'd give," Adele said.

"What's that supposed to mean?" He barked at her.

"Well, you wouldn't have bought your sister a scarf or a pair of leather gloves but you might have given her a sweatshirt with the Bills on it. You do love them."

"It's an enclave of witches here. That's what this place is," he said. "Tell you what should happen. They should all be burned at the stake."

"That seems a bit harsh," the woman said. "You said you'd be open minded."

"I said I'd try," he said. "And now I'm done."

The word he should have used was coven. It comes from the Latin: *convenire*, meaning to come together, to gather, and later gave rise to the English word: convene. A gathering of witches, usually thirteen in number. He wasn't original. People have called Lily Dale a coven, they've called it a center for voodoo, they've called it a hoax, a circus, a little house of horrors, a pack of liars, even a bunch religious fanatics though technically spiritualists are not religious by nature. Most can simply communicate with certain people who have already passed. There are no neo-pagan religious organizations on the site. There are no by-laws, no agreed constitution, not even a code of honor. It is just a society with common goals and a board that makes all decisions with a guiding sense of good will.

They were standing only a few feet from where I was painting the dock. I was hidden beneath the branches of the trees though they could have seen me easily enough if they had been looking my way.

Adele put her hand over her eyes and searched out across the water. Cassadaga Lake was a clear blue that day.

You would not have thought something awful was going to happen to two of the Assembly's long time residents.

"The website said there were swans on the lake," she sighed. She was not mad but disappointed. The morning had been typical. She felt overlooked by life. Even at a reading by a spiritual medium given for her benefit, she had not been the center of attention. She never was. That was her destiny. Everyone else, so much more important. She wanted to see a pink swan.

"Do you notice there are no men here?" the husband said, as if that proved that my mother was out of her mind. "These women probably have cauldrons in their basements where they brew up potions to poison any who come too close."

The man from Erie was right — the ratio of men to women is out of whack in Lily Dale, which is one of the reasons the place spooks people. Had he compared it to Salem, he wouldn't have been at all original. There's something unnerving about a bunch of women together; the world mistrusts that — too much estrogen power or something. But sometimes it's just how it happens. More women are called to the profession, most probably because they're more open to it, and more women stick with it. Clients tend to be women. Women aren't afraid to admit that they want to know the future. Men tend to believe they're happy with the present.

I finished painting for the day and, on the way home, stopped at the market for turpentine. Robert, the owner of the market, one of two storeowners in the Assembly but the one who has the most selection, was on the porch rocking in his chair. It was his perch; from there he watched over the entire place.

"Here she is, the college graduate of the year," he said. "The little miss, who won a big fancy scholarship only to come home and paint park equipment like any high school drop out."

That was how Robert talked. He breathed venom and mean-spiritedness. The song changed but the tune was always the same. I had forced myself not to take it personally but that day, perhaps because of the dried paint on my skin, I lashed out. "You bitch for no reason now. But soon you'll have a real reason to bitch."

"What do you know, Ms. I got-my-college-degree-for-nothing?"

"Like I said. You'll get yours soon enough." I pushed my head forward and hissed at him like a snake going after its prey. It felt strange to be on the attack like that. For so many years I had let him talk to me like I was an idiot. I was never rude or minded what he said. He was a bastard and I accepted him for that. That day though, I was tired of him, tired of his words and his opinions.

He grunted and waved his hands in the air as if he could make me disappear.

The woman from Erie was standing outside the market. She wouldn't know who I was but I smiled and gave a short wave. Lost in thought, she simply looked past me as if I wasn't even there. When I first saw her, I thought she was crying.

I passed by her and stopped when I realized my first impression of her had been right. She had been crying.

"What is it?" I went over to her. Her Crocs were dusty, so was the skin around her ankles. She tried to talk but lost her breath. I thought she might faint; she was struggling that hard to breath between sobs.

"The air is so heavy here," she said. "I don't like it here. I can't breathe."

It's been said that the division between this world and the next is extraordinarily thin at Lily Dale. It's why the place was founded on this particular spot. Visitors sometimes feel a sort of looming presence in the air, which manifests itself in strange ways. Some people drive in, look around, and drive right back out.

"This place spooks me out," she complained.

Her husband was gone. He had left her there. Their argument must have accelerated as they walked through the old-growth forest, which was somewhat odd, as most people are so impressed by the size and width of the trees that they find some sort of peace or inspiration on the path.

"Do you need a ride somewhere?"

"He didn't take the car," she said and pointed to the parking lot.

"But he took the keys?"

"I have my own," she said.

It would serve him right if she drove home without him. Tantrums were childish and his anger had been caused by my mother, not by his wife, so to take it out on her and to leave her worried and alone in a strange place seemed an enormous waste of emotions.

"There isn't anywhere to walk. Lily Dale is in the middle of nowhere." I said. He might have tried to get a ride to the highway or a bus station in Jamestown but it seemed unlikely. Most likely he was stewing in the woods somewhere.

A police car pulled up and my guess was that they had found her husband wandering the lakeshore or the country roads and had brought him back home like a wayward child.

The driver had his window down. He leaned out and asked me where to find Robert Gleason.

"Right there," I said.

Robert heard his name and came down the steps of the market.

The policeman asked if they could speak somewhere privately. Robert hated authority and told the policeman to state his business.

There was no question of identity. They had the license plate and had checked the registration. "I'm so sorry."

I went over to Robert so that he would not have to lean on a stranger. He asked for details. "Tell me everything."

There had been two people in the car. Robert couldn't believe what he told them. He was frantic. At first with disbelief; then, as he came to understand that the men who stood before him were telling him something true and something that wouldn't go away, with grief.

The police car attracted attention. You could feel the energy created by all that curiosity in the Assembly. We were a protected place; the outside world rarely intruded and if they did it was easy to lock the gates and ignore the troubles.

Lucy Reims came forward and embraced Robert.

"What is it?" she whispered to me.

"Bella and Robert's-son are dead," I said. "A car accident."

"Oh lord, no," Lucy said.

Eighty years old, Lucy was a strong woman. She took Robert's arm and told him it would be best if they went inside the market with the policeman. "No sense making a spectacle out of a terrible situation," she said and he allowed her to lead him up the steps.

The driver who crossed the median was fifteen years old. He had no license and had spent the night out in the woods drinking bottles of alcohol stolen from their parent's cupboard and doing drugs taken from his older brothers and sisters. He most likely passed out and the car veered off, smashing into an eighteen-wheeler which then careened into at least seven other cars. In total, seven people lost their lives that morning. The fifteen-year-old and his friends survived. They had no memory of the event and when they later appeared in court pleaded not guilty because, as their lawyers pointed out, one has to be cognizant of a crime. Bella and Robert's-son were in the first car the semi smashed into, according to the coroner. They were dead even before the crash was over.

Bella's mother came running out of her house. She knew. Maybe it was a guess; Bella was away, the police were there. She feared the worst and when no one rushed forward to reassure her that everything was all right, she stumbled. She tripped on the root of the sycamore tree. She fell and gashed her chin against the rough bark. I helped her up. She put her entire body weight on me and I got her into the store.

"Out!" Robert cried when he saw me. "Get out of my store."

Bella's mother collapsed against the shelf and several cans of soup crashed to the floor. I knelt to pick up the cans, pushing them together into a small pile.

233

Robert went wild on me "Get out! Get out!" I let him have his raving without protesting. "This is my store. I own this place. Get out. Out!"

I left.

The Assembly and several visitors were gathered outside. Everyone had heard the news and they were weeping in sympathy and shock.

Bella and Robert's-son were people I had known all my life.

Robert came to my mother's house the next morning. He brought along several members of the Assembly and an accusation. He threatened her, demanding that she show herself in all her sinfulness. It was quite a show — one I might have enjoyed had it not been directed at my mother.

He pounded on the front door, calling out her name and cursing her for the entire village to hear. "Come out of there, you two-faced bitch. I hope you're ashamed of what you've done. We are finished with all your lies and deceptions."

She came to my room — it faced the front and we looked out the window to see Robert and his entourage, who were taking directions from him.

My mother clucked her tongue. "He's been up all night," she said. "He so loved his son. It wasn't right how he much he loved that boy."

"Are you suggesting something strange was going on?"

"Just that it was the two of them for so many years," she explained. "Robert would never have allowed him to marry. I'm surprised he got away for two days with a woman."

Robert's face was twisted in pain and loss.

My mother and I went downstairs to see why all the commotion. Robert was full of rage, not for the loss of his son, or so he claimed, but because he thought my mother knew something about the accident long before it happened. My mother was astonished but she was someone who has dealt with death every day of her adult life. She listened to his words, trying desperately to make sense of what he meant.

"I didn't," my mother said. "Where would you get that idea?" She was genuinely confused. But Robert couldn't see anything through his own fury, which had knocked all sense from him.

"You knew something bad was going to happen to Robert's-son," he said. "You owed it to me to warn me. You deliberately hid information that would have saved his life."

My mother strained for calmness but his accusations upset her and the tears started to flow.

Robert thought them a sign of guilt and tried to strangle her. We pulled him off. He wasn't strong.

Bella's mother was there. Also hysterical, she was the one who suggested they bar my mother from the Assembly. "That's what I think we should do. Make her leave this place. Get her out of here. Get her out of here."

I think everyone, except those personally affected by the tragedy, understood that the anger was directed at my mother because they needed a scapegoat for their grief. They couldn't bring their children back from the dead, but they could ruin someone's life.

I had forgotten about Adele. She must have spent the night at one of the Bed and Breakfasts. She was still wearing her long blue shorts, her white shirt and her clownish Crocs.

She joined in even though most of the people in the room had no idea who she was. She gave testimony against my mother. "She disappeared my husband," she said. "She did."

I stepped forward and told everyone to leave the house. "Now," I said. "If you're going to accuse my mother of something, do it the right way with the right people. But don't bring a lynch mob into someone's house and accuse her of causing everything that's gone wrong in Lily Dale in the last twenty-four hours."

"It's exactly what we'll do," Robert said. "Do not think you'll get away with this. I will see this crime punished!"

We talked long into the night. My mother cried some but after awhile we stopped talking about how we would set things straight. "I think it's time for us to go?"

235

"You'll leave because of Robert?" I asked. "He doesn't mean it. He'll get over it in a few weeks."

"If that many of my friends came out to accuse me of being dishonest, then it's time to move on."

I did not have her decision-making powers. She was all energy and force. She had decided on something and as far as she was concerned, that was it. We were leaving. Together.

"Besides, I think we're done with this place," she said. "It's very isolated."

"It always has been."

My mother took my face in her hands. She was used to comforting people.

I saw the accident without fear. The dark tire marks on the highway of a spring morning when there was nothing but clear blue sky. I saw the smashed chrome and fenders and the broken glass. I saw Bella and Robert's-son and the blood and broken bits of flesh and bones. I saw the ambulance attendant who had to pull them out of the crushed car by their legs. I turned it off.

"At least they were together," I told her. "At the very last minute, they were together."

They were driving north, back to Lily Dale. They were happy to be with each other. Bella saw where they were — right near Grove City.

"Will you think me stupid if I stop at the outlet mall?"

"You want to go shopping?" Robert's-son had been raised with a strict father. They did not spend money. As his father owned the only decent market in Lily Dale, they got everything from wholesalers. He had learned from his father that shopping was a frivolous activity; people with little intellect liked to shop all day. He was hindered in that respect, someone who had no clue to how the people of the world spent the majority of their days.

"I want to look at the shoe stores," she said, sensing that if he said no, it would be the end of her infatuation with him. She despised that kind of close-minded control.

Shopping for anything except the essentials was impossible in Lily Dale. The boom of the outlet malls across the border in northern Pennsylvania, where clothes were tax free, was her fashion salvation.

"I didn't ask if you wanted to skinny dip in the Allegheny River," she said. "I just want a pair of shoes."

He started to tell her what he thought about shopping but suddenly his usual thoughts went out of his head. "I think I've lived in the Assembly for too long," he said. "I need to get out and see the world. I need to change. Loosen up."

She smiled and reached over to touch his hand.

And then the young driver ended their lives.

My mother planned our preliminary leaving from the Assembly. Later, after the funerals, when things had settled down, we would return and collect our things, sell the house, and go wherever we were going to be.

I saw the woman Adele while I was packing the car.

"It's true," she said. "Your mother scared away my husband. She said things she shouldn't have. He's been tormented about his sister. He always thought it was strange that her heart just gave out like that. But your mother shouldn't have done that. People don't always want to know the truth."

"And some people do," I said. "My mother wasn't trying to be mean. She was just telling him what she thought he would want to know. It's not her fault the sister killed herself."

"But it is her fault that my husband is gone."

The ground was wet from the rains that had come during the night. The air smelled fertile, which seemed contradictory given the problems we were facing.

"Get yourself to a doctor immediately," I said. "Cancer is harsh and horrible but it's not always deadly when detected and treated early."

"Am I sick?"

"You knew that," I said. "You didn't need my mother to tell you that."

She gasped.

I nodded. "Lymph nodes. But if you have to have any cancer, that's the one you want to have. It's curable but you can't just ignore it."

"What about my husband?"

"He won't be any help," I said. "Not when you get sick. He'll find you unattractive when you lose your hair and when you lose all that weight."

I hadn't wanted to make her cry, only to get her to understand the work the mediums do. I didn't realize how upset she was and it was my mother who came forward and steadied her. "There, there," my mother said. "I think that's enough. I think you've had enough of Lily Dale. Why don't you go home? Talk to your husband. See what you both have to say to each other."

We drove out of Lily Dale like thieves sneaking away from the scene of our crime.

"That was quite a show," my mother said.

"She pissed me off," I said.

"You who always preached that that kind of honesty wasn't worth the pain."

"I just told her what she already knew," I said. "What she suspected, at least."

"You seemed pretty sure of yourself," my mother said. The two-lane roads were empty and open. Beside us were the acres of vineyards — mostly owned by the Welch's factory.

"It was you who said something to Robert, wasn't it?" she asked.

I was surprised. "Me? How's that?"

"He thought you got it from me," she said. "But you knew on your own. You were the one who saw that one coming."

"I just told old Robert to watch himself," I said. "I said he shouldn't be so smug when he didn't know what the future held for him."

"You told him something bad was going to happen to him."

"It didn't mean anything. I just wanted him to shut up."

She sucked in her breath, but didn't say anything. When I looked at her, she returned my gaze and nodded.

"Oh no," I said. "It can't be."

"I think it's obvious," she said.

I couldn't speak. Not for several moments.

"Have you always known?' I asked as we went through the New York tollbooth.

"I hadn't a clue," she whispered. "Not until yesterday."

"I don't believe it," I said. "I really can not believe this. How can it be that I'm the last to know?"

"Sometimes it just happens that way." My mother's wisdom never illuminated. This time it didn't have to.

Have you ever looked at the shadow of a spring tree and thought you could see the outline of a face? It's never clear but you think you recognize it? Have you ever turned your head and for a moment recalled a dream or a memory? It's vague and if you had the time you could put it all together. But for the moment it's only random images. You might think about sharing it but like that, it's gone?

The things in this world are not empty of meaning. They continually draw attention to themselves. They tell. They warn.

It's not so odd. There are just some of us who see it so clearly that it's impossible to ignore.

Sharon Dilworth has published two collections of short fiction, *The Long White* and *Women Drinking Benedictine*. Her novel, *The Man on the Street* is forthcoming. Contact: Sd20@andrew.cmu.edu

A DREAM AT THE END OF THE WORLD

—————————————— ℰᑕℛ ——————————————

Excerpt from the novel
by Ben Cheetham

Memories are funny things. You can build walls around them, try to dam them back. But you can't ever really control them. The floodgates can burst open at any moment, and when they do, you, along with everyone you ever loved, cared about or even hated, can be swept away like leaves in a river.

I hadn't been to the house in nearly fourteen years. From a distance it looked the same as I remembered. The window-frames, guttering and drainpipes were sky blue; the front door was post-box red. Just an ordinary terraced house in an anonymous London suburb. It made me tremble to look at it. Amy reached for my hand and gave it a squeeze.

Irritated by my show of weakness, I pulled my hand from hers. "Come on, let's get this over with."

We got out of the car and approached the house. I put my hand out to steady myself as my shoes slipped on the wet weeds sprouting through the path. All around I saw signs of neglect — overgrown grass, grimy windows, flaking paint. The small window at the centre of the front-door was boarded over. Shards of glass had been swept into a corner of the porch. It was stained glass that had depicted a full moon hanging in a starry sky over a forest. As a child I'd been fascinated by the way the sun shining through it projected the image onto my skin like a changeable tattoo. As I opened the door and stepped into the hallway, the smell of decay brought me to an abrupt halt. It wafted up from the foot of the stairs where dad's body had lain for over a month decomposing in the humid summer heat. The stair carpet had been ripped out. Men in plastic suits, I'd been told, had scrubbed the floorboards with disinfectant. But still the smell clung to the place like a curse that nothing could lift. And underneath it other smells lurked, making the one on top even worse. Amongst them I detected rancid cooking fat and the sour ammonia stink of old urine. Gone were the smells of fresh cigarette smoke, aftershave and fry-ups that had filled the house all the years of my childhood.

The place was squalid. Dead flies and mice droppings littered the floor, penetrating damp had reduced much of the wallpaper to black fungal mush and the ceiling was strung with cobwebs. "It looks like something from an old horror movie," said Amy, her voice a mixture of revulsion and pity.

I made a low noise in my throat. Her words were closer to the truth than she realised. "I expected it to be bad, but this . . . How did he ever let things get this bad?"

The lounge door would only open a couple of feet before it jammed against a stack of yellowed and faded newspapers. Apart from the thick talcum of dust and piles of unopened mail, everything was the same as in my childhood. The same battered leather sofa and armchairs that spilled their stuffing. The same photos, pictures and ornaments. The same deep-pile rug I used to love stretching out on. An empty packet of the same brand of cigarettes dad had always smoked lay on the sideboard. I quickly moved to the window and flung it open.

Amy picked up a framed photo of dad stood outside the half-built log cabin, arms crossed, stone-faced as usual. "This has to be your dad. You've got the same nose and eyes as him."

"I took that over twenty years ago."

"Where?"

"A forest in the Scottish Highlands."

"Were you on holiday?"

"Not exactly."

"What then?"

"It's difficult to explain." I puffed my cheeks. "It's going to take forever to sort through all this junk."

A look of annoyance came into Amy's eyes. "Don't try to change the subject, Mitch."

"I'm not."

"Yes you are, just like you do every time I ask about your family."

That wasn't strictly true. During the year and a half we'd been together, I'd told Amy a little about my family — as little as I could get away with. For instance, she knew I was an only child whose mother was killed in a random street attack — stabbed in the back as she walked to work — when I was too young to remember her. She knew my dad was a retired college lecturer. That was about it, though. She'd never met any of my family, and never would now. Dad had been the last of them. My reluctance to speak of my family hadn't caused problems with previous girlfriends, but they'd only been casual flings. Amy was something different. Recently things had been getting serious between us, and the more serious they got, the more my silence became a point of friction. If I wanted to be with her, I knew, sooner or later, I was going to have to open up. "Alright," I said. "But I warn you this is going to sound a bit, well, insane."

"Now you've got me intrigued."

I cleared my throat. "We were in the Highlands building that cabin in preparation for the end of the world."

Clearly uncertain how to react, Amy laughed and frowned at the same instant. "You're kidding, right?"

"I wish I was."

"What exactly do you mean by the end of the world? Are we talking God sending down another Biblical flood or aliens demolishing the planet to make way for an interstellar highway, or what?"

I smiled. "There wouldn't have been much point building the cabin if either of those things were the case. This was the eighties, remember, the era of Cold War paranoia. We're talking somewhere to shack up post-nuclear holocaust."

"That doesn't sound insane. A touch eccentric perhaps."

"Eccentric." The word had a bitter taste that made me want to spit. "People always said dad was an English eccentric. Makes him sound kind of woolly and harmless, doesn't it?" I took Amy's hand. "Come on, I want to show you something." I led her to the basement door. Behind it was another door — a steel one — which I unlocked and opened. Cool, stagnant air flowed out.

She resisted my pull. "What's down there?"

"You'll see."

I drew her down into the bunker. I fired up the petrol-run generator that powered the dim overhead bulb. In stunned silence, she struggled to take in the scene in front of her. Hundreds of newspaper clippings, maps, charts, graphs and diagrams papered the concrete walls. There were rows of metal shelves crammed with tinned and vacuum-packed food, nutritional supplements, jars of preserves, bottled water, gas canisters, crockery, cooking utensils, gas masks and water purification kits. One shelf was given over to books, board games, jigsaws and other non-electrical forms of entertainment. Sealed drums of powdered milk, salt, sugar, soybeans and wheat were stacked floor-to-ceiling against the walls. In the centre of the room was a table with a camping stove and a half-dismantled CB radio on it. There was a set of bunk beds partitioned from the rest of the bunker by a half-drawn curtain. The top bunk — dad's bunk — looked slept-in. A confused heap of clothes occupied the bottom bunk — my bunk. Clothes spilt out of a wardrobe onto the floor. A dozen brown pill bottles cluttered a bedside table. More littered the floor. At the head of the bunk-beds stood a padlocked metal cabinet.

"You really weren't kidding, were you," Amy said.

"We'd ride out the initial attack down here, if we didn't have time to get out of London." I pointed at a map of the city marked with radiating lines and concentric circles coloured different shades of red. "That's where the missiles would strike. We're in a light red zone here."

"Meaning what?"

"Moderate damage to buildings, third degree burns and flash blindness for anyone caught in the open, amongst other things." My voice came with difficulty. It's hard to explain how it made me feel to be in the bunker again after so many years. There was an air of unreality about the place, yet at the same time it was all too real. I watched Amy's eyes search the map for her apartment, then mine, and find them in the darkest red zone. "Dark red means total destruction."

She gave me a wry glance. "Yeah, I guessed that." She approached the shelves and ran her finger over the cracked spines of several books, reading their titles out loud. "The Alpha Strategy, Live off the Land in the City and Country, Life after Doomsday. These sound like interesting reading."

"Oh they are. They contain all sorts of interesting facts. For instance, did you know that missile early warning systems are notoriously unreliable? And that on more than one occasion the world has been brought to the brink of nuclear war by dodgy computer chips, weather missiles, even flocks of geese?"

Amy's brow furrowed. "Not a pleasant thought to take to bed with you."

"Yeah. Well, from the moment I was old enough to speak, dad drummed that shit into my head and I lived with the fear that an attack might come at any time. Can you imagine what that does to a kid? For years I used to have nightmares almost every night."

Amy slid her arms around me and drew my head onto her shoulder. We stayed like that a moment, her stroking my hair and neck. She pointed at the metal cabinet. "What's in there?"

"Personal documents, radiation medicine, guns."

"Guns." Amy frowned again, more deeply. "What did you need guns for?"

"Protecting ourselves against looters and enemy soldiers, hunting, that kind of thing." I felt around under the bottom bunk and found the key lodged in its usual place. I opened the cabinet and lifted out a handgun. "This is a Beretta 92." I proffered it to Amy. She hesitated to take it. "Don't worry, it's not loaded," I assured her.

She took the gun and studied it with a deep, uneasy fascination. "I've never held a gun before. It feels strange."

"You get used to it." I removed a shotgun, an air-rifle and a bolt action hunting-rifle from the cabinet and placed them on the table. Amy blinked as I drew the bolt back on the hunting-rifle to check the chamber. The rifle was clean and well-oiled — dad had always taken good care of his guns.

"Do you know how to use these things?" asked Amy.

"Sure, I used to be a good marksman. I once killed a deer with one shot from three hundred yards."

Amy looked as though she wasn't sure whether to disapprove of that or not. "And what did you do with it?"

"Cooked and ate it, of course."

"Oh, well, I suppose that's all right then." She handed the Beretta back. "That's quite a little arsenal. What are you going to do with them?"

"I don't know."

"You're not thinking of keeping them, are you?"

The thought hadn't occurred to me. Now Amy mentioned it, though, the idea wasn't without logic. After all, the city could be a dangerous place and I owned a lot of nice, expensive things. "Maybe just the Beretta." Such an expression of dismay flashed over Amy's face that I found myself hastening to add, "Although, I suppose, it'd probably be best if I just get rid of them all."

"I think so. Definitely." Amy's gaze travelled the bunker again, lingering on the map of the city. She gave a little shudder. "Let's go back upstairs, Mitch. This place gives me the creeps."

I returned the guns to the cabinet and we climbed the stairs. As I reached out to close the steel door, I felt something I hadn't felt in over sixteen years — a strange, heavy reluctance to leave the safety of the bunker. It wasn't as strong as it'd used to be — there was a time when I used to get panicky whenever I was more than four minutes away from the bunker (four minutes, of course, being the amount of warning we'd supposedly have had if the Soviets launched a surprise attack) — but it was there. I shook it off roughly and dragged the door shut.

We spent the next few hours working our way through the house, noting down what was to be thrown away or sold at auction. As far as I was concerned, I told Amy, nothing was to be kept. "Not even these," she said, when we found a box of photos, mostly of me and dad working on the cabin and the vegetable garden and orchard that surrounded it.

"Especially not those."

There were other things in the box, too — pressed flowers and leaves, fragments of bird eggs, old nests and unusual stones I'd collected from the forest floor as a child. There was also a collection of whittled wooden deer, rabbits, birds and fish. "Who made these?" asked Amy.

"I did. There wasn't much else to do at the cabin of an evening. I could lose myself in my own little world for hours at a time working on those things."

Amy picked out a rabbit and ran her fingers over its smooth-grained surface. "They're really lovely. Are you sure you want to get rid of them?"

I nodded. "Just mark the box for disposal. No, wait. Actually, don't bother, I've a better idea."

I took the box to the lounge, filled the fire-grate with newspaper, overlaid it with the photos and struck a match. Once the fire was burning strongly, I emptied the rest of the box's contents onto it.

"Can I keep this one?" asked Amy, holding up the rabbit. I shook my head. Sighing with reluctance, she tossed it into the flames. We watched in silence as the box of memories went up in smoke. I don't know what, if anything, I expected to feel, but I felt nothing.

When we were finished labelling everything for the house clearers, exhausted, I drove us to my apartment in Central London. As I pulled away from dad's house, almost unconsciously, I found myself watching the clock, silently counting down the minutes. One. . .two. . .three. . . When I reached four, tension cramped my stomach. A couple of bottles of wine later, Amy took my hand and led me to bed. Lying with her head on my arm, she said, "I'm sorry."

"For what?"

"Pressuring you to talk about your dad. I should've realised you had a good reason for keeping quiet."

"There's no need to apologise. I wouldn't have taken you to the house if I didn't want it all to come out."

"Well I just want you to know that if you never want to talk about any of this stuff again that's fine by me. The last thing I want to do is make things harder for you than they must already be."

I let out a sigh. "I'll just be glad when tomorrow's over with."

"Why, what's happening tomorrow?"

"I'm driving up to the cabin to scatter dad's ashes."

"I'd like to come with you, if that's okay."

"Fine with me. But are you sure you want to? The forest isn't exactly your kind of place."

"Of course I'm sure. No one should have to do something like that on their own. And when it's done, hopefully this whole unpleasant business will be behind you once and for all."

"It's already behind me."

Amy shot me an appraising look, as if not entirely convinced. She ran her fingers down my belly. "Perhaps we can find a nice little hotel somewhere, make a few days of it."

"Sounds good." I kissed her hair and murmured, "You know, you're the only person I've ever spoken to about these things."

Amy pressed her head more closely to my shoulder, eyes closed. I watched her face. After a while a faint crease appeared above her nose, her muscles tensed as if she was stiffening against a blow and she made a low moan. I gently shushed her until she relaxed and sank into a deeper, dreamless sleep. I closed my eyes. I knew the dream would come, and it did. As usual, I was stood in the street, air-raid sirens were wailing like lost souls. I started running for home, for the bunker. I could see my house, but it never seemed to get any closer, as though I was running on a treadmill. I began screaming for dad. Suddenly there was a startling white flash and a sound like a giant whip cracking. I was blinded and deafened, but I could feel my flesh being burned away, could smell it. For what seemed a long time, I felt myself tumbling through black space. Then I hit something with enough force to snatch my breath away forever.

Of course, that's when I woke up.

Neither of us said much during the ten-hour drive to the forest. It's hard to make casual conversation when there's a pewter urn full of a dead person's ashes wedged upright on your car's backseat. Amy spent most of the journey reading or dozing. I just drove as fast as possible, which is pretty fast in a Mercedes S600. Every so often, even though the urn's lid was tightly screwed on and sealed with adhesive tape, a faint burnt smell seemed to waft from the backseat. I imagined microscopic particles of ash escaping into the air and surrounding me like radioactive fallout. I imagined breathing in and absorbing them into my lungs, my bloodstream, my being. I opened my window and let cold air rush over me like a protecting shield.

Sometime in the late afternoon, the forest crept up on us. One moment we were driving through open countryside, the next the road was bordered by trees. Sunlight filtered through their leaves, dappling the windscreen with shadows. I turned onto a narrow lane that petered out into a stony path, its edges overgrown with brambles and other creeping plants. Birdsong and the rustle of wind in the treetops drifted through the open window. Somewhere off to my right, I heard the soft gurgle of a stream. Each fresh sight and sound caused more memories to bubble up from corners of my mind I hadn't visited in a long, long time. I pointed to a wooded hilltop a mile or so away. "The cabin's up there."

I picked the urn up hesitantly, as if it might burn my fingers, and we got out of the car and continued on foot. When we came to a wide stream bridged by two tree trunks tied together with mouldy old rope — rope I'd helped dad knot around them — I edged across the bridge testing the wood with my foot to see if it would still bear my weight. It creaked and sagged, but held. Amy followed on her hands and knees. It was the first time I'd seen her out of a city. We'd spent time in Paris, Barcelona, Vienna and New York, eating and drinking, shopping and sightseeing. Cities were her natural environment; outside them she looked a little lost, a little uncertain on her legs.

The path began to rise steadily, snaking its way up the hillside. I stopped to catch my breath, holding my hand over a stabbing stitch in my round bowl of a stomach. "Christ, when did I get so unfit?"

"It's all those long lunches you guys take."

"What long lunches? I've had lunch outside the office maybe ten times in the last year. So it can't be that. The fact is, I simply spend too much time sitting on my arse."

The further we went into the forest, the more densely packed the trees became. Overhead, the canopy was so thick it almost blotted out the sky. Occasional shafts of sunlight illuminated a carpet of mosses, dead branches and rotting leaves. The air was cool and earthy, like a cave.

The path got narrower and more overgrown until only a faint trace of it remained visible. Relieved for the excuse to do so, I handed Amy the urn and snapped a branch off a tree. The sound echoed like a gunshot amongst the gloomy tangle of tree trunks. A flock of rooks rose from the treetops, wheeled around several times cawing furiously, then settled back down. There was silence — deep, watchful silence, as if the forest and all its inhabitants were suddenly alert to our presence. Amy put her hand uneasily on my arm. I stared into the forest. All I could see in every direction was trees.

"I bet it's easy to get lost in here," said Amy.

"Even easier than you might think. I got lost for nearly a day once when I went wandering around here by myself." A shudder ran through me as my mind flashed back to that day. I was fourteen years old. I'd strayed from the path and gone into the forest alone in search of — of what? The secrets of another world, perhaps. Whatever, all I'd found were trees. Just trees and trees, and then more trees. I have only sketchy memories of what happened next. I remember running, not caring that thorns snagged and tore my clothes. I remember yelling myself hoarse for dad. I remember tripping, falling, tumbling over and over, bashing my head against a tree. Finally, I remember lying on the damp ground, my ears buzzing, my vision blurring. After that there's an empty space in my memory until dad found me several hours later, trembling from head to toe, arms clasped around myself. He'd hugged me with relief. But he'd been angry, too, and he'd made me promise over and over until he believed me never to stray out of sight of the path again.

"It's not far now." I began hacking away the undergrowth to expose the path. I went at it hard until a flap of skin peeled back on the palm of my hand. I leant on the branch, breathing heavily, while Amy nipped the flap off with her long, well-manicured nails.

She kissed my hand. "Better?"

"Much, thanks. I used to be able to do this all day without getting blisters."

"Times have changed."

"Yes they have. Thank God."

After another ten or so minutes of hacking, we emerged blinking into a broad, grassy clearing dotted with fruit trees and bushes, their branches heavy with crab apples, pears, damsons, gages, cherries, gooseberries and raspberries. At its centre stood the cabin — or rather, the remains of the cabin. Its roof had collapsed in, leaving only a rectangular structure of unpeeled logs so overgrown with moss and ivy it looked like some kind of weird natural sculpture. On three sides of the clearing a dark wall of vegetation blocked the view, but westwards the ground sloped away steeply. The forest extended in this direction for several miles, ending abruptly at an expanse of purple-flowering moorland. There wasn't a road or building in sight. In the evening sunlight, there was a hazy, dreamlike quality to the place, a sense of somewhere set apart from the everyday world.

Eyes closed, Amy raised her face to the sky, inhaled deeply and purred, "Mmm, just feel that sun."

Dozens of tiny birds fled the fruit trees as I approached the cabin and trod down the grass to reveal a rough stone hearth. The old memories pushed their way to the surface of my consciousness again. Memories of curling up beside the hearth in my sleeping bag, dad on the opposite side of it, both of us staring fixedly out the window at the night sky, as if watching for a sign of the coming of doomsday. Memories, too, of being lulled to sleep by his low, peaceful snoring. This was the only place either of us had slept soundly.

A breeze blew in from the exposed side of the clearing. Standing with my back to it, I unscrewed the urn's lid.

"Shouldn't you say something?" Amy suggested.

"Like what?"

"I don't know, some kind of goodbye. After all, no matter how you feel about him, he was still your dad."

I thought for a moment, but there was nothing I wanted to say — leastways, nothing I wanted to say in front of Amy — except, "Goodbye, dad." I emptied the floury white ash into the air, leaning

251

back so as not to get any of it on me. Most of it dusted the grass and the walls of the cabin, some of it was carried away, like a trail of smoke, by the breeze to the trees. I put down the urn, walked to the western edge of the clearing and sat down. Not for the first time, I found myself wondering if dad had died quickly or if he'd suffered. The cause of death was a subdural haemorrhage — whatever that means — resulting from a fractured skull. The coroner said that in such cases death was probably instantaneous, but was sometimes delayed for minutes, even hours. It often depended on how strong a person's will to survive was. In that case, he would've suffered for hours, at least. I thought about him lying undiscovered until swarming flies and the stench of decomposition alerted the postman. Amy put her arm around me. She said nothing. She seemed to know instinctively when to speak and when to keep quiet.

After a while, I looked at her face. Her cheeks were flushed, her lips slightly parted. I looked at her fine, straight brown hair. She wasn't beautiful, but she had a nice open face. She had a nice body, too, curvy, built to last. I felt the tension drain out of me as my gaze moved over her and, suddenly, I found myself thinking, I could spend my life with her, have children, grow old. I'd never thought such a thing before and it both excited and disturbed me.

I began kissing her. I kissed her gently all over her face and neck. I took her lower lip between mine and sucked it. She pushed me onto my back, unbuttoned my jeans and pulled them down to my knees. As we made love, the glare of the sun behind her head brought tears to my eyes. She dropped forward onto my chest and lay there, warm and heavy, breathing as rhythmically as a sedated animal. I held her to me, thinking of nothing, completely relaxed for the first time in as long as I could remember. It was as though, for a brief moment at least, she'd drawn all the bad memories out of me and absorbed them somewhere deep inside her.

Amy said something then that took me completely by surprise. "So do you think you could ever live somewhere like this?" She must have seen the look of startled bemusement on my face, because she added quickly, "Not right away, obviously, but one day."

"Do you?"

"Maybe."

"But you're strictly a city girl, Amy. What would you do in a place like this?"

"I don't know, how about raise a family. This wouldn't be such a bad place to bring kids up, would it?"

"That depends."

"On what?"

I didn't want to think about that. Not with the breeze still stirring up puffs of ash. Amy laid her head on my chest again. We watched the sun dip towards the horizon, its last rays glinting on the sea of treetops. "We'd better get back to the car," I said, lifting her off me.

"You didn't answer my question."

"Give me a little time to think, then I'll give you an answer."

"Take all the time you want."

Twilight fell as we hurried hand-in-hand along the path. My legs felt heavy and rubbery, most likely from the unfamiliar exercise, but it seemed to me as if some invisible force was reluctant for me to leave. My feet dragged, stumbling over stones and roots. A crushing pressure built across my chest like the onset of a coronary. It was the same way I'd felt upon leaving the bunker. The same, only much, much stronger.

Amy looked at me with concern. "You really need to start eating right and getting some exercise, Mitch."

I nodded, too winded to reply. This time both of us crossed the bridge on all fours. It was almost fully dark by the time we reached the car. I collapsed into the driver's seat.

"Maybe I should drive," suggested Amy.

"I'll be fine, I just need a moment."

I closed my eyes. In my mind, I saw missiles falling on London like burning stars, blast waves spreading concentrically from each explosion's core, vaporising everything in their path.

Amy reached across me and shut the door. At the sound of it closing, I snapped out of my daydream. A sudden overwhelming urge to get away from that place gripped me. Shoving the car into gear, I turned it around and accelerated fast along the lane. The car bounced around, branches scraping its sides as if trying to snag hold of something. "Slow down, will you?" said Amy, bracing herself against the dashboard. I ignored her. The closer we got to the forest's outskirts, the more the pressure in my chest faded off. "Slow down," she repeated, angry now. "What the hell's the matter with you?"

I eased off the accelerator. "Sorry, I just needed to put some distance between myself and that place."

"Well, I'll take that as an answer to my question then, shall I?"

Again I made no reply.

After we'd gone a short distance further, Amy turned to me with a start. "Hey, it just occurred to me, you forgot to pick up the urn."

"No I didn't," I said.

"Yes you —" Amy began to argue, then, catching my meaning, she fell silent.

We passed plenty of nice little country hotels, but I didn't stop until we reached Edinburgh. I booked us into an expensive hotel with panoramic views of the city and we ate in an equally expensive restaurant on the Royal Mile. After that we hopped from bar to bar, drinking wine and champagne, slow-dancing. And after that we returned to the hotel and made love again. Then Amy fell asleep and I stood by the window of the darkened room, staring at the streets — cluttered, narrow streets built over hundreds of years, crisscrossing in every direction, as confused as the thoughts whirling in my head.

After so many years, I hadn't expected the forest to affect me so strongly. The intoxicating sense of safety I'd felt there had got me drunker than any alcohol could. Mingled with it was an equally strong sense of unease and shame. Unease at what I couldn't, rather than what I could, remember. The lost hours, as I called them. It's impossible to say how many times I've scoured the recesses of my mind, vainly trying to recall what happened during those hours. The only thing I was certain of was that something happened. And shame at the thought of giving in to the fear dad injected into my heart.

I've spent most of my adult life trying to blot out that fear. I remember the exact moment I promised myself I wouldn't end up like dad. It was Christmas Day 1991, I'd just turned sixteen, the

Berlin Wall was gone, torn down brick by brick, now Gorbachev was following it into history. As we watched live television pictures of the Soviet flag being lowered from the Kremlin so that the flag of the Russian Federation could be raised in its place, a massive sense of relief surged through me and I said, "That's it, it's over."

Dad shook his head. "That's just the end of the beginning."

Part of me — the part that wanted to run away from life and hide in the forest — was drawn to his words. Another part of me — the part crying out for a normal teenage existence — was utterly repulsed by them.

Dad was sat scrunched forward in his armchair, a blanket wrapped around his narrow shoulders. His eyes were moist and sunken, and there was a feverish flush over his cheekbones. All year we'd been travelling up to the forest every weekend to work on the cabin, tend the fruit trees and vegetable patch, and lay a pipe to draw water from the stream to a tank nearer the clearing. The physical labour had taken its toll on him. He'd lost a lot of weight and what'd started in the damp autumn months as a hacking cough had, because of his refusal to rest, developed into lung-ravaging pleurisy. He'd ended up in hospital for two months. Just two months, but it was long enough to give me a taste of what my life might've been like if not for him. I'd gone out with friends, got drunk, overslept, skipped school. Christ knows how, but I'd even managed to get myself a girlfriend. By the time dad got out of hospital, the son who'd looked up to him with unquestioning reverence was gone. And now, faced with his refusal to accept even the possibility that the Cold War was over, I saw him for the first time for what he really was — a paranoid outsider who'd fritter his life away in the forest, and mine, too, if I allowed it.

That's when I decided that I was going to spend my life striving to be everything he wasn't. I was going to get a job in The City, climb the corporate ladder, buy a Porsche, have a string of girlfriends. Then, when I'd done the work-hard, play-hard thing, I was going to exchange the Porsche for a Volvo, marry a nice girl, have a few kids. In short, I was going to be a fully paid up member of society. Most importantly of all, I was never going to look back.

I didn't say anything to dad right then for fear it might make him even more ill. A month later, though, when he was well enough to start planning our first trip of the year to the forest, I said, "I'm not going."

Dad's brow furrowed. "Why not?"

"There's no need anymore."

He was taken aback. If he hadn't been so caught up in his delusions, he might've noticed that since Christmas I'd shown no interest in politics or the forest or any of his survivalist nonsense. "How can you be so naïve, Mitch?" He tapped his temple. "I thought I'd taught you to use this, to see the truth behind the things that appear to be true. The Soviets might be down, but they're not out. Soon the red flag will be flying over Moscow again, mark my words. And even if it's not, then the end of one cold war will just lead to the beginning of another. Look, it's already starting." He shoved a newspaper in my face. "Senior Chinese leaders have been quoted in pro-Peking newspapers in Hong Kong as saying that a new cold war between China and the West is in the making."

"I'm not interested."

"What do you mean you're not interested? This is your future we're talking about."

"Not anymore. From now on I don't want anything to do with the bunker, the forest or any of that stuff."

Dad looked at me pityingly, as if he was a priest listening to one of his flock confide in him about their loss of faith. "Well, of course, Mitch, you're free to make that choice." He was big on freedom of choice. Freedom of choice in the West, he believed, was an illusion. You only had to look at the ever increasing gulf between the haves and have-nots to see that. He might've been right, but what freedom of choice had he given me? He'd pointed his telescope into the future, forced me to look through it, and said: within our lifetime the world as we know it will be blown to pieces. My life had been built on that prophecy. I was so stuffed full of fear that at fifteen I used to be sick every morning before leaving the house. Well, no more. No more, no more, no more.

"And I've made it." My voice was set hard. I could be as stubborn as dad once I'd made my mind up about something, and he knew it.

"That's it then. There's nothing else to say." He turned away from me and continued making his list of provisions, building materials and tools needed for his trip to the forest.

That was pretty much the end of our relationship. Over the next couple of years we rarely saw each other and only spoke when necessary. I cooked my own meals, did my own laundry, went out and came home whenever I felt like it. I never brought anyone back to the house, though. Not once. This arrangement suited me, but even so, I couldn't help but feel bitter about the way dad was treating me. My whole life we'd spent every free moment together, talking, planning, working towards a common goal. Now that we no longer shared that goal, he'd simply lost interest in me. As though all I'd been to him was a pair of hands to dig, sow seeds, weed, fetch water, spread compost, chop down trees, saw up logs, hammer in nails, and all the rest of it. As though it mattered nothing to him, when set against his beliefs, his obsessions, that I was his son.

Freedom of choice was an illusion alright.

My 'loss of faith' was the end of dad's ambitions for building his own little utopia in the forest, too. He just didn't have the strength to do it alone. Not that that stopped him from trying. Week after week he travelled up there, each time returning a little thinner, a little frailer. It was obvious he was going to end up in hospital again. In February 1992, his pleurisy returned worse than ever. When I visited him in hospital, he was hooked up to an oxygen tank, barely able to move. His face was grey-blue and shrivelled, like something dug out of damp ground.

"You've got to stop this right now, dad, or it's going to kill you," I said matter-of-factly. He tried to speak, but all that came out was a hoarse, strangled sound. "Do you know what they said on the news today? The government's dismantling the four-minute warning system. They say the chances of us being attacked by air are so small it's not needed anymore."

Dad slowly shook his head and, with an effort that made an ooze of spittle muddied with blood dribble from the corners of his lips, he managed to utter two words. "Double-glazing."

I was bewildered and irritated. "What are you talking about? What's double-glazing got to do with anything?" Dad's lips parted again, but he couldn't force any more words out. He began coughing so hard that a nurse came over and turned up his oxygen. I took his hand. "Save your breath, dad. Let's face it, nothing either of us says will change the other's mind."

I stayed with him all night. Listening to the muffled moans from neighbouring rooms and wards, the thought occurred to me: double-glazing blocks out noise. So that's what he'd meant. They weren't getting rid of the four minute warning system because it was less likely the Russians would attack, but because double-glazed windows — which were being installed everywhere at that time — made it too hard to hear the sirens. That, as far as he was concerned, was the truth behind the thing that appeared to be true.

I almost laughed. Almost.

That was the last time I tried to convert dad to my way of thinking. A year later I left home to study business at university. I never returned to the house from that day until the week he died. In all the intervening years I only saw him three times. Once when he turned up uninvited at my graduation. Once at my Aunt May's funeral. And once when I chanced to bump into him laying flowers at mum's grave on the anniversary of her death. On that final occasion he was barely recognisable as the man who used to effortlessly carry me up the hill to the cabin on his back. His thinning grey hair was long and bedraggled, and he had a thick beard, stained yellow with tobacco at the edges of his mouth. His cheeks and eyes were so deeply sunken they gave his face a skull-like appearance. He looked like the kind of lonely old man you see wandering the streets, talking to themselves.

He acknowledged me with a nod and we stood across the grave from each other, staring at the headstone. He breathed in short pants, shoulders trembling with each in-breath, like a miner suffering from black lung. We stood in silence for maybe five minutes. Then he shuffled off. I remember thinking to myself, he'll be lucky if he lives to see the end of the year. Six months later I got the phone call to say he was dead.

I wanted to wake Amy and tell her this. I wanted to spill it all out, spill it into her ears until there was nothing left in me. She would take it from me gladly, I knew. But she looked so peaceful I couldn't bring myself to do it to her. I rested my forehead against the glass. The sounds of car engines floated up from the streets, faint as the murmur of a distant river.

"Fucking double-glazing," I muttered.

Ben Cheetham's stories have won awards and been shortlisted for several competitions, including The Scott Prize, run by Salt Publishing. He's also been nominated for a Pushcart Prize. His short fiction has been published in *The London Magazine, The Willesden Herald New Short Stories 3, The Grist Anthology of New Writing, Dream Catcher, Staple* and numerous other magazines and anthologies.

'*A Dream at the End of the World*' is an excerpt from his novel of the same title, for which he's currently seeking representation. The novel touches on themes including the corrupting power of money, grief, love, infidelity, murder, schizophrenia and end-of-the-world paranoia. It seeks to hold a mirror up to the modern world — its greed, paranoia and consequent loss of innocence. Ben Cheetham lives in Sheffield, UK. Contact: benjamin.cheetham@btinternet.com

BOISTEROUS DEVOTION

—————————— ℰℭ ——————————

Excerpt from the novel
by D.E. Tingle

Years after the fact, I still marvel at how rich I was then in the things
that were important to me but had no price. I was young — in my
early thirties, blessed with a job that paid me to ask questions I'd
have been glad to ask for free, and surrounded by women who
appeared to gain precisely the same benefits from me that I gained
from them. Life promised to go on forever. I'd been on earth as long as
I could remember, and I'd be on earth indefinitely longer, enjoying its
scrumptious fruits. I could even make a case for a kind of constructive
immortality that didn't depend on having a soul separable from the
body that housed it and provided all of its input, maintenance and
capacity for expression. I reflected that I had come into the world with
no history and no memory, and that I'd someday go out of it with no
future and no repercussions. The time between was all I had and all
I'd ever know. My entire experience would be the experience of life;
I'd no more remember the trauma of my death than I had anticipated
the trauma of my birth. That's as good as what most people mean by
immortality, and far less tiring. Or so I supposed.

In Ingrid's absence I found myself dabbling in this and similar
metaphysics. Like all metaphysics, it was silly stuff but selectively
reassuring, and it conferred a powerful sanction in favor of yet more
womanizing: see, *e.g.*, the metaphysical poet Marvell on sporting

us while we may. Susan Gold and Aurelia were good continuity, but not devoted enough to fill all of the time vacated by Ingrid. I took to socializing once again with Daphne Spencer-Underhill, a co-worker and former first-echelon lover of mine. Daffy and I had had a sexually torrid but affectively placid affair a year earlier that had lasted for several months, then tapered off as her fascination with me — not entirely explicable in the first place — began to wane. Daffy was drawn to men of power and wealth, neither of which I had. Her favorite situation was as the mistress of a man capable of flying her to assignations in five-star hotels in Paris or Rome. She was a woman of no conventional beauty at all, but glamorous beyond easy description. She dressed with flawless taste in all the proper labels, was extremely intelligent and well read in English and French, spoke in a voice that seemed confected from silver chimes, and packed a wit that could amputate limbs. At the piping peak of our sexual relationship, although her body looked like nothing better than a knackwurst fitted with the human parts required for foreplay and intercourse, she could seduce me with a smile and drain me like a succubus.

In this second, post-Ingrid round of our relationship, sex was infrequent but, if it happened, as spectacular as before. To stand any chance at all of making my way into bed with Daffy — or to inveigle her against a convenient wall, over a piece of furniture or to the floor of an intentionally-stalled elevator — I had to be careful not to remind her of my relatively low estate in the world. If I could manage to be funny without being modest, or ardent without seeming desperate, Daffy could be had. I never ceased to try.

Even without sex, moving in Daffy's company was worth the attendant trouble. Those friends who were not her lovers were nearly all gay men. She liked their subversive propensities and their inclination to read Marcel Proust. I felt the same way, and furthermore they flattered me with attentions that required no strenuous activity on my part. They required only that I be decorative and amiable, and provide a rationale for their continuing invasion of Daffy's privacy. After brunch one Sunday, her parting guest Anthony pecked her on the cheek and offered me some flaccid fingers, put on a tragic moue and said, "What a sad world, where you kiss the women and shake hands with the men." Such fun!

Except for an occasional round of slumming with mediums, tarot readers and the *I Ching* — and these things happened only when she was emotionally stressed by a transition among lovers — Daffy was as skeptical, impatient with hype and scornful of credulity as anyone I ever knew, man or woman. She was a mathematician by profession, and unwilling to accept an answer she didn't see supported. My favorite words to hear in her silvery voice, even if they were directed at me, were an exasperated, "Oh, please."

These women — Susan G, Aurelia and Underhill — two kinds of gold and perhaps a mine, accounted for my available time in the first few months after Ingrid went home to Sweden, although writing letters to her was another of my preferred activities. One Saturday afternoon Susan G and I were making our way to a New York-style deli she favored when we met Eric Patz on the street. I introduced la Gold, who was looking succulent as usual. Eric gave her an appraising glance, behind which almost anything might have been going on, and asked after Ingrid.

"We write," I said. "She's doing medicine in Stockholm. She asked about you, too. I'll tell her you said hi."

"Thank you," Eric said. "She's a beautiful woman."

"How're you doing?" My last previous news of Eric was that he had quit his job and entered seminary.

"I'm doing well," he said, and I seem to remember that he assigned to God the credit for his success. "I've discovered I have the calling to preach."

No revelation of Eric's ever truly surprised me, but this one was notable. The only time I'd seen him in front of a group of people — at the antiwar meeting where Ingrid had introduced us — he'd looked petrified, and on that occasion he was only trying to make a short statement. In close company he was given to introspection and long silences. The notion of Eric making a career of public speaking seemed preposterous, but I recognized that I might have seen him that first time on a bad day; and of course it's possible to be shy and insecure in company, but commanding before an audience. Some actors, reassured by pseudonymity and a script, are said to be like that. Eric was unknowable enough that anything seemed possible. "The calling to preach!" I said. "Are you going to do it?"

"Certainly," he said. "No one hearing a vocation from God could think of turning it down."

"I suppose not," I said, imagining how I'd respond if the sky opened and a Voice addressed me. "When do you start?"

"I've already begun," he said. "In a homiletics class, and once before a congregation."

"Wow!" I said. "Sounds daunting."

"No," he said. "Not daunting. When you're called, God gives you the means."

"Can I hear you sometime?" I was fascinated.

"Of course," he said. "Nothing could gratify me more. I expect to preach a couple of times this summer. I'll invite you."

"Wonderful!" I said. "I look forward to it. You still have my number?"

"Yes," he said.

We shook hands. He smiled tentatively, gave a quick nod of his head, which must have been an abbreviated bow in the direction of la Gold, and turned away. Susan and I walked on. "What was that about?" she wanted to know.

"You have nearly as much information as I do. A friend. More like a friend of a friend. Pretends to be cultivating a close working relationship with God."

"Which one?"

"The invasive, New Testament one."

"Oh," she said. Then she added, "Pretty fine-looking guy."

"Yeah," I said. "Interested? Feeling ripe for conversion?"

"Always feeling ripe." She was kind enough to grab my ass, which prompted me to stop, back her up against a parking meter and kiss her out of sympathy and gratitude. "Carry on," she said.

The thought of Eric's preaching beguiled me for a couple of days. I didn't foresee such an occasion as an aesthetic triumph, but I was determined to attend anyway, recalling Samuel Johnson's take on the horse that played a trumpet: not good, but impressive nonetheless.

I included the news in my next letter to Ingrid, largely without comment. I couldn't think of anything to say that wasn't snide, and Ingrid's radical kindness shamed me. She must have heard my skepticism anyway, because she wrote back something to the effect that Eric might do well, that his passion was authentic, and where his faith was concerned he seemed fearless. Her remarks gave me hope that I wouldn't see Eric embarrassed.

Several weeks passed before he phoned to announce the date and place of his sermon, a Sunday in June, at the same church, as I later learned, where he had once dragged Ingrid for what he hoped would be her religious edification. On the day, I left Aurelia airbrushed and asleep, put on a suit and proceeded to the Church of the Redeemer, taking in sights, sounds and smells that to me were quite exotic. The place was full of white flowers, green bunting and a low order of organ music, heavy on pedal and sparse on counterpoint. The church building was of recent vintage and didn't appear to have much money behind it. There were stained-glass windows featuring the usual Biblical cast, but the colors were plain and poor. I sat not far from the back, hoping to spare Eric from eye contact should my worst fears be realized. I spotted him sitting in a chair behind the pulpit, dressed in black robes, just like a real cleric, while fifteen or twenty minutes passed in invocations, prayers, hymn-singing (to which I didn't contribute) and the passing of the collection plate (to which I did). He looked calm, centered (as some of my friends had grown fond of saying) and ready to go. I believed he stood a chance.

When he stepped into the pulpit, my confidence increased. He moved with utter assurance, met every eye in the house, mine included, and began speaking in a voice of quiet, firm insistence. I sat back, prepared to enjoy myself. I ended by being amazed, and more entertained than I'd been at any public lecture in years. What he delivered was a jeremiad of astonishing complexity, fluency and auditory dynamics. In the process he decried virtually every phase of human sexuality of which I had personal knowledge. He wrenched Biblical passages from their context, which was the cultural mores of tribes that flourished in the deserts of Asia Minor thousands of years ago, and shaped them into rhetorical tools to rip the hearts, lungs and guts out of the audience he was holding in his thrall. He quoted Scripture that prescribed the death penalty for adulterers, and the stoning (also to death) of both partners in any adventure leading to the deflowering of a virgin by someone other than her betrothed, and recommending prophylactic self-mutilation to anyone at risk of sexual temptation through any of the senses.

This last was Jesus according to St. Matthew — the thing about plucking out the right eye. My own experience suggested that a scrupulous Christian so advised would have to sacrifice every organ of the body if he hoped to feel secure: in my time I'd been seduced by every imaginable combination of sights, sounds, smells, tastes and touches, not to mention the unprovoked activity of many glands, both ductless and otherwise. The Old Testament injunction to stone to death hapless virgin prospective brides and their seducers specified that the punishment should occur outside the city walls — a fine point perhaps having to do with the relative availability of loose rocks. If any of what Eric said had made the least practical sense beyond that poor standard, he might have terrified me. As it was, I almost wished I could sing along. His music was far more intricate than the organist's.

Eric's performance lasted nearly half an hour. By the end of it, many in the congregation showed signs of having taken the message seriously. Some were weeping, some appeared to be praying silently for their lives. It was a show unlike anything I'd seen. I couldn't wait to meet Eric and clap him on the back.

The organ poured forth the recessional, up-tempo but dour, and I flashed a thumbs-up at Eric as he marched past me in the aisle on his way to the church door. When the congregation began standing to leave, I dodged into the aisle and got to Eric near the front of the line. "Brilliant! Great! I loved it!" I told him. He smiled a little ruefully, I thought, and asked if I was alone. I was. He said he was sorry, although he didn't say why, and invited me to stay for lunch in the church basement. Of course I accepted. I was eager to talk with him about his sermon, and anyway it was time to eat. I moved onto the church lawn to make way for others leaving.

I watched the succession of parishioners congratulating Eric. After a couple of minutes I saw him point me out to one of them, a small, trim blonde woman in a green jacket, matching skirt and brown heels, with a green pillbox hat on her head. The woman descended the steps and walked toward me with her hand extended. "Are you Mr. Bartley?" she asked. "Eric says you're a friend of his."

"Rob Bartley," I corrected her. "Yes, we're friends. Who are you?" I took her very small hand and shook it.

"I'm Vera Reed," she said. "Eric is a friend of the family. My husband is one of his teachers at seminary."

"My congratulations to whoever taught him to preach," I said. "Eric's a phenomenon."

"He has the calling," she said. I looked her over. She was quite attractive, if bony, not more than five feet tall, and probably ten years older than Eric or I. Her eyes were greenish-grey, with something I can only describe as a questing look. There was no diffidence in her gaze. She stared straight at me, as if on a scavenger hunt of some urgency. Had I been more perturbable, she might have made me nervous.

"Who taught him to preach? Not your husband?"

"No, no," she said, and named a different professor. "But he brought the gift with him. He didn't need to be taught much."

"Interesting," I said.

"Have you known him long?"

"A little over a year, I guess. And not terribly well. We had a friend in common. But Eric's an interesting character. I wanted to keep track of him."

"He's more than interesting," she said. "He's important." I waited for her to elaborate, but she said no more, only turning her body half around to watch Eric greeting his congregants. After several seconds, she turned back to me. "Eric says we'll be having lunch together."

"Oh, good!" I said. "I'm glad you're invited. Maybe you can help interpret him to me."

"What do you mean?" The grey eyes were still probing.

"I wish I knew," I said. "He's a study. As a woman and a family friend, maybe you have the insight that provides the key."

"'As a woman.'"

"Sure. Women know how to evaluate the stuff that men don't know how to measure. It's not an invariable rule, but it gives me hope for lunch. Will your husband be joining us?"

"He's out of town, I'm afraid."

"Then we'll have to do without his input."

She nodded.

"So you'll have known Eric for just a few months. Or did you know him before he started seminary?"

"No. We met him last fall."

"You talk about him with a certain solemnity. Is that a clue?"

She laughed. "I suppose it is," she said.

"Here he comes." Eric had seen off the last of his flock, and he must have ducked inside the church door to doff his vestments, because he now approached us in a coat and tie. "Maybe solemnity's in order," I said. "He makes a powerful impression."

She smiled and turned to look at Eric. "I think he's beautiful," she said.

"I don't deny it," I said.

Eric arrived looking feverish. "You've met, then?" he asked superfluously.

"We have," I replied. "And are ready to break bread." Looking no less feverish, Eric escorted us to the scene of the repast, an air-conditioned, low-ceilinged room below ground, with a buffet along one wall and two long, covered tables with folding chairs for the diners, some of whom were eating already. Evidently the saying of the blessing was being left to individuals and their affinity groups.

We filled our plates at the buffet with hearty stuff: hamburger sandwiches, baked beans, two or three kinds of potato salad. I was entirely satisfied with the selection. Eric steered us to available space at one of the tables; we sat, and Eric said the blessing. It's not easy in retrospect to imagine why, but I harbored the notion that a lively conversation might ensue about the substance and merits of Eric's sermon. I had some ideas of my own that would no doubt have placed me in a minority, but I thought they were worth airing. I didn't suppose I'd be very effective with Eric's flock as an evangelist for humane womanizing, but I thought there might at least be room for a humanist counterpoint to his screed in defense of chastity-no-matter-what. Consequently I was disappointed when the conversation devolved into a farrago of commonplaces about the weather, sports teams and baby care. The only idea in the room to engage my attention was the idea of eating, so I resorted mostly to that.

As the titular host, Eric was gracious in the midst of so much mind-numbing triviality. Although I had yet to deduce how he ordered matters in his brain, I had to suppose he was ineffably bored. Vera Reed was quiet and may have been bored as well, but she was animated enough to divide her attention equally between Eric and me, a detail that was easy to ascertain, because her grey eyes fixed on us in turn with the same intensity I'd seen on the church lawn. In the absence of anything better to think about, I considered her potential as a sex partner. She was substantially older than I, married and a conservatively turned out churchgoer, so the auguries were unpromising, to say the least. On the other hand, I knew from observation and experience that she was equipped with the same necessaries for lovemaking as, for example, Daphne Spencer-Underhill, and on a body that evidently could not in fairness be likened to a knackwurst. The more I examined her green suit and her blond hair, the less I hewed to my original judgment of boniness, and the more I thought of her as fit, petite and probably capable of clinging to my body like a crazed vervet. I even considered inviting her home with me. Such are the vagaries of the under-stimulated mind.

If I hadn't been fairly certain that Aurelia was by that time up and gone from my apartment, my native devotion to sex might have driven me out of the church basement without further delay, and back to her airbrushed beauty, perfect though familiar. Instead I had to soothe myself with a third helping of potato salad and a speculative inventory of Vera Reed's secret treasures.

Half an hour into the spread, guests with a smaller capacity than mine began to excuse themselves and clear the hall. With the inconsequential nattering thus reduced, I tried again to engage Eric. "You are some preacher," I said. True to a propensity I was to notice in him throughout the years of our infrequent meetings, he shuffled all praise (and logically, although he'd have denied it, all blame) to the shoulders of his deity. God made him do it. "But while you were up there," I went on, "I was thinking: how's he going to sell this, really? Everybody in this room comes from sex. Maybe they won't say it in church, but they know it. And they want and value it. And here's old Eric, trying to discourage every natural impulse, or at least putting such strictures on their exercise that sedation looks preferable."

"Well," he said. "Don't you think that responsible, moral people should regulate their impulses?"

"Sure," I said, "but they should regulate them with reference to their potential harm to themselves and to other people."

"I think that's what I was preaching," he said.

"Yeah, but you were taking on a tiny fraction of sexuality and ignoring the vast majority of human experience with it. I've almost never seen sex do harm. Maybe I'm just lucky, but I keep seeing it doing nothing but good. It makes people happy. Women look better after sex. It's good for skin tone."

Eric was a little ruddy at the temples, but composed. I had no wish to make him uncomfortable, and I admired his sermon as cultural curiosity and *tour de force*, but it seemed to me that some of its implications needed answering. He glanced sidelong at Vera Reed, who was still dividing her attention between us; and because it was Eric's turn to speak, her eyes were on him. It occurred to me to wonder about the nature of their relationship. She seemed to hang upon his words as if they carried more freight than I could find in them, but the subject was sex, about which Eric perhaps knew nothing at all. I had to assume that her attitude toward him was that of a mother surrogate delighted by his precocity and confident of his preferment. Really, no other bond seemed plausible. Evidently the time would never come when she'd be obligated to tell Eric about the birds and the bees, since he appeared determined to have no use for such information.

"It hardly seems likely that God gave us our sexuality for its cosmetic benefits," Eric protested. "Surely something so powerful, in combination with the free will that He also gave us, is meant as a test of our fidelity to Him and a means of establishing a Godly, Christian bond between man and wife. Any other use must be a perversion."

"Then perverts reign," I said. "Consider masturbation, and ask yourself how many adherents it boasts compared with Christian marriage."

"I have no idea," he said, "but I know which cohort God approves."

"That's quite a claim."

"It is written."

"In a book that also describes the earth as flat."

"What passage is that?"

"Help me," I said. "Something about four angels standing at the corners of the world."

"Yes," he said, unperturbed. "In Revelation. 'I saw four angels standing at the four corners of the earth, holding back the four winds of the earth, that no wind might blow on earth or sea or against any tree.'"

"Somewhere else it says that the four winds are north, south, east and west. So the description is of a sort of rectangular slab with its corners pointing in the cardinal directions of the compass. If that's the earth, then maybe the pattern laid out for human nature also needs work."

"The Bible doesn't need work," Eric said.

"And the earth is flat."

"If that's what it says, yes."

Good old Eric.

"Okay," I said. "You're a hard guy not to like."

In the two days that followed I surprised myself and was surprised. My séance with the Christians kept recurring to me as an interlude out of time, quite unrelatable to my usual pursuits. During the valedictories in the church parking lot, I had acquired the name of Vera Reed's husband, and the fact that he was away from home on an extended walking tour, perhaps for the whole summer. Vera took Eric into her Oldsmobile and drove him home to his apartment; I hoisted my weight between windscreen and rollover bar and vaulted into the driver's seat of the Elva. The weather was fine, and with no roof over my head I was at large in the world, reflecting on Vera and her peculiar circumstance: left alone at home in her early forties by a husband who had gone for a walk. Her personality interested me too. She was quiet, but her manner was assertive, as if she were making claims on one's attention without specifying a topic. Primarily it was the eyes.

Some twenty-eight hours after I had shaken her hand and said goodbye, presumably indefinitely or forever, I found her husband's name in the phone book and called her number, though not without trepidation. I was generally bold in my approach to women, reckoning that nothing is accomplished without enterprise, and crediting each woman with the capacity to deflect me where I wasn't welcome. Even so, the idea of paying court to the wife, ten years my senior, of some sort of academic divine, daunted me a little. I dialed anyway. She answered, and I noticed again that small frisson that goes with hearing for the first time in the receiver the voice of a new woman.

"Hi," I said. "This is Rob Bartley. We met after Eric Patz's sermon."

There was a pause. "Rob Bartley," she said, and there was another pause. "Hello."

"I enjoyed the day and I enjoyed meeting you. I know your husband is out of town, but I hoped I could invite you out of your house for coffee or a drink. I apologize. I know this may seem irregular to you."

"Have you spoken to Eric since yesterday?" she asked.

"No, I haven't." I waited for her to say something that might reveal the basis of her question, but nothing followed. "I see him pretty infrequently," I said.

"I see."

There was another silence. In the period between the meeting of a man and a woman and the time they become lovers, silence is to be avoided. After they become lovers, silence can be a tribute. It was plain that I'd have to create some sound quickly, before my gesture with Vera became too awkward to succeed. "Do we both understand the nature of this conversation we're having? I'm trying to arrange to meet you again. I enjoyed it very much the first time."

I heard her laugh. "I get it," she said.

"Great!" I said. "And what's the answer likely to be?"

"It's likely to be yes, okay. But I don't know what the purpose is."

"I don't know either, but I'd look forward to your company."

"Well then, yes, okay."

"Wonderful! Unless you're busy, I'll come and get you now."

"It's six p.m."

"Perfect. I'll buy you dinner."

I fully expected some objection, but none came. The slight impression I'd taken away from church of Vera as less conventional than she looked was now reinforced. She might have offered a pro forma demur, which she could have withdrawn as soon as I insisted, but she didn't even do that. As I came to find out, she was impatient with every kind of ambiguity and indirection.

Her house was about what I expected: modest, two stories, on a suburban street. There was a room air conditioner in one of the windows on the front of the house, and when Vera opened the door and invited me into the vestibule, I could tell that a pipe smoker inhabited the place. Vera was wearing a print dress and flat shoes — a non-ecclesial version of the outfit I'd seen her in before. She picked up a purse from the hall table and led me onto the front porch, turning to lock the door behind us. I surveyed the environs. The neighborhood was too old to exhibit the sprawl seen farther out of the city center, but there was no look of community about it, and no sign of children. It seemed unlikely that the neighbors knew one another. We descended the front walk to the car, whose top was down. Sunset was still a couple of hours away.

I walked around to the passenger side, ushered Vera into the seat and closed the fiberglass door as smartly as necessary. Then I went to the other side, hoisted myself over the driver's door and dropped into the cockpit. Vera may have thought I was showing off. The truth is I'm lazy. "Got a food preference?" I asked her.

"What kind of car is this?" she said.

"It's an Elva. British."

"Oh," she said. "Cute." She poked an index finger here and there at the instrument panel and the upholstery. While I waited for her to answer the food question, I looked her over again. She was remarkably small for an adult woman, far from filling even the limited space in her half of the cockpit. On close inspection she still looked forty or so, but made a more youthful and athletic impression in her cotton dress than she had at church. She must not have been wearing a slip, because the dress followed faithfully what I took to be the contour of her legs. I had no idea yet of her sexual politics, but she certainly looked like fun.

"Like Italian?" I asked her at last.

"You mean like a Ferrari? No, this is fine."

"I meant food," I said.

"Oh," she said. "Yes, I like Italian food."

"Good." I reached to the right and buckled the lap portion of the racing harness across her middle, evidently without spooking her, then belted myself in. She must have seen by this ritual that I was both solicitous of her safety and unafraid to touch her — positive signals, should some kind of resuscitation be in order later. I fired up the engine and we moved off. I had a preferred Italian restaurant a few blocks from my apartment, so I headed there. Seduction was not so much on my mind that the choice could be seen as tactical. I liked these events to fall organically out of circumstances consensually arrived at: no love potions, empty gas tanks or obligatingly large dinner tickets. I liked my Italian restaurant because there were booths, it was flatteringly dark, and the prices hinted at no obligation whatever.

Vera conveniently wore what was known in those days as a poodle cut — hair short enough that travel in the Elva didn't muss it. She appeared to enjoy the ride, smiling as the wind buffeted her blond curls and tried to lift her skirt. I hoped she was also appreciating the purposeful snarl of the exhaust, since the combined noise of it and the wind discouraged conversation. At the restaurant we parked in an adjacent lot and Vera combed her hair with her fingers. Inside we took a booth. Although the sun was shining outdoors, we were to dine by the light of a five-watt bulb protruding from the neck of a Chianti bottle heavily swaddled in wickerwork and red candle drippings. I suppose either the municipal code or the restaurant's insurer forbade the use of an open flame. We ordered pasta.

"Tell me your story," I said while we waited.

"White Protestant Christian female, age forty-two, married twenty-three years to a kind, intelligent, fascinating man. No children. No job. Do some volunteer work. Sing solo in church."

"So much for the stats. Make it interesting."

"It's not interesting."

There was no edge of rue, self-pity, self-mockery or challenge in her voice or look when she said that. It was simple declaration. Accordingly, I decided not to greet the statement with pity either. "Interesting," I said. She laughed.

"But chances are there's something going on in your head," I said. "What gets you out of bed in the morning? "

"Passion," she said.

This was the earliest I could remember being stopped in a conversation in many years. I had always regarded passion as a strong motivator for getting into bed, not out. If I'd been more single-minded in my work as a physicist, I might have understood immediately what she meant. "Beg pardon?"

"Passion," she said again. "Something has gotten away from me. I'm looking for it. Every day."

"Wow," I said, and maybe in the subdued light she saw me lift my eyebrows. I consulted my own experience for something I might relate to her remark, but nothing matched. I so little understood what she might be talking about that I couldn't even frame a question. I waited.

"I want something," she said.

"You're religious," I ventured. "Is it a religious quest?"

"I imagine it is," she said.

"I wish I could help," I said. "I don't do gods very well."

"You don't do gods at all," she said.

"Not strictly true," I said. "I don't doubt that there's some invisible stuff going on in the world. In fact my job is to pin it down. But it generally ends up being quantifiable and impersonal. Kind of dull, if you want your gods to be slippery and quarrelsome. If you want 'em to be human."

"I don't look for God to be human," she said. "But when He embraces me, I want to know it."

A bottle of Chianti arrived, full and without wax dribbles or a light bulb in its neck, and immediately after it the pasta. I poured and we ate. I hadn't noted Vera's dining style after church, but I noted it now. She was quietly voracious. The brittleness I thought I'd seen when first I laid eyes on her was entirely absent. We both looked softer under five watts than in direct sunlight, but there was more to her softness than that. It was not the softness of the diffident feminine; it felt like the softness of a warm death by rising bread, the sort of thing that might happen to a baker cornered without warning by a loaf. All at once I felt as giddy as if we'd already finished the wine, although we'd barely started, and in as little doubt of a sexual conclusion as I'd ever been in my life. "Come home with me," I said. Vera looked up from her plate and nodded.

After that, we ate like prodigals, and together we polished off the wine. The promise of intimacy breeds intimacy; we talked like old friends. Her whole frame of reference as we talked was religious and mine was skeptical, but the effect was the same. What we had in common was passion, the thing that would draw us into and out of bed. For a woman with a pillbox hat and a four-door Oldsmobile, she was astonishingly unconventional.

We left the restaurant at dusk too drunk to drive, but not too drunk to walk. The Elva stayed where it was. I folded tiny Vera under my arm and we meandered the six blocks to my apartment, growing sober as we went, through June weather so mild I wanted to cry with happiness. I let us in and lifted Vera's print dress up and off her body, then carried her in her underwear to my bed. Her shoes fell off en route. The bed was a king-sized waterbed, *de rigueur* for any serious bachelor in those days. Atop the single sheet draped over the mattress, I unhooked and threw away her bra, then pulled her panties off and tossed them too. I took the nape of her neck in my teeth and began to graze. The bed bore us up like a tide in the Bay of Fundy. I was in love with all of nature.

D. E. Tingle was born in Iowa City in 1938. Following a narrow escape with an A.B. from Harvard in 1959, he married and worked for eleven years in the early U.S. space program with the Smithsonian Astrophysical Observatory in Peru, Argentina, Spain and Cambridge, Massachusetts, before graduating into renewed bachelorhood and self-employment as an automobile mechanic. He has two children and four grandchildren. His first novel, *Imperishable Bliss* (2009), appears at www.tingleslotus.com. Contact: tingletlc@gmail.com

JAMESON'S LETTERS

————————— ℰᴑℭℛ —————————

by B.R. Bonner

Jameson's letter came to me thirty days after its postmarked date, stamped with the face of a dour-looking Nepalese ruler. Within its tattered envelope I found shreds of wrinkled rice paper, scribbled with the indecipherable yet undeniable handwriting of my friend and climbing companion.

I envisioned Henry huddled in his tent, tucked into the crags of Everest, his headlamp illuminating his quivering writing paper, blowing into his blackened, frostbitten hands as he gathered his thoughts to tell me what he then had on his oxygen-deprived mind. His letter appeared to have once been crumbled into a ball, as if he'd given up in frustration and had tossed it away, only to reconsider and iron it out as best he could. Exhaustion must have weighed on him, his vision blurred from the onset of snow blindness. In spite of this, he renewed his effort, striking through words, cursing in whispers, giving up again, and finally ripping the sheet into small pieces and stuffing his scrambled thoughts into an envelope with a laugh.

From the day I announced that I was hanging up my crampons and no longer accompanying him on his increasingly risky climbs, Henry never forgave me for abandoning him, for dissolving what had been a solid partnership — I, his trusted Sancho Panza, loyally following him on his journeys of peril and absurdity.

His letters came to me from all over the world, randomly, unexpectedly. On one occasion he sent me a small package from Africa following his descent from Kilimanjaro. It contained a large ball of dung formed by the endless rolling of that famous beetle. "This is my friend, Matt," said the note that came with it. "A well-rounded individual, to be sure; but in the end, still a turd."

A year later I received a letter from China that contained nothing more than a page torn from a Beijing newspaper. He had circled a cluster of characters and scrawled into the margin: "They're at it again." Neither of us understood a word of Chinese. But to Henry, that was precisely the point.

Forever spotlighting the inscrutable, Henry religiously believed that exploring the unknown was our highest calling. We had experienced much together on our travels, helping each other down from high altitude peaks and marveling near death at the unexpected lengths of our own limits. We'd nursed each other back to health from infectious diseases, lacerations and broken bones; gotten drunk on the local spirits; bailed each other out from foreign jails; and, when the gods smiled down on us, slept with the local women. He thrived on this camaraderie, his spirit quickly dissipated by anything that smacked of inertia or complacency. It was not thrill-seeking that motivated him. No. Whatever wanton demon it might be named, it drove him to the ends of the earth with an ever-increasing obsession. He wanted desperately for me to rejoin him on his quests to explore what he cryptically referred to as "The Tangent," and though tempted by this siren call, I knew I could no longer go on with it. The money wasn't there anymore. The seasoning that age brings opened my eyes to my own mortality. Pragmatic concerns now dominated my thoughts: The need for higher education. The struggle to make a living. The desire to find a woman, win her affection, make a home, raise a family. The usual stuff of life, all of which now stood between Henry and me. And, of course, he would not abide any of it.

"Dear Infidel," he once wrote me from Karachi. "Abandon your false gods. Save your withering soul. Come to Pakistan and climb Nanga Parbat with me." And that was the last I'd heard from him.

I poured the bits and pieces of Jameson's letter onto my writing desk and arranged each shred flat, ink side up, in the right order. "Meet me at the Hotel Florid Nepal in Kathmandu," it read. "I found Mallory's camera."

Henry's latest ploy to lure me out of the suburbs brought a smile to my face. "The Tangent" in this case was a mystery that dates back to June of 1924, when George Mallory, the English mountaineer who famously retorted "Because it's there" to the question of why attempt Everest, made the tragic first attempt. He and his climbing companion, Sandy Irvine, were last seen on the Second Step of the Northeast ridge, a few hours below the summit. A cloud of mist enveloped them, and they were never seen again.

Mallory's bleached white body, well-preserved in the anoxic environment, was found in 1999, lying face down in the snow and scree at 8,160 meters altitude. His pockets contained various artifacts: a folding knife, altimeter, goggles, bits of twine; but nowhere to be found was the Vest Pocket Kodak camera that was known to have been carried on the climb. Neither was found the photo of Mallory's wife, which Mallory claimed he would place on Everest's summit, leading many to believe that since it wasn't on his corpse he likely made it to the top after all. If indeed he had made it to the top, then surely he had taken a picture with his Kodak. So the theory went. But the expeditions launched to find and retrieve the cameras of Mallory and Irvine had been in vain.

For days I tried to shrug it off, but the astonishing declaration in Jameson's letter was impossible to ignore. It haunted my thoughts, distracted me into states of forgetfulness, and drove impatience in my replies to those around me. Why this letter, out of all the letters he'd sent littered with outlandish statements, had so knocked me off balance, I can only attribute to the inescapable possibility that *it might actually be true*.

Much to the chagrin of my friends and family, whose concerned looks clearly indicated a loss of faith in me, I flew to Kathmandu and inquired for my friend at the hotel desk. It was a hostel, actually. Frugal. Sparsely furnished. Adorned with faded posters of Annapurna and Everest. The rooms were less than three Euros a night, which attracted many of the poor wayward youths of the world who shared Henry's wanderlust. Climbers constantly came and went from this place, some crackling with a familiar electricity of anticipation, others carrying their sunburns and climbing injuries like badges of honor.

The face of the little man who ran the place lit up when I mentioned Henry's name. "Yes, I know him," he said, in a harried tone. "But I have not seen him in two weeks, so I had to rent his room to someone else. He owes me one week room charges."

A group of young climbers sitting on a bench against the wall suddenly grew quiet. One of them, a red-headed, lanky twenty-something dressed in a black North Face jacket, approached me.

"Are you a friend of Henry Jameson?" he asked.

"Yes," I answered. "Do you know him?"

"I knew him," he said. "He was our guide."

He introduced himself as Steven Walcott and asked if I was Matt Sawyer.

"Yes. How did you know my name?"

"Henry told us you might be coming. He talked a lot about the trips you guys made together."

"You said you knew him. Have you seen him recently? He wrote me that he was here in Kathmandu, staying at this hostel."

"I'm sorry to have to tell you this," the young man said. "But Henry died on Everest five days ago from cerebral edema. We found him staggering outside his tent at Camp 3, rambling incoherently about a camera that he'd found recently on the Tibetan route. Believe me, we did everything possible to stabilize him so that we could take him down. We gave him dexamethasone and put him in a hyperbaric bag, but he was too far gone and couldn't be moved. He died that same morning as the sun came up."

A few of the other young climbers had gathered around us. Some of them gripped me by the shoulder and expressed their sorrow, lamenting how losing a good friend is one of the worst of all pains in life, that they had also lost good friends to the mountain, and though they had not known Henry for very long, they liked him immensely and were very saddened by his loss.

They informed me that his body still lay on the mountain, covered with rock cairn, marked with his ice ax as a make-shift cross. Steven wrote down the coordinates for me, which he had taken on his GPS, in case I wished to visit him. "None of us knew if he had any family," he said. "You were the only one he ever spoke about."

"We have his gear with us," a tall Danish-looking girl told me, her English heavily accented. "We weren't exactly sure what to do with it. But I think if anyone should have it, it should be you."

She brought me his pack and a nylon carry bag. I thanked them for their kindness. They shook my hand vigorously, and some of them said goodbye with sympathetic hugs, displaying all the camaraderie that Henry had relished, the bond among climbers that he'd wanted to reconnect between us. I would never again feel that tie with him. But I took solace in the fact that he died doing that which he loved best.

On my return home I found it difficult to go through the motions. Work. Eat. Sleep. Worry about job security. Stress over financial volatility. Battle with insurance companies. Saving for college. Saving for retirement. The struggle against entropy, the inexorable deterioration of all things . . . All this now dominated my thoughts. And while immersion in good books, time with family, dinner with friends, laughing at stupid jokes, made up for the nagging sense of loss, I still could not shake the desire to strike out into the unknown, into "The Tangent" that had seized the imagination of my friend Henry and men like him. Men like Hillary, Mallory, and Irvine.

Naturally, Mallory's camera was nowhere to be found. I looked for it in all the pockets of Henry's gear, but there was no Vest Pocket Kodak. What had become of it, whether it had really been found or was simply a delusional fantasy of Henry's, would never be known. But I did discover one camera — a digital camera that belonged to Henry. On its storage card I found a photo of Henry standing on the top of Everest with a big shit-eating grin on his face. There were other photos too, including one of us together on the top of Aconcagua, a peak in Argentina we'd climbed in February of 2004. The photo sits on my desk as a reminder of what we had once accomplished.

A month or so after my return, in preparation for a summer camping trip to Colorado, I pulled out Henry's backpack again to look for a First Aid kit I'd seen amongst his belongings. As I pillaged through the pockets, pulling out sundry gear and piling it onto the floor, a crumpled pad of paper, bundled in one of his shirts, spilled out onto the mound of equipment. I flipped through its pages, full of scribbles, doodles, drawings, and bursts of cosmic wisdom, and found, at the end of the pad, a letter addressed to me.

"I'm back at Everest Base Camp," it read. "On the Southeast Ridge this time, doing some guide work to earn some money so I can travel on foot to Llasa, like Heinrich Harrer described in *Seven Years in Tibet*. I have Mallory's camera with me. I have sewn it into my jacket so it will not be lost again. What do you bet it will have pictures of Mallory's naked wife on it? By the way, what's keeping you? Come to Llasa with me! Shangri La is real but it's no fun going it alone. Your friend, Henry."

I promised myself then that I would go back to Nepal, that I would locate my friend's grave with the coordinates Steven had given me and put to rest once and for all whether Mallory's camera had been found. But no, it will never come to pass. The drive is gone. My will is shot. I cannot look at my friend Henry frozen in death, the way they found Mallory. Let them both lie buried on the mountain where they belong.

B.R. Bonner lives in Austin, Texas. *Jameson's Letters* will be his 13th published short story. Previous literary credits include: *South Dakota Review, The MacGuffin, Matter Journal, Words and Images, Buenos Aires Literary Review, Existere — Journal of Arts and Literature, Chaminade Literary Review, Mind in Motion, Takahe, You Are Here,* and *The Wanderlust Review*. Contact: bbonner3@austin.rr.com

I'M PRUDENCE

— ℰℐℂℛ —

Excerpt from the novel
by Joanne Groshardt

Sometimes my brain goes faster than I do, and I go faster than anyone I know. Mother calls me when she needs something. "Have you seen my sterling silver leopard pill box with the ruby eye?" she'll ask.

Helga, my governess, calls me things under her breath that I can never quite make out.

Daddy doesn't call me, but I answer to Prudence. Prudence Peppinger.

I told Daddy I wanted to be 16 so I could have a sweet 16 party, decorate the yard with pink and blue balloons and yellow crepe paper, and hire a band with a singer in a long, black-sequined dress to sing "Happy Birthday" to me! He didn't answer me exactly.

I'm four-feet-six-inches tall, which is enough to reach the cookie jar on top of the kitchen counter. My hair is auburn, and when the sun bounces off of it you can see ruby flames. It is very beautiful, and hangs down the entire length of my back and touches the top of the blue satin bow of my dress.

My eyes are blue. Not just any blue, but the blue of a morning glory in full bloom on a summer day! When I stare at people, they stare back. When they do that, I stare harder. Pretty soon they start to twitch and turn red and get nervous, but I keep on staring.

My nose is small and nicely rounded at the end, unlike the large pointed noses of my Mother's bridge club friends. This nose is very becoming to my face and very useful. If people do something I disapprove of, I toss my auburn-and-ruby hair over my shoulder, give them a sideways glance with my blue eyes, lift my head as high as possible, elevate my heels, and point my nose toward the sun. Then I strut away looking as stately as old Aunt Mildred.

"Who is that young lady?" they ask among themselves. I don't answer.

I live in a stately state, in a stately section everybody has heard about if they are anybody. Chauncy Square is the name of my stately street. My house is the fifth stately house from the corner. Mother painted it a stately pink that I myself chose from the Sears catalog when I had the measles. "We need to call our stately house a stately name," she announced, "like Peppinger Manor or the Stately Estates of the Peppingers." Finally she suspended a huge, stately sign from a brass chain on the outside gas lamp reading, "The Pepp-in-the-Box."

Sitting on my front steps and counting the number of people who walk by is amusing. An ancient man walks past every Saturday morning. He can't hear very well. Sometimes he says, "Huh?" and sometimes he doesn't.

"He hasn't seen a barber in years," states Mother with authority. The old man's shoulders are humped because he has a large lump on his back. I guess he can't see very well either. He always scuffs his feet very slowly so he can feel the pavement while he sings, "Mares eat oats and does eat oats and . . . "

Eight o'clock is when I usually get up every morning. Helga serves me oatmeal in bed at 8:13. "Pru — dence!" she yells. "If you don't get back in your room and eat, I'll . . . " as she carries breakfast on a huge tray that has a picture of Niagara Falls decoupaged on it. I like using big words.

There are always two spoons, one for my sugar and one for my oatmeal. As I eat the oatmeal and get closer to the bottom of the cereal bowl, I get to see a circle of flying, winged, cupid babies, wrapped with garlands of flowers, holding hands. Mother makes Helga give me Mother's old monogrammed pink napkins, the ones she got as a wedding present, but I prefer the linen napkins we use at Christmas because they're red like my hair. Helga always remembers to put a red plastic rosebud in my favorite milk-glass vase. "Someday," she threatens, "I'm going to pull that old rosebud off the stem and attach it to my Sunday hat!"

I usually sit in my room after eating to think about all the things I could be doing but am not doing, because I am up in my room thinking about all the things I could be doing. Alfreida, my cat, usually comes to my window. Of course, I always let her in. She chases mice all night and then eats them. Alfreida is pretty worn out by the time morning comes.

Instead of eating lunch at 12, I'd rather go outside to play with Sam. Sam and I always go to the sandbox at the back of my yard and bury my four baby dolls. "Bury them deep," says Sam, "we don't want them crawling out of their graves."

I place a cross made of paper at each headstone and sprinkle grass cuttings over the graves. Solemnly we stand over each grave. "Magnified and sanctified be the name of the Lord," Sam recites as I say, "And may the souls of the faithfully departed rest in peace. Amen," throwing rose petals over each doll. We burn a candle and bow to the East three times with our eyes closed. After the service, the Windley's dog unburies the dolls. His tail wags so fast that it looks like it will become detached and continue to shake in the air by itself.

It's time to practice the piano at three o'clock. I hate the piano, and I hate to practice. Mother thinks if I play scales every day, I will soon play as well as Rachmaninoff. Faithfully I trudge up my front steps when Helga calls to me that it is time to practice. "Prudence, get your little bottom on the piano bench!"

My piano teacher, Miss Crimshaw, has had me working on "Spring Ballet" forever. "Practice," she says, "and maybe you will play to a full house at Carnegie Hall when you are 18, as I did."

When I play, Alfreida goes behind the sofa and shrieks every time I hit a C-minor chord.

If he's home, Daddy yells, "Deaf! I am going deaf from the likes of you!"

Helga starts pulling anything resembling a weed, grinding her false teeth saying, "The world, it will all end soon. Please God!"

Mother screams, "I'm off to the furrier again," and goes shopping.

At 29 minutes past three, I close my book, slam all 10 fingers on the keyboard as hard as I can, stick my tongue out at Rachmaninoff, and run outside to play.

Daddy's always late for dinner. Once I asked him why it took him two hours to get home when I could walk the distance in a few minutes. He blushed a strange shade of crimson and said, "Eat your peas."

A tear ran down Mother's face. Never did Mother ever allow anyone to see a tear run down her face. She curtly said, "Eat your carrots," but we only had beans and potatoes that night.

Darkness reminds me that it is time to read my nightly chapter from the Scary Hour book. Then Helga tells me to go to bed. Last night she started off with, "There was a beautiful princess who had three pet pigs and an evil sorcerer for an uncle who changed into a wolf each night."

Making her pretend she was the evil uncle, I bet her that she couldn't blow down my house of cards. (I glued them.) She got really mad. Now she has to give me a week's worth of bubble gum!

My days keep me pretty busy. That's why I get enough sleep every night, so I can start all over again in the morning.

Joanne Groshardt, after many career attempts, combined writing skills with a computer background and was a technical writer for over twenty-five years. During her latest (and hopefully last) career of screenwriting, three of her shorts have been produced and the psycho-female killer feature "13 Knots" will be released in 2011. "I'm Prudence" is excerpted from her unpublished novel *Views from Four Feet Six Inches* written while she was in high school and college. She is listed on imdb.com. Contact: joannegroshardt@yahoo.com

BUCKTOWN

—————————— ℘∞℧ ——————————

by Dave Woods

Maurice stood before the mirror, glaring at the small trickle of blood running down his chin. He had, months ago, packed away his Norelco electric in favor of a return to the comfort of a straight razor and lather brush in the solitary morning ritual. Yet he now seemed defenseless against intrusions upon even this one tranquil moment. Irritation bred difficulty, difficulty bred distraction, and distraction had already left its nasty imprint when, just yesterday, Maurice had nicked himself while trimming off the annoying growth on his nose. Now an additional tiny band aid would be applied just below, in absolute cosmetic symmetry.

"Mooooor . . . ," shouted Bev from the kitchen, "the real-estate lady just called and she's bringing a group through in two hours."

Here was one intrusion: the neighborhood was changing. Nearly a decade had passed since Maurice and Bev had migrated into this forgotten pocket on Chicago's near northwest side, drawn by its mix of poetry hideouts and Polish holdouts, of wit, charm and cheap shelter. Back then you couldn't touch these low rents anywhere livable. And with its attraction of hipster and post-punk sensibilities, you couldn't touch Bucktown's iconoclasm anywhere at all.

It had been tough at times — car batteries had been boosted, *cars* had been boosted. Still, even the two or three break-ins over the years had been accepted as tribute to an edgy co-existence with the street element.

But today, it wasn't the bangers as much as the developers with Bucktown in their crosshairs. The place was too close to downtown, far too promising as a residential layover for the army of twenty- and thirty-somethings recruited to the cubicles of Chicago's resurgent financial and legal industry, and to all the feeder businesses the big dogs supported.

As a result, Maurice and Bev's little rowhouse rental was forever on the market. With faceless investors in and out, the property had turned ownership no less than three times in two years, further deteriorating with every transfer. Each turnover was preceded by packs of gawkers, consumed more by the interior's eccentric furnishings and untidy state than by the building's structural tilt and foundation cracks. Worse, Bev seemed incapable of insisting that tours of the couple's cramped quarters were inappropriate before noon.

And with each turnover came a rent increase.

Here was another intrusion. The nineties had landed on Maurice's lifestyle like a bomb on butter. A skilled graphic designer for many years, Maurice had lingered at the layout table far past the digital dawn. While he had once commanded top dollar and set his own schedule, Maurice now continued to stubbornly insist that talent would trump technology. And he steadily lost clients. Just this week, his biggest account replaced him with a twelve-dollar-an-hour grad student from a local art school. (An exchange between Maurice and the project lead hadn't helped. "No, no, no, Maurice, it's got to go Pop! to go Bang! to go Pow!" "Give me *colors*, not sounds.")

Today's troubles only reinforced how comfortable things had once been. A lifetime ago. A different age, when two part-time incomes accommodated free time, easy time, time to embrace the arts, time to watch CNN. You could "make the rent in a day," as Maurice and Bev and like-minded friends who followed them into the area used to brag.

Alas, now even these like-minded friends had deserted the old Bucktown. They had actually bought homes, homes in stable areas of the city, or even the suburbs. They had settled in, had calmed down and grown up, despite Maurice and Bev's sometimes envious, private whispering. Maurice would never confess that each departure sparked a tumultuous self-examination of his own past choices and present trajectory. Many of the friends had received, from the passing of aging parents, sums adequate for entry into lovely two-flats. Maurice knew at heart that this was also his only way out. He would never confess this either — it seemed a pitiful passage to adulthood. Yet the predacious hour would likely come sooner rather than later. And until then, Maurice and Bev would be forced to swim alone, fleeing the sharks, or dressing the wounds, whichever the case may be.

Well, not exactly alone. For at Maurice's feet sat the one connection to that other, elusive universe.

"Dad."

Here was another intrusion.

"Dad, could you buy an ax?"

Young Ken obstructed the bathroom doorway, facing the ceiling, his attention absorbed by a spider suspended inches above his head. A small gust, whose origin was a splintering window frame, blew the spider off track. The bug began moving up instead of down. Ken was disappointed.

"Not now, Kenny," said Maurice, "I'm shaving."

Ken ignored the rebuff as usual.

"Dad, *could you buy an ax?*"

"I don't know, Kenny," said Maurice. Today, thought Maurice, we must be on lumberjacks.

Ken's genesis was accidental. In retrospect, Maurice and Bev's decision to carry though with the pregnancy had provided, despite financial burdens, the new glue to a tired bond. What was really planned these days anyway, wondered Maurice. What could be? One might accept the consequences of accidents, and grow to love them, and this he had done, and so had Bev.

Maurice turned the handle on the sink for more hot water. The pipe spat mist, then rust, then a tepid brown fluid. Maurice took this particular inconvenience in stride, focusing his resentment instead on the property's latest manager, whose answering machine was always inaccessible, its tape filled with messages.

"Dad, could you go to the store and buy an ax?" persisted Ken.

Maurice threw in the towel. It was no use resisting the coming onslaught. Solitude, after all, was an inner journey, immune to worldly assault. All Maurice could do was keep on shavin'.

"Yes, Kenny," Maurice said, a shade more engaged. "I suppose I could go down to the hardware store and buy an ax if I really wanted to."

Maurice took a half-step closer to the mirror to examine a job half-finished. He stubbed his toe on the tip of a nail he himself had driven to secure a linoleum tile loosened by a leak in the roof during the last few rains.

"Dad, if you bought an ax, could you chop down a tree?"

"Sure, Kenny, chop down a tree. Sure."

A home. A nice neighborhood. Sharing a fence with a Certified Public Accountant. A Republican City Council. A big, goofy Weimaraner. Three nights ago, an old man was stabbed just up the alley, not fifty yards from Maurice and Bev's back door.

"Dad," said Kenny, "If you chopped down a tree, could you build a house?"

"What? What did you say, Kenny?"

"Maurice!" shouted Bev. "They're here! They said two hours, but they're on the porch right now!"

"Sonofabitch," grumbled Maurice. Another little band aid would be needed.

"Dad," came the voice from the floor. "Why don't you buy an ax?"

Dave Woods lives and works in Sacramento, CA. Contact: dwoods2020@comcast.net

THE CATALYTIC SEDUCTION OF BRIAN WHITE

————————— ℰᑐᑕᗅ —————————

Excerpt from the novel
by Andrew Binks

Sixteen and never been — '75 and barely alive — graduated, never been dated. The tuneless verse pestered Brian's sleep — never been dated — rated, just disturbated — to the core.

Winter blasted through Ottawa and whined at his basement window finally waking him. The snow piled, darkening the room into a perpetual night. He lay on his back, one hand clutching his scrotum and the other resting on his chest, staring at the constellation of sterile dots in the acoustic tile ceiling. Seventeen and never been — graduated and never — class of '75 and never been — — laid, never traveled, never seen a Goddamned thing, never, never, never. Least likely to do anything at all. They could put all of it in the yearbook, next to his picture. Fuck the yearbook. He let go of his balls, reached for the radio and turned the knob, " — AND TO HONOUR HER FILING FOR DIVORCE, HERE'S AVERAGE WHITE BAND'S LATEST PICK UP THE PIECES, WAY TO GO CHER, I GOT YOU BABE!" — radio off. Snow whistled at the window. Way to go Cher for living somewhere warm.

He stepped into the bathroom, dropped his boxers and stood naked, leaning over the sink, pressing his pelvis against the cold porcelain while he searched for blackheads and burgeoning whiteheads. He didn't know which was worse, the pimples or the tell-tale welts from having squeezed them. He shaved the young stubble off his face, blood running down his neck from nicked bumps. And later as he washed in the shower, he soaped his crotch until the wet skin stung, and when he rubbed dry, brought himself to the brink of pleasure. That will happen soon, he thought. He closed his eyes and ran his hand below his navel, imagining the touch of another man. Here the fantasy derailed. It was a betrayal to everything he had ever learned, to everyone who had ever loved him. To his dead mother, although with her death came a kind of understanding. He somehow believed she would understand him, forgive him, and know that what he was wasn't wrong, somehow. But to his oblivious father and most of the rest of the living world he felt like a sinner.

He dressed silently and listened for his father's steps on the floor above, the only sound to penetrate the walls. He crept up the stairs and retrieved jacket, boots and keys. He left the quiet house and crunched on the hard snow down the walk. In spite of the wind chill, he decided to catch the downtown bus as far away as the mall. Otherwise his father might see him waiting at the bus stop on the corner. Aside from the business commute, no one in his neighborhood ever went downtown. Nor did he. The stores in the mall had been good enough.

He sat in the bus midway back, wipers erratic and heavy, a thick whiteness enveloped the bus and created a darkened silence. Hot air from under the seat lulled him like a drug. From time to time the driver glanced into the mirror. What was *he* looking at? Keep your eyes on the road. If you can see it. The hospital where his mother died sat stoic, somewhere beyond, in the white.

Just over a year since mother died, and the year before that of knowing she would. If he trudged through the snow to the hospital maybe she would still be there, waiting, in her bed. He always imagined he would wake from a very long dream in which he was captive; every morning when he woke he pretended he had woken from the dream in which his mother had died, and that she would be right where he'd left her — —

Fortunately the blinding snow made this leg of the journey the easiest it had ever been.

And it had been right before Christmas when she died, for God to really rub it in that she was gone and there would be some readjusting to be done. "I was born too early," she'd said, "I'm just a frustrated flower child." And like paint brushes being cleaned, the colour in their lives was washed away for good, leaving father and son in a winter of discontent. Two men who had been taken out of their unflappable selves by her pranks, now sat solemn against one another in the land of supposed-to-be.

And how can funerals be nice, for God's sake? Was there anyone who didn't think that it wasn't nice — — that lilies in December weren't nice? That new fallen snow in a cemetery wasn't nice? That cake and home cooking and gallons of tea weren't nice? He drank for the first time, really drank — that was very, very nice. Even retching was nice. It freed him from what she didn't want him to feel. Now he had to deal with the remains. The living ones — — the man who lived upstairs on the main floor, who was known as his father. His father the high school principal. The man who got to school before he did, and home after. The one who reminded him that he wasn't doing enough schooling or enough of anything, to be precise.

And here he was on the bus, escaping for a dirty little tryst that years of fantasies had finally forced him to make happen in the real world. His pulse raced and slowed. Well, what was he *supposed* to be doing? Mother had left no specific marching orders before she left. Maybe he was to follow her example and lighten up. But alas, there was too much of his father in him he feared. To let go guiltlessly would be an uphill battle. The bus plowed along, funneling a grand wake of snow as they tobogganed down what may have been Main Street.

When the bus stopped he stepped down and gasped for the breath that a gust of cold wind had quickly snatched from him. What had possessed him? He knew exactly. But in a blizzard? The blizzard helped to make the whole undertaking that much more accidental: show up at the teacher's door, feigning frostbite, be invited in, find out what a man's warm hands felt like on his chilly white skin — — he would be a victim of happenstance. He had no alibi if all went wrong other than, perhaps, to blame his irrational behaviour on the stress of his mother dying. Exactly. If that didn't fly there was always the public library nearby or the French bookstore. Who could dispute a visit to the French bookstore?

A small storefront with a warm glow appeared unexpectedly out of the blizzard on an empty Sussex Drive. Perhaps he could collect himself for a moment — be calm, and catch his breath. He pushed open the door, stepped inside, the wind sucked it shut again, a bell pitched above him, he puffed, stamped off the snow, slapped his arms against his side, and, fanfare finished, stood still until the faint tinkle of a piano came to him from a distance, a radio perhaps.

"It's just too cold."

A woman's voice wafted from above, out of his view. He looked around quickly, still concerned that someone might recognize him.

First it was the bus driver and now he had to worry about another witness.

A thick sweet smell mingled with a mothball scent and drifted out of the yards of fabric and garments hanging from the ceiling. Orange light from glass lamps weakly pushed back the darkness. Several wire racks held bundles of yellowing postcards. Others displayed pages and covers from magazines: starlets from the past; old ads for gadgets he did not recognize were preserved in plastic. Another skeletal rack held nothing, but looked like it might have been intended for hats. Everything was faded, forgotten, steeped in exotic incense, like the sweetness of marijuana (although he had been warned against it), and the musty scent of mildewed books.

Rows of heavy clothing and furs disappeared towards the back. He couldn't see any walls. Magic, he thought, like the fairytale of the wardrobe.

"Eighteen inches," came the woman's voice again.

He squinted and shaded his eyes from the lamps to see nothing in the darkness. He boldly stepped closer to the voice.

Again she spoke. "We've had eighteen inches of snow in the past twenty-four hours. How many centimeters is that?"

"Lots more," he said, speaking into the dimness, still looking up.

"I'll never figure it out," came her reply.

"It'll take a while, I guess, before we get used to it —"

"— The snow or the centimeters?" She laughed.

"It smells nice in here."

"Patchouli, it's supposed to hide the mustiness."

He waited to breathe for a moment, until the delicate form of a face emerged from the shadows above, along with the realization that he had been looking in her direction all along. She seemed to float in midair. Now he regretted coming into the store. He would have to commit to more than just small talk about the weather in order to be polite. Why had this happened? There was a heated bus depot nearby where he could have stopped, even if it was populated by transients. He was now obliged to make conversation. He hoped she would leave him alone and not ask any questions. He shifted towards the door.

"Sorry. You're my first customer and I've been stranded here since yesterday, otherwise no one. That's the only reason I'm here. Besides, I had it so warm I couldn't bear the thought of going out into that." She gestured towards the snowy street, the fine bones in her hand and wrist catching the shadows. She sighed theatrically, "I suppose I'll have to go home sooner or later," and laughed. "Probably the only customer I'll have," she continued, mostly to herself. "Do you live nearby? You must. Why else would you be out?"

He smiled. She didn't treat him like a stranger. However, he did not want to explain, or lie, while he still felt ashamed that temptation could drag him this far downtown.

"I'm on my way to the French bookstore," he said, stepping closer to the door.

"In this weather?" Even when she was not laughing she had a naturally subtle smile.

"I need a book for my class." There was nothing but silence and the room swallowed up his words.

"I doubt they're open."

"You look like you're levitating."

"Oh." She disappeared from her dark perch; he heard her shoes finally click against the wooden floor, then silence until she reappeared much closer. She still seemed to be floating until he realized she was at least as tall as he was. "Make yourself comfortable."

She was like her surroundings, draped in faded layers of skirts and textured fabric. Not just a dream, yet he was under a spell. She and this place existed, and were offering him refuge from himself.

Her eyes, heavily outlined with black, stared intensely, as if she were looking for someone. "How old are you?" she asked and then, as if not expecting him to answer, walked past him. She moved between hanging coats, used hats, pieces of aging furniture, towards the door, and reached for the handle. With little help a gust of wind pressed the door against her narrow body, pushed her off balance, blowing her hair back from her face. He remembered again the story of the snow-queen who lived beyond the wardrobe in a country of perpetual winter. Then the cold blew crystalline flakes of snow past him too, making him shiver. She turned to look at him and the wind wrapped her hair around her face. Inclined against the door, she firmly shut out the winter. Everything settled. A bell tinkled above her and she rolled her eyes in mock annoyance.

"Cold out," she said.

"In Celsius or Fahrenheit?"

"That will be the next thing, and by then I will have given up completely. I'm just too old, or old-fashioned." Still her spell continued. She leaned into the bay window by the door, and over a dusty pile of hatboxes. Her narrow shoulders shrugged up around her neck. Her red hair hid her pale face. What did she see? He watched her profile, dark against the light from outside. Beyond, the wind howled and curled each drift, leaving a frozen seascape.

The music continued to chime quietly from an old radio sitting on top of an older, larger one. It was a silent battle between the raging winter outside and the meek but determined warmth inside.

Hands resting on hips, she silently strode back to her cocoon of darkness. He pretended to be interested in the clutter: luggage, floor lamps, a cavernous chair, ornate dishes set for a meal on a dark table. All seemed to be waiting. But the jewelry display of red-speckled glass beetles and orange fireflies caught his attention. He bowed over the display case hoping she would not speak to him again.

"Do you like them?"

Her fingers tenderly handled the pins. She looked up into his face, catching him by surprise. It was impossible to hide. Her green eyes were too much. He stepped away, behind a rack of clothes.

"Men's on the left, some nice women's things — for your girlfriend."

With her chin resting on the back of her hand, she watched him. He pulled off his mitt to feel a dusty silk robe between his fingers.

There was a crinkling of cellophane from behind.

"It's not — really — for sale. You know, more for decoration than anything. Peppermint?" she asked.

"No thank you."

"You're polite."

"Pardon?" Was she mocking him?

"You're polite. It's a virtue."

"Is it a woman's?" He gently held out the silken arm of the robe.

"Men's — it's Indian. Nearly perfect condition," she said proudly.

He held it up. "Looks like something Omar Sharif would have worn." His face heated under her continuous stare.

"He's Egyptian."

" — Yul Brynner? The King and I?"

"Siam." She slipped off the stool and stood beside him. A scent of patchouli enveloped him. She pressed close to him, her hair tickling the side of his neck. This close he could see that she was only slightly taller. She clicked the candy on her teeth.

"I know: Peter Sellers —

" — what on earth?"

"in The Party. Then he was Indian."

She interrupted. "Look at this." Her thin fingers followed the black and white piping around the lapel, and her white nails glowed against the dark lining. Blue veins showed through her pale skin. Ink smudged the tips of several of her fingers.

"Except for the cigarette burn on the cuff, it's in perfect condition." Her breath was warm. She dug at the little burn hole with her thumbnail. "I don't imagine you smoke. Try it on. It's probably your size." She looked directly at him. He tried to look away, but ended up staring at the small depression just below her throat.

"It'll fit . . . go ahead."

303

He handed the robe to her, pulled at his sweater, shirt riding up his back, the sweater popping over his head as his hair flew with static. He tossed it away and was lost in a struggle to pull his shirt down.

"Go ahead. Take off your shirt."

He turned his back to her and undid the buttons. He let the shirt slip. Goosebumps spread across his skin, his nipples grew hard and he crossed his arms over his chest. He exhaled slowly, angered that his planned rendezvous, his dreamed about liaison, his reason for being downtown, had come to this. Just his luck.

"Turn around."

He uncrossed his arms, hoping the goose bumps would disappear.

"Relax, I'll put it on."

She gathered the fabric and ran the sleeves up his outstretched arms. Did he smell too much of the cologne he had doused himself with?

Her reflection over his shoulder startled him. Her face was pale in the dim streaky glass of the mirror, but it was his own lacklustre grayness that disappointed him. As if the winter had stolen his being. As if he would disappear if he didn't get sun and a tan sometime within the next few months. He crossed his arms and turned from left to right, avoiding her stare, looking at his own pale face, and not really even noticing the robe.

"It's nice." But when he finally looked, the whole picture disappointed him. He could not *just look* at the robe.

"It's you," she smiled.

But she must have registered his disappointment. He smiled back.

This time it was she who looked away from him. "What I mean is that it looks good on you."

"I know. I mean I agree. It — makes me look good. I don't do it justice but it manages to make me look different."

"Different?"

"I haven't looked this good since my mother's funeral." He swallowed. He wanted to stop.

"You look good." She clapped her hands lightly as she said each word.

"Like a matinee idol?"

"You look good. With or without the robe."

He closed his eyes and brought the fabric close, to smell the mustiness. "I like it," he whispered, pretending not to hear her last remark.

"You do it justice. Not everyone can wear something like that. I've only ever — — " but her voice drifted off and when he looked up she was back behind the counter.

His face was still hot. With his back to her, he undid the robe and pulled it over his head, and gathered his shirt and sweater.

"You're a student?"

"Class of '75."

"Graduation?"

"Still five months of torture." He hung the robe back on its hanger, keeping his back to her.

"I'd say you're about seventeen."

"I'll be eighteen in the —

" — spring? If you'd like, you can borrow the robe."

"Well, no, it's, it's just not — It's beautiful. It's just that I can't see myself — "

"I can. You could wear it to your graduation."

"Well —" He quickly pulled the shirt and sweater over his head.

"Back out into the snow?" She became polite again. "Don't get snowbound. Drop by again. I'm Daria." She leafed through a tall old magazine as she spoke, not looking up.

"I'm Brian." He swallowed. Was she angry? Did she *really* know why he was downtown? Where would he go now? Continue? Wander past the Latin teacher's building? Fantasize about the hot cocoa he would offer him as he massaged his tough shoulders, having to kiss his feet like the Roman *pueri* did, as he tirelessly recited *amo, amas, amat.* Getting it wrong. Being punished. As in his childhood fantasies, playing the part of the Roman slave boy, bringing water, cleaning his master's back with oil and scraping the skin clean with the sharp *strigiles.* Wandering endlessly through the atrium, behind pillars of marble being taunted by some hunky Gladiator — looking for his master — forever being punished — forced to do their bidding no matter how degrading — licking the marble floor clean. He'd heard all about it. And it all seemed so plausible in his little dark imagination at home. Now? He felt foolish. Lost his nerve. Father's voice punched through with an *only fags take showers*, after he had steamed up the basement one hot afternoon releasing the forces within that had caused so much confusion. There were the warnings about taking candy from strangers because they'd want to touch you-know-what in exchange. Big deal. What did that make him? He wanted desperately to be touched. Was he destined to be the world's youngest dirty old man? Didn't anybody else want to touch anybody or was it merely old men and young boys? His parents never touched. Proof. Saint Mom didn't mind, took it in stride until she died. All these thoughts had led him to a self-imposed abstinence and denial of anything sexual around him or on him or in him. Don't look when you dry yourself down there. Don't linger too long. At fifteen it all came crashing down when he washed a little too long in just the right spot. The world would never be the same. He had stuffed the guilt of it into a compact black smudge and dated girls, fantasizing about boys, and never reconciling sexuality with emotion. And this the biggest of big fantasies, the Latin teacher, had now run his adrenaline dry. His reddened complexion, warm smile, acute pronunciation. His *cutius buttius*.

Outside he took a deep breath of cold air and immediately coughed. The previous anticipation had exhausted him. He wandered along the street, shop windows dark, nothing shoveled, all waiting for the tempest to blow itself out. He struggled through the snow, around the city block. He passed the bus depot, and the bundled wanderers. Wind howled through an empty parking garage. Sixteen and never been — he thought, not by man nor even by woman — afraid, afraid to face the truth. It would have been absurd now to show up at the Latin teacher's door and say he'd been out for a stroll or to exchange last month's Christmas gifts, or visit the French bookstore —

Life hadn't done anything but work against him, in that department anyway — what was life saving him for? Thoughts broken by the sound of the crippled car crawling past him, windshield wipers scratching at crusted ice, the futile zippering of its tire treads. At each corner the wind struck a little harder.

Finally a narrow path in the drifting snow led him directly back to her store. He slowed. The wind pushed him past the bay window and into the doorway. He cupped his hands on the door's window. Candles, faint pins of light glowed now among the racks of clothing. Gripping the door handle, he was once again blown into the store. He shoved the door shut, stamped his boots and hit his arms against his sides, hoping he'd been gone long enough. Relief embraced him. Candles flickered one by one.

"Still winter?"

"Colder now."

"Furnace is off. Wind blew it out I guess." She rolled her eyes. "That's why the candles." Her delicate arms motioned to the surrounding room.

"Looks nice."

"Warm up. It's still warm. Let me take your jacket." She lifted the jacket from his shoulders. Once free, he squeezed his hands between his knees and shivered.

"Bookstore?"

"Closed." But he hadn't even checked, to cover his story.

"Sit down." She laid a heavy fur over him, as he sat back in the chair.

"Is this your store?"

"Not really. No. Not at all. I'm just doing a friend a favour."

"A big favour being here in a blizzard."

"It's no trouble. It wasn't. I just do my thing. I didn't really expect anyone."

"Do your thing?"

"I draw. People come in, poke around. I draw until they need help. Here." She handed him a steaming mug. "Very hot tea. Don't burn yourself."

"Inky fingers." He inhaled the vapour. Smiled at her.

"You noticed."

"Either that or you've been picking blueberries."

"I guess you could say I'm passionate about it, art, whatever form it takes. What's your thing, your passion?"

It was a question that made him want to explode. "Well, I don't know if I've found my passion, or discovered it. Not yet."

"You'll need to. It's all we're here for. Our passion." Now she sat facing him on a stuffed footstool, the likeness of a large pink cake. Long layers of skirt draped between her legs. She held her own drink with both hands. "Assam tea, from India — *excellent in winter and foul weather*, as the box says. Part of my personal stash."

"Of Indian things?"

She looked into the cup, blew at the steam. Fine lines traced her lips. The candlelight softened her white skin giving it the same translucence of the lily petals on his mother's altar.

He spoke quietly, "It's strong, the tea."

"Improves with age."

"I love the robe." Senseless words started to flow: "Do you work here all the time?" It sounded an awful lot like do you come here often.

"Just helping a friend." She rescued him from his stream of awkward drivel. "If Justine needs help then I come in. She's in Montreal. I offered to help. No trouble. It's a change. Poor Justine. It's never busy. Not at this time of year." She stopped talking and laughed lightly.

"Finish your tea. I'll look at your leaves."

He picked the stray leaves off his lip and flicked them into the cup.

She turned the cup over and several drops fell to the floor. "Oh. You'll cry a few tears. Perhaps you already have." She looked into the cup, "I see — well — I see myself, a tall redhead, how odd, that's never happened before. I see a dark man and the beginning of a very long journey. Perhaps you, to find your passion."

"I should get going." He regretted speaking these words. "I mean, to find my passion."

"I have something for you."

The layers of her skirts fell into place as she rose. Her breasts and soft profile arced and she concealed a yawn with the back of her hand. Cords of her hair fell behind her shoulders as she wandered back through the forest of garments.

He hoped she wasn't going to give him her phone number. Obligation frightened him.

She returned from the twilight, blowing out the candles one by one, as she came forward, letting the darkness reclaim its world. She

308

put on a cape that covered her to the floor. "Here." She handed him a parcel wrapped in brown paper and string. "I've been saving it."

He looked up at her and then at the parcel.

"Let's say it's on loan. Therefore you'll have to see me again. Come on." She reached out her hand. He took hold of it, feeling the fine bones through his wool mitt. She pulled him to his feet.

Out in the cold she locked the door. The air immediately turned her fingers red. With her back against the wind, she pulled on a small woolen cap that covered just the top of her head and her ears, but couldn't control her wild hair from whipping into his eyes. She turned, shoved her hands into a large muffler that looked like a fat raccoon. "Which way?" she shouted.

"South."

"I'll walk you to the corner." She put her arm through his and shoved her hand back into the muffler. Her body pressed close, as if she were escorting him away from a precarious route. They walked through the blowing snow like an old-fashioned couple, leaning into each other, having done so for years.

At the corner she released her hold. "Thanks," she shouted. She turned, her cape and hair funneling madly, wind quickening her steps like some character in an old black and white film played at the wrong speed. Dusk and winter swallowed her away. He turned too, and headed south.

Andrew Binks has won honorable mention in the Writer's Union of Canada's short prose contest, Glimmertrain's Family Matters contest, and he was a finalist in the Queen's University Alumni Review poetry contest, and *This Magazine's* "Great Canadian Literary Hunt."

Binks' first novel, *The Summer Between*, was published by Nightwood Editions in Spring 2009. He received an MFA in Creative Writing from the University of British Columbia. His fiction and non-fiction has been published in *Joyland, Galleon, Fugue, Prism International, Harrington Gay Men's Literary Quarterly (U.S.), Bent Magazine, The Globe and Mail,* and *Xtra,* among others. His poetry has also appeared in Quill's "Lust" issue and Velvet Avalanche Anthology. Andrew's satirical play, *Reconciliation,* about Native land claims, Japanese internment, and political corruption, will receive a staged reading in Toronto as part of the Foundry Theatre play-reading series.

Andrew spoke at the AWP conference in New York City in 2008 on the merits and challenges of multi-genre writing programs. This excerpt is from the yet-to-be-published novel, *The Catalytic Seduction of Brian White.* www.andrewbinks.ca, Contact: binksandrew@gmail.com

LEARNING TO CRAWL

---------------- ☙☞ ----------------

Excerpt from the novel
by Ben Mattlin

On their first date, she dolled up in more makeup than she'd used all year and, after six changes of clothes, decided on the fire-engine-red silk tank-top and matching harem pants that her summertime employer, Edna Dorritt, whose five-year-old son she was looking after, had given her as a graduation gift. No underthings — on the pretext of preserving the appearance and feel of feathery smoothness.

She drove into the city — that mystery place where grunginess was raised to a majestic height — and ascended to his apartment with her eyes fixed on the surprisingly unpolished black wingtips of the silent elevator operator. A heartbeat and she was there. The foyer had textured tan wallpaper. She pushed the buzzer at the only door — 18-J.

"C'mon in! It's open."

Open? As in *unlocked*? In New York City?

He was in jeans and a gray cotton sweater.

"Oh! I hope I didn't — didn't dress wrong," she said.

"What? Come in. Have a seat. You look terrific!"

He made a slight movement that caused a series of mechanical clicks, and his heavy motorized wheelchair glided backward into the living room. A large room with lots of windows — Western exposure, judging by the light. A white shag rug lay at the center of the parquet floor, surrounded by what looked like expensive modern furniture. She chose the suede couch.

"Want a drink or something?" he asked.

What did he mean — beer, Coke, mineral water, gin? "No, thanks," she said.

She'd met him just a few weeks ago in Connecticut, when little Brian had gone over to play at a friend's house. Brian was the five-year-old boy she was looking after for the summer. The friend had an older brother — much older, a half-brother — who was home from college. Edna, Brian's mom, had told her that the brother lived most of the time at his mother's, in the city — though his mother had died a year ago. He'd been in a wheelchair his whole life, as far as Edna understood it. One thing Edna hadn't said, but was readily apparent: he was a boob man.

"Shall we go?" he asked now, raising his eyebrows upward toward her face, over the top of his tortoise-shell glasses. "I figured we'd walk to the pier. Do you like walking? New York is a great city for walking."

"Sure," she offered enthusiastically, suppressing the urge to giggle on hearing him talk about walking — and her own insidious regret at not choosing more sensible shoes. But of course it wouldn't be too far. How far could he go? "The Pier, you said? Is that a restaurant?"

He laughed. "No. It's a pier. There's a concert tonight. I hadn't really thought about food, I'm afraid. Not this early. I'm sure there'll be stuff to eat there, or we can stop on the way. Do you like Squeeze?"

"What?"

"You said you used to like Elvis Costello. Squeeze is sort of similar."

She was wearing high heels and silk to a rock concert?

It was a warm summer evening, the kind you don't get in San Diego. Humid and still. After five blocks she was so hot and sticky, she thought she would die.

A guy sitting on a parked car holding a bottle in a brown paper bag hollered, "Mm-hmm! You're beautiful, baby!"

And her date, rolling along beside her, said, "Sorry. Maybe I should have picked a different route."

Sweet, he was. But really! She'd heard worse — from her own father.

Onward — through even seedier parts of town. Much as she tried to ignore her environs, she was overcome by the smells. Buses with their diesel exhausts, pretzel vendors, the occasional horse poop and ubiquitous urine stench, and the cigarettes! With all the other pollutants in the air, you really couldn't blame people for smoking — for creating their own personal little fume-clouds. "This would be a great city to be a dog," she said.

"You mean because of all the fire plugs?"

"No. No. The olfactory variety. The piss and the automobile exhausts."

"I never noticed."

Suddenly, in the middle of a crosswalk, he stopped. He mumbled something.

"Excuse me?" she said.

"No curb cut. No ramp," he said, as if translating. "Could you give me a push?"

"Sure."

He instructed her to tip the wheelchair back. It flew back in her arms. She caught it — and her own equilibrium.

Once the front wheels were up over the curb, she tried to pull the rear up. Finally she decided to crouch a bit and push up from underneath the handlebars. Voila!

"You okay?" she asked, catching her breath abruptly. "Wasn't too rough or bumpy?"

First he didn't answer. She panicked. Then he said, "Nope. I'm fine. But how about you? Not so bad, was it?"

"Now that I've got the knack . . . Sort of like a big baby carriage."

"*Baby* carriage?" he snapped, like a rubber band.

From then on he took to riding in the streets, alongside the curb. Cars whizzed past and made her nervous.

They got to the pier in one piece, however. It was a madhouse. He didn't so much as pause. He cut through the crowd savagely in his miniature tank — not caring whose shins he rammed or toes he crushed. Which was fine, considering this was New York, but everybody who got out of his way ended up trampling on her!

He even bypassed the ticket booth and ushers and led her to two seats on the aisle. He parked next to her.

"You've been here before?" she observed.

He seemed full of secret knowledge, the arcane mysteries of Wheelchair Life — and City Life. Perhaps that was why she had accepted his invitation — to experience the city *not* on her own or with a child in tow. She was so bored in Connecticut!

Sometime later, the band — Squeeze — showed up. Everyone rushed toward the stage or stood on their chairs. She couldn't see. Didn't matter — she could hear. Boy, could she hear! They sounded oddly familiar. An eerie memory filtered into her consciousness — the dorms. She recalled the music from the scratched-up radio in Jim's room, next to the bed.

Her mood dropped lower than the pit of her stomach. This guy beside her now, in the wheelchair . . . Others had seemed gentle and wise, before. Surely, this one could not dominate her, and that made him stand out from the others. Well, no — not *stand* out. The crowd was suffused with the sweet smell of pot and though she was not a stoner herself, she wouldn't mind getting hold of some. She kept expecting him to offer her something — a joint. Or a drink, from a hidden flask tucked into his chair — a nice bourbon-and-soda, like mother used to make.

After several million decibels of rowdy fun, she was feeling lightheaded and enthusiastic again.

"Want to stop for a bite or a drink?" he asked her when the concert was over.

If he wanted her to go back to his place, why didn't he just say so?

"To break up the walk," he added, flashing a sort of sideways smile.

He led her to a small purple-neon cafe on what she thought was Columbus Avenue. Smartly dressed people were smoking cigarettes and exchanging business cards at a curved bar at the back, while old-fashioned jazz came through invisible speakers. She wondered if she looked okay, not too sweaty and disgusting. Clothes here in the city tended to a more fitted look, and she hoped her outfit wasn't too suburban: women here wore dark textured panty hose, which seemed odd in the summer. No shorts, as you would certainly see in San Diego this time of year.

He approached the hostess. "Could we sit out front?" he asked.

The woman nodded and walked briskly to a small round table on the glass-enclosed patio. A Perrier bottle in the center, illuminated by a tiny white candle, held yellow daisies and baby's breath. A quick look around confirmed they were the only ones out here. The wicker chair was comfortable — a good choice. She wondered if he had been here before. With — who knows? — other women?

They ordered a round of Black Russians. She couldn't recall exactly what they were but thought she remembered liking them.

"I'm actually underage," he whispered, once they were alone. "My birthday's not till November."

"We could have coffee instead . . . "

He laughed. "Nah, I'm kidding. I _am_ underage, but they never bother me. One of the advantages of using a wheelchair: people are afraid of me. And one of the disadvantages."

Great! she thought. I work as a nanny and I'm going to get arrested for corrupting a minor. Not that he wasn't already corrupt. "My ears are still ringing," she said.

A steady stream of taxis went by outside, horns beeping continuously. A symphony of the streets! And their lights shone through the glass walls with shimmering vibrancy — random, independently flickering. Flashes as animated and mesmerizing as a fireplace. A slow saxophone echoed out of the bar area. She nodded at him, as if she understood all.

The drinks came. "We'll run a tab," he told the waiter with authoritative ease.

A tab? How much were they going to drink? What did he have in mind?

Halfway through the first round, her answer came.

"So tell me your life story," he said.

It was a line, right? A bad one. She gave him a look that she hoped said "Give me a break!"

"Knock down the wall of ice," he said.

It started raining. And they still had . . . how many blocks to walk? In San Diego it almost never rained, and when it did it took all day about it. This seemed impossibly sudden, impossibly dramatic, and, in a way, wonderful. She reminded herself that here storms blow over as quickly as they come. She pocketed the matchbook off the table and wondered, without much concern, if she was already losing her head. "What wall of ice?" she asked.

He was kind of cute, with his understanding. She signaled the waiter for another Black Russian and chewed on an ice cube in the meanwhile. The pitter-patter of rain hitting the glass grew louder, more urgent. Her brain was clouding over. Was he really still only two-thirds through his drink?

"You're not drinking," she said.

"I put it down and can't get it back up," he said. "Hold it for me, would you, and I'll sip it through the straw."

Outside, pedestrians — there were still pedestrians, at this time of night! — ran for cover and men selling umbrellas appeared like moles out of the ground. There was a tremendous, triumphant crash — then lightning. The whole wonderful array of nature's might!

The excitement was infectious. Even for supposedly jaded New Yorkers. Folks at the bar actually pointed as if they'd never seen a thunderstorm; one woman came to the patio for a better look. The roar of the storm melded with the trumpet and sax from the speakers.

She must have had a goofy smile on her face, because he suddenly said, "Y'know, Black Russians can be deceptive. They're so sweet, you don't realize how potent —"

The waiter came over. "Another round?"

Before she knew what she was doing, she nodded yes.

"You wouldn't be trying to get me drunk, would you?" he said.

"*Qui, moi?*" she said.

He chuckled and made a slurping sound with his straw until the last drop. He raised his eyebrows. "Would you put my glass down, please?" he asked.

Their fingers touched briefly. His seemed as new and pink as a baby's. The dregs of their candle danced light off his nails.

316

Midway through the next round she said, "What, me imbeedriated?" He laughed. "No, Ocifer. I'm sotally tober!" she continued.

He cracked up. He'd never heard it before. She could never make anyone in her family laugh — not the way her mother could, the lilting way she told long stories . . .

He raised his dark eyebrows again. It was a signal, she realized. She lifted his glass.

They decided at the end of this round to stop and brave the weather — emboldened by alcohol, no doubt. He slipped some bills out of somewhere in his lap.

"I don't usually allow a man to pay for drinks," she said. She thought it sounded worldly and sophisticated.

It was still sprinkling outside, but refreshingly, like champagne bubbles. And the streets were amazingly dry, only damp enough to reflect the city lights like in movies. The air felt clean and rejuvenating.

"Did I mention the time I thought I was pregnant?" she said at the corner.

The light turned green, and he turned around to bump down the curb backward.

"No," he said, betraying minimal shock. Then: "I'm sorry." As if there was a death in the family.

Clunk! He was down. The other side was ramped. She was not sorry she'd told him, though she wasn't sure why she'd done it either.

They proceeded slowly. Evidently he accepted her confession; they paused at store windows to ooh and ah over the more provocative displays or giggle over the garish ones, and he didn't ask her any questions or tell her what she should have done — didn't try to take charge, like most men. She wasn't sure she could deal with that!

"What's your favorite flower?" he asked at a florist's that was still open. Still open? She looked at her watch. This city really does never sleep!

He went inside. "No!" she objected.

He smiled. She pointed to some purple freesias. "How much for a bunch of those?" he asked the clerk.

She laughed and said she would accept only one. She carried the single stem out into the street.

New York looked beautiful in the dark — its peerless, towering architecture. Perhaps he had chosen a better course than before, for their return journey.

A scruffy-looking couple was standing under a signpost holding hands. On the West Coast, you never saw people holding hands. Everybody was always in cars. And the scruffy people — the real ones, not the fashionably-scruffy Hollywood types — were all homeless or illegal Mexican migrant workers. New York was so romantic! She could scarcely admit it to herself, but she was swept off her feet — the corniest feeling! The lights and all put her in mind of Christmas.

"It's not like I'm some kind of slut," she said.

Just then, a Chasidic Jew jaywalked toward them. She giggled — though his stare did look slightly demonic.

"What are you talking about?" her new boyfriend — or was that presumptuous? — asked. But he knew what she was talking about. "Pregnancy scares happen to everyone, at some time."

She wasn't entirely sanguine about his casualness — how everyday were such experiences for him? — but she wanted to take off his glasses. She wanted to tell him it was with her first boyfriend, and if not for her inexperience and subsequent guilt, she would never have thought . . . It was like her punishment, her comeuppance.

But she didn't need to tell him any more. "I thought I was in love," she said wearily. "You know?"

A few blocks later he asked, "Would you ride on my lap?"

She stopped, looked at him. "You don't know how much I weigh! I'll — I'll hurt you."

"Well, how about if I asked for a kiss?"

He thought he was pretty smooth, didn't he? Only later would she understand that everything had to be verbal with him. Other guys might grab her passionately and plant one on her mouth, earlobes, neck — but he had to ask.

She saw the Art Deco spires of his apartment ahead, rising above the others, and bent down. Why? What moved her to wrap her arms around his neck and press her lips against his so hard?

Still he wasn't startled. How experienced *was* he? She slipped him her tongue.

When he started playing his own gingerly back and forth along the ridge of her top lip, she wanted to dive in, to be swallowed. His mouth felt warm, and the tip of her spine sent ripples like cream in coffee. But wait. He was too aggressive, too hungry. She pulled away as a flock of pigeons ascended in a sort of spiral-funnel formation.

He mumbled "Good evening" to the doorman, then the elevator man — who didn't have to ask what floor. Alone at the vestibule of his apartment — the private entry — he asked, "Spend the night?"

Joy and panic — panic like a migraine — shot through her. "I have to get back to Connecticut."

Why, she wondered, do I want to burst into tears?

"Sober enough?" he asked like a concerned father.

She nodded and kissed the top of his head. "Yes. I think so."

"If it's diseases you're worried about —"

"No."

"Well, I don't have any anyway."

Diseases — it seemed funny coming from him, in his wheelchair. Nothing infectious, he'd probably meant, which was good.

What should I do? How does one handle a proposition from a handicapped guy? He was a charmer, but he was rushing her! She pushed the elevator button.

"Some other time, perhaps?" he said.

She had to admit, she was intrigued. What would his needs be? Probably he had a lot of needs. She smiled wanly and moved her fingers in a sort of wave. She didn't have the confidence. The elevator opened.

She waited. Should she say something?

"All aboard!" scolded the elevator man.

"Thanks for a lovely evening," she said reflexively.

She stepped into the elevator, turned around to face him once more, and blew what she hoped was an enigmatic kiss.

The doors began closing. "Wait," she said, sticking a foot out.

"What is it?" he said from the apartment doorway.

"Can you get in and everything all right by yourself?"

He pursed his lips. "Got that covered."

"Okay. Good night," she said, stepping out of the elevator into his vestibule and signaling the elevator man to go without her.

Ben Mattlin is an NPR commentator, a contributing editor at *Institutional Investor* magazine, and a frequent contributor to other financial and general-interest publications. His credits also include *Newsweek* and *Self* magazines, the *Los Angeles Times*, the *Chicago Tribune*, and *USA Today*.

Mattlin has written for the Mark Taper Forum, Blonde and Brunette Productions, and the children's television program *Biker Mice From Mars*. He has appeared on ABC's *Prime Time Live*, CNN, and E! Entertainment Network; been interviewed on radio stations KKFI and KPFK, Los Angeles, and KSLC, Salt Lake City; and been quoted in *The Wall Street Journal*, *U.S. News & World Report*, *Penthouse*, and *USA Today*.

Born in New York City in 1962, Mattlin graduated *cum laude* from Harvard University in 1984. He lives with his wife, two daughters, and a cat in Los Angeles. Contact: bmattlin@earthlink.net

Remordimiento

———————— ℰↄ◌ℛ ————————

by Hélène Valentina de Portu

"Padre, tengo mucho remordimiento." The prisoner lay in the shadows, looking at me. I stood two feet from his hospital bed, the only one of three being occupied in the whitewashed room. The semi-darkness sharpened the contrast of his jutting cheekbones and deep-set eyes.

"Father, I have sinned."

The fifty-year-old former officer had been convicted of ordering multiple cold-blooded political killings, but it was cancer that came to claim his life. He was at death's door and I had to overcome my repugnance to his crimes to minister to his soul.

The prisoner's admission of guilt did not surprise me. Other convicted murderers, suddenly confronting their mortality and the fear of hell, had cowered and cried in my presence, and begged for God's mercy before it was too late.

Dusk made it difficult to see the expression in the man's eyes beyond the pool of light of the bedside table lamp, so I moved the light slightly and leaned in closer to the man. What I saw in his eyes was not fear at all. It was torment. Knitted brows, tight pupils, and liquid green irides reflected this emotion however fleetingly.

I made an involuntary movement with my right hand toward his, as I clutched a bible against my chest with the other. "Confess your sins, my son. God will absolve you." I took a seat and waited for him to begin.

"Padre, I've killed my brother. I've killed my brother." He stopped.

"What do you mean? I don't recall that being on your record."

"My brother, padre, the man I should have considered to be my brother."

The prisoner, although ill and weakened, had a vitality that caught me unawares. Was it the oblique cut of the heavy lids or the feral intensity of those eyes?

"Ah." I spoke slowly, deliberately. "You mean you've killed a fellow man, someone you actually cared about. Is that what you mean?"

"That's just it, father. I hated him. I hated him with an intensity I didn't feel for anybody else. It consumed me at times, how much I hated him." The man lay still and closed his eyes, as if to remember.

"Gabriel and I grew up on the same street. Things came easily to him. His family had money and he was gifted. He had looks and he was charismatic. I had to work hard at everything. My family was of modest means. We weren't poor, we weren't rich. We were somewhere in the middle and struggled to make ends meet. Gabriel and I attended university together. We both studied politics and went to the same rallies, at first. He was so eloquent, crowds listened to him. I never had that talent. This was over three decades ago — eight years before the coup."

The man opened his eyes and looked as if he suddenly became aware of me. He may have found me, on closer inspection, somewhat younger than he had thought at first. My chubby cheeks, wisps of light hair, and small blue eyes have long lent me an appearance at times elderly and at other times almost cherubic. In fact, we were about the same age. Like Gabriel, I was born in a well-to-do family. My father was a lawyer; my mother, a schoolteacher; my grandparents on both sides, successful merchants. Like Gabriel, I took an interest in politics and became an activist. When the coup d'état instituted fascism, I joined the priesthood. When friends "disappeared," I led their vigils. There are different ways to deal with opposition.

"Gabriel and I socialized together as students; if girls ended up falling for me, it was because I paid attention to them. Gabriel was more interested in politics, and in Elena.

"Elena was in the first class we attended at the university, and we both noticed her. Her straight dark hair flowed like silk down her back, her small face was expressive, and her smile radiated energy. She soon became Gabriel's girlfriend. One day, when Gabriel was detained by a bus strike, I kept Elena company while she waited for him at the university cafeteria. She spoke clearly in a low, melodic voice. Her chiseled lips fluttered like red butterfly wings and her almond-shaped eyes studied my face without any timidity. I fell hard for Elena.

"When Gabriel arrived, he stood, framed by one side of the cafeteria's double glass doors, and looked around for her. I watched the ease with which he carried himself — his shoulders, at rest in a corduroy jacket, evoking power; his square jaw and bronzed leonine features commanding attention. He ran a hand nonchalantly through his mane of brown hair and smiled when he spotted us. Elena followed my gaze. Her face lit up, and jealousy grew in my heart. As I said, everything came easily to Gabriel. He never struggled for anything or anyone, things just came to him. Father, it never occurred to me to think that when she graduated, Elena actually left Gabriel to go abroad. I just remembered that he got the girl.

"Our paths separated when I began a military career at the academy. At the time of the coup, I was in the military police and Gabriel, an assistant professor at the university. He got involved in underground politics. One day, the police cracked down on suspects and he became a prisoner. My prisoner. For weeks, I vowed to make him confess the names of his fellow conspirators. Gabriel looked at me with disdainful resistance, his lips shut and lids half lowered. Once, when I'd hit him hard, he spat in my face. I wiped my cheek and struck him again. He fell unconscious on the ground, and I told my men to pick him up and throw him back in jail.

"The next time I saw Gabriel, he was standing in front of me while I finished eating my lunch. The white shirt and khaki pants he had been wearing when we arrested him were now dusty and tattered. He was gaunt and a film of sweat covered his body. The two guards who had brought him there stood on either side of him. I asked Gabriel, 'Why do you defy me like this? Don't you know your fate is in my hands?' He said, 'Yes, I know, Tomás. You've made sure I knew. But my heart is in the hands of my friends and I won't betray them. Do what you will — my heart has more value to me than my life.' So he would not see I was rendered speechless by his temerity, I bit into a piece of bread and motioned to the guards to take him away. As Gabriel walked out the door with slow steps, I hurled one last comment in his direction. 'We'll see who gives in first, you or me.'

"Gabriel and I met one last time, for his execution. We were ordered to leave and regroup in another town, and that is when I exacted my vengeance. It was early dawn and everyone was asleep. When I pushed Gabriel out to the courtyard in the back of our barracks, he knew his last hour had come. He kneeled down and muttered a brief prayer under his breath — the Ave Maria. I lifted my revolver, his face in my line of sight. The most extraordinary smile hovered over the corners of his lips and I thought it was at my expense. I pulled the trigger and all I saw was his smile mocking me, even when he fell to the side, dead."

Silence fell over the hospital room. I felt sad. Deeply sad, as I do every time I contemplate man's capacity for evil. I could not help thinking that it could just as easily have been me at the end of that gun barrel. Me, a young, plainer Gabriel in those days. Born to money and ease, indifferent to both, and determined to have a meaningful life. Only, Gabriel's was cut short. Mine wasn't. Why?

The former officer narrowed his eyes, fixing a spot on the wall. "For years," he muttered, "that smile haunted me. I chased it away but it returned. My life disintegrated as I went from camp to camp, woman to woman, and drink to drink. As much as I tried, I could not reach oblivion. For years, I felt Gabriel had won the war between us even if I'd taken his life. My hatred persisted and with it, my fears. I had killed the man but not my obsession with him. For years, I struggled to gain control over myself through the ups and downs of my life during the regime, my failed marriage and many affairs, and my children's estrangement. Without my enemy, I seemed to have lost my touchstone. Then cancer came and with it, for the first time in my life, a bit of peace."

What kind of peace was that? I wondered.

As if he had heard my unspoken question, he continued. "One night, I dreamt about Gabriel. He was not the gaunt, bearded shell of a man whom I killed. Instead, he looked exactly the same as on that day at the cafeteria, with his strong shoulders and thick, wavy hair. In my dream, his dark eyes were smiling at me, and he ran his hand through his hair in the old familiar way. He explained to me, 'Tomás, you were the furthest thing from my mind in the moment I died. All my adult life, when things came easily to me, as you so often told me when we were students, I practiced non-attachment to personal outcomes. Whether things worked out or didn't work out, my goal was to let them go. Before I experienced a success, I had let it go. Before I experienced a failure, I had let it go. Then, when I saw the hatred you had for me and when I knew I was about to die at your hands, I let it all go. I felt no regret, no resentment, only peace. I had overcome the limitations of my own self. That is why I smiled, brother.' In my dream, he called me brother.

"Padre, when I awoke, I was suddenly released from my old anger, my fears, and my obsession. Something else came over me. A knot in my throat constricts me so hard, at times, I have difficulty breathing and swallowing. This enemy, this friend whom I killed, why, he looked as if he could be my son. I'm middle-aged, and suddenly he looked so young. What have I done? What have I done?"

The sick man fell silent. He closed his eyes and, for an instant, I had the crazy notion that he was perhaps dead.

I took his hand in mine and prayed. "Holy Mary, Mother of God, pray for us sinners, now and at the hour of our death. Amen."

When I raised my eyes to the man's face, his lids were still closed. Down his right temple, tears had left a shiny track. To my great surprise, the corners of his mouth were upturned in a ghost of a smile.

Born in Tokyo and raised in Paris, **Hélène Valentina de Portu** is an award-winning educator, executive editor, and coach, now living in New York City. French and Japanese by birth, she has been in fifteen countries, and spent much of her life in the U.S. Over the years, Valentina has learned Japanese, French, Italian, Latin, German, English, and Spanish.

Valentina holds a Ph.D. in Comparative Literature from Harvard University. For over two decades, she has fostered linguistic, transcultural, and ontological competence among adults worldwide and U.S. college students. Valentina is currently at work on her first novel. You can visit her website at http://valentinadeportu.com. Contact: valentina@manhattaneditorial.com

DON'T THINK YOU'RE CALLING TOO MUCH

————————— ℰ❧ ———————————

Excerpted from the novel
by Wickham Boyle

It's 3:23 a.m. and the Humvees are driving across North Moore Street, where I've made my home for over 25 years. It's a street that has seen a huge suspicious fire in an old warehouse waiting to be converted, a migrant worker buried alive by errant Con Edison workers, and the death of our neighbors John and Carolyn Kennedy. But this is war and it is different.

I have been up all night, between the phone calls from around the world — Australia, Finland, Italy and France — and the blaring light of too much TV. The adrenaline is pumping and, although I feel like passing out, a part of me doesn't want to lose consciousness because another explosion, another crash, another cloud of noxious smoke and debris may wash over what I thought of as my safe, calm, sweet TriBeCa home.

I heard the first plane rush over my loft, felt the impact, ran to the roof, saw the second plane hit and the tower burst into flames. At first, I couldn't believe it was anything but a horrible accident. Then it began to sink in, and I wondered how long those towers would stand before they tipped over. Such a gentle word for what would happen, but that was all I could think of: a child's tower built too high, now tilted by the bully's block thrown in malice. They would tip over; I knew it. My husband and my neighbor told me to stay calm.

They wouldn't collapse; the school would evacuate the kids But my mother's instincts took over.

I jumped onto my three-speed bike and headed over to my 12 year old son's school, P.S./I.S. 89, about four blocks from the towers and right in the path of the terrible tipping I envisioned. I broke through the crowds, brandishing my press pass. When I arrived, the school was a beehive. Teachers were sending parents upstairs for the elementary kids and to the cafeteria for the middle schoolers. I left my bike with my purse in the basket but wasn't going back. Anyone could have my money, the bike, my stupid useless cell phone. I didn't care.

I saw my Henry — goofy — with a bunch of friends. I told the principal I was taking as many as would come. "Who's coming with me?" Henry's crowd raised their hands; there were about a dozen of them. The principal and I discussed it for a minute and quickly wrote a makeshift sign-out sheet. Before we hit the streets, I gave perfunctory directions: "Stay together, hold hands. You will see people crying, screaming. Don't look back, keep moving forward. Listen to me and do what I say."

We made it across the West Side Highway and by then a third of them were crying. I kept switching partners in mid-run, pairing the calmer kids with the more hysterical ones. I had seen people flinging themselves out of the towers on the way over and I wanted to shield my kids from that sight. So I said, "Just look ahead!" Then I looked back — the mistake of Lot's wife — and, although I didn't turn into a pillar of salt, I was frozen for a second. The south tower was dropping in a horrifying cascade; a huge column of smoke rose and rushed toward us, swallowing everything in its path.

The escaping crowd was careening into the middle of the West Side Highway. We were alongside the Borough of Manhattan Community College, another neighborhood landmark, and I yelled, "All my kids against the wall of the college. All my kids stand still!" They obeyed immediately. I counted; I had them all. We waited for the tremors to subside — five seconds, maybe ten — then we ran like hell until we got to my loft. One kid was crying because his mother works in one of the towers. I kept saying I knew she was OK and she would expect me to get him home safe to her. My son Henry was like a soldier, never balking, simply following orders: "Hold her," "Take this one across the street," "Get your shoes off upstairs." Kids installed, I headed out again to buy some food. I cried in the deli, then wiped away the tears. I wanted to be strong for my kids.

When I came back, we had to turn off the TV because the remaining tower had crumbled to the ground and the kids lost it. Henry put on Charlie Brown's Christmas video and that seemed to work. I made sandwiches, which were hardly touched. Chips were devoured. One by one, parents and children were reunited, even the kid whose mom worked up there — she had been at a dentist appointment that morning. All were returned home, shaken but somehow safe.

My family ate pasta, toasted our good fortune in having each other and were pretty quiet. My 16-year-old daughter and I went out for a walk, a nod to our normal warm weather postprandial wanderings. She veered off with another neighborhood kid and I gave out water to the rescue workers. One young cop asked me for scotch so I went back upstairs and got some good single malt. I gave him a plastic cup and he asked if we could toast his friend who had been crushed that day. We raised our glasses. "To Wally," he said and burst into tears. I hugged him, then he downed the scotch and went to the next corner.

Back home I wanted a shower, but we had no water. I wanted to sleep, but there was no air and the phone never stopped ringing. I sat in the window seat overlooking my too-quiet block. That's when the National Guard rolled past, changing the landscape forever by punctuating my poky streets with tanks and illuminating our new found fear.

Sometimes the platitudes our mothers or grannies espouse over the years never come to be tested. The lesser of two evils is presented as a choice between two poor options. Should I stay with the deadbeat spouse or head out on my own and attempt to remake a life from scratch? Quit the low-paying job with good benefits or clump out into the world to find a dream career with uncertain support? These are light choices between minor evils, nothing akin to the choices I witnessed on a clear, bright September morning.

The towers were ablaze; the news told us it was the work of terrorists. I saw it from my roof ten blocks north. There was an explosion of flame, followed by billowing black smoke and debris floating down onto the streets like an early fall snowstorm. The world stood dumbstruck, and I watched with clenched teeth from my rooftop — the same perch I had occupied to view the innocent fireworks of past Independence Days. Sound, light, explosion — this time giving way not to joy, but unimaginable fear.

As I rushed closer to the scene in an attempt to find my son, who was sitting in history class and felt the rumblings of this assault, I began to see the choices being made. Bodies were launching, gliding, tumbling from the high windows of the towers. Were they hurtled by the force of explosions . . . pushed by crowds gasping for air . . . or had they flung themselves out in a final act of free will?

This was not a scene to be watched. When I grabbed my son and his pals, I warned them not to look. I cautioned them to avert their eyes. I had to shield their young psyches from this abomination. But as Biblical scholars will point out, all we humans need be told is "don't look," and that is all we want to see. So we glanced again and again in disbelief. Perhaps we thought that, like scratching a scab, the repeated action would assuage the pain. It didn't.

On that morning, we witnessed a terrible choice between the lesser of two evils: to die immolated or to fly like Icarus toward the Earth in the hope that such a mythic action would render some peace. I believe that all who perished are heroes in different ways, but I believe the flying bodies, holding hands in their final moments, offered a kind of proof that humanity and the power of partnership are unshakable, even in extremis. Will I hold hands differently now? Will I leap from the tall, quarry cliffs in New Hampshire into the clear water below with the same abandon? I do know that when I brush my teeth, using my silly electronic toothbrush that counts out what seems like an interminable two minutes, I wonder: did it take this long? Would I have had the courage to launch myself in order to grasp some semblance of self-determination in a world instantly transformed into hell? A friend expressed his belief that the light emanating from the 16-acre disaster site was so strong because it contained the pellucid gleam of all the souls that had been released there. Perhaps he's right.

My eyes search the horizon from my TriBeCa home; they roam over the landscape idly like an errant tongue groping the empty socket that earlier held a gleaming tooth. Over and over, my gaze comes to rest on the spot where the twin towers of the World Trade Center held sway as mighty landmarks. "Go south toward the towers," I would direct endless foreign visitors.

Now in the darkness of the third night there is a crescent moon and stars, unusual in downtown Manhattan. But after all, these have been three glorious Indian summer days with crystal-clear skies, shockingly filled with acrid smoke and choking particles. In the streets, I've seen children whose loud mouths are covered in gas masks and hollow-eyed neighbors' faces obscured by knotted bandannas or construction masks.

My daughter, who was born in this loft, is frustrated because she wants to work; she wants to feel the heft of steel and wood . . . to do something of consequence, to help. My 12-year-old son's school was covered in dust and rubble. He ran hand in hand with me from the devastation of the crumbling towers, and now he just wants to fall asleep without seeing bodies tumbling from the massive burning hulks.

Today he and I went to one of the few local markets still open and bought the dusty flowers that languished outside. The young Korean manager gave them to us with a smile saying, "Very dirty, very dirty." We took the bundles, shook them vigorously, then ran them under our shower. They revived much more miraculously than the buildings or the people around us. We carried these bouquets and placed them ceremonially but swiftly into the host of crushed cars that abound in our usually quiet, chic neighborhood.

On Hudson Street, two unidentifiable vehicles were flattened into a sort of double-decker car sandwich; we left deep pink lilies. Across the street, a Con Edison van was twisted, burnt and filled with dust; we left white lilies. The repair crew whose car it had been thanked us and told us that one of the other rescue workers had not made it.

331

We continued our grim reverie, pausing, inserting flowers and reflecting. Henry told me, "No one can really understand why this happened. People keep asking me if I understand, but grown-ups are just as clueless." We talked and walked and paused. We wanted, above all, to make a small mark in the ugliness of the rubble by inserting something beautiful. The flower bouquets were full of color in a world of lingering summer turned to gray winter by this unspeakable act of violence.

We are alive and breathing down here, blocks from the devastation, searching the landscape with our eyes and groping our teeth with our tongues for assurance that some things remain in place.

When they yell, "Quiet!" at the top of the pile, it becomes so silent it is surreal. What it means is they've found a human.

Four young, wildly handsome doctors strode down my street in the first hours of the third day after the terror and destruction. They told me they had just been at Ground Zero and helped pull two men out alive. These four, a year out of medical school, were jubilant, ecstatic and solemn, the emotions radiating out of their soot-caked pores.

Doctors Kayan Amini, Keyur Trivedi, Alan Singer and Marcel Marcet seemed to represent the four corners of the world. These diverse Americans were thrown together in catastrophe and bound by a brotherhood they described as "the powerful need to physically assist, to actually do something."

They spoke simultaneously, words tumbling one on top of the other.

"We were right in the rubble, the only docs, everyone else was firefighters, cops and rescue workers. We don't even think we were authorized to be there, but when they pulled the guys up, we were more than welcome. Did you hear it on TV? Did they announce the men were found? Did you hear the cheering?"

We live ten blocks from the World Trade Center; its precipitous lights were a dazzling backdrop at night. My children played in a soccer league on a field that bathed in the long shadows thrown by the twin towers on beautiful fall weekends. But now, in the pre-dawn hours, we were out in the rain unloading 80,000 pounds of water, food, dog chow, work gloves, coolers, ice, granola bars and baby wipes onto the former warehouse loading docks of our TriBeCa loft buildings. The donations came from Long Island, where they were gathered by radio station WBAB and trucked in by Liberty Van Lines. They were unloaded simultaneously by chanting Buddhists from North Carolina, Salvation Army Volunteers from all over the city and stalwart neighborhood teens who refused to be displaced from their homes.

When the trucks rolled in, we heard the commotion and descended to work. We were eager to finally get tired from honest work, rather than the airborne soot and detritus invading our homes, not to mention the draining emotions provoked by the devastation. "Let's do this like Buddhists," was the loading chant, and two lines of people passed huge boxes of clothes and tight, heavy bags of animal food along the chain onto loading docks that are normally reserved for strollers, suitcases and bicycles.

Suma Ching Hai is a meditation group from Durham, North Carolina. They drove up the day before with twenty-five volunteers, all wearing bright yellow polar fleece vests and wonderfully calm expressions. Jeffrey Dubransky was 23, a sweet-faced strawberry blond who was remarkably focused as he hefted box after box, emptying one truck and moving quickly to the next. His demeanor was offset by Robert Guzzon and Vinnie Miano, truckers from Liberty, who bellowed instructions and then paused briefly to reflect. "Hey, we're doing whatever we can. We're truckers, we have trucks, so we're carting whatever they need. We just came to help. It's that simple."

Seventy-plus-year-old Ho Ng was side-stepping the heavy labor but encouraging the group with chants. He came from Vietnam over twenty years ago, now resides in North Carolina, and he was here to make his contribution. As neighbors passed by with dogs or precious groceries garnered from uptown beyond the cordoned off area, they paused to help. No one felt extraneous.

We were adjusting the mountain of boxes when the four doctors from Saint Vincent's and Mother Cabrini hospitals marched down the street, electrifying our block. They were all so vibrant, so full of hope, buoyed by the notion that they had finally put their education — years of brutally long hours and hard studying — to work and truly made a difference.

"Hey, tell everyone that we're all single," one of them yelled over his shoulder as they began the two-mile hike back to their hospitals. "But don't make us look desperate." Desperate is the last thing any of us are. We are working together, side by side, chanting and hoping — and there is the strength in this crisis.

Last night, I ate at famed chef David Bouley's newest establishment, unofficially dubbed The Green Tarp Café. The food was superb and the patrons brave, appreciative and exhausted. The site faces Ground Zero, the epicenter of the World Trade Center's demise. It is a black and white world of unimaginable weirdness; it is also part of my neighborhood.

I finally ate after six hours of feeding firefighters, construction workers, rescue experts, police and medics. The food service site on Cedar Street abuts the debris pile. Night after night, David Bouley, his chefs and volunteers attempt to inoculate the workers against their ordeal by fortifying them with food.

My mother is Italian, and I descend from a long line of people who were comforted by food. My childhood was a whirl of nutritional vaccinations — pastas, pizzas, pastries, fruits and salads. Every disturbance and every fete was marked by the solace of food. Even now, nearly three weeks into this turmoil, I have joked to friends that if the world ends I plan to go down at "Maximum Chubby," my version of full alert.

My grandfather used to regale us with tales of his mother making an Italian version of pancakes every winter morning. She would carefully wrap them and line his thin jacket with the steaming cakes. He told us how they kept him warm on his walk to school and were still edible by lunchtime. We thought it was silly, but last night as I stood on the line serving workers, I had a vision of my Grandpa cocooned in cakes.

I stood and served food well into the night. I worked the salad and dessert station — a hard sell and an easy fix. I joked that salad is a necessity for men who pile their plates with roast beef, macaroni and cheese, and baked ziti. I made special plates with greens and Jersey tomatoes. For breads, we offered baguettes and focaccia. As he returned for seconds, one construction worker from Alabama quipped, "I can't pronounce it, but I sure can eat it." He hauled back a stack of focaccia for his table.

At a break, I walked past The Green Tarp to the edge of the rubble: acres and acres, a mountain really, where eight gigantic bulldozers dig and shovel and it never seems to diminish. The pile steamed. Everything was gray, save for the flags flying and the intermittent smiles of the workers. The drone of machinery was comforting, but crashing steel girders and chunks of wall made me jump. I was unprepared. There is no precedent for seeing such a familiar landscape jumbled, twisted, smashed and sucked colorless.

The mood in the café was subdued, the air was heavy and the work back-breaking and depressing. The normally bubbly noise of lunchrooms was missing. The grimy faces on the workers were punctuated with eyes so tired that, as a mother, I wanted to put them all down for their naps. These guys were not broken, but they were disheartened. The crews were mostly men. They spoke with Polish, Italian, French, Ecuadorian, Brooklyn and Southern accents. They had spiky punk hair, graying ponytails, buzz cuts and heads obscured by hard hats. I ladled salads and made them all promise to return for dessert, a medley of peach clafoutis, apple strudel, brownies, and a worker's wife's cake topped with fluorescent green icing. Most said they would be back, but one young man with blue eyes and a shock of black hair stubbornly showing under his "Probie" firefighter hat told me his captain had admonished his men to "eat dessert first, you may not live till dinner." I told him not to believe that just for tonight, promising him dinner then dessert. He laughed at me and crooned, "Oh, so you're one of the glass-is-half-full people."

After the shift, I stumbled out into the night air. It was brisk and the smell less acrid. I washed at a special decontamination station. A place where all workers had to wash their shoes so they didn't transport dust from the site out into the real world. I rinsed my shoes. I trudged on toward home, beholding a horrific movie set . . . the fallen Tower of Babel. I looked around at ceaseless activity brought on by senseless violence, and I put one foot in front of the other.

Still numb, I thought of the smiles and the heartfelt thanks for food, for service, for flirting, for warm desserts, for a pile of greens. It was fabulous homemade fare, the fortification of my childhood, of my children's youth and now of a small army. As I trudged along, a golf cart filled with emergency equipment and two firefighters pulled up to me.

"Hey, aren't you the lady who made us eat salad and gave us two desserts?"

"That would be me."

"Come on, we'll drive you home."

I jumped in. They wanted me up front because the terrain was treacherous. We drove through the checkpoint, past dump trucks and cranes. The sirens were pretty quiet by now; there were no more people to save.

They dropped me at home and thanked me again for the food. I reminded them that I just served it, Bouley cooked it. "Whatever. You made us smile. So get some sleep."

By the time I walked up the stairs I was exhausted, but not too tired to eat some toasted *prosciutto* bread and wash it down with a glass of milk. Inoculated, I slept like a baby.

This weekend I had an affair with geography. I ran away and caressed the coastline with my smoke-stung eyes. I inhaled the forgotten aromas of tangy salt air, felt the wet grass between my toes and reveled in escapist conversation. I consumed this feast of forbidden pleasures like an Italian downs his espresso at the bar. I stood, tilted my head back, and devoured the furious waves cutting across the Atlantic Ocean. I gazed out from the porch of a pink house so picture-perfect it erased the memory of the stark gray relationship I had left after nearly three weeks of steadfast determination and loyal devotion.

Like a guilty, liberated spouse, I broke free. I drove the length of Long Island to the enclave of the Hamptons, leaving my TriBeCa neighborhood steeped in smoke and wallowing in a miasma of misapprehension. We saw our son go off to a temporary school while his regular one was converted to a command post. I celebrated my birthday in a series of smoky local establishments and we all toasted the sweet notion of being here, alive, in one piece. We had been loyal, monogamous residents and then I bolted, I balked, I ran away in search of sheer, unadulterated pleasure.

At first, as I breathed deeply of the country air and felt the roll of waves echo my heartbeat and the salt air fill me with giddy joy, I knew I had done the right thing. I was young and unattached again. I was in the moment, and that present tense was all about hedonism — the pristine landscape, the sleek automobiles, the gourmet cheese puffs hot from a giant oven, the cold champagne bubbling just for me. I slept with the wind rustling aged maple trees and the coolness of fall seducing me with color, harvest plenty and an intoxicating taste of freedom.

But all this ended in the morning light. It was the crush of ill-gained ecstasy, full at the expense of another. Commitment is difficult, and there is always another whose jubilant laugh promises wonderment, or whose cottage begs no work, no laundry, no dishes, no tough times to navigate. Perhaps we have taken refuge in the arms of others; maybe these easy seductions have thrown us off course in the space of our lifetime.

I see my own existence as a hyperactive, interactive work-in-progress. I change, the seasons change. I learn, I am challenged and I get my rudder back and return to what I love, what has supported me, nurtured me and consistently allowed me to be all the inconsistent things I am.

One of the anchors in my life is TriBeCa, my home for nearly three decades. This neighborhood has taken in my two babies, embraced me in my endless quest for the perfect career, and married me in its opulence. My children are home-grown and I have come of age listening to the buzz of cobblestones, the clip-clop of horses' hooves, the bustle of the big city all around and above us and the neighborly smiles, nods and waves in our streets.

I may on occasion want my affair with the geography of perfection. I am fickle when it comes to travel, but my heart is housed here. I may visit, lollygag or dawdle with another place, but I come home to TriBeCa. There is so much to be said for commitment.

It's a Monday morning in early fall, 2001. The kids are off to school and my husband is scurrying to assemble his bags, trying to make an early morning flight from New York City to Dallas. I am sitting down to beat deadlines and perhaps even have a thought.

It's business as usual, yet I am terrified.

This is the first flight Zachary has taken since the assault on the World Trade Center, the U.S.A. and my life. This is his first departure in nearly three weeks. Every other regular activity in our lives has been canceled or postponed. Everything has changed — Zach's work, our son's school — which is a command center lying perilously close to Ground Zero — and my work, which is now obsessively focused on chronicling life downtown.

Zach used to take day trips to Dallas. He'd fly out early and be home for the news and some late-night snuggling. He counsels professional athletes, giving workshops on life skills, basically teaching them how to be better players off the field. He has to travel; there are only a few teams in New York City and the rest of them are strung out across the country. Zach flies over 100,000 miles every year. Although it was sometimes exhausting, it was never terrifying. Until now.

He packed a simple bag. He clipped his nails last night, thus obviating the lethal clipper-in-the-carry-on bag syndrome. He left his computer, stuffed an extra shirt, some drawers, and his toiletries into an overnighter and then started to kiss me good-bye. He mushed my face, held me, kissed me again, told me he loved me and then left. Then he came back up the stairs for something he forgot. I grabbed him again and kissed him, really smelling his shower-fresh skin, his crisp shirt. I felt the slight prickle of his moustache and held his beefy hand for a brief second as he charged out the door striding to the limo that would meet him outside the barricaded zone where we live.

I yelled after him, "Don't think you're calling too much." He laughed that resonant guffaw I love so much. I meant call me from the airport, tell me how it is. Call me when you arrive in Dallas, tell me you're safe. Call me when you get to the hotel, let me hear your voice. Call me in the morning when you leave. Call the minute you touch down in NYC and then again when you're out of the airport. Call me from the barricade if you can't get home because you still haven't changed the address on your driver's license after all these years. Call me to say you love me. If you call me every minute then perhaps you'll be safe, I'll be safe, the children will come home and I'll be able to get some sleep.

Wickham Boyle, known as Wicki, wears many hats: journalist, writer, finance consultant and theater producer. She writes about the arts, finance, parenting and travel for *The New York Times, Savoy, National Geographic, Budget Travel,* and *Downtown Express.* She was one of the founders of *CODE Magazine,* and editor-in-chief of *THRIVE.* Her essays can be heard on the AARP radio stations during their Prime Time show. Boyle was executive director of La MaMa Theater and produced over 60 shows during her tenure there.

Her 2001 book, *A Mother's Essays From Ground Zero* garnered excellent reviews and raised over $20,000 for schools closed downtown. It was adapted to an opera, titled *CALLING: an Opera of Forgiveness.* She has lived in TriBeCa since 1977 and holds an MBA from Yale University. For more info: www.wickworld.com. Contact: wixboyle@mac.com.

SCHERZO

———————— ℘ℭ ————————

Excerpt from the novel
by David Landau

I grew up in Graumark, the rain-soaked northern province of Feierland, not far from the Karelian Sea. My father was a navy man, a classmate of the first famous admirals. I later went to war under their command, but I never knew my father. He died in a duel when I was a baby; my mother died soon after. I was left to my father's elder brother and raised on the family estate.

Our home was called the Stork's Nest, because much of our ground was a wading area for those long-legged, tough-billed birds. The house was a brick rectangle the color of ox-blood. The main entranceway was a barn-style door with a swinging top, flanked by a pair of cannon from the Twelve Years' War. A wagon-ride south across a yellow sand marsh were Uncle's grain fields and a broad evergreen wood. On our northern side was the sea, whose long, spindly fingers reached almost to the house. On even the dullest, foggiest days we could look out and see a maze of canals, inlets and coves, all teeming with life and beckoning to us with a mysterious power.

On spring evenings, in brilliant lantern-lit processions, Uncle and the servant boys set out for the coves to scavenge for crabs. And at all seasons they brought back eels, prized creatures that were a delicacy in restaurants and homes throughout Feierland. The swampy reaches beyond our back yard overflowed with eel-beds. Once a week or more, the servants carried large nets full of shiny, serpentine fish to the distillery that occupied almost our entire barn. There they processed the eels for shipment to all parts of the country. This they accomplished by stuffing the eels' mouths with rags soaked in potato brandy. The intoxicated creatures remained still in their packages, reaching their destinations fresh and live.

"We make our livelihood from those eels," I said one day, as soon as I was able to encompass the notion of a livelihood.

Uncle dismissed my idea. "That's only a small part of what we do," he said brutishly.

"Actually," Auntie chimed in, "your uncle is extremely skillful at making moves in the grain market." Out of respect, she lowered her voice and explained: "To look at him, you wouldn't really guess, but he is a financial genius!"

Apart from our exotic sea-life, we didn't have many animals on the estate: one or two rickety horses, a handful of chickens and pigs. I was fond of the pigs. One of them, a blue-eyed creature called Engelbert, was a fine conversationalist.

"What do you think, Engelbert?" I often asked him. "Are we going to see the sun today?"

He moved backward with a chafing gesture and fixed me with his frank, sociable gaze. "Probably not," he meant to say, "but one should never lose heart."

"How do you put up with it?" I wondered. "Don't you get tired of all the rain?"

Engelbert stamped and snorted. "My feet are on the ground," he was telling me, "and I always enjoy a good bath."

The animal I knew best was Uncle's hound, Theophil, who dwarfed me in size even on the day I left the Stork's Nest for good. Though not so gifted a raconteur as Engelbert, Theo had a thoughtful attitude. His preferred activity, in which he engaged for hours without stopping was to sit guard at the main entrance beside the cannon, his front paws resting assertively on the ground before him and an imperturbable look on his face. Whenever a guest carriage pulled up to the Stork's Nest, the passenger froze in consternation before the noble beast until the servants, wielding umbrellas in the rain, could coax the newcomer around this formidable sentry. All the while Theo kept sitting to attention without moving a muscle or eyebrow, as inscrutable as an Imperial guard.

In exchange for this important service, Theo asked only the customary recompense due to all beloved pets, along with one other: a release from the obligation taught to him in house-training. Theo knew perfectly well to attend to himself outside the house; he even knew the virtue of discreet distance. He simply preferred, every now and then, to relieve himself in our sitting room, smack on the rug before the hearth. Whenever it happened, Uncle stormed into the sitting room and snapped at the servants: "What is this here? Why does no one clean this up? This is not a riding stable. This is the house of Leiden. Get to work, or I shall dismiss all of you!"

One day, while the servants hurried to do as Uncle commanded, I asked my favorite among them, a tall and sympathetic fellow named Walther, why they didn't save themselves the trouble of dealing with Uncle and clean up the mess before he noticed it.

"Then we would be poor servants," Walther said. "We wouldn't be doing our jobs."

"Isn't it your job to keep the place clean?" I asked.

"It is, in part," he explained. "Our most important job is to please the master."

"But he wants you to clean it up!"

Walther smiled and said, without a trace of ruefulness: "Actually, he enjoys discovering the mess. If we didn't let him find it and scream at us, we would be taking away one of his greatest joys. So we just leave it alone until he mentions it."

When I heard that, I began to understand that life was full of hidden complexities.

Uncle fancied himself a drawing-room personality, but he was much happier in his peasant vest and mud-spotted riding boots. At times he took me on wagon rides into the forest, where he could let loose. When we got to the woods he jumped out of the wagon, stretched his arms and wheeled about like a child, kicking his legs in those enormous boots.

"Look at the forest, Gerhard. It's a work of God. Thousands of years go into its making. And it will last for thousands more. The forest is a mighty presence. Once it's here, it's here to stay."

To prove his point, he took an axe from the wagon and struck a tree with it. He thrust his large body forward and grunted with every blow, cutting into the tree from all sides; working sometimes for half an hour before he could put his heel to the trunk and fell the huge being with one last kick.

"You see what it takes to destroy a forest, Gerhard? That is just one tree. Think what it would take to destroy a thousand of these, or a million. No, Gerhard, it never would be possible — not in a man's lifetime. Always remember: the forest is mightier than any one man."

As we rolled back to the house, the horses bellowing under Uncle's lash, I wanted to murder him for what he'd done. How defenseless the tree had been! It could only stand there in mute magnificence as Uncle hacked into it. How many times I'd nearly cried as he chopped, and had had to hold back from swinging my fists into him. On the way home, I looked over to see whether perhaps he shared my thoughts and regretted killing the tree. He was only swigging beer, making loud gulps as the butt end of his bottle swung aimlessly in the sky.

In my soul, I raged at Uncle for those exhibitions of his with the axe and beer-bottle. I was sure he was the most heinous of all creatures to inhabit the earth. Now I think differently. Uncle was an innocent. Even as he cut down a tree, he never imagined felling the forest at a single blow. He wielded an axe, never thinking to use fire.

The people of Graumark are intensely attached to their terrain. I've often wondered why. At times it seems that the harder a fatherland is on its children, the more deeply its children care for it. Or maybe they don't; maybe they're just more vehement about their fatherland because at bottom they loathe and fear it.

One thing is for certain: this feeling of fatherland belongs to grownups. Children, by and large, do not share in it. When I lived in Graumark, I wanted to know why the sun hardly ever appeared — why it was cloudy and rained nearly every day. When my aunt saw me running around the house in my father's old sailor hats, she knew I was upset and tried cheering me up.

"You're not sad again, are you, my sweet? What is it?"

"I want to go outside, Auntie. But it doesn't stop raining."

"What do you want outside, my child? You've everything you need inside, don't you? You've your toys and your father's things and your friends, the youngsters of all the fine people who help us in the house. Aren't you happy with all of us?"

"Yes, but why doesn't the sun come out?"

"There isn't anything to do about that, my little one. If the old man in the sky wants to be gray and stormy, we can't change that down here. Do you know what my grandmother told me? When I was a girl I also wanted the sun to shine, and it hardly ever did, so Nana said: 'My love, if your happiness waits on the sun to shine you will never be really happy. You must learn to be happy without the sun.'"

Sometimes I frolicked with the servants' children in the shadow of the house, or I went on trips to the wood with Uncle. Mostly, however, the house's big public rooms, with their spare furnishings and dull, simple colors, were my playground until I was nearly five. Then my aunt introduced me to the piano.

It was a grand instrument, made of mahogany, with ivory keys a bit yellowed from age — the finest piece of furniture my uncle owned. Auntie could read music and play some simple tunes. That was quite enough to get me started. I played everything I wanted to play on the first try. Reading music was so simple. I read a piece on sight, and when I'd played it once or twice I had it memorized.

In a week or two I'd run through all the printed music in the house. Auntie had to send to the nearby towns for more. In a few weeks more she was sending to Torlag. She sent for teachers too, since I was far beyond her in no time at all. They came from all the towns and universities within a few days' journey of our house. Professors arrived to teach me big concert pieces, bringing baggage for several weeks. I learned and memorized their pieces in a day or two. By age ten I was playing the basic repertory: the sonatas of Laune and Steuermann, Strahl's preludes and fugues, Le Frêne's studies and nocturnes, and of course those gems of piano literature, the 33 concertos of Kutsche.

Almost as soon as I'd started to play, Auntie and Uncle were giving thought to my public début. The inspiration for my career, however, came from one of my would-be teachers, who reported to Uncle in frustration: "The deuce take it! That boy could play the piano with his hands behind his back!"

That fixed me. Uncle decided that if I was so gifted at playing the piano hands forward, it shouldn't be hard for me to play hands backward. Of course Auntie and Uncle didn't want to be hasty about it. They wrote all over Feierland, inquiring after teachers who might have some expertise in this matter. After a time they found just the man they wanted: the renowned Doctor Junius Spiegel of Lichtenstadt, a pupil of the virtuoso Redek and a venerable musicologist who had spent some decades perfecting the knowledge that he had lately delivered in a scholarly article, "Über die durch die Ruckwärtshandstellungstechnik des Klavierspielens zu ermöglichen Neugestaltung und Verbesserung der grossesten Musikmeisterstücke" — "On the Reinterpretation and Improvement of Music's Greatest Masterpieces, Made Possible by the Hands-in-Reverse-Position Technique of Piano Performance."

One day a carriage rolled up to our house. Out into a colonnade of umbrellas stepped a squat, mincing man with plastered white hair and a gaping mouth. His skin had a yellowish tinge; his countenance was most exotic. As he tiptoed around Theo and came inside the door, Auntie and I could see by looking through his spectacles that each of his eyes turned outward. That gave him his curious slant-eyed appearance.

As the Doctor was shown to his room, Uncle said: "I'm not fond of him. There's something funny about his eyes. A man should face you squarely when he talks. This one looks around you on both sides."

"Don't be harsh, Uncle," Auntie entreated. "He's a perfectly delightful man. And I'm fond of his eyes. I think it's a virtue that they turn outward. That means he can read both sheets of a musical score at the same time."

At dinner Uncle asked: "I'm curious, Doctor, why it is that you've devoted so much of your time to this unusual technique of playing the piano backwards. Does it have advantages that playing in the normal way doesn't have?"

"It's a difficult question, sir, a difficult question," the Doctor answered between slurps, for he was busy getting to the bottom of his dish. "Playing the piano hands forward is also perfectly fine! But playing hands backward makes possible a very valuable and stimulating extension of our knowledge about traditional technique. Whoever learns the hands-reversed position will only increase his mastery of the conventional position."

"But which is really the better technique, Doctor? This is what I should like to know. Could it be that what we are calling the reverse position might be, if not the more natural or obvious position, in the end the more advantageous and reasonable position?"

"It might be so, sir — it might just be so! Sometimes I would like to say one thing, and sometimes I would like to say the other. If I may relate a curious history, sir, I shall always remember what my first teacher of piano said to me when I was a boy. For most children, even the ones who like music, playing the piano is an arduous, complicated business. When you begin, your fingers and hands are so stiff they feel as if they are made from stone. You must work for a long time to make the left hand work properly with the right. When you play anything by Strahl, with the hands moving in completely different directions, it can be almost painful. One day I said to my teacher: 'This is a strange, unnatural thing you are asking me to do!' I will tell you how he answered me. If I may be suffered to stand up, I will demonstrate how he spoke."

The Doctor stood to attention with arms drooping at his side. His stomach protruded beyond his waistcoat, which he had long since unbuttoned to make room for his meal.

"First my teacher said: 'Chimpanzees stand like this.'" The Doctor swayed on his bulky legs and turned his palms forward.

"Then he said: 'Humans stand like this. '" The Doctor turned his palms inward to make a normal posture.

"At last he said: 'This is how pianists stand. '" The Doctor turned the backs of his arms forward and raised his knuckles. His hands were in keyboard position.

347

It was a splendid argument. The Doctor had shown us that the pianist's posture is as different from that of ordinary humans as the chimpanzee's.

"So," the Doctor concluded, "it is only a careless man who is willing to pronounce on what is natural and what is unnatural. For all we know, the hands-reversed position might be just as correct as the more familiar one. Who are we to say?"

With that, he plunked himself down and dispatched the rest of his meal.

I studied for some time with old Spiegel. Each morning I sat on the piano stool with my back to the instrument, turned my elbows inward and placed my hands on the keyboard behind me. As the Doctor watched my every motion, I went through the routine of exercises — scales, arpeggios, octaves, thirds, tenths and so on — with everything exactly reversed. Long wood strips were fastened to the pedals so I could work them with my heels. I was learning the piano all over again, using different muscles in my arms and shoulders, pedaling with opposite feet and not seeing anything I did.

This blind playing was not difficult for me, since a pianist doesn't really work with the eyes. I was more disturbed by never seeing the reactions of my teacher, who had to stand behind me to watch my hands. He remained, during my lessons, a voice from over my left shoulder. If he let loose a string of grunts, I knew I was doing things correctly. If I made the slightest error, he halted my playing and lectured me on the relevant laws of his theory. He corrected me by moving my fingers in the proper way, or by poking at the muscle in my arm which he said I must use to execute the required motion. Even during these little lectures he would not stand in front of me and speak face to face.

"I'm sorry, lad," he explained, "I must not come around and look at you. It's not that I don't *wish* to look at you. But it is bad for you to acquire the habit of any visual stimulus while you sit in this position. It would hurt your playing, I'm quite sure of that. I don't mean that you should shut your eyes or see nothing at all. Pick out a stationary

348

object, a curtain or picture frame or doorknob, and rest your eye on it. That isn't to say you should dwell on it. But your eye will want to rest on something, just as a stroller puts his walking stick on the ground at every pace. Most of the time the stroller doesn't need his stick, but he wouldn't just carry it in the air, would he? Of course not! He steadies his stick by tapping it on the ground. This is rather like what the pianist does with his eyes in playing. Only when something unfortunate happens does the pianist really need his eyes. Of course, you in your position must never look around at the keyboard. If you turned your head, your whole kinetic system would be disrupted and you would miss all your notes. To speak frankly, my boy, this is a question I am still trying to answer. Of what use are the eyes in hands-reversed playing if one is not permitted to look at the keyboard? But this much I am ready to venture: you will want to steady your eye, just as that stroller steadies his stick."

I don't mind admitting I had a devil of a time with parts of the new technique. Chromatic thirds, for some reason, were especially difficult. I studied a good long time before I could play one of Redek's tone poems with hands reversed. But after five or six months I had it all down pretty well. Soon after Spiegel and I started out together, it had become customary for him to embrace me at the end of our lessons. As we went on, his embraces grew more and more effusive and his praise was almost an embarrassment.

"What a miracle! How brilliantly you learn. I would never have thought it possible that such a lad could master my technique. Until now it's been just a theory. If I had been an astronomer and I had stated a new law about the motions of heavenly bodies, I should not have dared hope that the stars would descend to visit me in my laboratory, to sit with me and say, 'Yes, Doctor Spiegel, your theory is correct! This is exactly how we behave.' Well, my child, you are the one who has fallen from Heaven. May the sun, the moon, the stars and all of earth pay homage to you."

I was sorry on the day the colonnade of umbrellas went up again outside our door and old Spiegel was on his way. I sent many a shipment of eels to the Doctor's home in Lichtenstadt so he might not forget me. His thank-you notes were prompt and characteristically effusive. He wrote often, once my career was under way, full of excitement at the reviews and reports that reached him. A year after his parting, I made my début with the Torlag Philharmonic, playing Redek's Concerto in G-flat — hands forward, of course. On that occasion he wrote: "Heartiest congratulations, my boy. You have become the virtuoso I always knew you to be." Reading that, I wept for old Spiegel and for our time together, when under his sure and steady guidance I traversed the literature of the piano with my hands behind my back.

The men who followed Spiegel to the Stork's Nest were of a less distinguished stamp: artists' managers and talent scouts, ready to snatch up the wonder-child whose fame had spread far beyond our rain-drenched fields. For my part, I would have been happy to play an occasional concert and keep most of my time for myself. All I wanted was my music and a bit of sunshine. But Uncle wasn't going to be satisfied with that. He was scheming to profit from my talent. Despite his pretense of being a businessman, Uncle had driven the estate to the point of ruin. He needed my help to save it.

"We must not fall into a common condition, Gerhard. We must not be made to join the middle class."

A nobleman's life was much more than I could provide with typical concerts. Every manager who came to visit said so. The world already had a surfeit of good pianists. But if I were to go on stage and play the piano hands-backward, people would come in large numbers and pay plenty of money to see me.

It sounded sensible, so Uncle and I gave our consent to one of those managers and we worked out a simple act. I would come on stage and sit with my back to the piano, clad in Zanni's motley garb. I would play a brief number, a Laune sonata or a Redek study, both of which, even in reverse, lay splendidly under the hands. Then I would stand up and bow. This, by the way, was my biggest difficulty. I took a long time and many instructors to learn to bow properly.

I prepared for adventure. I would travel across the continent in comfort and style. I would mingle in artistic circles. I would be toasted on the Altbäumekolonnade and the Boule des Roses. Adorable young ladies would pine for me. I would unbutton my overcoat on

350

clear, windy nights and worlds would sweep themselves up before my breast.

So I wasn't all that sad to be leaving the Stork's Nest. Of course I couldn't let the others observe this. Whenever my departure was mentioned I put on a melancholy face, my little mask of heart and pain. One day the row of umbrellas went up, this time for me, and I embraced Auntie as tears filled both our eyes.

Uncle gave me a crushing handshake. "Very well then, son. The house of Leiden carries on through your work. You're a man now."

I was eleven years old.

Hardly had I foreseen how my adventure would unfold. Instead of lodging in grand hotels, I went from flophouse to flophouse. My roommates were singers who couldn't sing, jugglers who couldn't walk a straight line, and other assorted fakers. My audiences did not keep quiet for more than a few seconds at a time. I got almost no pay for my performances, as most of the money, or so I heard, went straight to my manager. To top it off, it rained nearly everywhere I went.

The rough conditions never got to me. Kids don't care about such things as long as they can get some conviviality, and I never had to complain for lack of that. I just got tired of playing the piano with my hands behind my back. When I had soured on the instrument, I knew it was time to take off. One night I stole away after my performance and didn't turn back.

This time it was the open road, because I wasn't going home. I couldn't face them back there; and I suspected that Uncle's conniving had played no small role in my misfortune. So I just kept moving from town to town, with a single objective: to get south and find the sun.

Music was the only thing I could do to make my way, so I played — played for coins at some inn, played to provincial mayors for festive meals and the keys to their towns, played to prosperous travelers for a ride to the next town. I played all the way down through Strední, Schwarzberg, Dobraja and Polloi. I walked into a tavern or café, sat down at the piano and thought for a minute about what I wanted to rattle off. Even for a thirteen-year-old I was small and childish-looking. The men at their tables poked fun at me or came over to show me a one-finger tune. Then I let loose with the "Unchained" *étude* or something like it. The café-talkers gave me bit of pocket money and I went on to the next town.

At last I reached the city of Thanakos. I stayed there for weeks and weeks, just playing in cafés. I had no idea I was in the seat of classical culture. It was just the warmest and sunniest place I'd ever dreamed of, that's all.

One day a lady heard me play — a lady from Esmeralda who spoke Feieran. She offered to take me on a steamer cruise through the Pollonian isles if I would play on board. I don't remember anything about the lady except the beautiful white clothing she wore. I'd never seen anything like it.

We were out on the boat for a week. I had my own stateroom and plenty to eat. When the lady and I went to see the ship's piano, I got upset because it was inside one of the ship's lounges. If I played in there I'd miss all the sun. The lady asked the steward whether he might have the piano moved out on deck during the daytime, and he at once agreed.

I hardly looked at the islands as we sailed by them. I just played for the passengers on deck and baked in the sun. If ever I've known happiness in my life, that's where it was, on the deck of that steamer.

It was the first time I'd been at sea; a fine thing, for a boy whose father had been a sailor and who'd grown up with the waters of the Karelian in his back yard.

At first I felt dumbfounded by the sea. It's odd, sometimes, that when a man stands in front of his destiny, he can look straight there and not see it. It might be a fresh young thing — a girl to fall in love with — or a thing as deep and wide as life itself, like the ruins of an ancient temple. A fellow catches his breath and doesn't know what to think. So he thinks nothing at all and goes his way. Still, the deed is done. He's looked his life in the face. If it takes a day or a month or a score of years he'll know it again, and he'll be back.

Well, there it was and there I was. The cruise reached an end; my Emerald lady went back home. It was getting to be summer, even a bit sunnier than I liked. I thought I should go up to the Cumbrias, our biggest mountain range, which I'd heard of all my life but hardly ever seen.

352

I played my way back up to Schwarzberg. The fabulous cafés of Waldorf were full of excellent pianists. I reverted to my music-hall act in order to set myself apart. That was my mistake; no sooner had I started to earn a livelihood than the police came and dragged me away in chains. If I had remained an ordinary artist, they might never have found me out; but even the dullest of constables can track down a youngster who plays piano with his hands behind his back.

Escorted from town to town across the Triple Monarchy, I was at last returned to Uncle's estate. Auntie met me at the end of the umbrellas with a great hug-and-kiss. Uncle gave a prepared speech.

"How could you abandon your post? You have brought shame upon us all. But I have seen to it that you will never do so again. I have arranged for you to enter the naval academy. This I have done on the strength of your father's name, of our family name. You leave for the academy tomorrow morning. When you arrive there, you will be on your own. You are not to set foot in this house again."

Next morning I said good-bye to the servants, to the old mahogany piano, to the chickens and other animals, to the distillery in the barn, to our backyard swamps and ramshackle grounds, now in serious decay. I shed a tear for my friend Engelbert, who had passed from this world. I bade a long farewell to Theo as the servants loaded me into my carriage.

Auntie was too overcome to say goodbye. Uncle didn't bother. It was all the same to me. From now on, my home would be the academy — my gateway to the sea and to the world beyond.

Best thing of all: I would never have to play the piano again.

David Landau is an essayist, novelist and translator as well as the publisher of Pureplay Press, www.pureplaypress.com. "Scherzo" is part of a novel-in-progress. Contact: pureplayed@live.com

What Happened to My Mother

—— ৪০ଓ৪ ——

by Paula Brancato

My mother taught me to iron. Just as she washed my hair in the cold metal basin in the cellar, using beer and eggs and experimenting with other household items (lemons, brown soap and anise), she had her own way of ironing. She'd pull the board out from under the queen-sized bed, strands of red hair swinging into her eyes, flip the contraption over, smack the board on its back, then reach under it, prying its pinions. Voila! Its praying mantis legs would sigh and open. Bearing down on the board, she would rock her body gingerly shifting the rubber feet, waiting for the soft ca-chunk that indicated the stand had locked in place. Then with a frown and quiet tilt of the head that said she and the board understood one another, she'd run her palms over the board, straightening its cloth, tucking it in here and there like she did with my father before he left for work everyday, even when he didn't need straightening. Women find incredible satisfaction in straightening out a man, in oh so many ways. The smart man simply gives in to it.

The iron itself was an entirely different matter. She'd grab the appliance by the handle and rapidly unwind the cord, disregarding how the wire smacked again and again across the metal body, until the cable was played out and she could plug it into the wall. She would pour in water from the tap, using a coffee cup and a funnel, filling the appliance to the brim, but turn the iron on cool, no steam.

She'd get the clothes, the sheets and linens, the towels, already sitting in a wicker basket, in color and texture-coded piles: slick slight polyesters, aerated chiffons, raw then smooth linens, flannels to be ironed inside out, starchable cottons, cottons unstarched, and fluffy things, whether bath sheets or athletic socks. At first I thought she was merely sensuous, but no. In this way she could work methodically from items requiring a cool/no steam iron, like a polyester blouse, to those requiring high heat/steam, like bath sheets, lost in her own parade of thoughts.

What did she dream of? Musicals, mostly. The leggy Cyd Charisse, forget about Debbie Reynolds, Singing in the Rain. Gene Kelly's solo, dancing under umbrellas, hopping off curbs. Esther Williams and her synchronized swim team, the swimmers' scissor legs opening and closing like petals of a perfect flower, he loves me, he loves me not. Of Ginger Rogers and Fred Astaire, tapping down the ceramic steps of La Chiesa di Santa Maria in Caltigirone, which they may never have done, but which was one of the highlights of her mother's childhood. The church itself, I mean, in Sicily where my grandmother grew up. At the thought of the church (which she had never seen) my mother would slip from reality. She could act, she could dance, she could sing. I caught her once in a Viennese waltz, led by, I believe, a starched white blouse. And then a rumba. Missing a step, she was cross with me for hours.

This is what happened to my mother.

April 10th, 1958. My little brother Anthony had just been born. My father and I, in excitement's after-crash, were home, fast asleep. My 25-year-old mother and the new baby, in separate rooms, were resting at Jamaica Hospital, where she had delivered satisfactorily and where my musical Uncle Sal, her younger brother, had inveigled himself a late night visit. True to form, he'd chatted up the nurse, singing a verse or two of Old Blue Eyes' Luck Be a Lady, and trading cigarettes, Marlboros no doubt, with a young hard-working doctor who, like my uncle, might also have joined a big band once were it not for the rules — no smoking, no drinking, no girls. So my Uncle

Sal said "No Frank Sinatra!" And though he never joined up with Frank Sinatra and his big band, he had been allowed in toward the end of visiting hours to see my mother.

The hospital rooms were dark. The patients in the maternity ward, all new mothers with looks of beatific relief on their faces, were fast asleep. Sal easily found my mother's room, number 405. Drumming on his leg a swing tune — In the Mood was one of his favorites — he opened the door and danced, in time to the rhythm, inside. The air was cold, thin, antiseptic. The floor was yellowed linoleum, peeling. The beige walls were bare. Jamaica Hospital catered to a population of immigrant families and blacks and did not have much money at that time. It was the Appalachia of hospitals.

Uncle Sal was wearing leather shoes that my grandfather, the cobbler, made him at the front of his store, blocks away, while chomping on cherry wood cigars. The shoes were a perfect fit. So when my uncle soft-shoed across the slick linoleum, wet with god-knows-what, he was in the middle of his dance routine before he slipped and fell on his back, the beginning of lifelong sciatica. He flailed around a bit. It hurt. And there was plenty of water in the puddle. His jacket and pants soaked, he flipped over, got up and hit the light switch. I can only imagine the look on his face, the narrowing then widening of his soft young eyes, the trembling of his lip: shock, fear, disbelief. There was blood on the floor, spreading everywhere, tendrils opening to the light like the edges of the petals of a flower, thick pools here, luminescent fragments there. The bed itself soaked. All of it red. All of it coming from my mother.

Uncle Sal immediately called for the doctor who, once he was pried away from the night nurses' (plural) kisses, called in the specialist post haste. Words of surprise were murmured under the specialist's breath. An emergency bell also sounded, squealing and honking through the quiet corridors, stealing away the other mothers' sweet, fat, baby dreams, tempering them with a fearful under-net of whispers.

"Who is it?"

"A baby?"

"A mother?"

"403?"

"405?"

The attendants wheeled my mother, IV attached, white sheet clinging to her, into operating room 102, the mistake room, not the room for deliveries. That night, she became the watched unlucky one, pasty-faced, moaning, "What? What is happening? Why?" They rushed her past all those questioning faces, the other mothers spared her fate only by the grace of luck and God. And those who waited to deliver, praying for themselves. Then they had at her again.

In the hours that followed, my mother took 14 pints of blood. All the relatives donated and some neighbors, the blacks, the Jews, even the Mick-Micks, the Irish, though, I am told, some who could have helped did not. Older folk, for instance, believed they could lose their souls. The doctors stopped the bleeding, sewed her up rather indelicately and wheeled her back to her room. She hemorrhaged that morning again, blood spreading across the mattress. She would hemorrhage two more times, they would operate two more times, before they decided to put her in the IC unit and, finally, to perform a hysterectomy. Still the bleeding came. Days and days of blood. Like thick rich orchids, blood inhabited her pelvis. The petals blossomed, shrunk and convulsed. Until, like any wound, whether one lives or dies, the flowers grew smaller and smaller, the tendrils slowly retreating into muscle fiber and bone.

My mother was in intensive care, I was told, for three or maybe four months depending upon which relative told me. She had had the equivalent of three bodies full of blood. She was open the whole time, saline solution keeping her moist, until the doctors felt safe to close her up. What I overheard was this:

— She was perfectly alright.
— She had the cancer.
— The doctors left something inside.
— They took something out.
— It was congenital, inherited.
— It was a tipped uterus.
— It was malpractice.
— Someone/God made a mistake.

— You're her daughter. And it could happen to you. But it probably won't.

It took over 40 years of secrets and whispers to piece together the truth. That my mother was not the schizophrenic I thought she was. That brain damage, which triggers violence and cannot be reversed, is more shameful to a family than insanity. That my mother had been suddenly physically and psychologically disfigured — whatever happened to Baby Jane had happened to my mother. And that my family had slipped into a state of shock and disbelief that lingered for decades.

Only my father, grandparents and an occasional aunt or uncle — from my mother's side, not my father's - were permitted to visit my mother during those three or four months she wove in and out of consciousness. My brother and I, safe and sound in some ways, in others not, were cared for by relatives. Our physical needs were cared for. There was food on the table, we were clothed and held and bathed. But every day at home, seeking her voice, her touch, her smell — like cold cream and White Shoulders — I stood on tip-toe outside her room, clinging to the doorknob and peering through the keyhole. Catching my breath I saw her shadow once. An unfinished dress, pink organza, waved to me from atop her sewing machine, an ephemeral net — empty — caught by the sun and swept up in the summer breeze.

When she was awake in the hospital my mother called for my brother, her baby, and sometimes, they say, for me. "Where is my baby?" she asked. "I had a baby, where is he?" And then, meeting stony faces, more quickly, under her breath, "Is he... is my baby...?"

For the doctors, in their barbarous wisdom, had forbidden my family to mention to my mother she'd actually had a baby. Saying the patient had actually had the child or even been pregnant could, they warned, cause my fragile mother such great pains of separation, such intense anxiety, that she would surely suffer an irrevocable psychological rift, not to mention physical relapse. The doctors, apparently, did not consider what kind of rift might occur in a woman who knew she'd been pregnant, remembered entering hospital for the purpose of delivering a baby, gone through labor, a thing no woman forgets, delivered said healthy baby, then woken up an indeterminate period of time later in ICU, possibly brain-damaged, trying to hold onto whatever shred of reality might have existed and whatever comfort might be recalled (a fine, healthy baby?) only to find everyone she knows and trusts in firm denial of her slim, painful grasp on reality, the baby gone, relatives too abandoning her, not answering if her questions were too insistent. She was only able to get fragments of information, as she replayed the scenes over and over again in her drugged and adulterated mind, milking the sad, moist-eyes of her guilty visitors (or were they?), who looked down or aside (or did they?), her relatives, gritting their teeth and clenching their jaws (am I dying? Am I dead? she must have wondered) and, finally, shaking their heads in silence. She was in Siberia with only a match for warmth. Families are where we learn to lie.

My terrified family was, thus, not permitted to discuss the pregnancy, the child, the state of the child's health or any of what had happened to my mother with my mother as she suffered those long months. They handled her like this.

"Where is my baby?" my mother moaned through a morphine-induced haze. Her eyes darted around the room like a trapped bird. She was so tired, so endlessly tired. She fixated on the shadow of the daffodils my father brought her, blueness falling across her bed.

My father sat up straighter in the chair beside, tugged at his shirt cuffs and suit sleeves. He kept his jacket on, the first two buttons buttoned tight as the perfect vest beneath, his black shoes carefully shined. "The daffodils?... They. . . they're flowers. . . " He took her hand, noting her vacant stare. Her being awake, in any event, was a good sign. "Pauline?"

"I had a baby, didn't I?"

He stared hard at his shoes, clenched his jaw. He had seen people die.

She looked at her reflection in the side table. The pale face of a stranger stared back, elongated by the convex steel. "I had a baby, didn't I?..." She had lost most of her hair. "My lipstick," she moaned. "My lipsh," my father heard. She had trouble keeping her eyes open, making her mouth work. The drugs pulsed in her veins.

"You're beautiful." My father winced, helplessly. The first time he'd made this particular face, cheeks up, mouth open, pain behind his eyes. We would grow to know those hardened lines.

"Why? What is it, Sam?"

"Rest, now, Pauline." He held her hand between both of his, a moth protected from a flame. He cleared his throat, a man that never cried.

She wanted to say she loved him, as the walls of the room dissolved. She wanted to tell him about the boy she kissed once when he was in Korea, as she slipped into that night of mermaids and moons, of impossible twinnings. Under the boardwalk. The sand cold, her feet bare. It was my father she missed but the boy with the clean shaven face, the smell of citrus and the dark dank hair was indisputably there. His hand brushed her cheek as their lips met. The sea roared on.

"Everything is fine," my father cooed, to soothe himself, for she was fast asleep already. He looked down. Something electric hit his heart and he dropped her hand. The wedding ring wasn't there. Then he remembered. It was home in the jewelry box he'd bought her in Korea — beside a small jar of cold cream, cover off, exposing the swish of her fingers. "Everything is fine."

He was holding her waist, so small, like the tiny dancing girl inside the jewelry box, a ballerina, who twirled and twirled, the tinny melody, the fullness of my mother's hips under his hands, the timbre of her voice, not low, not high — in his dreams she always laughed — my cries and the babbling of my brother, the tick-tock-tick of the starburst clock in our hall, the dripping sink, dishes piled high, wet clothes that flapped into the laundry bag. And footsteps. Such are the echoes of a family, no one there. Every night, it was like that. "Everything is fine."

Every night she was here.

My father stood, dying for a cigarette but he could not smoke in these sterile rooms. He shifted his thoughts to his work, because chemistry was always easy, thinking of the titration he must make next morning. The solution. How life was like a saturate, its sudden crystallization from the falling of a final grain. Of the toughness, the viability of petrochemical plastics. How capable they were. My father

361

was a "Plastics" man. Using the handkerchief she ironed for him, he blew his nose, wiped his eyes.

She only saw his shadow then, heard the faint hum of the machines, morphine dripping into her veins. Drifting, she smelled the smell of him, her husband. Her fingers traced his lips in the dream. The salt of his skin, the starched crispness of his collar, the heat of him like an iron, the oily coils of his hair, faintly mixed with the scent of tape and saline, the metallic taste of the IV feed. The light was out: he'd turned it down, set the stage. Somewhere in the dark, a baby cried. She was the baby. She was on someone's knees, bouncing, an aunt's, an uncle's, she was passed from hand to hand. There was a bright beach ball, red, yellow, green, and laughter. The ball, thrown with speed, flew toward her. Bigger and bigger. She grew frightened, suddenly. It would fly in her face, no one to stop it. It would obliterate everything. "No, no, please, don't go. Please!" she shouted. Or thought she did. At the height of this eclipse, she tried to sit up but her box of a body fell back.

My father, hand on the doorknob, heard her moans. "I'm here," he said, and turned back. But he wasn't. He too was lost. Thinking of the national athlete he once was, running the 440 around an asphalt track. The all-night lover he could have been with Giselle or Gertrude or Pru, given half the chance. The IBM VP climbing into his Olds in Poughkeepsie. The Princeton scholar, finishing his masters, my mother and brother and I applauding, as photographers snapped pictures and he alone explained how plastics would save the world. That beautiful mistress he might have had if he wasn't a good Catholic and didn't turn her down. They would be in Peru or Fiji, stripped down in a bed, bathing in the heat of one another. But at that moment, there was only the honorable husband, the benevolent father, the good son left to him, the terror of raising me and my brother very possibly alone, a piquant scent of hospital, and the remembered touch of my mother's sex the first time they'd made love, her legs wrapped around him. So away he was, though, of course, he turned back and ever so carefully, placed his arm under her shoulder.

"Sammy?" she said, closed her eyes and smiled. He would have crooned to her but he was not that sort of man. His body rocked back and forth, ever so slightly, as he sat on the edge of the chair. He hummed, perhaps he whistled, but the immovable arm lay anchored beneath her pillow, his fingers searching her hair. He leaned in, breathed her breath, the perfume of her sweat and wear. The night this baby was conceived he had felt her flush, felt her pull him in, then release, then pull him in again. He wanted her lips, the taste of them. She looked so like a child, her face pale, her eyelids lavender. He kissed her forehead. When she fell asleep again, he removed his arm without displacing the folds of her hair on the pillow. And kissed her lips, parting them.

My father stepped outside. He looked around at the night — how odd that it was night, that it was anything. He took a deep breath of the cool night air and then he ran, my mother's kiss inside him. He flew down the block, over to the bus stop, all the way to the end of the line, racing that bus, just racing it, though he could easily have caught it and paid the fare, his heart bursting inside, before he stopped, broke down and cried.

My mother lived in this twilight, this medicated comatose state of disinformation, until my Aunt Clara in the third month, unable to take it anymore, standing over her, sponging her forehead, finally burst out, "You had a baby, Pauline," she cried. "You had a baby! And the baby, a boy, is fine."

By that point, like the soldier in the film Jacob's Ladder, given LSD and sent out into the world without being told he'd taken the drug, my mother could no longer distinguish imagination from reality. In Jacob's Ladder, Tim Robbins is taken to a hospital, tied to a gurney. The deeper he travels the more the place is filled with mad people and then blood and body parts strewn all over the floor. The people she loved had held back the only piece of information that could keep her sane. One tiny piece of truth. But unlike the film, there was no end for my mother. The mind plays tricks sometimes. Who has not imagined stepping off the cliffs of the Palisades, for instance, into sheer atmosphere and, after a lovely, windswept, all too brief drop, being embraced, caught by the beautiful swaying maple trees, their arms outstretched with longing, far, far below? Only one step more to crazyland. Not that difficult to imagine. Most people live in a false sense of reality anyway. So, why not this mother. My mother.

363

Crazy as could be, she was then sent home, without any fucking help, to care for a one-and-a-half year old and a four-month old. Her illness granted a certain degree of freedom. I forgot to pick up bread and milk at the supermarket because I'm crazy. I forgot to walk the rabbit and feed the duck because I'm crazy. I forgot to pick up my daughter at whatever school that was, oh, yes, kindergarten, because I am stark raving nuts! I was very, very jealous of her for years.

My aunt entered the house the next day and found my mother in the kitchen, banging her head against the wall, me running about buck naked except for my shoes, with which, from time to time, I stomped on my infant brother who lay in his crib and whose bottle I sorely wanted. I had, apparently, just palmed the bottle, and was climbing out through the bars, when she grabbed me. It took longer to stop my mother. She had, apparently, been going at it — the head banging — for an hour and a half, though I have no recollection of this fact.

She would beat me into a damp cemented corner of the basement. I learned early that the back is strong. Much stronger than the stomach, throat and eyes. When your nemesis has cunning, of course, you must never turn your back. But when she is weak and out of control, you must, so as to save both of you. At such times, hunched up, contracting and expanding like a drum to the rhythm of her blows, covering my face with my arms and trying to make the rest of me very small, I could feel the grind of the cement walls as I pushed up against them.

Loose mortar, like hard uncooked rice, the crumbled bonding material indented my forearms, wrists and shoulders, burning when I moved. It was meant to hold things together. So real it felt, so much realer than what was happening, that I could actually taste its grit in my mouth. Synesthesia they call this, when one sense supplies the input for another: hearing colors, tasting shapes, seeing tastes. When you see green and taste lime for instance, or flex a muscle and release a color, say pink, against the sky. Or when you orgasm and, opening your eyes, spy those large frayed purple and green petals, after-images of sex, giant dying flowers. At such times we enter the realm of poets. We are sensorially privileged, hypersensitive to life's antipathetic connections and disconnections. Crumbling bonding material. This was what I tasted through my skin, the very walls reinforcing the true state of affairs. She was not always this way, of course, or I would not be here. Let me make one thing clear. I loved my mother.

This happened more than once. I faced it alone.

Over the years, the family, unable to grasp the tragedy, looked to lay blame. My father's sisters, Zia and Tina, said it was my mother's sister Clara's fault, for telling my mother what the doctors clearly said should not be told. My mother, Pauline, said it was my brother Tony's fault for kicking both before and after he was born. My maternal grandmother Rose said it was my father Sam's fault for (sanely) not wanting to marry her daughter Pauline at all. For being pushed into it. We would not have had Sam, she said, except Pauline wanted him and that was all. My paternal grandmother Concetta blamed my maternal grandmother Rose for passing on her crazy schizophrenic genes. We kids, all cousins — Lisa, Maria, Gianni, Frankie and Mike - blamed my paternal grandmother Concetta for the vendetta she waged against my maternal grandmother Rose, where relatives from one family would never set foot in the houses of relatives of the other family — so my poor parents had to drag us back and forth, back and forth every weekend, Saturdays with the Sepia's and Sundays with the Corrado's — a war that went on until both grandmothers died. My maternal uncles — there were several — Tony, Sal, Nunzio and so on — believed it was my harmonica playing uncle Sal's fault for not finding my mother soon enough, specifically for dilly-dallying with "those nurses, Norma, Miriam and Aretha and his songs". They were just jealous. Both grandmothers blamed their husbands, I never knew their first names, because that was how women kept men in line. Not to be outdone, my father thought it was my fault, for having weakened my mother by using up all of her calcium and iron, though I later made sure she ate spinach and steak all the time. My harmonica-playing uncle Sal, thoroughly pissed off by now, insisted it was my mother's fault for turning down the Fred Astaire college scholarship to marry my father, thus dissing the greatest dance-man of all time. My littlest cousins, Loretta, Joanie, Annette, Steven, Ernie,

Laura, Gianni, Craig, who were not even born then but felt a need to pontificate, believed it was mostly the fault of my gay closeted cousin Junior, who still thinks we don't know. My poorest uncles — there were nine — blamed my one rich uncle and his Westchester country club clan. My less religious, more feminist second cousins — fourteen of those — blamed the young doctors, the old nurses, the impoverished hospital, the over-prescribed medications and fundamentalist belief in God. Friends who were like family and my one Jewish aunt, Merele, still having to cultivate favor, took a distant route and blamed the Pope, the church, the priests, the nuns and God. Our pets Pooki and Lewis pointed paws at everything from kitty litter to old shoes. Even our goldfish, Jim, blubbering in his glass bowl, had a point of view, blaming my mother's unfortunate proximity to his fish food. In the end, this was what the family told me, the credo I learned to live by. There was one fact upon which we all agreed: "There's nothing wrong with your mother. Tina your mother is fine."

This would have been a good time for re-gifting. But I was a greedy child.

The beatings, I thought, were what it would be like to be in prison. Sensory explosions. Far, far away. I could see, I could hear, I could feel her touch, hot and rapid some times, slow as a boulder at others, but like a sedated patient, none of what I sensed was actually happening to me. My pain was over there somewhere in a corner across the room. I have always been mistaken in this way, my world filled with ambiguity and surprise. "I will give you a ring tomorrow" might mean someone would actually give me jewelry. I would spend days thinking about the actual kind of jewelry. Italian 14 k gold. British crown diamonds. The jade of Nefertiti. When I was beaten or brushed aside in any way — "I'll give you a ring tomorrow!" — my mind would go elsewhere, to the seashore where we had been a handful of times, or kneeling in front of my vanity, praying to the Virgin Mary for deliverance, placing in front of her statue a fistful of the finest dandelions. Dandy lions. Fit for a Queen.

Sometimes my mother was not so fast. Her darting, dashing energy would turn back on itself — she was in the service of it and not the other way around — sending her over and over the same ground until she would get confused. Then I got away, on good days as far as the yard when she chased me, where I crouched in the sun against the grounding wall, wet grass cushioning my knees, and hugged the bricks of the house. They were so red, so gritty. I wanted to swipe myself against them and just bleed, as if that would release me.

My mother said words too. She screamed then. *Che stupida!* How stupid I was. *Egoista!* How selfish. *T'uccidero!* How, in particular, she planned to tie me up and kill me. What saved me during the beatings was that I knew things existed other than her. Yellow sun, red bricks, green grass, yellow, red and green lights made white if you swirled them together. Mixing them as pigments made black. Yellow, red and green were also the colors of certain sickly sweet lollipops and candy canes. The sugar-coated guilt she would feel after, that I would have to save her from, sometimes for hours, sometimes days, several years when she knocked my teeth out. "It's only baby teeth," she insisted. But they were adult teeth. I was 10.

I thought of the orange soda pop my grandmother sometimes gave me mixed with tablespoons of red wine. I thought of the thinness of my legs and would I ever get any hips or breasts. I thought about places I'd read about in books, the snowy Russia of Tolstoy's *War and Peace*, the fiery attic in *Jane Eyre*, Narnia in the *Witch and the Wardrobe*. I put myself there. Anything till the beating was over. Strange thoughts appeared. Do your eyes get squashed when you sleep and is that why, when you wake up, it is always so difficult to focus? Or how much I really wanted to kick Terry Dorino's ass in the 50-yard dash because she had long blond curly hair, almost perfect. I was taller than her, than most girls, until the second grade. She was a big girl, Terry, and never let me forget it, slapping the basketball from my hands as I dribbled full tilt across the key, making an empty-handed jump shot. She swatted my victories away from my fingertips and into her own large mitts as casually as she picked a nit off her sweater. Anything to get the hell out of there. It was then I began to write stories.

I often wondered during these beatings, many of which were sustained, or came in chapters, wasn't my mother getting tired already? She was breathing hard but her breath was never acrid. And her sweat, even as her hands slipped off me, was lovely, a mix of eggshells, salt and sand.

No one likes trouble. An abused child reeks of trouble: trouble that bore them, trouble that is happening to them and trouble they will one day turn on the world. Our neighbors could see but they too turned their eyes away, filled with the guilt of knowing that this concerned them, and not just the neighbors who were family either. It was happening right out there on the stoop and on the lawn, for goodness sake, which, in suburbia is like a happening in international waters. Everyone's touched by it, perhaps, but no one's quite sure whose jurisdiction should fix the problem. "Pull", my mother would plead with those tiger lily eyes. That is what I thought she was saying, "Pull." She would want the devil out of her. I too wanted an exorcism. Or at least, not to be hit again. I wanted to pull the devil out and put her soul back, but I was only a wild intractable child, unable to hold her pain inside. I was only able to hold her, finally. No mean feat, as she was flapping about like a windmill. To wrap myself around her big black heart, like a straight jacket, straining to calm her down. Until I too would mew like a kitten, my own black heart, beating, finally. My own tiger lily eyes.

Paula Brancato is an award-winning fiction writer, poet and filmmaker, currently on faculty at the University of Southern California. In 2008, her book *Club Paradise* was a May Swenson and Holland Prize finalist. Additional awards include the 2008 Robinson Jeffers Tor House Prize for Poetry, the 2007 Brushfire Poet Award, first prize Chester H. Jones Foundation, the Karlovy Vary film festival award, National Screenwriters Award, Pacific Northwest Writers Association and the Organization of Black Screenwriters, SCIFF Family Focus and WINFEMME awards. She has been a Sundance finalist twice.

Paula has been published by *Mudfish, Georgetown Review, Litchfield Review, Southern California Anthology, Rattle,* and *Natchez Anthology,* among others. In 2010, Finishing Line Press is publishing her second chapbook *Painting Cities.* Poet Ilya Kaminsky selected her first chapbook, *Dar a Luz,* for publication by the *pacificREVIEW.* Paula has studied with poets Mary Stewart Hammond, Jill Hoffman and Philip Schultz in NY. She earned her MBA from Harvard Business School and is a graduate of the Los Angeles Film School and Hunter College. Contact: BrancatoNY@aol.com

WHEN CONRAD AIKEN LIVED UPSTAIRS

———————— ℬ℘ ————————

by Kalman Applbaum

It is night-time, and cold, and snow is falling,
And no wind grieves the walls.
In the small world of light around the arc-lamp
A swarm of snowflakes falls and falls.
— Conrad Aiken, *'Improvisations: Light and Snow'*

Once again they had parted from each other in argument. After six days with Pam and her parents in Connecticut, Vance Norman had left in a pique and was returning to Boston. Pam had been incensed at his departure — what would her parents think? For his part he dreaded the prospect of celebrating another New Year's, which also happened to be his birthday, with his in-laws. Sixteen years of marriage and still they did not accept him. They had complained about his sullenness to Pam, who in turn upbraided him for spoiling the holiday. Their quarrel had escalated to new territory when he had barked the word *divorce* at his wife.

"*There*, you've said it," she said. "You weren't going to be satisfied until you crossed that line." She grabbed the Christian Lacroix shawl he had given her for Christmas and flung it at him before storming from the room.

371

He abided in the darkening room like a child banished from the dinner table. At last he folded the shawl on the table and wrote a brief, unconditional apology. Then he packed his valise, thanked his flabbergasted in-laws, and started home.

At least he was in the clear geographically, driving homeward through dark New England. He pulled off I-95 for gas and McDonald's. Vance was a large, thickset man, a wall of flesh plodding up the walkway with downward gaze. Adolescents cleared out of his path with mocking gestures, but he was too self-absorbed to notice. He moved swiftly to the stainless-steel counter where he promptly requested two Egg McMuffins, fries and a vanilla shake, and rapidly downed all of it in the same fit of obliviousness. He gave another fleeting and regretful thought to Pam, who never let him eat this way; and he brooded over his brother Jack's recent diagnosis of diabetes. The two of them shared a common build, and Vance — a physician, after all — should be wise enough to take heed. He would make a fresh resolve of his diet in the New Year. This year, he swore he'd stick to it. He was turning 38, the last year he could even daydream about applying youthful malleability to his life's course.

By nine thirty he was in their Longwood apartment.

They had moved to Boston in September at the start of Vance's sabbatical from the Centers for Disease Control. Vance had accepted an affiliate's position at the Harvard School of Public Health. He had proposed research but even before arriving he knew he lacked the interest to carry it out. Administrative responsibilities at the CDC had dulled his inclination for research — as had the continuous stress at home. Now he was back in the city of his youth, meandering idly in a way he never had when he was young. He sat in coat and tie in the public library's august reading room, or in cafés, or on the ledge of the fountain downtown. It was an innocent deception to let Pam think he was in conferences or at the medical library. She, meanwhile, took courses in museum studies and socialized with her classmates.

They had arrived on a radiant September day, when the university neighborhoods were coming alive with preparations for the new school year; they had rented the second floor of a brownstone on Huntington Ave. Vance was unloading the car when Pam called to him from their window. When he reached her she was kneeling naked on the bed. His heart leapt from gladness as much as from arousal, and they had made love. So they did several more times in those first days. Afterwards they lay staring at the ceiling, admiring its irregular shape and crown moldings. Their condo in Atlanta had low drywall ceilings, like a tomb.

"Let's be lovebirds again," Pam had said with unwonted ardor; she, also, was stout and middle-aged.

Now alone in the place, Vance hung his olive-drab raincoat on the bedpost on Pam's side, removed his shoes and plopped down without taking his cholesterol medication, brushing his teeth or shutting off the hall lights. He lay with his face in the pillow and tried to dispel the thought of their argument. He summoned images of that first afternoon in the apartment and of their courtship in Boston seventeen Septembers earlier when he had been a senior at Harvard and she, two years older, a museum intern.

Their early idylls had given way to times of trouble. For three years they had tended Vance's father, who was wasting away from Parkinson's disease. They had failed to conceive, and Pam, diagnosed with endometriosis, had undergone a hysterectomy. As Vance's father endured his final illness in what would have been the baby's room, their time for considering adoption also crept past. Each of them had quietly lapsed into premature menopausal resignation.

When the Boston offer came through, they grasped at the opportunity to recharge their flagging life force. Something venturesome had accompanied the noise and humidity of those first nights, as though they were making love somewhere outside their apartment, in the center of the city. But then their patterns of blandness crept back. Conversations ran aground in mundane matters. One day Pam bought a TV. Winter came on, the rooms turned drafty and the traffic on the avenue ministered to insomnia.

Tonight, lying on their bed in his clothes, with the dim hall light casting shadows over his rumpled suit, Vance felt anger at his wife for abandoning him on his birthday and for not nurturing the hopefulness they had experienced in the autumn. The fault was not solely Pam's, of course, but in the character of their interdependence he allowed himself to blame her for their mutual disappointments. With the consolation that she would pity him if she saw him this way, lying on the bed like a discarded teddy bear, with the dim hall light casting shadows over his rumpled suit, he drifted to sleep.

He awoke to a cobalt-blue sky shuddering through the windowpanes. He dialed Pam from the phone in the entryway. She answered from the kitchen in her parents' house. In her voice, he could sense remorse and reconciliation. He wished to talk privately but she said they were about to sit down to breakfast. At the Wolcotts', every meal was a formal production. She suggested he call again in an hour. He said he wouldn't be near a phone in an hour (his resistance to cell phones was a source of dispute between them). Pam's response was "Fine," followed by a public "I love you. We'll speak later."

Blast it! Why couldn't she make a priority of talking to him? She hadn't even remembered to wish him a happy birthday. Why did she allow them to take her over so completely? Those miserable snobs, happy-hour drunks, Republicans.

In a mood to spite the resplendent sky, he hurried to the office to retrieve a small stack of verse he had left on his desk. He had started writing in September, at the weekly departmental presentations he was obliged to attend. He sat in the back playing a game in which he listened only to the musical aspect of the words, the inelegant meters of scientific jargon. How could a branch of learning associated with such discordant sounds be true? He composed unrhymed couplets, and he incorporated caricatures of the speakers into his verse. These comprised the sole output of his sabbatical thus far. He sifted through the piles of unread avian flu reports in search of his poems.

"Ah, here they are," he said aloud when he came upon his pages. "What's that? Gold among those hills?" spoke a voice behind him.

Vance turned around to see the grinning red face of Bernie Gladstein in the doorway. Gladstein was the man responsible for bringing him to Harvard. It had been a big favor. Vance was no longer producing cutting-edge research and wasn't connected to anyone else at Harvard. Gladstein, on the other hand, was professor of tropical public health and the world's leading authority on schistosomiasis. They had met at the Centers for Disease Control, where Gladstein was a frequent consultant. In one of his poems, Vance referred to Gladstein, an avid participant at seminars, as 'Backslapping Bernie'.

"Only fool's gold, I'm afraid," Vance said. "How's the holiday? Or since you're here, how's work?"

"An epidemiologist's work is never done. I thought you went to Atlanta for the break."

"No, we were with Pam's folks in New London."

"Ah."

"They're not too bad. Good at holidays, anyway. How about you? You celebrate Hanukkah?"

"No, not since the kids got big. Say," Gladstein continued, "would you like to join us tonight? Linda and I are going to the Hatch with some friends to see the Pops. Afterwards we'll ring in the New Year at our place in Cambridge. Unless you have plans."

"That's very nice of you, thanks. Thanks really. I'm here only in between. Pam's still in Connecticut and, uh, I'm headed back myself."

Vance looked toward the door. He didn't like to lie, but lately many of his movements seemed to require alibis. At any rate, he did not want to spend New Year's with Bernie and his gang.

"Oh, well, have a happy happy and my best to Pam. She's enjoying Boston?"

"Yes, we both are. We met here, you know. Pam went to Boston College. Good old days. Well, I'd better get going. Not the best day for travel."

Vance collected his poems and stuffed them in his briefcase like contraband. As he was stepping out, Gladstein flagged him from down the carpeted hallway.

"One more thing, Vance, if you don't mind," Gladstein called out, brandishing a sheaf of papers. Gladstein's comportment, like his fondness for clichés, suggested ungainliness, but his carriage, like his mind, was agile, even athletic. No doubt he exercised every day.

"Uh-huh?"

"These wouldn't be yours, by chance?"

He held out some pages. Vance had to keep from bugging his eyes when he saw them. They were his poems, complete with his parodies and caricatures. How on earth did Gladstein get these? It was a magic trick. Vance had placed them directly in his valise not two minutes ago.

"What are they?" he asked, trying to suppress alarm from his voice.

"Someone's crappy doggerel. Showed up in the department printer."

Vance leafed through the pages, using the glancing-down time to race through the question of how they were sent through the department's printer. Had someone been on his computer? The mysterious "network administrator"? Why would anyone wish to embarrass him?

"That's odd," Vance offered. "Maybe they were sent from a student dorm, or another department. Our printer in Atlanta once coughed up a whole mystery novel. Two hundred pages. We never figured out where it came from. The virtues of virtuality, ha ha."

Gladstein frowned and took the papers. Vance continued on his way, feeling Gladstein's eyes on his back. He counted the steps out the door.

The sky had become as gray as the sidewalk. Vance did not resist the gathering fatigue as he trudged home. He would nap and then start fresh with a plan for the evening. On his birthday and New Year's Eve he would not stay in the apartment.

In the entryway his German neighbor, Karolin, was retrieving mail from her box. Her husband was a post-doc conducting sleep research on rats. Karolin hadn't found much to occupy herself with while Joerg was at the lab, and she complained to Pam of homesickness. The two women often had coffee together and this obliged Vance to be amiable in the hallway. To complicate matters,

Karolin was gorgeous in a way that induced Vance to avoid looking at her directly when they met, lest his attention be taken for staring, which it could easily become. Joerg, with his commitment to work at the lab, seemed indifferent. He apparently had no idea how fleeting a gift it is to have a beautiful young wife.

"Happy New Year, Karolin."

She turned to face him, blocking the passage.

"Good morning, doctor! You are back."

She smiled and looked up at him from close enough to let him inspect the soft cleft in her nose and make out the soap-scent from her bath. She was wearing a headband and a kind of tunic flattering to her bust. He gave his usual closed-mouth smile and asked if they had had an enjoyable Christmas.

"Oh, it was very well, doctor, considering especially this is the first time away from either — or is it both? — of our parents. I wonder which is it, either or both?"

"Either. Or both."

She giggled. "You are funny."

Karolin's beauty didn't inoculate her against being a bore. She recounted how Joerg enjoyed her Christmas *Sachertorte* more than his mother's, even though it was her "first time in the making it." Vance smiled stupidly on. Standing so close to her weakened him.

Karolin stepped aside, and he went on to the second story.

For years, the endometriosis had spoiled Pam's interest in sex. She sometimes recoiled when he went to caress her, as though forewarning him to expect no reciprocation. Then she had the hysterectomy. So far she had had no recurrence of pelvic pain. In the summer she said she couldn't face the prospect of sex just yet, and when they arrived in Boston in the fall they had made love. Then the well had dried up again.

Oh, what was the point of grievances? The charge of neglect had been on his mind when he argued with Pam yesterday. (Was it only yesterday?)

He did love her, though lately, he admitted, in a shabby way. She was his first love. He recalled her maternal, effusive sensuousness during their courtship. Her affections were straightforward, and in that way more mature than his. Vance's father had adored her. In his last years, cut off by illness, he expended his waning energy in pleasing Pam. Even through his Parkinson's mask she could elicit laughter and joy from him. Children were drawn to her. Childlessness was far more tragic for her than for him, and resigning herself to it had changed her. In part, Vance grudgingly admitted, he was judging her for *that*.

Sleep dropped upon him. When he awoke, darkness was descending. He found a box of samosas in the freezer and chucked the lot into the microwave. He emptied his briefcase to review his poems. The thought of Gladstein's discovery made him gulp the food.

He thought back to Gladstein's dismissal of the verse. Was it so crappy? Some of the lines were quite handsome with their internal rhymes and metonymy. As an undergraduate he had taken a course from Seamus Heaney, to whom he showed some of his compositions. "Not bad, not bad," the poet had remarked.

"Do two half negatives make a positive?" Vance asked.

"Sure, sure," Heaney had replied.

Vance had decided that he lacked the self-possession to make a career in the arts. His mother's protracted illness had disposed him towards the role of healer. After college he married Pam. She came with him to Chicago for medical school and postgraduate studies in virology. Looking back, he could see how, despite his accomplishments, he had never made any positive decisions, but had only passed through channels of least resistance.

What would he do from now on?

He had often heard the story of how he was conceived less than one block from People's Park the day it was so named, when his parents were undergraduates at Berkeley. Such a birth augured a higher calling than bureaucrat. And why not at last challenge himself? All his academic achievements, so impressive to others, had come easily to him. That lack of struggle seemed a betrayal to human possibility. What if he were to alter his life so that years hence report of his former occupation would surprise new acquaintances? What if he and Pam sold their well-lit mausoleum in Atlanta and bought a farm in New Hampshire, grew vegetables and lived a life of physical exertion and contemplation?

Vance could think of only one destination for the evening: Harvard Square. The memory of the day his father drove him from New Jersey to Cambridge had never grown stale. It was in September 1986, and life had started anew. His mother's illness, his brother's firefights with their father, the industrial suburb in which they lived, all of it dissolved the moment Vance and his dad pulled into Harvard Square.

Nowadays, the Square had become commercialized. The chain stores made it feel like a mall. Harvard itself had become forbidding, an exclusive club where he was no longer a member.

Tonight, everything would be different. Tonight, he would reclaim the future he had prematurely surrendered. He placed in his jacket a fifty-dollar bill, the silver pen that had been his mother's last gift to him and a dozen index-cards on which to draft poems.

He emerged at Harvard Square Station to find a Guatemalan quartet playing panpipes. He had no specific program. The greasy spoons were all gone — just as well. He thought to visit the library, but realized he had not brought his ID.

The temperature was dropping. His raincoat sufficed for Atlanta winters but New England was colder. His large hands reddened. He peered in from the Mass Ave side to his freshman dorm room in Wigglesworth Hall. He remembered the thrill of encountering its fireplace and exposed wood floors for the first time. In the New Jersey of his youth, it seemed that the whole interior of the state had been carpeted.

What a redoubtable fortress, Harvard. So much academic *gravitas* by day. And now by night the potency of youth, sexual in its fecundity, took over.

As the night deepened, the moods and attire of those out and about became celebratory. One could cut New Year's Eve with a cake-knife. He headed to the Charles River, past Dunster House where he had lived. As he turned the corner of Flagg Street, he nearly collided with a man.

"Watch where you're going," the man growled.

Vance watched him lurch away. Something familiar about him— Christ! It was one of the homeless people from the Square who had been around even in Vance's time! The guy who had always looked like a werewolf. His still-upward-pointed beard was yellow, and Vance could swear he was wearing the same parka as then. What a thing!

Astonished, he paused over whether he might run after the man and give him money or invite him for a meal. He had, at least, affluence to share.

The chill in the air was pleasant to his skin, as if he were cooling a fever from the outside in.

Presently new voices were approaching — a party of adults enjoying the gayness of the evening. Their voices and the tap-tap of their shoes echoed off the brick of the undergraduate houses on either side. Vance stood and watched them approach; swaying in their wide outerwear and silhouetted under the half-waning moon, fixed and lucent among the stars. Two women and two men, all in dark coats, voices ringing as they neared. Then they stopped.

"Vance Norman! What on earth?!"

The taller man, no longer smiling, was Bernie Gladstein.

"Bernie." Vance cried out weakly.

"I'm disappointed. I don't know what else to say."

"I decided I couldn't bear to be with my in-laws for New Year's," Vance said, as if that had been the issue.

"I pulled strings to get you here. There were people who would have made better use of our resources."

"I . . . I . . . "

Gladstein's face flushed dark pewter in the silvery light.

"I read what you wrote. Mockery you didn't have the nerve to own up to. I'd have given them back right there, your miserable, lampooning doggerel about what the rest of us have dedicated our lives to. Did you want me to read them? So I could see for myself what a bunch of pricks you think we are? Priapic quacks? Grant-getting fools in league with hair-splitting knaves? Monsters of humanity and enlightenment? Sure, Norman, we're serious about what we do up there. We believe there's something at stake. I should have thought the same of you. Just so you know, I defended your aloofness. I actually argued to bring you here for a position in our department. It turns out I'm a much bigger asshole than you made me out to be. Backslapping Bernie. I'm not your mother to tell you how to behave, for God's sake, but I think we can agree that more by way of professional decorum was in order. I'm done," Gladstein said, grinding the words out. "I'm not going to let you ruin my evening. But at some point I think an apology is in order. And you should consider returning to Atlanta before the new semester."

Vance stood dumb as the group departed, humiliation drenching his forehead. What consolation is there for the wasteful loss of what might have been? To have shamed his host? To have squandered the possibility of a position at Harvard? Had Gladstein just made that up to torment him? What report would travel back to Atlanta? He was kneeling to withstand the brunt of the blame, his hands braced on the gritty pavement. What would he tell Pam? How could he have let this happen?

He careered like a drunkard down to the Charles River. He chose a bench and collapsed on it. His mind vaulted from one incomplete reckoning to another across the night-time river of conflicting emotions and desires that had brought him here, to this unforgiving place, a grown man beset on his birthday by a calamity suitable for a youngster. He fell asleep with his face pressed into the sleeve of his raincoat — his feet going numb from the sweat that had frozen in his shoes.

Then, rising up from mourning, shivering, emptied, he started towards the Square. With each step he surveyed his feelings. No, he was not too disconsolate to recover. He would apologize. He would explain that his waywardness had no bearing on his professional sincerity. He would solicit pity, if necessary, by telling Gladstein about his father's protracted illness—about their infertility, even. Gladstein would forgive him. A mid-life crisis—his first time applying that diagnosis to himself, and it made him wince a little—that's all. Nothing was irrevocable. He gave in to the realization that he had abandoned his career months or even years ago, and tonight was a belated rite of recognition. The New Hampshire farmhouse rose again like an image of salvation.

How long had he slept? With an immediate sense of where he must go, an instinct untouched by twenty years of living in other cities, he felt his way to Mt. Auburn Street and turned up Plympton, passing the entry to Adams House and The Crimson. He stopped beneath an iron lantern and a shop sign: Grolier's Poetry Bookshop. His watch read 9:50. He climbed the granite stairs and peeked through the door. The proprietress was inside. He squeezed the handle and the door yielded.

"I'm closed," the woman said.

"Oh, please, ma'am. I've come all the way from Atlanta. I wonder if you remember me, I used to be a regular here. I have longed to be here, really, especially tonight. If you would just stay open a few moments I'll gratefully make a purchase and be on my way."

She eyed him suspiciously. No doubt he cut a paradoxical figure. A bear in formal dress, his face purple from the elements, eyes bloodshot with self-recrimination and park- bench sleep. He remembered her. She had withered but the glower of mistrust hadn't faded. Her mistrustful gaze was if anything exaggerated by a mild, asymmetrical Grave's orbitopathy. Her right eye protruded like a quail-egg. Before the etiology of Grave's disease was discovered, one of Vance's medical-school professors had related in a lecture, the bulging eye had been taken as a sign of madness.

"Please, you see," Vance urged with a smile, "this is no ordinary night for me. It's my birthday. I am, well, a physician with a weakness for romantic poetry. I'll accept a recommendation, a poet for the New Year. You won't remember, but you suggested one of my favorites, many years ago . . .

"Who?"

"Pardon?"

"Which poet?"

"Francis Thompson. Francis Thompson. I can show you from which shelf you took it."

"I know the shelf. What poem of his do you like?"

"Oh, let's see. 'As lovers, banished from their lady's face/And hopeless of her grace,/Fashion a ghostly sweetness in its place,/Fondly adore/Some stealth-won cast attire she wore,/A kerchief or a glove.' "

"Lovely, isn't it? Today they'd call that perverse. A fetish. Come in, don't stand at the door, I don't want anyone else thinking I'm open. What are you looking for?"

The door tinkled when he shut it.

"Thank you. Shall I lock it? I've been reading the high romantics, Tennyson and Whitman, Browning. Ezra Pound."

"H.D.?"

"No, I haven't gotten to —"

"She was Ezra Pound's lover and a great poet in her own right. Tea?"

"T?"

"I'm about to make tea. Would you like a cup?"

"Oh, I hadn't thought! Yes, please, thank you."

The hotplate was on the desk at the front. She poured with a slight tremor and dropped in two teabags." A doctor who loves poetry. William Carlos Williams was a doctor, too."

"Sure, *Patterson*. I'm from New Jersey myself originally."

"Not a high romantic."

"I've thought of him as a kind of romantic, a low one, perhaps. "Queen Anne's Lace," for instance. 'Her body is not so white as/anemone petals nor so smooth — nor/so remote a thing.' "

She took a cigarette from her pocket.

"That'll make your eye worse," he said, gesturing at the cigarette.

She paused, as if evaluating his intentions again.

"How long has it been that way?"

"A year, about. The other eye went down."

"Hmm. Unusual at your age. Bother you much?"

"My doctor didn't say anything about smoking." She placed her cigarette tentatively on a bookshelf ledge.

"Let me give you the name of a good endocrinologist, a friend of mine at Mass General. William Cole. Tell him I sent you, he'll see you right away. Here," he said, scribbling on an index card, "that's my name."

"Why, thank you. That's very kind of you. I haven't known what to do." She did not move but seemed to settle in her chair a little, alternatively examining his card and then him. "When were you here? Here, right?" She gestured towards the Yard.

"Class of 1990. I was a chemistry major but I took some poetry. Helen Vendler, Seamus Heaney."

"Before the Nobel."

"He was inspiring. Made it come alive when he read, in his dreamy Irish lilt."

"Divorced?"

"Oh, I don't know anything about his personal life."

"No, you. I meant you. Don't mind. Most people don't go out alone tonight, unless they're alone."

"No, it's okay. I'm married. My wife's in Connecticut with her folks." He spread his fingers. "I find rings uncomfortable."

The woman shifted, reached for the cigarette and put it in her mouth, but didn't light it. Her hair was gauzy so that the roundness of her skull, protruding eye, breasts and stomach made him think of how she might be sketched by drawing different-sized circles crowded in upon one another.

"Dr. Vance Norman. From New Jersey," she said, squinting at the card.

"Originally," he corrected.

"Josephine. I've lived in this building almost my entire life."

"Really? When did the store open?"

"1927, the year I was born. Nothing to do with my family, except my mother was a poet, never published. Wasn't originally a bookshop, either, but fine arts for a few years."

"How did you come to own it?"

"I inherited the building from my parents. The store my late husband and I bought in 1968. Now Harvard owns the building, and I live at the back on the third floor." She replaced the cigarette on the ledge. "Vance, was it?"

"Yes."

384

"Let me tell you. When I was a baby, in this room, poets met, tested their creations on each other. T.S. Eliot dandled me in his arms. Why, I was passed around and read to. My mother told me. e.e. cummings took me for strolls in the park. Pound, too, but Pound I've never confirmed."

"Fantastic! I'll bet this room hasn't changed in 80 years," he said, glancing up and about. "Who else was here?"

"Oh, many famous writers, not just poets. But in the early days the most regular was Conrad Aiken. Read him?"

" 'Tetelestai.' There's a recording of him reciting it."

"People don't read him anymore. In the twenties and thirties he was very popular, more for his novels and stories. Now people ignore even those."

"He was here often?"

"He lived upstairs. Right there. First in 1927 when he was a tutor at Harvard, then again ten years later, he stayed in the same apartment. For a few months after he returned from England and was divorced from his first wife. Then he went down to Mexico, where he remarried."

"So you were ten when he was here in 1937. Do you remember him? What was he like?"

"Oh, he was many things, not all nice. You can read biographies, there's a very good one by Edward Butscher. He was a sentimental man, they say, full of himself, a depressive and a drinker — on account of his father, also a doctor, killing his wife then himself. Aiken was a boy of ten or eleven. They lived in Savannah. He discovered the bodies himself."

"How awful. I never heard that."

"He tried to kill himself a few times also. May have even when he was here, in 1937. I'm not sure. My mother died when I was 13 and we moved away." She picked up the cigarette and put it back down. "But to answer your question, from my point of view, I was a child. To me, Aiken was kind. You might imagine how he appreciated childhood."

"Yes, remarkable, isn't it. And you say he might have tried to commit suicide here?"

Josephine shifted her weight and sipped tea. "Can I ask you something personal?" she said.

"Sure."

"Have you ever been in love with a woman who isn't your wife?"

"Well, no, I don't, no. Maybe my wife and I aren't as close as —"

"You bottle it up inside, then."

"A lot of life that's way. Not just marriage," he blurted. He thought of horribly bumping into Gladstein.

"That's not how Aiken saw it. He felt everything intensely and didn't try to hold it down. He translated his emotions into poetry and acted them out, the devil with the consequences."

"That is a way to live. I'm sure I could be more expressive."

"A man like Aiken, you see, all the poets, they don't have a choice. It all comes out. Writing is a symptom of too much feeling. That's a harmless overflow. Others are more detrimental."

"Like trying to commit suicide."

"Of course. And drinking too much, or trying to make love to every woman."

"Did Aiken do that?"

"He returned to Cambridge because he was in love with my mother."

"Your mother! You don't say! How do you know?"

"Ha! How do I know? He was the death of her! He wrote poems about her. She inspired a few of his best." She let the frisson dampen to silence as though to evaluate the effect of her statement — who would not doubt such a claim?

He wondered why she had told this to him. Was it his desperation, or hers? Two lonesome souls on News Year's Eve." Your mother told you of her love for Aiken?" he said at last.

Josephine stood, walked to a cabinet above which hung a dozen framed photographs of well-known poets, and from a drawer pulled out a manila envelope. She sat back down and removed from the envelope a sheaf of stiff, unmatched photographs. She shuffled them until she came to the right one, whereupon she examined it for a moment before handing it to him: a candid shot of a woman, perhaps in her thirties, with a face of arresting clarity and beauty.

386

The lady's hair is pressed back above her forehead, as from perspiration on a hot day, and a slight smile is breaking across her lips — a face overtaken by joy. She is wearing a summery dress, and cantered upward from her lap is a mandolin. Her fingers are on the instrument in a way to suggest she's being captured in mid-song.

"Your mother? Extremely beautiful."

"Aiken took that picture."

"Really? I wonder what he said to make her look up like that."

"For the world, my love, comes round,/round as the dance of ancient oaks in spring/or the song the enchanted pinkwinks sing,/ the world is round as a ring."

"You know that!" he cried.

"Turn it over."

The words were there, scripted in an elegant penmanship that has faded into history with the fountain pen.

"No wonder," he said. "What power, to capture the attention of a woman like that. She is so alive, you feel her in the room right now."

"That was my mother. She took her own life three months later."

Vance's eyes grew moist. Josephine looked away to avoid multiplying the dread of her own sorrow, which they could both feel very close. They sustained a long silence, and longer still.

"I don't know what to say. Thank you for showing me."

"No one could forgive Aiken for what he did. But people are responsible for their own emotions. My mother didn't have to fall for him. She was a married woman. And the poet," Josephine gestured desperately to the walls of the room, "the poet is an emotional invalid. Well, maybe it's a noble weakness."

"I never thought of it that way. Why have you chosen all this?"

"Don't confuse the poet and the poetry. Poets may not be able to help themselves, but they see clearly. We hardly have a truthful path to our feelings without them. Forget the damn psychologists—you're not—"

"No, I'm in public health."

"You read poetry or do you write also?"

"After what's just been said . . .

"Oh, never mind. By the time you're my age there's no choice, we all become poets emotionally."

"How's that?"

"Ambition and vanity disappear. All that's left is sentimentality and the gift of sight for the present. Unwilling alertness, your eyes pinned open to the truth. That's what counts for the poet, who knows which way the future points. 'The peak that stays in view wherever we go'. Philip Larkin."

"At my age I guess I'm just starting to think that way. But the wakefulness you describe, I've never thought that way about aging."

She sipped her now-cold tea and observed him. He knew that her distended eye was the product of hyperthyroidism, but couldn't help thinking of her statement, "eyes pinned open to the truth." The correspondence was poetic, not medical. "It's snowing," she said at last.

Turning to see out the window, he noticed the small Christmas tree in the corner for the first time. "Look how big the flakes are, and how swiftly they're falling."

"Aiken was fascinated by the snow. His most famous story was called, 'Silent Snow, Secret Snow,' about a boy who goes mad, but it's secretly wondrous to him because he's always seeing the world through snow. He also wrote a series of smaller poems called *Lights and Snow* which I believe to have been inspired by my mother."

"What makes you think so?"

She recited:

> *The girl in the room beneath*
> *Before going to bed*
> *Strums on a mandolin*
> *The three simple tunes she knows.*
> *How inadequate they are to tell what her*
> *heart feels!*

"Wow, what a remarkable connection. I can see now. One can hardly imagine how that must have been for her, for him. Do you have any of their correspondence?"

"Listen, Dr. Vance Norman, it's eleven fifteen. I'm tired. Let me give you something and send you home."

"I'm so sorry, I didn't mean to pry."

"No, it's not that. I'm tired. And even after all the years this subject . . . Yes, there must have been letters, but my mother probably destroyed them. Only a few slips of paper seem to have escaped. I have them somewhere. Here," she said, climbing to her feet, "let me give you a gift of something, a book of poems you wanted."

"Oh, please, let me buy it . . ."

"A souvenir. For you to tell your wife how you spent New Year's keeping an old woman company."

"The pleasure has been mine. You have no idea. I mean it. I wish there were something I could do for you. I feel somehow changed, about many things."

"Your wife will enjoy those. Up there, on that shelf. The thin yellow one about ten from the right."

"Conrad Aiken. *Turns and Movies*."

"The original is 1916. This is a reprint." She raised her reading glasses from her chest. "Here, see, dedicated to his first wife. His poems have a beautiful music to them if you mind the numbers."

"You mean the meter?"

"Yes. Read this one, for instance. 'Evensong.' See how sweetly it begins: 'This song is of no importance,/I will only improvise;/Yet, maybe, here and there,/Suddenly from these sounds a chord will start/And piercingly touch my heart.' "

Vance watched Josephine recite the lines, and he thought how love of life must increase with its waning, if only one has the wisdom to embrace it.

On his way out, Josephine patted him maternally, and he kissed her cheek.

Boston was blanketed magnificently, from one end to the other, in snow. The taxi glided softly over it as if floating beyond time itself. Vance understood that his impulse to crash his career was not a longing to write poetry. He lowered the window and let snow in to rinse his face. How alive he felt.

He let himself into the apartment, hung his coat and filled a glass from the kitchen tap. The bedroom light was on and cast still shadows into the hallway. Not unpleasant, the dim light, he thought, and then a shadow moved. He caught his breath and went through the doorway. He felt his mind skip a stair and what he glimpsed more than momentarily was Pam, on the bed, kneeling, nude under the sheer wrapping of the Christian Lacroix shawl. She was fresh and unspeakably beautiful to his eyes. She began weeping from happiness at the sight of him, too.

"Oh, Pamela! It's as if I'm waking up to you after a century of sleep. Dearest, most darling —"

The phone startled him from his reverie. He let it ring several times before going in to reach for the receiver.

"Hello?"

"Vance, sweetheart. Thank God you're safe. I was frantic with worry. Happy birthday, darling. I wish I were with you!"

Kalman Applbaum is associate professor of anthropology at the University of Wisconsin, Milwaukee. His research is in the fields of global mental health and pharmaceuticals. He has also written two novels. Contact: kalman.applbaum@gmail.com

Soldier Red

℘ℭ

by Lauren Handman

At first he didn't register the ringing of the telephone, immersed as he was in the creation of a sharp, hooked nose. He had already formed the face with broad, careful strokes of the brush, but it was the details that entranced him. Anyone could have a face like that, a triangular face with a mop of black hair atop it, but the hook nose gave the image character. He was filling in the shadows, concentrating on a small depression on the left side of the proud nose, when the ringing finally pierced his oblivion. He almost dropped his paintbrush, so startled was he by the sound, and it took him a moment to collect himself.

He grabbed a cloth from the small worktable beside him and quickly rubbed paint from his delicate hands. The wall in front of him was alive with color, a jovial woman with a basket of flowers bowing demurely to a soldier painted all in red. It reminded him of childhood games, of the days when boys wanted to be soldiers. It is easier to make-believe when reality has not set in. He doubted boys played soldier in the streets anymore.

The insistent ringing continued. He took the small funnel-shaped receiver off its hook and held it to his ear, leaning down to speak into the telephone. These days it was often crackly — he was surprised it was working at all. The lines had been down for the past week, but someone must have climbed up despite the cold and fixed them, because he heard no static from the other end.

"Hello?" he asked in Polish.

"Jakub," a sharp German voice responded. "Speak German."

"My apologies, Herr Müller," Jakub answered in German. He pushed unruly hair back from his face, his fingers nervously brushing against each other, and tried to clear a lump from his throat. "How can I help you?"

"My wall is looking very bare, Jakub."

"Ah, yes, of course," he said. He nodded his head nervously, a part of his mind aware that he couldn't be seen, and scratched at his earlobe. "I was low on paint, you see, and— "

"You'll be here tomorrow to finish it." It was not a question, but Jakub responded as if it was.

"Yes, of course, Herr Müller, of course. First thing in the morning?"

"As soon as curfew has ended."

"Of course."

There was no goodbye, just a quiet click and then dead sound, indicating that Müller had hung up the phone.

Jakub shook his head, replacing his own receiver in its claw-like cradle, and let his exhausted body collapse into a seat. He should not have wasted so much red on his bright soldier — he would have to make some more before going to sleep tonight.

"Pardon me, my friends," he whispered to the figures on the wall, the familiar sounds of Polish a comfort to his throat. "You will have to go unfinished awhile longer. I must please my Herr Benefactor." He said the words with a curl on his lips, then shook his head sadly. "Forgive me, Adonai, I should be grateful, I know. I am still alive, no?"

He dropped his paintbrush to the side, abandoned for the moment, and set to work mixing colors for another man's wall.

He had been granted several days off from his work painting for Feliks Müller — it was strange that he was being called in so soon. Most likely it meant a purge was coming. He would want to make sure Jakub was safely tucked away, where no stray bullet or careless baton could rob Müller of his precious resource. Jakub felt too tired to shudder. He would have to warn his friends, if he could, tell them to stay inside their houses. These days of blood were coming more often now. It would not be long before Müller could not protect him from them, and it had been long since he himself could protect anyone.

Jakub dressed for the day, donning his least-patched pair of trousers and the blue shirt with only one hole in the sleeve. From under his mattress he carefully collected the pile of papers that were the last chapter of his manuscript. On top of the pile, her spidery writing a contrast to Jakub's careful calligraphy, was his last letter from Salcia. He touched the sheet, his lips working soundlessly as he traced the almost-memorized words. He told himself he was silly for hiding his manuscripts, silly for sending them to Warsaw as if they were secret documents; but this letter could truly be a death sentence. A promise of safe passage, from one of his only friends. How many years had it been since he had seen Salcia? Two? Three? He remembered a red scarf on a cold day, the sharp taste of her too-bitter coffee as he announced he was moving home. She advised against it, said his career would do better in the big city, but he wanted to go. He hated the crowds in Warsaw, hated the games he had to play with editors and publishers. No, better a silent studio and a paintbrush; a little café and a pad of paper. Salcia had once said that genius allowed eccentricity, which of course he told her was nonsense, but there it was. He joked that she cared about him for his writing, not for him, and she only smiled and said they were one and the same. If only he had listened that day. Warsaw was safe in Soviet hands, and the days of this place being a home had faded to distant memory.

He put the manuscript in an envelope and carefully marked down Salcia's address. This package he hid in the sleeve of his worn brown jacket, which he slid on, fastening the few chipped buttons. His fingers danced around the left lapel, tracing out the shape of the star, faded from yellow to a greasy, bone white. He should re-dye it soon. No reason to draw attention to himself. These were dangerous times for his people. He should be grateful — he was lucky to be alive.

Curfew had ended only a half hour before, and the streets were still mostly empty as he locked his front door and descended the steps. The quiet was eerie — Drohobycz was not a large town, and even before the war it had not been prosperous, but it had always been full of life. That was what Jakub had liked about it, what had drawn him back to his childhood home to stay. No matter how quiet it was in his house, he could go to the window and peer outside, and life would greet his eyes. Not so anymore. He was more likely to run into a marching square of soldiers than he was a woman with a basket of flowers. He had no models for his mural, only his own memories.

He had thought when the Soviets had marched through the tight, narrow streets that it was the worst thing that could have happened to his home; he had never imagined the Nazis would turn on their former Soviet allies and make a nightmare into a hell. He should have known — he should have thanked Adonai at the time, instead of cursing the Soviet troops and their unwanted communism. But how could anyone have known?

He would have to hurry if he did not wish to be late. Müller could be cruel when angered, but this was a necessary visit. Mrs. Wysocki was a notorious gossip, and would have the word spread through the ghetto faster than he could do on his own. One must use the few advantages available. Down the street and around the corner, Jakub climbed a flight of steps and pulled the bell outside the house. It was answered promptly by the frightened face of a young woman, which melted into a smile at the sight of Jakub's thin, nervous face and bobbing head.

"Good morning, Irina," Jakub said.

"Good morning, Mr. Schenker. Are you off to work already?" She was tucking stray strands of hair behind her ears, adjusting the once-bright apron that was hugging her slim waist. He tried not to look at her, but she kept smiling, trying to catch his eye, and he was forced to meet her gaze.

"Yes, yes . . . is your mother home?"

"She is, but I think she's still sleeping," Irina said. "I can give her a message, though, if you'd like."

"Yes. Please do. Tell her there are rumors the soldiers will be out today. People should stay inside."

"I'll tell her — thank you, Mr. Schenker."

"Of course," he said, guilt and nervousness making his fingers dance against his pockets. While they cowered in their homes, listening for the sound of footsteps on the stairs, he would be inside, putting color to plaster, making a life come alive in still frames. He had not thought the Nazis could pollute painting. Life, religion, the world, yes, even his books, burned or hidden away, but not painting, no, not his private world. That was supposed to be inviolate, locked deep within himself. This guilt, though, this ever-present guilt . . .

"I finished your book last night. It was beautiful," Irina said, her eyes lowered, a nervous twitch coloring her smile. She had caught him half-turned, lost in his own thoughts, about to depart without further incident. He hesitated, not sure what to say, and nodded once, almost sharply.

"Well . . . good. Yes. Thank you," he acknowledged, and then hurried away. She watched him for a moment before closing the door.

He always hated walking up those steps for fear young Irina would answer the door. She caught him speechless, never sure what to say. If only he could live and write and paint without ever meeting another human being, without having to acknowledge their praise. Salcia always laughed, told him he was born to be a hermit, and he supposed it was true. There was nothing to be done for it, though. If he could have lived on his art alone he would have, but one had to feed oneself somehow.

He reached into his pocket, double-checking that all of his transit-papers were there. He had reached the checkpoint once only to discover himself without the important documents, and had been forced to flee pursuit through the ghetto's streets, hiding in a trash can in an alley for three hours while the sounds of laughter and idle gun-fire echoed close-by. It was not a mistake he would make twice, and now he checked his pocket every few minutes as he walked. It was not far to the edge of the ghetto, a handspan of streets and shuttered windows. Every week, the inhabitants became fewer and further between, more and more houses truly empty instead of only appearing thus. He did not know how long this war would go on, and some days he wondered if any of them would survive it. Soon there would be more ghosts than people wandering the roadways. There were already more funerals than bar-mitzvahs. Two weeks ago, a mass grave had been dug in the Jewish cemetery, and filled with the men and women who had dug it. The mind shied from such atrocities. Better to think of his flower girl, his bright candy-cane soldier.

He saw the checkpoint ahead, and pulled his paper out of his pocket with trembling fingers. Every day it was the same. He wished there were work for him within the ghetto, but in reality he was one of the few lucky ones. Work of any kind was hard to come by. At least he could still mail packages, buy bread. Most were cut off entirely. His papers were signed by Feliks Müller, but they did not protect him from harassment by the soldiers. They were more than aware that he was here on the whim of one of their superiors, which was a double-edged sword.

A familiar figure greeted him, charcoal eyebrows shadowing a face too cold to be beautiful, and he held back a sigh. Today was not going well for chance encounters — Karl Braun was standing at the checkpoint, chatting with the soldiers there. Like Müller, he was an officer of the Gestapo, but a rivalry between the two Germans led to a greater-than-normal level of animosity directed towards Jakub. He wondered, in that moment of stillness before fear took thoughts away, what caused so much hate between these two. Did Müller see a Jew in Braun's stocky build, his dark complexion? Or could there still be petty hatred, divorced entirely from the occupation? Were there still spurned lovers, promotions denied, little hates, in a world so overcome? He wished he could pretend he was going somewhere else, divert his path up to one of the nearby houses, but so close to the border of the ghetto, they were all empty. He had no choice but to plough forward, and hope this day would come to an end soon"Papers," one of the German soldiers barked, somehow managing to sound sharp and bored at the same time.

Jakub handed the papers over quickly, not wanting to draw attention to himself. Keep your head down, he thought, and perhaps . . .

"Where is your star?" Braun barked.

"Here, sir," Jakub replied in German, pointing to the faded star on his chest.

"I can hardly see it. Are you trying to hide it?"

"No, sir," Jakub said.

"Are you calling me a liar?" Braun asked. There was something dangerous in his voice. Better not to answer at all.

Jakub shook his head.

"The officer asked you a question, Jew!" one of the soldiers snarled.

Jakub felt the sharp impact of a rifle-butt on the tender flesh of his side. He stumbled to the side, holding in a grunt of pain, and felt tears prick his eyes. "I'm sorry," he said.

"You know, my daughter said that she thought a Jewish child would make an excellent pet. How do you like being a pet?" Braun asked.

"I am honoured," Jakub murmured, holding back the anger and embarrassment he felt welling inside him. Adonai help me, he thought, help me be still.

"Speak up when you're spoken to!" the same soldier declared, giving him another sharp shove with the rifle. It sent him reeling a few more steps, mercifully outside of the range of another blow, though closer to the soldier on the other side. He seemed uninterested in the game, keeping his eyes fixed on the street in front of him.

"I am honoured," Jakub repeated in a louder voice.

"Well, I don't think I would want a Jew in the house. Filthy things," Braun said.

The soldier with the rifle nodded in agreement. "I always wash my hands after handling their papers," he said, and held the papers out towards Jakub.

Jakub scuttled forward to receive them, and got another hit in the back for his trouble. He started to scurry away, and felt a hand close on his curls, yanking his head backwards. His teeth smashed shut, and he had to blink back fierce tears.

"I didn't tell you that you could go," Braun said. He turned to the soldier, still holding Jakub's hair tightly in his hand, and inquired about the soldier's sweetheart, back home in Germany. A casual conversation followed, in which Jakub's scalp began to burn from the pull on his hair, and his back strained from holding his body at an awkward angle. Minutes passed, past the point where Jakub thought he could go on, but go on he did. Finally, when pleasantries had been exchanged to the German's satisfaction, Braun let Jakub go with a shove. "Go on, out of my sight," he snapped.

Jakub dashed away, quick as he could go without running. He rubbed his hair, massaging the aching flesh, and with the other hand gingerly tested the bruise on his side. All in one piece. Perhaps it wouldn't be such a bad day, after all.

Safely out of sight of the checkpoint, Jakub pulled his manuscript from its hiding place and ran his fingers over the edges, ensuring it was safe. He wanted his writing out of this cursed country, out of this war. With any luck, this package would be the last. He wrapped his arms tightly around the bundle and hurried through the cold November streets; he had a very small margin of error to get to the post office and still get to work on time. Sometimes, if he was late arriving, Müller would force him to work late, not caring that he would be skirting the safety of curfew. The guards at the checkpoint would follow him in a jeep as he ran back to the house, their eyes on their watches, a malicious game to see if he would make it before the short arm hit the hour. He had no neighbour on the floor below now. He had watched them gun the old man down.

He opened the post-office door, and scuttled into the warmth. For the first time today luck greeted him: it was Mr. Zajac working behind the counter, and not Mrs. Adamski. She often told him there was no mail, only for him to discover a few days later that she had thrown it away, and Mr. Zajac had rescued it, surreptitiously, from the trash. He waited his turn behind a woman wrapped head to foot in scarves and coats, and then put his package down on the counter.

"Good afternoon," he said.

"Mailing something to Salcia?" Mr. Zajac asked.

"Yes — some letters," Jakub said.

"And how is the lovely writer? A Polish treasure, that's what I tell my wife. We should all be proud to have someone like that representing our nation."

398

"Yes. She's very good," Jakub said. He preferred to talk about Salcia than himself. He owed most of his popularity to her — she had helped him publish his first story. "A good woman," he added.

"Yes, yes. I believe she sent something for you, actually. Let me go and get it." Mr. Zajac disappeared into the back, returning to the counter a moment later with a small package. "Here you are. Please sign," he said, and Jakub carefully sketched his signature on the page in front of him. "Now I have an autograph," Mr. Zajac joked. "This will be worth a lot of money some day."

"How much for the package?" Jakub asked without replying. He handed over the requested amount of money, sighing at the fee.

"I'm sorry for the cost," Mr. Zajac said. "They are charging us sur-fees now. Soon it will be too expensive to send anything, I think."

"Yes, I think you're right. Perhaps this will be my last package."

"Have a good day, Mr. Schenker."

"And you," Jakub said. "Good day."

He did not dare open the package at work, but he could not bear to spend the day praying it contained what he hoped, so Jakub took the risk of another minute and ducked into an alley. Safe as he could be, he opened Salcia's package with trembling fingers. Out flew a folded letter, some papers, a small sheaf of money, and a little glass jar. He opened the papers first, praying they were what he had been waiting for, and felt his entire body lighten as he read them over. German had never looked as lovely as those letters of transit, declaring him a good Christian man en route to Warsaw. Freedom in every black block; a possibility of life in that squirrelly signature at the bottom. He could kiss her — he would. He would kiss her when he saw her next, plant his lips on her cheek. Maybe even hug her. He flipped through the money, counting quietly to himself, and then murmured a prayer of thanks. It was easily enough to finance the trip; and a little extra besides, bless her heart and every thing about her. He would be free of this place, free of this ghetto and the gunfire that would ricochet outside his windows. It was too much, too much goodness. He did not deserve such good fortune.

He turned the small jar between his fingers, watching the glint of sun against the dark colour. Rosy pink, it was a hard colour to mix — a treasure almost greater than the money. It would be perfect for his mural at home. His soldier looked far too grim — with such beautiful flowers, and such a beautiful woman, he should have a smile on his face.

He wanted to leave, to turn on his heel and run back home, back through the checkpoint, pack his bags and leave this hell behind. But with Müller expecting him, he would instantly be looked for, and he did not wish to raise suspicions so soon. But these papers, the freedom they granted him! Warsaw was still controlled by the Soviets — he would be free from the Nazi occupation there. Free from the star on his breast and the casual torments of men made monsters.

If he left early in the next morning, he would have several hours before Müller knew he was late, and likely several more before Müller roused himself enough to go looking; by then he would be out of the city and fading comfortably into obscurity toward Warsaw. So he walked through familiar streets made foreign, skirted groups of soldiers and their women, kept his head down and his posture cowed, all with his heart in his throat and a barely contained smile on his reedy lips.

He knocked on the bright green front door and was admitted into Müller's home by a frowning, tight-lipped woman with hair pulled into a twist on the top of her head. They had never been formally introduced, but he assumed she was Mrs. Müller. He did not know her name. She walked him into the library, watching him as if he might slip trinkets into his pockets, and as soon as he was in the library she exited, shutting the door sharply between them. He heard the rusty creak of the lock sliding shut, keeping her safe from the Jewish taint that was invading her home.

He enjoyed the solitude, and the break from terror-filled tedium. Painting murals, no matter whom they were for, made the day seem easier. He spent several hours immersed in a cerulean mountain, kissing its tip with the faintest of white clouds. This would be a landscape, rather than the human figures of which he was more fond, but he wanted the left wall to be dominated by the proud image of a man conquering a mountain peak, and didn't want it to be overwhelmed by busyness around.

He was just beginning to add a shading of trees to the mountain when he heard the sound of approaching voices, and then the *shiink, click* of the key turning the lock. Müller marched in, his wife close on his heels, and surveyed the work he had just completed with a critical eye.

"But what if he retaliates, Feliks?" the woman said in a tone that implied it wasn't the first time she had raised this objection.

"He won't," Müller said with a dismissive wave. "The man is a coward. It amazes me that he has managed to become an officer at all; the Gestapo should be more stringent about who they let in."

"But Löwe *was* under his protection. He will consider it a personal insult, that you killed his . . ." she trailed off, waving her hands in the air, clearly at a loss for the appropriate term.

The irony was not lost on Jakub. The Party said Jews were animals, literally lower than human, yet these situations were not unheard of, Gestapo giving Jews protection in exchange for services they desired. A mural on the library wall. An accountant who was a master of numbers. A dentist — now just another body, hidden in the mass graves where the cemetery used to be.

"Filthy Jew," Müller said, miming as if he would spit, though he glanced at his wife out of the corner of his eye and refrained to follow through on the motion.

"No one is arguing that point, dear. *I* certainly wouldn't let one near my mouth, can you imagine what you might pick up? What on earth possessed Braun to keep one on as a dentist I will never be able to fathom. But he —"

"Never mind Braun. What's done is done," he said.

"But the Jew wasn't even in the ghetto, Feliks. Whether or not you did this intentionally, Braun will see it that way. He will think you're taking revenge for his embarrassing you at the State dinner. You'll have to tell him something," she said.

"I'll tell him that if he objects to the killing of Jews, he should defect to the losing side before someone discovers his true colours and shoots *him*, that's what I'll say! Now get out of my hair!" he said, his tone harking to the barking commands of the other soldiers. A man used to being obeyed.

In response to his words she threw up her hands, half-rolling her eyes before thinking better of it and sweeping out of the room.

Müller, meanwhile, seemed to have forgotten the conversation completely as soon as the words had left his mouth, and was busy scrutinizing the painting in front of him. "Beautiful," he finally announced. "You may stop and have lunch, then keep working."

"Thank you, Herr Müller," Jakub murmured.

"There is something so creative about your paintings. I feel as if I am looking into another world. A better world, perhaps," he said. He nodded once again, considering some inner thought, and then disappeared from the room. A faint click signalled his departure.

By the end of the day the mountain was covered in trees and shadows, rocky outcroppings and faint wispy clouds, and Jakub felt exhaustion seeping through his bones. He bid Müller goodbye without betraying a hint of his true emotions, and descended the stairs for the last time, back onto Drohobycz's streets. He almost did a dance as his feet touched the cobblestones, but stopped himself just in time. He must betray no hint of the change boiling within him. He had to be calm, as apparently clear as glass. In less than twelve hours he would be on his way, moving towards freedom.

It would be a long trip, and he stopped in at the baker's for a loaf of bread to make sandwiches. It was late enough in the day that the bread was on discount, and he used the last of his own money to purchase it, grinning in his heart. It would be the last time that he bought bread here; the last time that he left this store on his way to the ghetto. It would be the last time that he felt his heart skip a beat at the sight of armed guards on his quiet streets. The last time he would reach into his pocket, feel for the familiar weight of his papers, double- and triple-checking to ensure they were there.

He had them half-out when he neared the guards, and saw the familiar face of Karl Braun watching his approach. Braun stepped away from the guards, meeting Jakub several feet from the barrier of the ghetto. As his steps approached and stopped, fear finally overwhelmed the joy that had pervaded him for the past hours.

"Herr Braun?" he asked. His voice quavered.

Braun never answered his query. Instead he pulled a dark metal pistol from the holster at his waist, aimed and fired before a thought could form in Jakub's head. He felt a sudden coldness in his side, and for an instant he was sure Braun had missed, that a gunshot could not feel like this. He brought his fingers to his side, felt the world sway and spin, and saw his fingers covered in blood. The world began to fade, colours leeching out until all that remained was his bright, red fingers, and he thought with a smile that it was the perfect colour to finish his soldier, and then he thought no more.

Lauren Handman is a novelist, fiction writer, and playwright. She received her BFA in Creative Writing from the University of Victoria, and is currently pursuing an MFA in Theatre and Playwriting. Her short stories have been published in such literary magazines as *Crow Toes Quarterly*, and anthologies such as *Revolutions of the Undertones*, while her plays have won critical acclaim (Best New Play, Victoria Fringe Festival). Lauren is currently working on a novel series, and residing in Vancouver, BC. Contact: lauren.handman@gmail.com

REUNION

— ❦ —

by Walter E. Gourlay

On a crisp, beautiful autumn day, Dr. John J. Ackerman, Emeritus Professor of Anthropology at Michigan State, got into his new Lexus, intending to stop at the Faculty Club and have a couple of drinks with the dean before going home. Instead, he went to California.

He didn't know he was going to California. He was thinking of the empty house awaiting him. And the barren years he'd spent driving the same route, back and forth, literally and figuratively. Today, on a sudden impulse he went directly home, packed a light suitcase, and drove to the Interstate with no conscious destination in mind. Goodbye, he thought. Goodbye to his books, his house, his routine, his scholarly pretensions. Goodbye to all that. Goodbye, Professor Ackerman, Ph.D. Goodbye to the man he'd become, the man he'd once thought he wanted to be. He'd leave it all. Tear it up and throw it in the wastebasket. God, it felt good! The most impulsive, irresponsible thing he'd done in years. In how many years? Since before he'd married Harriet.

He remembered being just plain Johnny, before becoming Dr. Ackerman, Ph.D. Eager for adventure. He'd gone mountain climbing in the Adirondacks and the White Mountains, a glory of orange, red and yellow in the fall, with the crackle of oak leaves underfoot. A year driving cattle in Wyoming and another ranching in Big Sur near

Cambria, then hitchhiking back to Manhattan. There his freedom ended. His draft board zonked him. Greetings. Classified 1-A. Fit for combat. The price he paid for good clean living. A ticket to hell in the Pacific.

He didn't want to remember the war. It was sealed up somewhere in a dark corner of his memory, not to be looked at again. After his discharge, complete with a Purple Heart, he'd tried to put himself together again. Pick up the pieces. Start a new life. He'd gone to sea on a tramp steamer for a couple of years, then gone on a long fishing trip in the Maine woods. When he decided he was ready for civilian life he rented a cold water flat on Bedford Street in the heart of the Village, where he met Harriet, and entered Columbia on the GI Bill.

Harriet was pretty, blonde, brown-eyed and direct. The only daughter of a wealthy Republican broker, she'd been very properly brought up, and properly educated at Bryn Mawr. She'd decided to lose her virginity, she told him in her direct no-nonsense way, and was bestowing the honor on him. That was probably the most daring thing she'd ever done in her life, he thought, her one token of resistance to dear Daddy. Naturally, he did what was expected of him.

Why had he married her? Because she helped to wash away memories of the war, helped him to settle down and lead a normal life. He'd been seduced into marriage, not so much by Harriet's considerable charms, but by the post-war recession, by the comfortable niche that awaited him as the loving husband of the darling sweet little girl of her multimillionaire Daddy.

She had cheerfully given up ballet lessons and in due time produced three children, two boys and a girl, all now grown and each of them respectable, Republican, and as predictable as Harriet herself.

After earning his doctorate, John J. Ackerman, Ph.D. got a job as an Instructor at Michigan State, quickly rising to Full Professor. When Harriet inherited her father's wealth they became a popular couple socially, bought a huge house overlooking the Red Cedar River in Lansing, and hired a gardener, a maid and a part-time cook — "so you can entertain your colleagues" — she explained. As a rich man's daughter, Harriet had inherited a First Class ticket and a First

Class attitude to life. As was expected of him, he joined the Faculty Club and the exclusive Country Club and hobnobbed with General Motors executives in the state capital. As expected of her, she became a volunteer at several local charities, and made sure that everyone knew that her husband was a university professor and that she was a graduate of Bryn Mawr. By the time he admitted to himself how little they had in common, the first child came, and then the others, and he resigned himself to being a token husband and father, bought and paid for. He buried himself in his research, and became a workaholic.

He'd been highly successful professionally. His doctoral dissertation had been seminal, was widely cited, and led to his appointment at Michigan State. He'd published several textbooks and numerous monographs, had held a prestigious Guggenheim Fellowship, had become chairman of his department, and before his retirement had been elected president of the American Anthropological Association.

Of course, Harriet thought all this was wonderful. She made sure to go to every black-tie reception, and saw to it that their acquaintances and the local press were duly informed of his various successes. But to his amazement, she'd never once looked at any of his books or articles, attended any of his lectures, or even asked him about his work. "I'm just a simple housewife."

And so his best years had gone dribbling away.

Impelled by some inner directive that he couldn't name he took the Interstate south to Chicago, and U.S. 80 due west, intoxicating himself as he had done in his youth with the immensity and infinite variety of the continent, staying in Ramada Inns, Great Western Motels, Motel 6's, Quality Inns, and dingy mom-and-pop places smelling of mildew and insecticide that you'd never find in a Triple A guide book. In search of... In search of what?

Or was the trip itself the answer? He was renewing his acquaintance with America in all its spectacular beauty and all its man-made ugliness. The sprawl of filling stations, mini-malls and tract housing endlessly replicated like the marching morons who'd built them.

He took back roads through the cornfields of the Midwest, then Interstates through the lonely prairies, the magnificent Rockies muscling themselves up from the bedrock of the Americas, searching, yearning, for something the sense of which eluded him. Across the Sierra Nevada into California, over the hump of the Coast Range to Big Sur, to Cambria where he'd worked on a ranch in those days before the army grabbed him.

When he saw the Pacific ahead, its gentle blue sparkling under a milky sky, he felt he was getting close to wherever he was going. Up through Big Sur on the narrow ledge of Highway One, sculpted between the mountains and the terraced waves of the sea, and then on the freeway through Monterey without stopping.

On his left, through the dunes, he caught glimpses of Monterey Bay. Squawking gulls spiraling and soaring, pelicans gliding effortlessly above the wind-drift, the surf barely audible. The waves in wave language telling tales of the distances they'd come, led, like him, by the wind, to California on the edge of the great continent.

He passed Seaside on his right: a dismal congery of strip malls with a K-Mart just off the freeway, presided over by a ten-story box called the Embassy Suites Hotel, lonely and badly out of place.

He hadn't been to the Peninsula since the war. 1943, to be exact. There hadn't been any Freeway or Seaside then, only a tiny no-name huddle of rickety shacks. Monterey had been a town full of decaying adobes, booming with raucous soldiers, honky-tonk bars and hookers. But now the Embassy Suites reminded him that he'd have to find a place to stay for the night, and it was already getting dark. Still, he kept driving. Suddenly, ahead of him, a sign. Fort Ord.

He'd been stationed at Ord, in the fall of 1943. "Planet Ord," the soldiers had called it, or sometimes just "The Planet."

Out in the middle of nowhere, usually surrounded by fog so thick that it seemed an alien world floating in space and time, disconnected and unrelated to the rest of the Peninsula and to the rest of the earth. "Go to the end of the world and turn left," they used to say.

A couple of years ago he'd been surfing the Internet for an article on Native Americans of California. He'd found a reference to the Ohlone who'd left middens of abalone shells and primitive tools in the Fort Ord area. Mildly curious, he'd opened a link mentioning that Ord had been closed down and that Stilwell Hall — which he'd known as the Soldiers' Club — was on the brink of demolition because the bluffs on which it stood were being eroded away. The Club. He hadn't thought of it for years. Now, strangely, here he was. Fort Ord.

The Club had been the inspiration and gift of General "Vinegar Joe" Stilwell, who'd wanted the lowly GI's to have a place of their own, and had beaten back persistent attempts by the brass to build an Officers' Club instead. Later it was named Stilwell Hall in his honor. Beautifully constructed and furnished as one of the last Federal Arts Projects of the depression-era WPA, the Soldiers' Club had sat among the dunes overlooking Monterey Bay. Was it still standing?

Without stopping to think, he turned off Highway One at Marina and took the bridge leading toward the Club. Yes, there it was.

Silhouetted against the sky, dark and abandoned, not yet fallen into the bay, the Soldiers' Club stood proudly among the dunes. On a night like this, he remembered, near the end of September 1943, the Club had officially opened. At that time it stood the length of a baseball field from the dunes that buffered it from Monterey Bay, the dunes that were eroding away. Like us all, he thought. Give us time and we all erode away.

Two stories high, California Spanish in architecture with a terra cotta roof, the Soldier's Club was an enlisted men's palace. It had a vast ballroom with parquetted teak floor, crystal chandeliers, frescos and murals by local artists, a library, meeting rooms, and a forty-foot bar said to be the longest in California. Big dance bands — the most noted in America — performed on the ornately furnished mezzanine high above the ballroom floor. On opening night, he recalled, more than a thousand women, carefully selected by the Red Cross and the local U.S.O., had been bused in from San Francisco and elsewhere to dance with the soldiers. General Stilwell was absent; he'd been put in command of the China-Burma Theater, so his wife dedicated the Club and stood in for him on the long reception line.

Other dances, other parties, followed. And one memorable night in October, just before his battalion shipped out for the Pacific, he'd met Terry. Terry. Tall, redheaded Terry with the blue-indigo eyes. That party — the dance. Was it almost sixty years ago? Eons in a man's life.

God, but he was really bushed, suddenly exhausted. Very carefully, he pulled over to the shoulder near the Club to rest a bit.

He awoke to the sound of his radio. Funny, he didn't remember having turned it on. Tommy Dorsey's orchestra, playing *Boogie Woogie*. He hadn't heard that in years.

Directly in front of him was the Club strangely ablaze with yellow lights, music, and the sound of voices loud, the wind fresh and sea-scented with a slight hint of kelp, the sky clear with its stars winking at him, as on the night he'd met Terry. This is a crazy dream. He found himself walking toward the entrance, toward the music and the voices, the laughter. In uniform, young, vigorous, virile, the warm, familiar but long-forgotten touch of dog tags on his chest. He stroked his left hand, searching for the shrapnel wound that had earned him his Purple Heart, but his fingers were supple, his skin smooth. If this is a dream, I don't want it to end. He pinched himself to make sure he was awake. Not a dream.

If not a dream, then what was going on here? Einstein. Einstein said that past, present and future exist side by side, like bends in a river. That was it. He must have stepped right over a time loop, like in a science fiction novel, back to 1943. October 1943, to be exact. He really was walking toward the Club, in October 1943, toward the lights and Big Band music. What were they playing? *Tuxedo Junction*. He was young again, new corporal's stripes on his sleeve, dog tags jingling, his carriage erect.

Tonight was one of those rare starry nights in October, Indian Summer on the Peninsula, just before the rainy season, when the skies are clear for weeks on end and the days are warm and sunny. The caressing whisper of the surf, the green scent of the dune plants instantly familiar. Tonight a slight haze, a gentle breeze, unusually warm, as he remembered it had been that time long ago. Everything seemed more beautiful, more vibrant than before. Was this what it was like to be young? Did young eyes see everything with this crystalline brilliance?

Feeling unreal, in a trance, he showed his dog tags to the bored MP at the entrance and pushed his way into the lobby. The Club, aromatic with cigarettes and beer, was cheerfully noisy and jammed

410

with soldiers and assorted women — wives, girlfriends, Red Cross girls and even a few enlisted WACs in uniform. A pair of broad stairways on either side of the lobby led to the mezzanine, where a band was playing *The Last Time I Saw Paris*. He thought he saw several men from his platoon, but ignored them as he pushed into the ballroom. Terry. Was she here?

Yes. Terry, a vision in a long emerald green taffeta dress, was there as he remembered her, standing at a table across the room, talking to a couple of overly attentive soldiers who looked vaguely familiar. Yes. That same dress. Terry. And she seemed to have expected him.

"Johnny!" she called. "You're here!" She pulled a red rose from a vase on the table and put it in her hair just as she'd done that time so long ago. She ran over, her face radiant, and hugged and kissed him. There were those indigo eyes — such a deep blue that in the world he'd just come from he would naturally have assumed they were contact lenses. But in 1943 contacts weren't even imagined and her wonderful eyes were colored as if by magic. He took her hand. Warm, perfectly manicured fingers, nails neat, not long, a reasonable shade of pink, not colored claws like some women back in the time he'd come from. She wore those same beautiful jade earrings. Why had I ever let her go?

It struck him that the band in the mezzanine was playing a rumba.

"Do you remember, Johnny? Do you remember what I said when I walked over to you that night?" Oh yes, he remembered.

"Yes," he said. "You asked me if I could rumba."

"And you answered 'I can do anything you ask me to.' And that's when I began to fall in love with you. And then you said that my eyes were indigo. And I thought that you were probably the only soldier in the Club who knew what indigo was. But Johnny," she grinned, "you couldn't really rumba, you know. We won that dance contest because of my dress."

He looked down at the long dress almost covering her pumps and remembered how later he'd pulled that dress up to her waist and they'd made love under the stars.

"It was this long skirt," she said. "It covers my feet. You kept missing the beat and you couldn't lead and I had to keep shifting my feet. Nobody could see it because my dress was so long. And so we looked like the perfect couple. And of course we were. And are. What a woman will do for a man," she said, rolling her eyes. "Tell me, Johnny, can you rumba?"

"Whatever you ask me to do."

They began to rumba. Johnny was a bit awkward at first, but helped by Terry he got into the beat of it, and remembered to keep his hips and knees loose. "I wish I could do this forever," he said. "Be with you forever."

"You can, Johnny, you can." She kissed him. "Do you remember what we did that night?" She gripped his hand, looked into his eyes and grinned mischievously.

Oh yes, he remembered. Remembered telling her that they would be shipping out the next morning, remembered their mutual hungriness, remembered taking her out there where the dunes began. Remembered the two of them returning to the Club, hand in hand, sand on their clothes and in her hair as his buddies hooted, hollered and applauded, Terry looking embarrassed but somehow triumphant at the same time. He remembered. Oh yes, he remembered.

They walked back to the table where she'd been sitting. "Johnny, You remember Bryan Wilson and Joe Biondo." They didn't get up, but made space for him.

"Hello, Joe. Hello, Bryan."

"Hello, Johnny."

"What's new, guys?"

"Nothing much. The latest scoop is we ship out tomorrow. Five a.m. Eat, drink and be merry, as the man says. Especially drink." Bryan hiccupped. Big, blond Bryan had lost his leg to a land mine in Okinawa, back in what was now the future. Back in the future? I'm not going to rack my brains trying to figure that out. Could he go back to his own time? Did he want to? Suppose he stayed here with Terry now. He'd survived the war, he knew. Survived, and married Harriet and became a professor. That was a million years from now. But maybe he had a second chance, a chance to start over, Terry and he. He pulled Terry to the dance floor. High above, the chandeliers twinkled and cast fleeting shadows. "Tonight is beautiful," he said. "You're so beautiful." They danced. *Chattanooga Choo-choo*. "Pardon me, boy, is that the Chattanooga choo-choo? On track twenty-nine." God, that brought back memories.

What had happened between him and Terry? After he'd gone overseas there'd been letters back and forth. Passionate, erotically explicit at first, pledging eternal devotion, then his gradually becoming fewer and more distant until she'd stopped writing. Distance fatigue, he'd called it. A "red shift" of emotions and memories as the distance increased. A casualty of war. She'd sent a snapshot of her in a two-piece bathing suit that he'd posted by his bunk in the barracks, to the whistling admiration of his buddies. Somehow between invasions, he'd lost it, and then lost her address. He'd filed away the memory of her as a wartime souvenir. He thought he'd turned over the page she was written on. But the page was still there, he realized.

"If only we could live over again," he said.

"Sorry, it doesn't work that way." She rested her head on his shoulder.

The White Cliffs of Dover: "There'll be love and laughter and peace ever after, tomorrow when the world is free." *Were we really that naive?*

"What is this, some kind of time warp?"

She raised her head and studied him. "You could think of it like that."

"How should I think of it?"

"It's reunion time. Your class reunion. Your going-away party. Our anniversary. Come on, Johnny, loosen up. Live a bit, if you'll pardon the expression."

"I wish we could be this way forever," he said.

"We have now. Now is forever. We can be together now." She pulled his head forward and kissed him. "Please Johnny," she whispered, "please make love to me again."

He took her out to the dunes as he had on that night so many years ago and pulled her dress up to her chin as she whispered his name and clutched his back and it was all as beautiful as it had been so many years ago.

Then they walked back hand in warm hand, under the powder-soft stars, the whispering ocean breeze on their skin, surrounded by the susurrus of the surf, the scent of the sandy grass. "They're all gone now," he said, sadly, waving his hand at the shadowy dunes they'd just left. "Eroded away."

"Now? What is 'now'?" she said. "Now is now. Even when the Club is gone, we'll be here and we'll be now." He looked at her in puzzlement. "Oh Johnny," she said. "You'll see."

This time there was no sand on them, no cheers or whistles, as they walked into the ballroom alive to the beat of *The Jersey Bounce*. "If this is some kind of mixed-up dream," he said, "I don't want to ever wake up."

"It's no dream, Johnny. It's the way it was meant to be." She gripped his hand, hard. " I've missed you. I've come back every year looking for you."

"Every year? You do this every year?"

"It's the anniversary. The anniversary of the battalion's going away party. It's our anniversary too, Johnny," she said, pulling him closer.

He had to excuse himself to go to the Men's Room, since he always had to piss after sex. This can't be a dream, he thought at the urinal. You take a leak in a dream and it wakes you up. This is damn real. About as real as you can get. I wonder where she's been all these years. Maybe she's married now, has kids. But not in this crazy dream or time travel or warp or whatever we're in. The orchestra. What was it playing? "We'll meet again/Don't know where, don't know when/ But I know we'll meet again some sunny day." His eyes were moist as he walked back to her. *Must be the cigarette smoke.*

"I'll get us a pitcher of beer," he said. He turned brusquely and shouldered his way through the crowd to the Tap Room. Behind the bar were those amusing, corny paintings he remembered so well. Cartoons, really. Blackbearded whalers and fishermen in floppy oilskins, like in Moby Dick. But the beer, damn it, was that awful insipid 3.2 percent alcohol. Under pressure from America's mommies the Army had decreed that no military installation could serve anything stronger. But what the hell. It was better than nothing. It was only two-bits a foaming pitcher and it was drawn from kegs by smiling, bouncy-breasted, patriotic young barmaids with upswept hairdos, their every flounce and bounce studied avidly by the lonely soldiers lined up at the double brass rails. If you wanted stronger stuff, buddy, either female or liquid, take your hard-earned bucks to Lower Alvarado Street in Monterey, the center of sinful life on the Peninsula. And watch out for muggers.

On his way back, carrying a pitcher and two glasses, he bumped into Tommy Goodson, beaming, full of life and spirits. It opened a wound, seeing Tommy. Tommy. Screaming, screaming, screaming after his guts were blown open on Okinawa. "Johnny boy! Good t'see ya!"

Johnny forced a smile. "How ya doin' Tommy?"

"Great! How're you, Johnny?"

"Never better!"

"You can say that again! Ain't this a great party? You with somebody, Johnny?"

"Terry. The tall redhead."

Tommy whistled. "The ice woman? Let me tell you, Johnny, you're wastin' your time. She don't let nobody but nobody get near her. Oh well, best of luck, Johnny."

When he reached Terry, Billy Larsen was towering over her. Big, brawny Billy. The poor creep had lost it at Iwo Ie. Panicked under fire, he abandoned his squad, was court-martialed and dishonorably discharged. Here he was, showing off his new sergeant's stripes.

Male buddy talk:

"Hi, Johnny."

"Hi, Billy." You miserable sad sack.

"How's it goin'?"

"Can't complain."

"Great party." Billy drifted away. Good riddance.

Terry was looking at him curiously. "What's the matter, Johnny?"

He shook his head. "Nothing."

He told her what Goodson had said. She threw back her head and laughed. "Me? The ice woman? I've been saving myself for you, Johnny. My Johnny. I knew you'd come back some day."

God. Where had life gone wrong? Don't let this end. Terry reached out to him. "C'mon, let's dance." She led him out on the crowded floor. The chandeliers were winking. The band was playing *Stardust*. "This is my favorite," she said. She rested her head on his shoulder. Her fragrance smelled like lilac, her breast pressing against him. They held each other very close. This is where I belong. I'll settle in here and stay forever

He looked about the room. All of them were here, he supposed, the five hundred men, more or less, of his battalion. He recognized many of them, but could recall the names of only a few. Even some of the officers were here dancing with army nurses and WACs. Funny. They don't usually mix socially with the enlisted men. Of course this was a special night. A reunion, no less. Their last night at Ord. There's that arrogant Captain Leary and beetle-browed Lieutenant Vogel, and ninety-day wonder Lieutenant Franco who always looked confused and ill at ease in his uniform. Should have stayed a civilian. Fat bottomed Major Callahan, pudgy, sweaty, and self-important as always. Third Platoon almost all wiped out because of his stupidity. Ordered them right into an enemy ambush. Naturally they promoted him to Lieutenant Colonel. It figures.

What a miserable bunch they are. Were. *We* were. The "Greatest Generation." Who the hell said that? He shook his head. The phrase eluded him.

Sneering, loudmouthed Sergeant Truax, whom he instinctively disliked and always avoided. And poor sneaky little Gorzinsky, who'd be caught cheating at poker and have his life made miserable. And Sonny Quinlan that illiterate retarded hillbilly. How the hell did he ever get in the Army? He'd raped a teenaged girl in Japan after the war ended and wound up in Leavenworth. One by one they came over and shook his hand. It was a shock to recognize Sergeant Lacey, whose head would be ripped off at Iwo, spattering Johnny with blood just as he himself was hit by shrapnel and earned his Purple Heart. Here was Hummins, who died of pneumonia. Hennessey, who was killed by a land mine. Fat crazy Sam Goldman, who'd bitched and griped all through basic training, but would single-handedly hold off a Japanese platoon and earn a battlefield commission.

"You're a good man, Sam," he said. Goldman looked puzzled, but grinned back at him.

"You're doing okay yourself, Johnny," he answered, looking at Terry.

Didn't any of them know? Was he the only one who could see ahead? He gazed at Terry. How much did she know?

He looked for his best drinking buddies, Joe Vaccaro, who'd been seasick and puked his way all across the Pacific, and Benny Segal, who got V.D. in Guam and swore off women forever. And kept his vow until that uproarious night in Kobe after the war was over. And got the clap again. Terry took his hand. "What's the matter, Johnny?"

"A couple of guys are missing. Not everybody's here."

She looked at him and smiled. "Of course not. But they'll come when they're invited. Maybe you'll see them next time. Or the time after. Sometime soon, anyway."

"You mean we'll do this again?"

"We'll always be here. Every year. You'll see."

"How come I wasn't here before?"

"You have to be invited."

"And tonight I was invited?"

"Oh yes, Johnny," she said, taking his arm and cuddling close to him. He smelled the lilac. "You were invited."

They danced for hours, joking and laughing, bodies moving in wondrous unison. Jitterbugging. *Cow-Cow Boogie. Pistol Packin' Mama. Praise the Lord and Pass the Ammunition.* They held each other close for more sentimental tunes. *White Christmas. You'd Be So Nice to Come Home To. Sleepy Lagoon.* Johnny hummed as they danced, surprising himself that he remembered the words to all of them. *When the Lights Go On Again. As Time Goes By. I'll Be Home For Christmas.* Terry seemed tireless and so was he. Then, all too soon the band was playing *Three O'clock in the Morning* as a sign that the festivities were over, and Terry led him out to waltz.

"Terry, can we stay together tonight?"

She gazed at him in surprise and then with tears in her eyes. "Oh Johnny, dear Johnny, you still don't understand, do you?" She stopped dancing. "You can't change the past. This is all we had. It's all we'll ever have."

The evening was winding down. One by one, the others had disappeared. Even the band was gone. A cold wind was blowing from somewhere.

"The last one to arrive is the last to leave," said Terry. "That's you, Johnny. That's the rule. That's the way it is."

"Terry, I'd give ten years of my life to stay with you tonight."

"Oh Johnny, please try to understand. You don't have ten years." Then she suddenly vanished.

The vast ruined hall was silent, a dark and empty vault. A chilly fog smelling of kelp drifted through broken windows. Seagulls flapped their wings flying through the panes. Gone were the chandeliers, the murals on the walls. The floor was buckled, encrusted with animal dung and bird droppings. And the sea roared closer, much closer, beyond the dunes, sounding angry. There was a louder roaring in his ears, and now, finally, he understood it all.

From the *Monterey County Chronicle*:

PROFESSOR FOUND DEAD BY STILWELL HALL

The victim of an apparent heart attack, Dr. John Ackerman, a retired professor of Anthropology at Michigan State University, was found dead in his car at 7:30 A.M. yesterday near Stilwell Hall on the site of the former Fort Ord. He was discovered by workers who had come to partially demolish the building, which is in danger of falling into Monterey Bay. When contacted by telephone, a university spokesman in East Lansing, Michigan, said they were unaware that Ackerman had gone to California, and suggested that he may have been doing anthropological research on the Ohlone Indians, who used to inhabit the area. After a medical investigation into the cause of death, his body will be sent back to Michigan. Professor Ackerman is survived by two sons and a daughter, none of whom was available for comment.

Johnny walked up the path to the Soldiers' Club, lively again with light, laughter and music. A band was playing *Boogie Woogie*. He was in uniform, young and vigorous. And happy. He knew he'd see Terry again. And again. And again. Even if the Club slid into the sea. She'd always be there in October 1943.

Walter E. Gourlay is a retired professor of Asian History, specializing in Modern China. He was an Army MP in North Africa and Italy during World War Two. He has taught at Michigan State University, Cabrillo College, and the Naval Post Graduate School in Monterey, California. In other existences he has been at various times an aircraft machinist, a union organizer, a publicist, editor and writer for pulp magazines, as well as a part-time manager of a concert hall in Manhattan. A former New Yorker, he now lives on the California Central Coast, and when he can get his computer to work, is doing historical research and writing short stories as well as his wartime memoirs. Contact: Waltergo@comcast.net

This story has been adapted from a version published in *Monterey Shorts* (Thunderbird Press, Carmel, CA, 2003.)

PERMISSIONS

The Ground beneath My Feet, by Paul-Anthony Delor. © Paul-Anthony Delor, Brussels, 2010. Printed with permission of the author.

Dark Lady of Hollywood by Diane Haithman. © Diane Haithman, Los Angeles, 2007. Printed with permission of the author.

Consultation by Ruben Varda. © Ruben Varda, Brussels, 2009. Printed with permission of the author.

Gates of Eden by Charles Degelman. © Charles Degelman, Los Angeles, 2005. Printed with permission of the author.

Under the Poinciana Tree by Carlos Victoria. © Estate of Carlos Victoria, Miami, 2007. This translation appears by gracious permission of Carlos Victoria's executors.

The Vale of Cashmere by Sean Elder. © Sean Elder, New York, 2010. Printed with permission of the author.

A Cultural Revolution by Teresa Hsiao. © Teresa Hsiao, New York, 2010. Printed with permission of the author.

Patchwork by Dan Loughry. © Dan Loughry, Los Angeles, 2010. Printed with permission of the author.